BLOOD HEIR

ILONA ANDREWS

Blood Heir

Copyright © 2020 by Ilona Andrews, Inc.

Ebook ISBN: 978-1-64197-158-4

KDP ISBN: 979-8-56015-220-8

IS POD ISBN: 978-1-64197-165-2

Cover and Interior Art by Luisa Preißler

NYLA Publishing

121 W 27th St., Suite 1201, NY 10001, New York.

http://www.nyliterary.com

To the fans of Kate Daniels World who refuse to let it go.

The moon was full and silver. It peeked at me through tattered clouds as I rode my horse down the old I-20, staying in the center of the highway. Magic had been chewing on the edges of paved roads for decades, and the asphalt near the shoulder often crumbled under the weight of a horse.

Nothing to see here, moon. Just a lone woman in a tattered cloak riding her horse into her home city after being gone for far too long.

Around me dense pines towered on both sides of the once busy highway. Glowing eyes watched Tulip and me from the darkness between the roots and branches, yellow for racoon, white for deer, green for foxes, electric red arranged into a triangle for hell alone knew what. The forest critters gave me the stink eye but kept to themselves.

The trees stopped abruptly, replaced by fields wrapped in razor wire. A sign loomed ahead.

WELCOME TO ATLANTA
We're Glad Georgia Is on Your Mind

A bit optimistic of them.

Below someone had scribbled in white ink.

"Praise the Lord and get the fireballs ready."

That was more like it.

A dark shape swooped above my head. The moonlight slipped over it, dancing on its feathers, and then it soared into the endless indigo of the sky. Like most eagles, Turgan didn't like to fly at night, but something must've unsettled my raptor. He'd taken off the moment we left the ley line and refused to land on his perch on my shoulder.

Another sign jutted into the night.

ALL VISITING SHAPESHIFTERS
Present to the Pack in 24 hours
Take I-85, head northeast, follow your nose.

Twenty-four hours? When I left eight years ago, foreign shapeshifters had three days to introduce themselves to the Pack. Times had changed.

A high, eerie howl floated up to the clouds on the night breeze. Not a shapeshifter. Just some garden-variety monstrosity venting to the moon. Too far to worry about. Tulip flicked her ears and kept going.

Shapeshifters were a paranoid, suspicious breed. Lyc-V, the symbiotic virus that gave them the ability to change into animals, came bearing many gifts. Some, like enhanced strength, speed, and senses, were beneficial. Others, not so much.

Those who changed shape lived lives of discipline and self-control. The other way lay loupism, a catastrophic plunge into hormone-addled hell that turned shapeshifters into sadistic spree killers. Loupism had no cure, except for a blade to the neck or a bullet to the brain.

Shapeshifters required the kind of structure that regular

society could no longer deliver. They set themselves apart in packs, and the rest of the population, acutely aware that each shapeshifter was a spree killer in waiting, was happy to let them govern themselves.

Of all the shapeshifter packs active in the continental US, Atlanta's Free People of the Code were the largest and by far the strongest. Most packs rarely reached over a hundred members. Atlanta's Pack counted nearly three thousand shapeshifters and seven different clans, defined by their animal forms and unified under the rule of a Beast Lord. It was so large, that it was known simply as the Pack. Only the Ice Fury Pack in Alaska was larger.

A long time ago, I was one of the rare humans who were considered members of the Pack. I had lived in the Keep, the massive shapeshifter fortress northeast of the city. All my friends had grown fur and claws. Back then, the Pack had had a different Beast Lord, and he'd treated me like his younger sister.

The fields ended, and ruins began. I adjusted the weight of the spear in the sheath on my back, nudged Tulip, and she picked up speed. I had a morning appointment to keep on short notice.

The highway narrowed. We took an exit to the left onto Basilisk Road and followed it as it looped northeast, climbing through the exposed corpses of once tall apartment high-rises.

Magic hated technology. It came in waves, flooding the world, snuffing out electric lights and gasoline engines, chewing on skyscrapers, and spawning monsters. Then, as unpredictably as it appeared, the wave would wane, and technology once again came out on top. Spells fizzled, and guns once again spat bullets.

The taller the building, the harder magic gnawed on it. Most skyscrapers and office towers had fallen long ago. A lot of the overpasses had crumbled to dust or collapsed. The old skyline was but a distant memory.

In its wake, new buildings sprung up, built by craftsmen

3

mostly by hand to minimize magic erosion. Here and there, the new structures hugged the road, solid homes and offices with thick walls, strong doors, and narrow windows guarded by steel bars. The soft yellow glow of electric lights fought with the gloom. The magic was down now. If it had been up, some of the grates on the windows would shine with silver and the blue radiance of fey lanterns would replace the electric bulbs.

The city looked the same as when I left it. It felt the same too, dangerous, indifferent, watchful, yet somehow still achingly familiar. Home, despite all the years I'd been gone. I'd been almost eighteen when I left. I was twenty-six now. It felt like a lifetime ago.

I never meant to be gone this long, and this wasn't how I wanted to come back to Atlanta. My biological family was dead, but my found family was alive and well, and they'd wanted me back for a long time. In my mind, I would've called ahead, and they would meet me at the ley line, mob me, hug me, and we would all go home. That was the original plan.

But if I went home now, I'd be signing their death warrants. I had to stay off the radar, and I couldn't afford to be recognized.

Not that I would be recognized. When most people came home after a long absence, their family said things like "You lost weight" and "Is that a new hair cut?" If I went home, my family would ask, "Who the hell are you?" Nothing about me was the same. Not my body, not my face, not my voice, or my scent.

A hint of movement on the left jerked me right out of my memories and into the present.

I was several blocks deep into a deserted street. On the left, a ruined heap of a building crouched, still steeped in night shadows. On the right, a wall rose, new construction, solid, thick, and topped with razor wire. Ahead, the street ended, as if sheared with a giant's knife. A chasm gaped, dropping a full fifty feet down below, about a third of a mile across.

The chasm was new, but not surprising. Magic waves didn't just birth monsters; they produced new rivers, raised hills, and split the ground. Atlanta had dealt with the chasm, as was evidenced by a single-lane wooden bridge spanning it.

The bridge wasn't the issue. The three shapeshifters that moved out of the shadows to block it were.

There was absolutely no reason for a Pack patrol to be here at this hour. Their territory was all the way on the other side of the city. The timing wasn't right either, just before dawn, when they should've been returning to the Keep, to perform their morning meditation and curl up for a nap like well-behaved monsters. Yet here they were, dressed in matching Pack sweats and blocking my way.

Atlanta was a bitch of a city.

All three were male and young and showed no intention of moving out of my way. The itty-bitty welcoming committee.

"Hi there!" I called. "I need to get on this bridge."

The middle of the shapeshifters, who looked about twenty, tan, with longish dark hair, smiled at me. "Password?"

Aren't you cute? "Why do I need a password? Is this bridge in the Pack's territory?"

"That's not important," the leader said. "What's important is that there are three of us and one of you."

Well, look who learned to count.

"If you want to cross the bridge, you have to give us the password," the shapeshifter said. "If you don't know it, you'll have to pay the fine."

The smaller shapeshifter on his right grinned and let out an eerie cackle. Boudas. Of course.

Boudas, the werehyenas, belonged to one of the smaller of the Pack's seven clans. There weren't many of them, but they were dangerous and utterly nuts. Wolves, jackals, rats, all of them could be reasoned with. Boudas did things like climb into a captive polar bear's enclosure and tickle it with their claws to see what would happen.

Fine. I'd go around.

I tensed my right leg a fraction. Tulip turned, more anticipating the command rather than obeying it, the sound of her hooves clopping on the pavement too loud in the night. Two more shapeshifters stepped out of the shadows, blocking my exit.

Right. The story of my life.

"Did I say three?" the bouda called out. "I meant five."

A normal Pack patrol had two shapeshifters, three if it was on the border with the People, because necromancers made a dangerous enemy. Five shapeshifters meant a strike team. They had run some sort of mission in the city, and it was my bad luck to run into them as they were coming back. They saw a lone woman in faded jeans, old boots, and a tattered cloak riding a horse late at night, low threat and an easy target. If they'd been wolves, jackals, or Clan Heavy, I'd be halfway across the bridge by now. But they were boudas and they liked to play.

I guided Tulip into continuing the turn until I faced the bridge again. Five boudas would be a tough fight, and the moment they realized that I wasn't playing, it would escalate into real violence. I really didn't want to kill anyone. I didn't have time to play games either.

"Still waiting for that password," the leader of the boudas said.

"May 15th," I said.

"What's that?" the shapeshifter on the left asked.

"Andrea Medrano's birthday," I said. "Good enough?"

The shapeshifters paused. It was a funny thing to watch: one moment, they were oozing arrogance, the next they simultaneously lost their steam as if someone popped them on the nose with a rolled-up newspaper. To them Andrea Medrano was Boss, Judge, and Executioner. They called her Alpha. I called her

Andrea. Or Aunt Andy when I was sucking up to get her help for some nefarious deed.

The trio by the bridge eyed me, their expressions cautious. If they kept blocking me and I turned out to be someone Andrea knew, there would be hell to pay. The only way to check that would be to call the Bouda Clan House and talk to her, which meant they'd have to answer uncomfortable questions about why they stopped me in the first place. The Pack took pains to maintain a cordial relationship with humans in general, and the city of Atlanta in particular. The punishment would be swift.

A tall shadow stepped out of the ruins, as if congealing from the darkness, and glided forward with easy grace. Broad shoulders, long legs, a large guy, same grey Pack sweats. He took another step and I saw his face. It was a face that wouldn't just stop traffic, it would cause a pileup.

His eyes caught the moonlight. A blood-red sheen rolled over his brown irises.

"Now, that's an interesting development," Ascanio Ferara said. "Please, tell me more."

Damn it all to hell.

Ascanio glanced at the boudas by the bridge. All three promptly looked down. So, stopping me was an unsanctioned bit of fun.

When I left, Andrea and her husband Raphael, the alphas of Clan Bouda, were grooming Ascanio for the beta spot, which would've made him second in the chain of the clan's command. He'd wanted that spot more than anything. Apparently, he'd gotten what he wished for and all the headaches that went with it.

Ascanio turned back to me and looked me over, slowly.

I made a conscious effort to not hold my breath. Ascanio knew me. We'd met when I was fourteen and he was fifteen, and we'd spent a lot of time together.

We haven't met.

His nostrils fluttered slightly. He was downwind from me, and the night breeze had brought him my scent.

I'm a stranger. You've never seen me before.

Ascanio inhaled deeper. His eyes narrowed.

My heartbeat sounded too loud in my ears, but it was slow and steady. He wouldn't know me. Sometimes when I looked in the mirror now, I didn't know me.

Time stretched, slow and viscous like molasses. He stared at me, and I had no choice but to stare back.

Ascanio had been beautiful as a teenager, almost androgynous. The beauty was still there, in the bottomless eyes under the sweep of dark eyebrows and in the perfect lines, but his face had gained strength. His features had broadened slightly. Time had contoured his jaw. No traces of softness remained. It was a man's face now, with harsh edges and defined angles, and eyes that radiated authority and power. If I didn't know him, he would've knocked my socks off.

"You dropped my alpha's name," Ascanio said. "Care to explain?"

"No."

Red flashed in his irises. "You know confidential information about my alpha. I need to know how, because I've been with her for over a decade and I've never met you."

"And what will you do if I don't tell you?"

"I'll have to insist." His voice told me I wouldn't like it.

The first time we'd met, he'd decided it would be a brilliant idea to kiss me. I'd shoved a handful of wolfsbane in his face, dumped him on the floor, and tied his arms behind his back. And then I'd asked him if the spoiled bouda baby lost his bottle and his teddy.

"So, let me get this straight," I said. "Five of your shapeshifters detained me without cause outside of the Pack's boundaries, demanded that I pay a fee to cross a public bridge, and now you're threatening me with assault."

His eyebrows furrowed slightly. All of those would've been a violation of the Pack's policies eight years ago.

"I haven't threatened you yet."

"I feel threatened. I'm trembling with fear."

"I see a distinct lack of trembling," Ascanio said. "This is very easy. Tell me how you know Andrea Medrano's birthday, and you're free to go."

"You're missing the point. You have no right to detain me in the first place." To escalate or to back down? That was the question.

"You seem suspicious. I'm not sure you should be wandering around unsupervised."

Ascanio would require nothing short of complete submission to let me go. Once I took a step back, he would want my name, my reason for entering the city, and, once he saw my face, my address. Backing down would cost more time and require too much lying.

"And you seem like an idiot, yet somehow nobody prevents you from wandering around free."

One of the boudas by the bridge giggled and clamped his hand over his mouth.

Ascanio raised his eyebrows. "An idiot?"

"One human woman in the middle of a tech wave against six shapeshifters. Only an idiot can't understand how that math will look to civilian law enforcement or your alpha. Does she generally encourage you to hassle lone women late at night?"

He took a step forward. Menace rolled off him like air from hot asphalt.

"Since I'm an idiot, perhaps I'll pull you off your horse in my idiotic way, stuff you into one of our houses, somewhere with a deep basement, and wait until you decide to answer my questions. You can file a complaint if you ever get out."

"Is this you threatening me? I'm checking so we're both clear."

"When I threaten you, you won't have to ask."

"In that case, do it. Pull me off my horse."

He didn't move. I'd called his bluff. Ascanio had many faults, but he wouldn't hurt a random stranger, much less a human, without reason. If it got out that the Pack was kidnapping young human women off the street, the fallout would be catastrophic, and with five witnesses, it would get out. Shapeshifters gossiped worse than bored old ladies in church.

Frustration sparked in his eyes and died. I'd won.

Time to ease up. I didn't want to antagonize him too much. "Why don't we do this: you let me be on my way and I won't file a formal complaint. It's a win-win."

Ascanio held up his hand to stop me and turned away, looking at the wall across the street. A moment later the rest of the shapeshifters turned and looked there, too.

A boy leapt out of the darkness and landed on the corner of the wall, the only spot free of razor wire. He was solid and corded with muscle, only half a foot shorter than me. Dark brown hair cut short, tan face, and grey eyes that were so light, they were practically silver.

Conlan.

When I left, he wasn't even two years old. We'd seen each other hundreds of times over the years when visiting our grandfather in his otherworldly prison, but it'd been eight years since I'd seen him in person. If we were alone, I would've pulled him off that wall and hugged him so hard, he'd need all his shapeshifter strength to wiggle out of it.

Our stares connected.

He gave no indication that he recognized me. My brother, the master of subterfuge.

Ascanio heaved a mocking sigh. "The little prince graces us with his presence. You're a long way from your parents' territory, Your Highness."

His Highness sat cross-legged on the wall. "You're a long way from your Clan House, Beta Ferara."

Ascanio smiled slowly, baring his teeth. "Run along now."

"And if I don't?" Conlan squinted at Ascanio. "Will you try to put *me* in your special basement?"

One of the boudas chuckled and choked it off before Ascanio could glare at him.

"This doesn't concern you," Ascanio said, his voice harsh.

"I'll decide what concerns me." Conlan rested his elbow on his knee and plopped his chin on his fist. "Don't worry. I won't get in your way. Please go on with your attempted extortion, robbery, and kidnapping scheme. I just want to see how it all turns out."

"And then what?" one of the boudas behind me asked. "You gonna run home and tell your daddy?"

My brother turned his head and looked at him. Gold rolled over his eyes and flared into a bright glow. The bouda with the big mouth tried to hold his gaze. A tense second passed. The bouda looked down.

Ascanio couldn't let that pass. Conlan had just alpha-stared one of his people into submission. I had to diffuse the situation before it broke into violence.

"So it's not just lone women you hassle in the middle of the night. You also bully children."

Ascanio glanced back at me.

That's right. I'm still here.

"I'm going to ride across this bridge," I told him. "You're welcome to try and stop me. I'm pretty sure the kid and I can take you."

"You should try to stop her," Conlan called out. Flesh flowed over his left hand, snapping into a nightmarish half-hand half-paw, disproportionately large and armed with claws the size of human fingers. "It will be fun."

"We both remember what happens when you go looking for

fun," Ascanio said. "Do I need to remind you?" He made a show of looking around. "I don't have loup manacles handy."

He didn't have what?

Conlan's face rippled. He was a hair away from going furry. "That was a long time ago. Why don't we go find some and see what happens?"

Nothing. That's what was going to happen.

I nudged Tulip. She lowered her head and stomped to the bridge. The boudas blocking it hesitated.

I fixed them with my stare and barked in the same voice I used when I wanted soldiers in the middle of a slaughter to obey me. "Move."

The two on the left scrambled aside. The bouda on the right stood alone, not sure what to do.

Out of the corner of my eye, I saw Ascanio wave him off. The bouda backed away.

Ascanio had crunched the numbers and didn't like the result. In a fight with shapeshifters, there were no guarantees. If Conlan got hurt, or worse, if he hurt someone, there would be a lot of questions. I could just imagine how that conversation would go. *"How did Curran's son get hurt?" "Well, there was this woman..." "And what possessed you to detain a human woman in the middle of the night? Also, why is Bob missing an arm?"* Ascanio was an ass, but he wasn't a fool.

Ascanio flicked his fingers toward the city. The boudas shot past me, leaping onto the bridge, and broke into a run.

I glanced to the wall. Conlan was gone. Good job.

Ascanio turned to me. "You and I will meet again, soon."

"No, we won't."

Blood-red eyes fixed me. "Think about the things I asked you."

He sprinted past me onto the bridge, catching up to his crew with ridiculous ease. They dashed into the night with a speed that would make racehorses green and vanished from view.

For my first night back in Atlanta, it could've been worse. I still had all my limbs, and my hair wasn't on fire.

What was that about loup manacles? I'd seen Conlan every week or two for years, and my brother never mentioned anything involving Ascanio and loup manacles. In fact, he never mentioned Ascanio, period. I'd have to get to the bottom of this next time we talked...

A ghost of a presence tripped my alarms. The tiny hairs on the back of my neck rose. Something waited in the depths of the ruins on my left. Watching me. I couldn't see it or hear it, but I knew it was there, hidden in the darkness, the same way primitive people knew when a tiger lay in wait at the mouth of their cave.

I could get off the horse and say hello, but there was no telling what I would find, and every instinct warned me to back away. Tulip tensed under me. She didn't like whatever was hiding in the darkness either.

There was no point in looking for trouble. I'd lost enough time as it was. I shifted my weight in the saddle, and Tulip trotted onto the bridge.

Nobody followed us.

I sat on a big chunk of concrete in the middle of the street. Around me the old bones of Midtown spread under the pale grey pre-dawn sky. Jagged corpses of skyscrapers jutted from the sea of rubble. Some had fallen whole; others broke off midway, and their husks stared at the world with black holes of empty windows. Strange lichens sheathed their walls, some coiling in ridges on the brick and stucco like ancient fossil shells, others drooping in long crimson strands that moved and shivered without any wind. Decorative hedges that once bordered sidewalks had grown foot-long thorns. Other-

13

worldly vines, dotted with flowers, spilled from the gutted ruins.

The first magic wave had stabbed Atlanta in the heart, leaving a ragged, gaping wound that cut through Midtown. The wound bled magic even during the strongest tech, and its current had warped this area beyond all recognition. The locals called it Unicorn Lane. Nothing was what it seemed here, and everything tried to kill you. Even the biggest magical heavyweights steered clear of it. To enter Unicorn Lane, you had to be desperate or crazy. Good thing I was both.

In front of me, a small space had been cleared free of rubble. A ten-foot-tall stele thrust from its center, a narrow stone slab with four equal sides. A pack of small russet-furred beasts somewhere on the crossroads of squirrels and mongoose dashed down a narrow path and around it. The thing that chased them had no name. About the size of a large rottweiler, it scrambled over the refuse on six legs. Its fur was a forest of hair-thin black needles. It looked like a sea urchin, except for its head with long jaws and dinosaur teeth. The beast dashed after the pseudo-squirrels, slipped, and slammed into an abandoned car wrapped in orange moss.

The moss turned bright red from the impact. The beast staggered away, swayed, and collapsed, its side awash with scarlet. The needles drooped, liquifying. A thick puddle of brown blood spread from the creature. Dozens of critters no bigger than a rat streamed out of the ruins like a blue-grey tide to drink it.

Tulip neighed at me for the third time.

"Fine." I got off the rock and untacked her. "Don't go deep."

Tulip tossed her head and took off down the street, a splash of white.

"Is that wise?" a familiar female voice asked.

I turned. Sienna stood by the stele. She wore a long dark cloak, and her hood was down, revealing her face and strawberry blond hair shorn in a new short bob. Her skin was pale, her features delicate and gentle, and her eyes distant. Before the Shift, people used to draw fae like her. Nobody would ever draw a delicate fae again.

"Tulip will be fine. What happened to the hair?"

She smiled. "Needed power for a spell."

Sienna was an oracle who saw into the future. I had focused on her prophecies so much over the last four years, sometimes I forgot that she was a witch.

I walked over, and we hugged. She used to be sickly, almost skeletal, and sometimes she still forgot to eat, because she lived with one foot in another time. She felt solid now. Good.

"Why here?" I asked, nodding at the stele.

"I have my reasons."

Sienna looked at the monument and the single name chiseled on it. SAIMAN.

"I always wondered why nothing else was written here," she said.

"That's the way he wanted it."

I remembered the day we buried him. It rained so hard, all of us looked like we were crying. I wasn't sure if anyone actually had. He'd stabbed too many of his pallbearers in the back.

A grandson of a frost giant, Saiman had been an expert on magic. He'd also been a polymorph. He could turn himself into anyone he wanted, any age, any gender, any shape within human limits, and he'd used that gift to live a thoroughly selfish life, using people, manipulating them, trampling over them in a hedonistic pursuit of wealth and pleasure. Then the city had had to come together to face a terrible threat, and Saiman had one brief, shining chance to cast aside his cowardice and step up to the plate. He took it, and it killed him.

I hadn't mourned him, I'd never trusted him, but I was sorry he had died. A lot of people, better people, had also died in that battle.

Sienna looked at the stele, or rather through it, at something only she could see. I waited.

She'd called me yesterday. *This is your last chance to stop it. Meet me by Saiman's grave before sunrise.* Then she'd hung up.

Rushing her and asking questions would accomplish nothing. She weighed and measured each word a hundred times before she said it. And even so, most of what she said made no sense until it was too late. I just had to be patient and hope I figured it out in time.

Last chance. The very last one.

Four years ago, she'd called me in the middle of the night. Sienna had foreseen disasters before, wars, plagues, dragons. Nothing rattled her, but that night her voice shook. She told me that an elder god had been reborn as an avatar in Arizona. Moloch, the Child Eater, the deity of the Canaanites condemned in the Old Testament, who took his sustenance from infants burned alive in the fires of his forges and metal bulls. For nearly three decades he had been building up his domain, preparing to expand, and that night Sienna had seen his first target.

Moloch would kill Kate. The woman who raised me as her daughter.

Kate was so much more than my mother. She was the nexus, a point of connection for many people who would otherwise slit each other's throats. The Pack, who suspected all outsiders; the Masters of the Dead, who piloted vampires with their minds as if they were drones; the Witch Covens that guarded their precious knowledge with beasts and curses; the Neo-Pagans with a persecution chip on their shoulder; the Order of Merciful Aid, who maintained that their way was the only right way—all of them owed favors to Kate. She was respected by all, loved by some, feared by others, but none of them would treat her lightly. Kate was the only person capable of forging the factions of Atlanta into a unified force.

Eight years ago, she had done just that, and Atlanta stood as one against a danger that should have ended it. The city survived against all odds. Now Kate had moved on, to the coast near Wilmington, coming to Atlanta only for the summer, and without her the city had fractured again. But these fractures could still be repaired.

If Moloch killed Kate, Atlanta would collapse upon itself and fall to his power. Everyone I cared about on the East Coast would die trying to avenge her. The conflicts between the factions of the city would flare into war. On the West Coast, Erra, Kate's aunt and the woman I called my grandmother, was trying to resurrect the ancient kingdom she left behind thousands of years ago. My grandmother once lost herself to vengeance and became an abomination to protect her people. Kate's death would catapult her down the path of retribution once again, and this time she would not survive.

Sienna told me that I was the wild card. It was up to me to stop the prophecy from coming true.

That night four years ago I'd gotten off the phone with Sienna, and in the morning Erra and I were off to Moloch's fortress. He thought he was secure in his citadel. I'd gotten myself captured, killed his guards, cut my way to his workshop, and severed his spine. He tore out my eye. My grandfather had told me that Moloch's power was in his eyes, so I carved one of his out of his skull as he lay by my feet and put it into my head. Then I cut his body into pieces and threw him into his own forge. And then I set his hell fortress on fire.

Within two years Moloch regenerated, as my grandfather had warned me he would. I had bought us some time, but the future remained unchanged. Kate still died. From the moment I felt Moloch's eye root into my head, everything I had done was to prevent the prophecy from happening. I clashed with Moloch again and again, but no matter how hard I struggled, I couldn't alter Sienna's visions. If Kate met Moloch, she died. If I went home, she died. If I warned her, she died.

"Moloch spoke to me again," Sienna said.

Hearing the name said out loud was like being shocked with a live wire. I pushed the rage down. "What did he say?"

She glanced at me. "He taunted me. He can't see what I see. He worries."

Anything that worried Moloch was great for us.

"A holy man was murdered. His name was Nathan Haywood. Moloch sent his priests into the city. He wants something connected to this murder."

"Something or someone?"

Sienna shook her head. I wouldn't get an answer. "Find it before he does. If he obtains it, everything is lost. The future becomes a certainty."

Kate would not die. Not while I was still breathing.

"Julie," Sienna called.

I startled. I had left that name behind me years ago. Julie Olsen was gone, melted down in the crucible of magic. Now I went by Aurelia Ryder.

"Do not go home. If Kate sees you, she will recognize you. She will die. Curran will die. Conlan will die. Everyone you love will be gone."

A cold spike of fear hammered through my spine. "Conlan saw me."

"Conlan doesn't matter. Only Kate does." She reached out and gripped my hands. "You must stop him this time. No matter the cost. There are no more chances. This is it."

"I promise," I told her.

"Carry some lemon juice with you. Just in case."

She pulled her cloak around her and walked away.

Lemon juice. Right.

I stood by the grave and watched the sun rise, splashing pink and red across the sky. The night was still in full swing in

Arizona. Three hours from now Moloch would awaken and look at the sky just as I was. He was drawn to the sun. It was a ball of fire, and fire gave Moloch his power.

You sent your priests into Atlanta, huh? Don't you worry, Child Eater. I will take good care of them, and when I'm done, you'll wish you had never been reborn.

I let out a shrill whistle. Turgan took off from the ruin to the right and landed on my arm, all twelve pounds of him. Yellow feet gripped the padded bracer on my forearm with black talons. The golden eagle shifted his weight, wings fanning my head, and stared at me with his amber eyes.

Tulip came running around a heap of rubble. It was time for us to go to our new house and get the keys. I had a murder to solve.

[2]

Tamyra Miller chewed on her bottom lip. She was about ten years older than me, in her mid-thirties, with dark brown skin, a wealth of black hair she kept braided, and big round glasses, and she stared at the house in front of us with what could only be described as trepidation. I couldn't really blame her.

Built at the turn of the 20th century, the house used to be a sprawling antebellum mansion. When I bought it two years ago, it stood three stories tall, with white walls, a wide wraparound porch, and towering ionic columns holding up its gabled roof. Its twenty thousand square feet of living space had been divided into eight apartments, each with a separate entrance and balcony.

Eight months ago, I had hired Tamyra, a structural engineer, to wreck it. She went in with a team of masons and carpenters, reinforced the structure, reconfigured the floor plan according to my instructions, carving out a rectangular living space of about six thousand square feet inside the house, and then carefully collapsed the outer walls, piling additional chunks of concrete and wood from the fallen high-rises nearby.

From the outside, the house looked like a ruin, a heap of rubble topped with a roof, some columns scattered, some still standing, buried in debris. The reinforced stable with the armored door was securely hidden in the back. A narrow path led to the entrance, guarded by a thick steel door with a wooden veneer smeared with dirt. No windows, except for the small one located to the right of the door and guarded by a metal grate that gave me a view of the front yard from my kitchen. No weak points. No sign that it was even habitable, except for the balcony. Invisible from the street unless you climbed another building, the balcony sat recessed under the roof, shielded by thick steel and silver bars that ran all the way down to the cement foundation. I had already seen the inside of the house, and it was everything I wanted it to be.

Tamyra had come to a decision. "Ms. Ryder..."

"Yes?"

"I realize that you've sunk a lot of money into this home, but you can't really put a price on human life."

"Are you trying to tell me the house isn't safe?"

"The house is perfectly safe. It will withstand an earthquake. It's a fortress and I'm proud of it. I'm talking about that."

She turned left and looked west, where 17th NE Street rolled down hill, right into Unicorn Lane seething with magic five hundred yards away. Before the Shift, this was a neighborhood of stately homes and large yards, cushioned in greenery, with views of Midtown's office towers and price tags to match. Now the entire area lay abandoned. Unicorn Lane kept growing with every magic wave, creeping ever so slowly outward inch by inch.

"You wouldn't believe the crap we've seen crawl out of there over the six months we spent here," Tamyra said.

I would. That's why I'd paid them twice the going rate.

"There are other houses," the structural engineer said.

But none like mine. Ten years ago, when I was still Julie, I was coming home after killing a manticore. It had clawed my leg before it died, deep, almost to the bone. I was tired, dirty, and bleeding, so I took a shortcut, strayed too close to Unicorn Lane, and a pack of feral ghouls chased me to this house. Back then a pack of six ghouls presented a problem.

I'd climbed up on the roof to escape and watched the sun slowly set behind Unicorn Lane until Derek found me. He ran the ghouls off, tracked down my horse, and then lectured me on the benefits of not taking stupid shortcuts all the way home. The memory of it was vivid in my head. Me, on my horse, and him, walking next to me through the deserted night, chewing me out in his raspy voice.

That was long ago, in another life. Derek left Atlanta two years after I had. Nobody had seen him since.

An orange creature shot off the roof from across the street. I pulled my knife out, stepped forward, and sliced. A bat-like body the size of a medium dog crashed to the ground at my feet, jerking its limbs. Blood gushed from the stump of its neck onto the asphalt. Its head with long pointed jaws rolled and came to rest by my boot.

Tamyra grabbed at the gun on her hip.

"A shrieker," I told her and kicked the head back toward Unicorn Lane. "Nothing to worry about. Thank you for your concern, Mrs. Miller. I appreciate it, but I'm exactly where I need to be."

She sighed and held out a key ring and a bundle of rolled-up newspapers. "This is the only set, as requested. Here are all of the newspapers for the last week."

I took the keys and the newspapers. "Thank you. Would you like me to walk you out?"

She shook her head. "My husband is parked a few blocks down on 15th."

"Scream if you need help."

"Sure." She walked away.

I went to the front door and stuck the key into the lock. The well-oiled pins slid smoothly, and I opened the door and went inside.

The front door led straight into the living room, with a grimy wood-burning fireplace on the left. The inside of the house, about eight hundred square feet, looked like nothing special: old wooden floor, swept clean; battered walls that had seen better days; a shabby threadbare sofa facing the fireplace. On the right, a tiny square kitchen waited, with a derelict breakfast table and two chairs, clean but roughly used and worn out. A small dented fridge hummed in the corner. Straight ahead, at the other end of the living room, a short hallway led to a bedroom on the left and a bathroom on the right.

It seemed so familiar.

I hadn't realized it until now, but I had subconsciously recreated my first house, the one where I'd lived with my biological parents. It wasn't an exact copy, but it had that same vibe of working too hard for too little money and a stubborn refusal to admit to poverty. All that was missing were empty bottles of Tito's and Wild Irish Rose in the sink.

I walked into the kitchen and looked at the sink. Empty.

My birth father had been a carpenter. He died while building a bridge when I was eight or nine. A chunk of a crumbling overpass fell on him, crushing him instantly. It was too heavy to move, and they never recovered his body. We had to bury an empty coffin with some of his favorite things in it. I could no longer recall what he looked like.

I remembered my birth mother a little better. She was thin, bird-boned, with big brown eyes and blond hair. I used to look just like her. Her name was Jessica Olsen, and in my memories, she was always tired.

When my birth father was alive, we did okay. I had clothes, food, toys, even a skateboard. His death destroyed us. Shortly after the funeral, a man had come to the house trying to convince my mother to sell father's tools. She kept them and apprenticed to a carpenter instead.

Money became scarce. During the week, my mother worked long shifts. She wasn't really cut out for dragging heavy beams around, but she did it anyway. The weekends were the worst. There was nothing to do except remember that my father wasn't there. One weekend she started drinking and didn't stop until Monday. Next weekend she did it again. Then she started drinking after work.

All people struggle with the loss of someone they love. My mother wasn't a bad person. She just struggled more than most. She never meant to abandon me. She only tried to escape her misery, and somehow, she forgot I existed. I went hungry a lot. I wore torn clothes. Occasionally she would have a moment of clarity, see me, and then there would be food on the table and clean, mended T-shirts. But then she slipped away again.

I became a street kid. I starved, I stole, I took my beatings, and I learned that human predators were much worse than anything the magic waves could throw at me. I was so desperate for someone to love me, I'd thought the street kids were my friends even when they hit me and stole from me. At night I would go home. I still remembered the fragile hope I'd feel coming up to the front door. Maybe this time I would open it and Mom would be okay.

Then one day my birth mother went missing, and that's when Kate found me. Back then she worked for the Order of Merciful Aid, and she ran across me during a job. She didn't have to care about me, but she did, and she promised me she would find my mother. Things didn't go as planned, and my mother and I ended up in the middle of a sea demon invasion. The memory slapped me, clammy and revolting: me hanging off a cross, tied to it by ropes that stank of rotten fish, and a mass of sea demons below, scraping the flesh off my mother's body with their tongues. Her brown eyes had stared at the overcast sky, milky and empty...

I'd hung on that cross, watching the demons devour my mother's corpse, and hoped against all odds that Kate would rescue me. And she had.

I left the kitchen, crossing the living room to the short hallway that led to the lone bedroom and bathroom. The hallway wall was in bad shape, all plaster and old wallpaper, marked with holes where pictures must've once hung. I followed the hallway to where it made an L-turn just before the bathroom and stopped before the grimiest spot. They'd done a good job hiding the door.

I chose a big metal key from the key ring Tamyra had given me, inserted it into a nondescript-looking hole in the plaster about three feet off the ground, and turned it. A section of the wall gave way, as the heavy door swung inward. I stepped through it.

A large space spread before me, glowing in the flood of sunlight streaming through an enormous skylight above. Four gypsum columns soared toward the skylight, a pale, soothing cream, their finish slightly rough. The floor was limestone tile, the same sandy color as the columns and the walls. A two-foot-wide channel filled with clear water ran from the front door to the back wall, dividing the house in two. We had tapped a natural spring for it. The stream ended in a shallow basin, where lilies and lotus buds rested on the water.

On the left of the stream, three steps led to a raised platform, supporting a wooden desk. Past it a metal cauldron sat sunken into the floor, four feet in diameter, large enough for a small bonfire. Rows of shelves built into the walls offered endless storage space, and some of my supplies had already been delivered: bundles of different split wood, bags of dried herbs and minerals, and crates of glass and plastic jars and bottles waiting to be sorted. Behind them, by the blank wall, rested five long crates. My weapons.

On the right a kitchen was built against the wall, with a large island, a gas stove, a dining table large enough to seat eight, and a grouping of plush divans upholstered in green and blue. The shelves on this side of the room would hold books and pantry ingredients.

Here and there, small tables and plush cushions offered spots to sit under green diaphanous canopies embroidered with gold and scarlet. Plants thrived in big ceramic pots and vines dripped from the walls. Metal statues rested between the flowers, some delicate, some fierce. Beautiful glass fey lanterns and electric lamps dotted the walls.

Walking through the arched doorway at the back of the room would lead me to the bedroom and the bath with a luxurious shower and a square dipping pool, six feet by six, sunken into the floor.

Home... Well, almost.

I walked to the desk on the platform and pulled the lid off a small crate next to it. Inside lay a simple gladius in a plain sheath and a bundle of soft cotton. I took the gladius out, pulled the blade from the sheath, and placed it on the desk. The first sword Kate ever gave me.

The bundle was next. I unrolled it and took out a slender vase of seafoam color, with a second narrow bundle inside. I set the vase on the desk, pulled the smaller bundle free, and pried the cotton layers apart gently, holding my breath. A metal rose waited on the cloth.

Phew. It survived the trip. Derek had made it for me years ago when I first met him. Back then he'd been helping Kate with a job.

I slid it into the vase. There. Now it was home.

I spread the newspaper on the desk. It didn't take me long to find it. Pastor Nathan Haywood, fifty-two years old, Methodist, murdered in his own church, torn apart by something during the night. Three days ago. Why had Sienna waited three days to tell me?

I scanned the articles and the obituary. Pastor Haywood must have been beloved. The article spoke about him as if he were a saint. A photograph showed a line of mourners stretching around the city block. People weeping. People hugging each other. The death had stunned Atlanta. The city was grieving.

The most recent article mentioned the investigation being passed to the Order of Merciful Aid. Perfect. I had a way in. It was risky, but far better than trying to sort this out while dealing with Atlanta's Paranormal Activity Division.

It was barely eight in the morning. If I got a move on, I could get to the Order by nine.

I looked up. The blade of the gladius lay on my desk, reflecting the glow from the skylight.

Kate hadn't just rescued me. She'd taken me in. If something tried to hurt me, she'd kill it. If I had a problem, she would give me room to fix it, and if I needed help, she would help me. She enrolled me in school and nagged me to do my homework. She taught me to use weapons and gave me my first spear lesson. She loved me honestly and without reservation.

Her family became my family. Andrea Medrano, her best friend, became Aunt Andy. Kate's aunt, Erra, the City Eater, the ancient princess awakened into our age, became my grandmother. Kate's father, the immortal megalomaniac, decided to be my grandfather. Curran, Kate's husband and the former Beast Lord, took care of me like I was his own child, and when Conlan was born, I never once thought of him as anything but my brother.

We never used words like "mother" and "daughter" even after the adoption went through. She called me Julie and I called her Kate. She married Curran, and I called him Curran.

I slipped up only once. Eight years ago, I left Atlanta with Erra. I wanted to find my own way, and I had my reasons. Within two weeks homesickness had set in and gnawed on me, until I could stand it no longer. Three months from setting out, I'd called the house. Kate picked up. I'd meant to say hi, but what came out was "Mom?" She had said, "Yes, kiddo?" And then we talked like nothing had happened. Neither of us ever mentioned it again. She never blamed me for leaving. She had done the same thing when she was my age. She didn't have to tell me I was welcome back anytime. It was a given.

Kate, Curran, and Conlan, they were my home. My safe place, my shelter, secure, stable, and warm, where I was loved. It was my turn to guard them from danger, and my first step was to take custody of the Haywood case and keep Moloch's priests away from it.

[3]

The Order of Merciful Aid occupied a compound at the intersection of Centennial Park Drive and Andorf's Avenue. The five-story building, half fort, half bunker, had all the bells and whistles that came with post-Shift construction: narrow windows protected by metal grates with silver in the bars, foot-thick stone walls, and a flat roof, guarded by ballistae and M240 medium machine guns. A nine-foot-tall wall topped with razor wire and sporting guard towers wrapped around it all. Magic or tech, the knights would pulverize it.

I rode straight to the front gate and stopped before a squat guardhouse with reinforced walls and tinted windows secured by metal grates. The gate in the stone wall past the guardhouse stood wide open, and through them I could see stables and an exercise yard. The Order had upgraded. You could fit four of their old headquarters into this new place.

A dark-skinned knight about my age with a scar on his neck and black hair cut short came out. He carried a tactical sword on his hip.

"Name?"

"Aurelia Ryder."

"Purpose of visit?"

"I'm here to see Knight-Protector Nikolas Feldman."

The knight eyed me. "Is he expecting you?"

"No. But he will see me."

"What makes you so sure?"

"I hold the Tower."

The knight's expression didn't change. "Is that supposed to mean something?"

No, I'm a crazy person who came to spout random nonsense at your citadel of armed fanatics. "Why don't you call it in and find out?"

"Wait here."

He went back to the guardhouse.

I waited.

The Order originated in the chaos immediately following the Shift, right after that first wave of magic that dropped planes out of the sky and sapped all the energy out of the power grid. That wave raged for three days, birthing monsters and awakening powers at random. The apocalypse had come and shattered our technological civilization with one blow, like a cosmic hammer. During that wave, Jared Stone, a former Army Ranger, banded with a few of his neighbors to protect their houses from the magic nightmares ravaging their neighborhood, and the Order was born.

Stone patterned his creation after the medieval knight orders, emphasizing strict discipline, education, and, above all, competency, and gave it a simple mission—protect mankind from all things magic. The knights helped anyone who asked. Rich, poor, it didn't matter. If you ran into a magic problem you couldn't handle, the Order would accept your petition and solve your dilemma. On their terms.

Over the years, the Order grew. As the reach of the federal government weakened and the States gained power, law enforcement came to rely on the knights more and more. They had chapters in all the major cities; they were experts in disposing of magic hazmat, and they were deadly.

Unfortunately, the Order took its mission literally, and the knights' definition of human was rather narrow. Occasionally they would show their true colors, and society recoiled. The knights would adjust their policies, weather the storm of public opinion, and sooner or later the authorities would come knocking on their door, and all would be as it was. At least until the next massacre.

A skinny kid with tan and sandy hair, about sixteen or so, trotted out of the stables inside the walled perimeter. We nodded to each other.

The knight stepped back out of the guardhouse. "You may go in. Peyton will take your horse."

I dismounted and handed the reins to Peyton. He smiled at me and looked at Tulip. The mare sighed.

"Behave," I told her.

"Beautiful color," Peyton told me.

"Thank you." I headed to the building.

"Ma'am," Peyton called out.

"Yes?"

"Your horse has blood on her chin."

I turned around, pulled a rag out of my pocket, and wiped the bloody smear off Tulip's face. "There you go. All good."

Peyton gave me a suspicious look, and he and Tulip walked off.

I loved my horse, but she always was a messy eater.

A YOUNG FEMALE KNIGHT MET ME AT THE GATES OF THE ORDER. She was taller than me by six inches, brown-skinned, with a lean athletic build, light hazel eyes, and an intense, unblinking stare. Her dark brown hair, braided in cornrows, fell on her

31

shoulders in four thick plaits. She walked me through the front hall and a long hallway to Nick's office and pointed to the chair in front of his desk. "Sit. Stay. Wait."

I sat and held my fists in front of me like paws. "Woof!"

"Perfect." She turned, walked out of the office, and parked herself in the hallway by the open door.

The Order of Merciful Aid, the very soul of courtesy in this savage age.

I sat in the chair and studied the office. Plain desk, plain chairs; a row of bookshelves against one wall filled with an assortment of volumes, everything from forensic science volumes to bestiaries; a weapons rack against the opposite wall, holding three blades, a spear, a mace, a rifle, and a shotgun. A spartan, functional office for a spartan, functional man.

Nick Feldman and my family had a complicated history. He had a code of morals, to which he fanatically adhered. He was also deeply paranoid, resolute, and, once he decided that you were a threat, prone to sudden violence. This conversation would have to be done very carefully.

Steps echoed down the hallway. Nick Feldman entered and walked to his desk, and I almost fell out of my chair.

Nick had gone grey.

The last time I saw him he'd had brown hair he kept cropped. It was longer now, long enough to be brushed, but it was steel-grey. He had aged.

Oh wow.

Nick Feldman gave me a cold stare. His eyes were very pale, stark against the backdrop of his tan skin, and being on the receiving end of that look was like gazing into the barrel of a gun. I was probably expected to collapse to my knees and beg for mercy, but I was still grappling with the hair and the lines around his eyes, so I just stared back, my face blank.

How old was he now? Kate was...thirty-eight, so he was forty-one. Is that what people looked like at forty-one?

He didn't look weakened by age. If anything, it made him harder. Tall and broad-shouldered, his body conveyed harsh, sinewy strength. His cheekbones had grown more defined. He'd picked up a scar that crossed his left cheek, and his face radiated authority and stoic pessimism. If you catapulted him through time to the convoy of Crusaders with hollow eyes and worn-out armor cutting their way across the Holy Land after years of fighting, he would fit right in.

He motioned to me with his hand. "Let's see it."

I pulled the Tower out of my pocket and placed it on his desk. It was a metal badge about the size of a playing card with an image of the tower engraved on one side. Nick turned it over. The other side was embossed with number four. A signature ran underneath it, silvery and embedded in metal, as if someone had signed the badge with silver wire while the metal still cooled from the forge. *Damian Angevin.*

Nick picked up the badge and held it out. The female knight who'd escorted me in entered, took the Tower, and left.

Nick studied me with his pale eyes.

I had spent too much time with my grandmother. Technically, she was my adoptive grand-aunt, but we both agreed that "grandmother" was easier and shorter and better fit our relationship. Erra didn't age. She was millennia old, but she looked perpetually about forty, and it was an awe-inspiring, regal forty. Nick was forty-one and he looked like he'd seen hell.

"Have you been well, Knight-Protector?" I shouldn't have said that. It just slipped out.

Nick furrowed his eyebrows. "Do we know each other?"

"No."

Magic surged through the world, saturating it in a single breathtaking instant. Suddenly I was lighter, stronger, sharper. My sensate ability kicked in, and vivid color bloomed in my field of vision. Faint swirls of blue in every shade slid over the furniture and floor—recent traces of human magic from the visitors to Nick's office. A smudge of green from a shapeshifter, a hint of purple, old and fading—the foul track of a vampire—and Nick himself, an amalgam of azure and sapphire streaked with bright, electric yellow. I blinked to turn it off.

All living things emanated magic, and the intensity of the trail they left behind varied. A human mage walking down the street emanated very little, and that faint trail vanished within minutes. The same mage in a fight for her life would leave behind an explosion of blue that could persist for days, provided tech didn't wipe it out. The visitors to Nick's office had been under some pressure. Looking at his stone idol expression, I couldn't imagine why. He worked so hard to put you at ease.

In the hallway a woman bit off a curse. The Tower realized that the hand holding it didn't belong to its owner and activated. Asking the female knight if she needed some aloe for that burn wouldn't be prudent, but it was very tempting.

The female knight returned and deposited the badge wrapped in a rag on the desk. "It checks out." She turned and went back to her post by the door.

I picked up the badge. A tingle of magic shot through my fingertips and vanished, recognizing me. I slid it back into my pocket. The Tower granted me the right to call on the Order for aid and gave me authority equivalent to a Knight-Captain, which meant I outranked everyone in the office, except for Nick.

The Knight-Protectors oversaw regional offices, individual chapters of the Order, and their position came with a lot of autonomy. Only Grand Master of the Order and the Knight-Seneschal ranked higher. Technically the Tower constituted a direct order from the Grand Master to render whatever assistance I required. Practically, trying to strong-arm Nick would end in disaster. I needed his cooperation.

"To get a Tower you had to have performed a service of great value to the Order," Nick said.

I had.

Nick waited. I kept my mouth shut.

"What's your relationship with the Grand Master?" Nick asked.

"I'm not at liberty to answer."

Erra liked to describe her relationship with the head of the Order as "complicated." From my point of view, there was nothing complicated about it. Damian Angevin was desperately in love with my grandmother. After he granted her the first Tower, she gave it to me. He found out and presented her with another one, so she would have one of her own just in case. My grandmother liked him; however, her heart belonged to a man who'd died over two thousand years ago. Damian knew this, but he was never one to back down from a challenge.

Nick leaned back into his chair, doing an excellent impression of a granite boulder. "I've never heard of you, Ms. Ryder."

"I'm not famous."

"There are only four Towers in existence," Nick said.

Five, but who was counting?

"I know all four recipients of the Tower."

Great. Just my luck.

"Your Tower is registered to you, which means that one of the four granted you authority to use it. Who do you belong to, Ms. Ryder?"

I belonged to New Shinar and to my grandmother, the Plaguebringer, the City Eater, Rigmur Pana-Shinar—the Voice of the Old Kingdom. In the grand tradition of the royal line, I had earned my share of titles as well, the most famous of which was Dananu Edes-Shinar—the Strength of the New Shinar. Nick *had* actually heard of me. He just didn't know it.

Mentioning any of this nonsense was out of the question because Nick hated my grandfather, my grandmother, and anything to do with Shinar with the passion of a thousand suns. The Tower compelled the Knight-Protector to comply, but if he knew who I was, he would make things as difficult as he could.

This required tact. Of the four Tower recipients, Nick would likely view Hannah Salazar as the lesser evil. A former officer, she ran a small private army in New Mexico, and her people had saved the local Order chapter during the last flare at great cost.

"I belong to someone who values discipline and accountability, Knight-Protector. I swore an oath to follow orders, and those orders require me to maintain confidentiality. I don't enjoy the cloak-and-dagger act. I prefer simple missions where the enemy is clear, but this is the way my chain of command wants to play it, so I must do my best. I hope for your understanding."

There you go, I am a mercenary with a military mindset. Don't mind me. No deep dark secrets here.

Nick pondered me for a long moment. "Very well. What do you need?"

I LEANED FORWARD. "THREE DAYS AGO, A MAN WAS MURDERED. I want to take over the investigation into his death."

Nick sighed. "This is Atlanta, Ms. Ryder. Be more specific. Which of the seven murders on my desk would you like to play with?"

"Pastor Haywood's."

Nick thumbed through the stack of files on his desk, pulled one out, and offered it to me. "Fine. It's all yours."

Just like that. Huh.

Nick studied me. "Is something the matter?"

"I expected more resistance."

"And you will have it. Just not from me. How much do you know about Atlanta?"

"Not as much as I'd like to."

"Stay awhile and you'll wish you knew less."

Nick stood up and pulled at a cord hanging from a roll of plastic secured on the back wall. The plastic unrolled into a map of Atlanta with sections tinted with different colors.

"The lay of the land," Nick said. "At least as of last week. Atlanta is less a city and more of a collection of territories claimed by different factions. There are three main roads, I-20 that runs east to west, I-85 that runs north to south, and the Peach Loop, which is a new road that circles the city."

He pointed to the northeast where a grey icon depicted a stylized castle sitting in the middle of an area tinted with green. "The Keep, the headquarters of the Pack. Their territory extends almost to I-85."

Nick tapped a white palace icon located in the northwest, in the loop between I-85 and I-20, colored with red. "The Casino. It used to belong to the People, except now our particular People call themselves the Eastern Institute of Necromancy, also known as EIN. They're still the same People. They still pilot vampires with their minds, finance their research with gambling, and think they're better than everyone else and therefore are entitled to special treatment."

The People had been created by my grandfather. Thousands of years ago, Roland accidentally made the first vampire, and when he awoke in the modern age, he decided to make good use of them. Before his exile, he established the People, an organization of necromancers capable of piloting vampires with their minds. He gave them a modern name, because "navigator" sounded a lot less scary than necromancer, and sent them into the world. The People positioned themselves as part-corporation, part-research institute, and usually owned community-entertaining businesses. Casinos were their favorite.

Now that Grandfather was no longer in the picture, the People fractured into independent organizations. Atlanta's EIN was more independent than most. During the final fight between Kate and Roland, the Atlanta's People threw their lot in with Kate. A lot of other navigators viewed it as a betrayal.

Nick pointed to a grey section centered on a tower. "The Order's territory. You are relatively safe here."

He moved his finger to an area spreading north and south of I-20 stained with so many colors, it looked like an overenthusiastic toddler with finger paints had gone wild after a serious sugar rush.

"The Pagans. The Covens are here, the Neo-Vikings over there, then we have the Druids, the Greeks, the Volhvs, the Egyptians, the devotees of the traditional African religions…"

His hand flicked over the map to the southeast. "The representatives of the Cherokee, Apalachee, Muscogee Creek, and other tribes are here. Also, the major religions each have their own sphere of influence and center of power, dotted throughout the city, with the Christians being the most numerous. Apocalypse or not, we're still in the Bible Belt."

Nick stepped back and waved his hand, encompassing the map.

"It's about as fun as it looks. Occasionally, something gets them all united, but most of the time, they can't agree on where the sun will rise tomorrow. They are like rocks in a sack, grinding against each other. They all want to expand, but there is only so much city to go around, so they watch each other, waiting for an opportunity."

"What about that smaller blue-green area in the southeast?"

Nick grimaced. "That's the Lennart-Daniels gated community."

Really? "Gated community?"

"Yes. It's very exclusive."

I bet it is. "Meaning?"

"Stay out of there. Lennart once led the Pack, and Daniels has claimed—her word, not mine—the entire city in the past. Now they spend most of their time up in Wilmington because their son attends a private school there, but they come back in the summer to visit family and friends. That family is complicated."

You don't say.

"They have issues with the Pack and EIN, and they are not receptive to outsiders. The entire neighborhood consists of shapeshifter families that left the Pack with them. Imagine three streets full of werebears and former Pack heavy hitters fanatically loyal to Lennart and Daniels. If you trespass, I may not be able to get you out."

That was a lie. Nick visited my family on a regular basis. Kate considered him her stepbrother. Conlan called him "Uncle." Sometimes, when Nick did something particularly boneheaded, Kate referred to him as "Uncle Stupidhead" and not always out of his earshot.

If one of Nick's knights accidentally happened to wander into their neighborhood and made a mess of things, Kate and Curran would absolutely return the poor lost lamb to Nick. Besides, as the Knight-Protector, Nick could and would go anywhere in the city, and all the bigwigs whose territory he invaded would have to mind their manners when they politely asked him to leave.

"While you're at it, keep clear of the Mercenary Guild. Lennart and Daniels don't run it anymore, but they still own a chunk of it, so don't go in there looking for your people."

Well, my ploy to pose as one of Hannah Salazar's private soldiers worked. He thought I was a mercenary, clearly a profession he wasn't fond of. That and my barging in and taking one of his cases likely meant that if I did get in trouble, the Knight-Protector wouldn't be in a rush to rescue me. Good thing I didn't often require rescue.

"The murder of Pastor Nathan Haywood happened here." Nick touched an area in the southeast, close to the Peach Loop. "In no man's land. You have the Warren to the east. It's an impoverished area, full of the homeless and street gangs. The PAD doesn't make many trips to the Warren. Pastor Haywood deliberately chose this neighborhood. He was a true Christian. He lived simply, he was humble, and he worked miracles. This was a man who ministered to anyone in need, especially to the poor. He fed them, he healed them, and he spread the word of his god."

"You knew him?"

"I saw him cure people. He wasn't a fraud."

Post-Shift, faith had power. If enough people believed in a god, the deity would grow in power and sometimes its priests gained magic abilities. Nobody quite knew if those powers were the result of the deity imbuing its chosen with magic or if the faith of the congregation empowered the clergy directly, but their new abilities were a fact.

"Pastor Haywood never took any money or credit for what he did. His magic was faith-based, so it only worked on those who shared his beliefs, but when it worked, it was extraordinary. He was a good man, who thought he had no magic of his own and saw himself as an instrument of a higher power. Do you know how this kind miracle worker died?"

"No."

"Look in the file."

I opened the file. A colored photograph stared back at me. A stump of a body sprawled in a puddle of blood on the floor. The head was missing, torn off, judging by the ragged shreds of skin around the neck. His chest was a gory mess. Something with vicious claws had ripped him open, breaking his ribs, and their shards jutted out of the red-smeared flesh. Thick, dark blood pooled inside the chest cavity where vital organs used to be.

"It took his heart," I said.

"Yes." Nick sat back in his chair. "It's too early to say if the culprit is an 'it.' The force and the claws required to open a human being like that could indicate a shapeshifter or a vampire or half a dozen magical beasts seen recently within the city limits. Your guess is as good as mine."

He sounded bored. Nick didn't know how to be apathetic about his job. He never phoned anything in, but here was a holy man, a pastor he personally knew and clearly admired, murdered in a horrifying way and Nick was pretending not to care. He wasn't giving me any details either.

Why so indifferent, Uncle? What are you hiding?

"Did he have any enemies? Do you have any leads or suspects?"

"No and no. Pastor Haywood was beloved by his congregation and respected by his peers. The murder was announced in the paper two days ago, and there are still hundreds of mourners standing vigil at the church where he was a deacon."

I studied the photograph and slid it back into the file gently. I had seen plenty of dead bodies. I had made a lot of bodies dead, and sometimes my handiwork looked worse than this. But there was something profoundly sad about Pastor Haywood's murder. The brutality of it, the sheer savagery of it made you want to punch something. He was a man with a kind heart, and someone had literally ripped it out. He was a light in the world. We had so few lights.

I traced the body with my fingertips. *You won't be forgotten. I promise you I will find the one responsible and stop them from hurting anyone else.*

I realized Nick was watching me and closed the file.

"The Order was asked by the Methodist Bishop of North Georgia to step in because the manner of death makes this case a political time bomb. The PAD was overjoyed to send it over. It landed on my desk this morning. Everything we know is in that file and now it's yours."

Nick opened a drawer in his desk, took out a form, wrote on it in indecipherable cursive, and held it out.

"For the purposes of this investigation, we're going to make you a Knight-Defender."

Rank and file member of the Order. Perfect.

"Go down the hall, take a left, second door on the right, give them this paper, and they will make you your very own junior detective badge. While in possession of said badge, you represent the Order of Merciful Aid. Should you fuck up, you'll find me less than merciful, and no matter what favor your superior thinks they're owed, I'll kick your ass right out of Atlanta. Understood?"

Right. That's all he was going to give me. "Understood. Any advice?"

Nick grinned like a wolf baring his fangs. "Have fun, don't offend anybody, and try not to die."

[4]

Three minutes after I left the Order's chapter, I realized I'd picked up a tail. To be fair, the tail was almost painfully obvious, so it wasn't that much of an achievement.

I shifted in the saddle, turning my head slightly. The female knight who'd escorted me to Nick's office was following me on foot, making no effort to hide herself. She must've decided that even if I knew she was there, I couldn't do much about it.

I let her follow me down Magnum, across the post-Shift bridge that spanned the railroad tracks, and down the narrow Packard Street. Normally I would've just ignored her and let her merrily tail me wherever, but I was going to the murder scene, and I had a feeling there were things there I didn't want her to see.

Packard brought me to Ted Turner Drive, lined with reclamation shops and construction offices. Turner ran next to the ruined Downtown. Scavenging the ruins for metal and other usable materials was a big business. The traffic went from nonexistent to heavy, as the street channeled carts with supplies, craftsmen, and laborers. Both of my parents used to work here.

I should've turned south, to the right. Instead I turned north. The buildings at the intersection blocked me from the knight's view. I nudged Tulip into a trot. She picked up the pace, nimbly dodging the crowds. A collapsed building loomed on the left, pure white, its four remaining floors rising from the rubble. We reached it, I dismounted, and tapped Tulip's neck. "Around the block."

She took off down the street.

I ducked into a hole in a former office building. From the outside it looked like the interior had completely collapsed there, but there was a narrow gap on the right, if you knew where to look. I squeezed through it, into the gloom, jogged a dozen feet to the inner wall, and jumped up. My hands caught the familiar handholds on pure muscle memory, and I scrambled up, all the way to the exposed third floor. I padded to the half-wrecked wall and glanced out of the gap, keeping myself hidden.

The female knight jogged out of the traffic and halted below. If she was tracking me by magic, she would have no problem finding me. If she tracked by scent, she would likely follow Tulip. A horse's scent was stronger and easier to track than the rider's.

She looked left. She looked right. She looked confused.

Lost something?

The knight turned in a slow circle, scanning the streets, and went right, down Trinity Avenue. Neither magic nor scent then, just plain old eyesight. She'd lost me, and she correctly figured out that I would be going to the crime scene, so instead of wasting time on finding me, she decided to go to the crime scene as well and wait.

On paper, Trinity Avenue would be a good way to get to Pastor Haywood's church. But Trinity Avenue ran into Wolf Bridge, which spanned the rubble and crossed over I-85. This time of day the reclamation teams would be bringing in the first loads of salvage from Downtown. At the same time, the teamsters would be transferring this morning's freight from the north ley line to the west. Wolf Bridge would be packed hoof to bumper. It would cost her at least half an hour, forty-five minutes if it was a busy shipping day. She was likely a capable knight. Nick didn't tolerate incompetency. But she spoke with a touch of Upper Midwest, and I'd been running away from monsters on these streets for as long as I could walk. Atlanta was my city.

I climbed down and whistled. A few seconds later Tulip came trotting from around the corner. I mounted and headed south on Turner.

Twenty-five minutes later I dismounted in front of Garden Lane Chapel. If there were gardens here, no trace of them remained. The street bordered the Warren, a patchwork of ruined houses and crumbling apartments that had been hit by magic so many times, everyone who could afford to move had. The neighborhood looked bleak; abandoned buildings staring at the world with black-hole windows, ugly grey lichens on the walls that seemed to suck the color out of the paint and stucco, and black trees. The trees were the worst, their bark coal-black and slightly fuzzy. Even their leaves had turned dark and narrow, sharp enough to cut.

Against this backdrop, the chapel all but glowed. White and freshly painted, with a bright red door, it perched on the corner like a beacon of safety. A young cop stood by the door, a gladius on one hip and a service revolver on the other. Traces of magic sometimes lingered even during the tech waves now, and the revolvers tended to misfire less than semi-automatics.

Personally, I preferred blades. They always worked.

The cop tilted his head, presenting me with a flat expression. In his mid-twenties, tan and fit, with blue-black hair, he wasn't a rookie or a veteran putting in time till retirement. He was in the prime of his copness, and the way he stood told me he enjoyed every minute of it.

He took in the tattered cloak that hid most of me, the worn saddlebag on Tulip, and the bow protruding from the scabbard attached to her saddle and classified me as "move along." I clearly had no business on this street.

I pushed back my hood. He blinked. The flat expression slid off his face. Suddenly he was alert and professional. He was treating me to his "polite badass" persona.

The face strikes again.

Like many teenage girls, I had gone through a stage when I thought I was the ugliest thing on Earth, but by eighteen, I had realized that I was pretty. I used to have one of those pixie faces that could look beautiful or mousy. My old face was like a simple black dress. I could dress it up or dress it down.

That was no longer an option. My new face made an impact no matter what I did to it. Dirty, clean, makeup, no makeup, it didn't matter. The eye I had absorbed reshaped me. Nobody even remembered my old face except me.

"Can I help you, ma'am?" the cop asked.

I pulled out my freshly minted Order ID and presented it to him. "I'm here to take this murder off your hands."

"I haven't seen you before. I would have remembered if we met." His face moved a little. He had considered hitting me with his "smooth smile" but decided that the professional colleague angle might work better.

"I just transferred."

He gave me an understanding look. "New guys get all the shit jobs."

"Isn't that the truth?" I smiled at him.

He raised his eyebrows slightly. I waited, but nothing came out of his mouth.

"I would like to see the crime scene, Officer..." I let it hang.

"Officer Fleming. This way."

He opened the red door and walked through. I followed.

The inside of the church was clean and bright. Sunshine flooded through the windows and the round skylight right above where the pulpit would have been, so the pastor standing at it would have been bathed in light during the sermon. But the pulpit was nowhere to be found.

Fleming strode down the aisle between the pews. "You're not from around here."

"No," I lied.

"So where is home?"

"Small town out west."

He nodded. "Okay, Small Town. Forensics has been through the scene but try not to alter anything. Until your boss signs all the paperwork, this is still our baby, which means it's my head if you screw it up."

He thought I was fresh off the farm. Oh, this would be good.

Officer Fleming gave me his serious stare to communicate that he was about to pass on Important Information. "I'll give you some background. This area was hammered by magic. You saw the black trees?"

"Yes."

"It gets worse as you go deeper in. Everyone who could afford to move did. The church used to thrive, but after the first couple of flares, they closed it down, because everyone had taken off. It sat abandoned for a while, then Pastor Haywood asked if he could have it to minister to whoever was left in the Warren. They gave it to him. He lived here too, in a little apartment in the back. The church door was never locked, and if you rang the bell on the door in the back, he would come to talk to you, day or night."

"You knew him."

"Yes. Most people around here knew him. You see all sorts of shit in Atlanta. Most of it makes sense. Someone needs something, food, drugs, wood for the winter, so they steal. Someone gets mad, hurts somebody else. It's bad but it makes sense. This, this makes no sense. It's evil."

He halted. The raised platform where the pulpit should have been stood empty, littered with broken glass. Blood stained the pine floorboards, dried to a dark crust. The light streaming through the shattered skylight painted a bright circle in the gore, and the crushed glass glittered, like diamonds on burgundy velvet.

I glanced around. A heap of broken wooden shards lay crumpled against the left wall—the pulpit. Something had come through the skylight and batted it aside. The pulpit had flown into the wall and splintered into shards.

"First time in Atlanta?" Fleming asked.

"Mhm."

"It's a rough city."

You should see LA. It will turn your hair white overnight. "So I gathered."

"It can be tough to get your bearings."

"I can see that." Please, crusty veteran, enlighten this humble rookie.

"Have you found a place to stay yet?" Fleming said. "I can recommend a few of the safer areas."

The last thing I needed was him trying to find out where I was staying. I needed to shut this down flat. "The Order likes to keep an eye on us. I'll be in the barracks for a bit."

"Let me know when they let you out for recess and I'll show you around."

Recess? "I might take you up on that generous offer."

He grinned at me. "Happy to help."

I blinked, bringing my magic into focus. Translucent swipes of color appeared. Bright blueish silver, the color of human magic infused with divinity. Pastor Haywood. The flecks and smudges of silver were everywhere, but the bloody platform glowed with it. The twisted cascade of feathery magic stretched from the skylight all the way down, as if someone had taken a radiant spider web, woven of pure light, crumpled it together, and dumped it from the skylight onto the floor.

A bright trail of green, a familiar shade, led to the platform. Shapeshifters, too recent to have been involved in the murder. I crouched, getting a closer look. One particular ribbon of grass-green stood out. Ugh. Just my luck.

"Have any shapeshifters been here recently?"

"No."

Right. They didn't come through the skylight. The trail started at the door. Someone let them in, which meant either the cops owed them a favor, or some money had exchanged hands. Probably both.

I moved closer, into the space between the front row of pews and the platform. A second shapeshifter trail. These guys did come through the skylight and left only a couple of hours ago. Strange. Two separate crews? Why?

A single thread of green in that second trail caught the light, glowing with magic. It was the most beautiful mint green, translucent and pure. The other shapeshifter trails, grass-green or hunter, had degraded slightly, fading a little into the environment. But that mint green stayed, still bright and vibrant. If the other traces were watercolor, this was a metallic acrylic. It drew the eye. I had never seen anything like it.

As beautiful and strange as it was, the thread was too recent to be connected to the murder.

I stepped onto the platform and knelt down, trying to parse the explosion of silver. So much power expended so quickly. Death wasn't instant. Pastor Haywood had come face-to-face with his attacker, and he'd fought back. The struggle hadn't lasted long, but it was savage and brutal.

The magic was too dense. I needed a better point of view.

I lay down on my back and looked up into the funnel of silver stretching to the ceiling.

"Are you okay?" Fleming asked.

"Mm-hmm."

Some of the silver was tinted with gold. It spiraled down, feathery and gossamer, mixing with Pastor Haywood's silver blue. Yellow usually meant animal magic, but not always. When Nick went undercover with my grandfather's people, they had forced his body to absorb an alien power, which is why his signature had a yellow streak to it. Still, such light gold... A divine beast?

"Remember how I said not to mess with the scene? I don't know how to break this to you, but you're contaminating things all over the place."

"Since Pastor Haywood died, seventeen people have been at this scene. They walked all around the church, and a couple of them tasted the blood over there. If you're worried about contamination, that cat is out of the bag."

I crossed the platform to the right, taking care to avoid the blood, and saw a slight shimmer of purple in the corner. Hello.

I walked over. A sigil was burned into the wooden floorboards. A distorted stick figure with a circle where the head would be and a crescent moon instead of feet. Its right arm pointed up at a forty-five-degree angle. The left arm continued down, forming an H, while its right simply ended.

The sigil glowed with intense, electric lilac. Active.

A familiar rage stirred inside me. Moloch's priests didn't kill the pastor, but they defiled his sanctuary by leaving one of their own to watch it and taint it with Moloch's power. This was his holy place, a refuge where Pastor Haywood ministered, and they desecrated it.

Why watch a crime scene? What did they want from it? I had to pull Moloch's little helper out of its hidey hole and find out. Depending on who was hiding in the sigil, it could get messy.

The female knight would be here any minute. Anything she witnessed would be reported back to Nick, and I wasn't ready to answer the kinds of questions it would raise. I could try to come back tonight, but if the thing hiding in the sigil killed someone before then, I'd never forgive myself. If I was going to break the seal, it had to be now.

Getting rid of Officer Jaded Veteran would be a problem.

"Can you give me some privacy, Officer Fleming?"

"Nope."

Crap. "I need you to step back, please."

Fleming took two deliberate steps back. His face told me that was as far as he was willing to go. Doing anything too flashy with him here was out of the question. Fine.

"I'll be right back."

I walked past him, going outside. On the left some bricks had come loose from a flower bed. That would do. I picked one up and headed back into the church.

Fleming was exactly where I had left him. He eyed the paver brick. "Don't break any windows, Small Town."

I walked up to the sigil, put the brick on the floor, reached into my cloak, and found the handle of my knife. It was a simple knife, reminiscent of a Bowie with a nine-inch tool steel blade, full tang, and a stacked leather handle, so my hand didn't slip.

"Officer Fleming?"

"Yes?"

"Duck."

I yanked my cloak off and dragged my foot across the sigil. A man-sized clump of darkness tore out of it, like a ghost in a mantle of smoke. His hands ended in three-inch-long black claws, their tips glowing with red-hot fire. A ma'avir, one of Moloch's priests. A lesser one.

The phantom raked at me. I shied out of the way, letting the claws rend the air a hair from my throat, and stabbed the knife into the phantom's chest, hammering a spike of my magic through it.

The knife sank into flesh. I jerked it free. Fire bled through the smoke.

The ma'avir screeched and spat a torrent of flames. I dodged and slashed again, slicing at the creature's protective cloak, left to right and up. The smoke tore like an old tarp, betraying a glimpse of a charred body wrapped in flames.

The phantom flailed, trying to shred me with its claws. Fast, but not fast enough. I spun to the left, around it, bringing my arm in an arch from inside out and buried my blade in its back.

The creature shrieked.

I gripped the knife, feeding magic into it, and dragged it down, carving through gristle and bone, slicing through the sigils branded on its flesh, until I reached the main one in the small of its back. My blade bit into it. The sigil broke and vanished in a flash of lilac.

The smoke disappeared, like a length of black chiffon jerked out of sight. Fire burst out of the priest. For an instant, the ma'avir was engulfed in flames, a dark thing flailing within an inferno, like a blasphemous demonic candle. He burned and howled.

I swiped the brick from the floor.

The fire faltered, leaving behind a humanoid shape, desiccated, charred, bald, with his face covered in a metal mask. I kicked the creature's spine. He went down with a dry crack. I flipped him on his back and smashed the brick into his face. The mask clanged.

I hit it again, again, and again, with controlled, methodical savagery. The mask cracked. Another hit. The metal split. Chunks of the mask fell apart, revealing a nightmarish face. His lips were gone, teeth bared in a grotesque grin. His nose was a hole in the leathery flesh of its skull. He should have been dead but somehow he was alive, an abomination wrapped in foul magic, staring at me with wide eyes, its irises full of fire.

A raspy sound broke through the priest's teeth, a half-groan, half-snarl, so weak I had to strain to hear it. "Glory to the King of Fire…"

"Your god isn't here," I told him quietly. "He doesn't care. He won't save you."

"He'll come for you. You belong to him. The world belongs to him."

"The world belongs to me and my kind, ma'avir."

I plunged the knife into his chest and twisted. The priest convulsed, agony twisting his limbs.

"Tell me why you are here, and your death will be quick."

The ma'avir rasped again, "Mercy…"

"You serve the god who feeds on children burned alive in his fire. There is no mercy in the world for you."

I twisted the knife again. His shriek lashed my eardrums.

"Tell me."

"The priest's killer," he whispered. "Moloch wants it."

"Why?"

Fiery eyes stared past me at the piece of the sky through the ruined skylight. The magic that gave the ma'avir his perverse unlife was bleeding out. He was done.

Words of an ancient prayer in a language dead for thousands of years hissed out of the creature's mouth. *The Great Moloch, God among kings, I come to you…*

No. I leaned close, so close I could feel the dying heat rising from the priest and whispered into his ear in the same tongue as his prayer. *There will be no death rites for you. Die and become nothing.*

I rose, set the brick on the creature's face, and stomped down on it.

A fiery blast wave tore out of the corpse, roaring like an enraged animal. Every window in the church exploded. The building shook once, and then all was quiet. Smoke rose from the front pews, scorched by the heat.

The priest's body melted into nothing. Only my knife and

the brick remained, stained with soot and lilac magic. That was the problem with killing ma'avirim. When one of Moloch's assassin-priests died, their magic sullied the weapon that killed them, and, worse, others of their kind could track it the way bloodhounds followed a scent. The stain lingered until the next tech wave. I didn't want them to track me. Not yet.

I glanced at the lilac splashed on my hands and concentrated. Thin red vapor slid out of me, invisible to the naked eye, cleansing my skin. Didn't work on weapons or clothes, unfortunately. I'd tried.

A small noise made me turn to the right. Something moved between the pews. Slowly, gingerly, Officer Fleming stood up. Two wide eyes stared at me from a face smudged with soot.

The door burst open, and the female knight tore into the church.

"You missed it." I swiped my cloak off the floor, slipped it on, and walked off the platform.

She swore.

I walked past Fleming. "Sorry about the windows, Big Town."

He gaped at me. I winked at him and headed to the door.

[5]

I brought Tulip to a halt on the corner of Jonesboro and Gammon Street, two blocks away from Pastor Haywood's church. Around me black trees crowded the road, their sharp leaves unnaturally still despite a slight breeze. A small two-story building with boarded-up windows perched on the corner to the right, its grimy brown bricks stained with grey mold. Back when I ran the streets, this building served as a rallying point for the North Warren kid gangs.

Street kids knew Pastor Haywood. He fed them, he healed them, and he probably had hidden them when the occasion required.

I reached into my pocket, pulled out an ounce of silver, and held it up. Silver was the go-to metal for most magic-related work. It was easy to shape, took enchantment better than any other metal, even gold, and was poisonous to a wide variety of magical creatures, all of which made it hellishly expensive. It could be bought in several forms: dust, rod, bar, and wire. I was holding a one-ounce bar, five centimeters long, three centimeters wide, and about as thin as ten pieces of paper stacked together. On the street, it was worth roughly fifty bucks.

I tossed the bar into the air and caught it in my fist. "Silver."

No answer.

They knew all the cops in the area, so they realized I wasn't one. I was a stranger, and therefore scary, but I also offered silver. Paper money could be ripped or burned. Some of the older pre-Shift notes contained plastic and sometimes fell apart in the magic waves. But silver always held value, and it was easy to hide and sell.

"Pastor Haywood." I held the bar up. "Hurry up. I have things to do."

The boarded-up window on the first floor quaked. The entire section swung out, and a figure squirmed out and landed on the grass. A boy ran up to me. Ten, maybe twelve, skinny, filthy, smelly, his hair a brown mess on his head. A rat's tail hung from a loop on his pants. When I'd left, the Rat Tails were a small gang on the east side of the Warren. They must have expanded.

Light blue eyes looked at me from a grimy face. "What do you want to know, lady?"

I studied the silver in my hand. "Did anything strange happen with Pastor Haywood in the last couple of weeks?"

"Silver first."

I sneered at him and tensed slightly. Tulip started walking.

"Wait, wait!" The kid jumped in front of my horse.

Tulip bared her teeth.

"I wouldn't if I were you," I told him. "She bites."

He stepped to the side. "A guy came to see him. We know everybody who comes but we hadn't seen him before. We'd remember him."

"Why? Tell me about him." I dropped the bar.

He snatched it out of the air with a catlike quickness and let out a squeak. Shutters banged, bushes rustled, and five kids closed in, all under twelve years old, all equally filthy. They kept their distance in a ragged semicircle.

56

I took another silver bar out. "Tell me about the stranger. Where were you when you saw him?"

The leader stared at a small child, maybe about seven or eight, with twigs and beads in her dark hair. "Tell her."

"I saw him," the girl said.

"Where were you when you saw him?"

"Inside."

"Why were you inside?"

"Pastor had cookies," the girl said.

"What kind of cookies?"

"Oatmeal. If you got hurt, he would heal you and give you a cookie."

Ah. So that's where this was going. "You hurt yourself to get a cookie?"

She nodded.

"How?"

"I ran and fell."

"What happened when you went to see the pastor?"

"He magicked my leg and gave me milk and a cookie. It was this big." She held fingers of her small hands far apart.

"Did you eat the cookie in the church?"

She nodded.

"Then what happened?"

"I was eating the cookie and a fatso came."

Fatso meant someone well-off, good clothes, expensive jewelry, well-fed. A good mark.

"Did anybody else see the fatso?" I asked.

The kids shook their heads.

That's what I thought. It wasn't "we hadn't seen him before." It was *she* hadn't seen him before.

I needed to separate her from them. I'd get more information that way.

"You know where Central Market is?"

She nodded.

I leaned down and offered the girl my hand. "Show me and you can tell me about the fatso on the way. I'll give you this silver at the end."

The leader stepped in front of the girl. "No. We don't know you."

I added a second ounce to the first.

He shook his head.

The little girl tried to push past him, and he blocked her. "I said no. Not safe."

A street kid who took care of the younger children. Rare. He was probably new to the life. Some people thought that street kid gangs were like the Lost Boys from *Peter Pan*. It wasn't like that at all. On the street, it was all about survival. The stronger kids preyed on the weaker ones. This boy wouldn't last long.

I pulled out my Order badge and showed it to him. "I won't hurt her."

He stared at the badge, thinking. "Okay."

Yep, new. Still trusted law enforcement.

I reached down. The little girl grabbed my arm. I lifted her into the saddle in front of me. She weighed nothing. We set off north, toward the old I-75.

"What did the fatso look like?"

"Big."

"Tall or short?"

"Tall."

"What color hair?"

"Brown."

"Was his skin brown or pale?"

"Pale."

The little gang was trailing us, trying to be inconspicuous as they darted through the brush past the ruined houses.

"What did his face look like?"

She frowned. "He had fake eyes. Like he is nice when other people can see him, but not when he's by himself."

"Did he look like the kind of guy who would hit you if you stole from him?"

She nodded. Her shoulders hunched a little. She'd been hit before, and she'd learned to roll into a ball.

"Do you remember what the fatso said to the pastor?"

"He said he had a holy artifact."

Jackpot. "What kind of holy artifact?"

She shook her head. "I don't remember. I wasn't listening good. Pastor and he talked, and then Pastor said he would think about it, and the fatso left."

"Then what happened?"

"The next day a car came, and Pastor got into it. He never gets into cars. He came back later."

"Did he seem okay when he came back?"

She nodded. "The next morning, he got killed." Her voice got really quiet. "He was nice."

He was, and now he was gone. No more milk and cookies. No more healing when you got hurt. She'd lost the only safe place she'd had. She was the smallest and the weakest of the gang. I could feel her ribs rubbing against my arm. Starved. So starved, she'd learned to hurt herself to get food.

I wanted to take her off the street. I had to.

If I took her with me, where would I put her? I had a job to do. Sooner or later I'd become a target. Anyone close to me would be a potential hostage. If I left her in the fake shabby section of the house, she'd get bored and go out. She was a street kid, used to moving around. If I left her in the inner chamber, she wouldn't be able to keep her hands to herself. There were things in that room that could eat her or turn her skin inside out.

I had promised my grandmother that I would stop trying to rescue every homeless child I saw off the streets. It was a luxury I didn't have. As a princess of Shinar, my job was to see to all street children, not just the one in front of me, and to enact changes that would ensure no more kids would be thrown away like garbage. I had done that, and the New Shinar was on the way to being a place where no child went hungry, but New Shinar was far away, and the child in my arms was here now.

Erra had tried to save everyone, and she'd allowed herself to become a monster for the sake of her people. She didn't want me to go down the same road. She said it would unravel my soul thread by thread. My position gave me the ability to bring about sweeping change and I had to concentrate on that, because not everyone understood all that, but the little girl in front of me was so tiny.

Even if she survived for the next couple of years, I knew exactly what lay ahead: abuse, more abuse, rape, beatings, drugs, death. Few of the kids endured to adulthood, and those who managed it didn't live long.

But if the priests of Moloch saw her with me and got their claws on her, they would cook her alive just to hurt me. I had to let her go. Once this was over, I would find her again.

"What's your name?"

"Marten."

Usually street kids had nicknames like Rat or Weasel. "Who named you that?"

"I named me."

"Why Marten?"

"Because they're smart and cute. And fast. You can't catch them."

"Squirrels are fast."

"Squirrels are dumb. Pine Martens eat squirrels."

Fair enough. "There was a blue building on the corner of Harpy Street, Marten. Is it still there?"

She nodded.

I dropped the silver into her grimy hand. "They'll take it away from you as soon as I'm gone. Let them have it."

She sighed. "Dougie doesn't take our money. Dougie is too nice. He isn't mean. He is…"

"Soft."

Marten nodded. She wasn't soft. Not even a little bit. Dougie was bigger and older, but she would last longer.

"Give him the silver anyway." She couldn't protect it, and it would only make her a target. "Come to the blue building tomorrow. Go through the second doorway. Inside turn left, count eight steps. There is a loose board in the floor. I'll leave something there for you."

She squinted at me.

"Keep low for the next few days. If something else weird happens or if anybody else comes asking about this, hide from them and go straight to the Order and ask for Aurelia. They'll keep you safe until I get there. Tell the other kids, too. Anybody shows up with questions about Pastor Haywood, bolt and hide."

I let her off the horse. She ran back, skinny legs flying, the silver clutched in her small fist. The little gang closed about her. Dougie wrapped his arm around Marten's shoulders, gave me a wary look, and the lot of them ran away around the corner.

She was me. Except I was thirteen when Kate took me off the streets.

Suddenly I wanted to go home. It scraped at me like claws, ripping through my resolve to the vulnerable soft place I'd been trying to armor. I could picture it in my head, the sunlit kitchen; Curran gliding through the house, quiet like a ghost; Conlan leaping over the fence after running in the woods next door, the big, smelly poodle trailing him; and Kate standing in the kitchen, cooking something, her sword within reach. I wanted to go home and hug the three of them. I'd been gone for eight years. Talking on the phone wasn't enough. Meeting Conlan in Roland's magic prison was nothing compared to getting a hug in person. I was so homesick, if I were a wolf, I would've howled. I needed to see my family and make sure they were okay.

But if I did, they would die.

I exhaled slowly, reasserting control.

This city was bad for me. It was tearing wounds open that had long ago scabbed over.

I was a princess of Shinar. More, I was the child Kate raised. People in our family didn't waste time feeling sorry for ourselves. We killed the monster blocking the front door, so we could go home.

I urged Tulip on, and she started down the street, light on her feet. Although many denominations, Methodists included, rejected holy relics, the existence of magical artifacts and relics was a fact. Some religious items had gained magical properties after the Shift. Finding and selling these artifacts became a small but lucrative business and even spawned its own profession: relic hunters.

These hunters were a rough crowd. These were people with nothing to lose, who crawled into abandoned temples, opened cursed tombs, and dug graves out of sacred ground at a time when myths proved real and phantom monsters turned flesh. They would do just about anything for a profit.

According to Nick's file, Pastor Haywood had very few assets, so it was unlikely relic hunters had tried to sell him a magical artifact. Most likely, they'd wanted to know if the object they'd found was the real deal. As a man of his god, Pastor Haywood would have been able to recognize a relic of his deity and assess its power.

I was looking for someone who had or thought he had a Christian holy item. The first step would be to contact Pastor Haywood's chain of command and see if they referred anyone to him.

I didn't hold out much hope. Pastor Haywood was famous

enough that someone might have found him even without a referral. But it was still worth a try.

Unfortunately, all of that had to wait. I had to go home to put up wards, and I had to do it now.

When I'd mentioned shapeshifters to Fleming, he didn't contradict me, and he didn't ask questions. A law enforcement officer who'd had no idea shapeshifters had trampled the crime scene he'd been guarding would want to know the details. Why did I think shapeshifters had been there? How many shapeshifters? When did they visit? Fleming had just let it drop. He must've owed the Pack a favor or he had taken their money. Either way, he would contact them the first chance he got. A team would be dispatched to the scene, and they would track me.

There were ways to knock a shapeshifter off your scent. Wolfsbane worked well. It had the same effect on a shapeshifter as sticking your head into a bucket of pine pollen would have on a human. If a single shapeshifter was following my scent, using it might have been an option. But I wouldn't be tracked by a single shapeshifter. I would be tracked by a team, so sanding my trail with wolfsbane was futile. I might get the leading tracker, but the rest would just go around the wolfsbane, spread out, and pick up my scent again.

A confrontation with the Pack's people was imminent, and I wanted to have it on my home turf, safe behind my wards.

I'd been in Atlanta for less than a day. It was entirely too early to start killing people.

I WAS IN THE DECOY KITCHEN, SLIDING THE FIRST BATCH OF cookies into the oven, when something brushed against the edge of my outer ward. It was almost eight in the evening. Took them long enough.

I'd cut through the Central Market on my way back. They must've had a devil of a time trying to follow my trail through the open-air market. Hard to track a scent after a horse peed on it.

I draped the kitchen towel over my shoulder and walked to the front door, left open to vent the heat from the stove. The sunset burned across the sky, a gory, violent orange. I concentrated, sinking into my sensate vision. Three... two...

Contact. Magic nipped at me. A bright green flash pulsed in the empty air and vanished. To the left, a dark four-legged shape jumped out from behind some rubble and dashed down the street, little more than a blur in the fading light. The shapeshifter who'd found my house, hurrying to report.

I went back to the kitchen, sat at my strategically sad table, and waited. I felt spent. Fatigue wrapped around my shoulders like a heavy blanket. Too much magic expended too quickly this afternoon setting up the defensive perimeter.

I'd learned the art of wards from my grandfather. Roland loved to teach, and I'd been hungry to learn. Later my grandmother and her servants refined my education, but the foundation of my magic expertise was built by Roland. If you have to learn magic, studying under a brilliant megalomaniac wizard who thinks he's always right and can't wait to dazzle you with several millennia of knowledge was a really good choice.

In the few hours since coming back from the Central Market, I'd set three concentric rings of wards. The outer ward, undetectable by most of the people and creatures who crossed it, warned me that someone was coming, sampled the intruder's magic, and flashed it in a burst of color invisible to anyone who wasn't a sensate.

The middle ward wrapped around the building, shielding the front entrance. I'd chosen a rune ward, a simple defensive barrier that relied on Elder Futhark runes carved on bone stakes driven into the ground. Solid, powerful, and common enough to not raise any eyebrows. It was also the first ward the Order's Academy taught to prospective knights, so it went along with my disguise.

The third ward sealed off the hallway leading to the front bedroom and to the secret door, protecting the entire inner chamber. I had raised Enki's Shield in four hours instead of the full twelve it usually required and got a throbbing headache for my trouble. Still, Grandfather would be proud.

I missed him. He was the monster in our family of monsters, but he was still my grandfather, if not by birth then by choice. When my grandfather wanted to be liked, he was an unstoppable force, and he wanted me to like him. Roland wasn't bored in his prison—he was far too brilliant for that—but he planned to get out, and Conlan and I were his link to the outside world. It had been over six weeks since my last visit. I was overdue.

Magic pinched me. I peeked out of the kitchen in time to see the street light up with green through the doorway. Ascanio walked out of the shadows and strolled up to my house. I'd thought that trail of grass-green magic I'd noticed at the murder scene looked familiar.

Someone from the Pack was interested in Pastor Haywood's murder and they'd sent Ascanio to figure it out. Why? Had this order come from the top, or was this a Clan Bouda affair? Was someone pulling his strings or was he doing it on his own? All good questions.

Ascanio was never big on following orders. It wouldn't be out of character for him to do this on his own, but he never acted without aiming for some sort of benefit.

He knocked on my doorframe. I walked out of the kitchen and to the front door.

"The shapeshifter hero. We meet again, and so soon."

Ascanio froze.

Before I'd been on horseback, in the dark, a dozen yards away with my hood up. Now less than three feet separated us. He could see my face, and it burned a fuse in his brain. For a moment Ascanio forgot to be suave and simply stared with unnerving, focused intensity.

My timer went off.

Ascanio blinked. "Are you baking cookies?"

"Yes, I am. Excuse me."

I went into the kitchen. Behind me, magic tolled through the house, like a gong. Ascanio had tried to follow and walked right into my second ward.

I pulled the batch of cookies out of the oven, slid the second tray in, reset my mechanical timer, and went back to the door.

Ascanio leaned in the doorway, arms crossed, a slight smile on his lips. It had to be his sexy, nonchalant pose. I wasn't sure if I was expected to toss my underwear at his feet or just fall back with my legs in the air. He must've realized that he'd stared like an idiot and overcorrected, like a driver who drifted onto the shoulder and jerked the wheel trying to get back on the highway.

"Nice ward," he said.

"Keeps out the riffraff."

A ruby light rolled over his irises. "Can I have a cookie?"

"No."

He gave a mock sigh. "I have a feeling this conversation has gotten off to the wrong foot."

"Not just a hero, but a master detective as well," I kept my voice quiet and friendly. In my head, I grabbed him and shook him until all the things I wanted to know about Pastor Haywood's murder fell out of his shockingly handsome head.

He winked. "I'm not just a pretty face."

"I don't recall saying you were pretty."

The smile stayed on his lips, but his posture lost some of its slouching. "Let me tell you what I've detected."

I smiled back at him. "I can't wait. Dazzle me."

His gaze snagged on my lips. He blinked again.

Lost your train of thought for a second there, buddy?

"You pretended to be a lightweight on the bridge. You visited the Order and you have an Order ID, which says you are assigned to Atlanta, except you're not, because the Atlanta chapter never has more than twenty knights and with you, they are up to twenty-one."

Fair enough.

"You've used your brand-new ID to gain access to a crime scene, but you aren't staying in the Order chapter. Instead you're living in a hovel on the edge of the most dangerous area of the city, flirting with disaster and baking cookies with expensive chocolate chips."

Here it comes, the brilliant deduction.

Ascanio hit me with a direct stare. "I have to ask why the Order is so invested in Pastor Haywood's murder that they would bring a Knight-Crusader in for it?"

It wasn't a bad assumption. When the Order had a particularly nasty mess on their hands, they threw a Crusader at it, who would either clean it up and disappear or die trying. Crusaders worked undercover, used unorthodox methods, and enjoyed a lot of leeway. If they screwed up, the Order had plausible deniability.

Crusaders were dangerous as hell and often crazy. They didn't do what they did for accolades. They did it because they believed in their cause. Before Nick Feldman became the Knight-Protector, he was a Crusader, one of the Order's best.

"No answer?"

I smiled at him again. "Did you expect one?"

Ascanio pushed away from the doorway and looked past me, at my humble abode. "This place is a dump."

"Thank you."

"Whoever rented it to you should be barred from owning real estate. Nick should've never let you stay here."

Dropping the Knight-Protector's name like you are bestest friends. "I like it here. Quiet, picturesque, but now that you've visited, I'll have to put a 'No solicitors' sign up front."

"I'm not here to sell you anything. But I can offer you better accommodations. You're new to the city, and this really isn't a good neighborhood."

"People keep telling me that."

"Because it's true."

My timer went off again. "Hold that thought."

I went back to the kitchen, rescued my second batch, and turned the oven off. It was good that gas still burned even during the deepest magic waves.

"I can put you in a better house," Ascanio called from the door. "Free of charge."

Too crude for him. He was trying to gauge my reaction. I came back to the front and raised my head, inhaling deeply, the way shapeshifters did when they were trying to catch a scent on the breeze. His eyes widened.

"Do you smell that?" I asked him. "What's that odor, I can't quite place it..."

He frowned.

I opened my eyes wide. "Bribery. That's it."

He recoiled with theatrical shock. "I come here, I offer you a safer place out of the goodness of my heart, and you accuse me of bribery."

"I have to ask why the Pack is so invested in Pastor Haywood's murder that they would send the beta of Clan Bouda to investigate it, bribe the Atlanta PD to gain access to the crime scene, and then stalk and attempt to intimidate and coerce a knight of the Order?"

"I don't recall intimidating you. If I wanted to intimidate

you, I would break through this ward." He smiled, showing me his sharp white teeth. "And take all of your cookies."

He promised to break the ward with complete confidence. That wasn't arrogance; that was experience talking.

The runic ward would stop an average shapeshifter, but then Ascanio Ferara had never been average. All shapeshifters had two forms, one animal and the other human. Those with talent had a third, the warrior form, a blend of human and animal devastating in combat. Curran considered Ascanio's warrior form to be one of the best, a high compliment from a man who was once Beast Lord.

Looked like I wasn't the only one who'd gotten stronger. I'd have to readjust my expectations.

I went to the kitchen, took a cookie, whispered a bit of magic from a forgotten language into it, walked back to the door, and dropped the ward.

Ascanio blinked.

I held the cookie out to him. "You think it's the ward that's keeping me safe. You want this cookie? Take it."

He studied me for a moment, his face calculating. He was lighting fast, and he was ninety-nine point nine percent sure he was faster than me.

The cookie lay on my palm, waiting. Perfectly harmless.

Ascanio's nostrils fluttered slightly. He was sampling the air looking for the scent of poison. Not that it would hurt him. Lyc-V, the shapeshifter virus, ate poison for breakfast and asked for seconds.

I sighed. "Do you want the cookie or not?"

He moved so fast, his hand was a blur. His fingers touched the cookie and went right through it, brushing my palm, so light, like the tap of a moth's wing. When I was a street kid, I thought I had a light touch. I thought I was quick. Compared to Ascanio, I was a rank amateur. If I ever held something in my hand and he wanted it, I wouldn't even notice him taking it.

Ascanio stared at the perfectly solid cookie in my hand.

"What's the matter?" I asked. "Don't you want it?"

Moth wings on my palm. He'd tried again.

"Nice trick," Ascanio said.

"You said you could take all of my cookies and you can't even grab one. I'm disappointed." I raised the cookie to my mouth and took a bite. "Mmm. Delicious. You really don't know what you're missing."

He swiped at the cookie, trying to take it out of my mouth. His fingers fanned my lips.

"Hey! Personal space."

Ascanio opened his mouth.

A female shapeshifter dashed across the yard and slid to a stop next to Ascanio. "I saw him!"

Red burst in Ascanio's eyes. "Are you sure?"

"Yes!" She waved her hand in front of her. "I saw his face."

"We'll finish this later." Ascanio spun to her. "Show me."

They sprinted off into the darkness.

I stepped out and yelled. "Wait! You forgot your cookie."

A distant howl from Unicorn Lane was my only answer. That was fine. I knew he'd heard me.

I went inside, sealed the ward, and closed the door behind me. So, the Pack, or some part of it, was definitely interested in this murder. Unfortunately, I still had no idea why.

Let's see, things I learned from this encounter: Ascanio was amazingly fast and he wasn't shy about using money to get what he wanted, and what he wanted was Pastor Haywood's killer. Not a complete waste, but not terribly useful either.

If the Pack required access to a murder, they could request it through proper channels. Most of the time, the city let them in. They were the best trackers, and they made efforts to play nice with law enforcement. They also took care of their own criminals, so if a shapeshifter had committed this murder, the Pack would do an internal investigation, apprehend them, and either punish or, depending on the political situation, turn them over to city authorities. It was a win-win arrangement—the Pack avoided unnecessary suspicion and the cops bled less trying to do their job. Subduing an enraged shapeshifter wasn't a walk in the park.

But the Pack hadn't requested access. They'd bribed a cop instead.

So far both Ascanio and Nick were interested in this case and pretending as hard as they could that they weren't.

Nick's interest worried me. Years ago, before Nick became Knight-Protector, he was a Crusader and his last assignment before his promotion was to infiltrate Roland's organization. Grandfather had done something to him, something awful neither of them ever talked about. The assignment had ended in a disaster, and Nick watched the entire chapter, seven knights, be slaughtered by my other uncle who wasn't in his right mind. He never broke his cover. I couldn't even imagine how much of his soul that had cost him. He watched as the knights died and would've carried on his mission, except the asshole who was the Knight-Protector then exposed him as he lay dying and made sure it was all for nothing.

Nick had been volatile to begin with. That experience crystalized every crazy tendency he'd had. He had dedicated himself to opposing Grandfather and everything he stood for. Nick used to call Kate an abomination to her face. Kate didn't mind. He was the only son of her former guardian, and she viewed him as a brother and helped him any chance she got. That was the way she moved through the world.

I should've resented Nick, but I didn't. He was a knight of the Order in the truest sense, and he dedicated himself completely to the Order's mission of protecting humanity against all threats. Kate represented a potential threat of catastrophic proportions. Kate was also Nick's friend, and if she needed help, he would drop whatever he was doing and ride over with guns blazing and swords bared, as he had more than once. He simply refused to see the conflict between those two things. He worked with Kate, he was genuinely fond of Conlan, and he went over to Kate and Curran's house for dinner, but he was always alert for any signs of Kate descending into madness. If she chose to become a tyrant, he would be first in line to run her through with his blade.

It was possible that his years as the Knight-Protector had stabilized him, but I highly doubted it. His paranoia was a bottomless, dark lake, and he was excellent at subterfuge.

I went to the hallway, slid the secret door open, entered my real home, and shut the door behind me. It clanged in place with a reassuring thud. The Enki Shield flowed closed, cutting off the outside world.

I whispered a word, and the fey lanterns ignited, bathing the chamber in bright yellow light. Yet another benefit of a classical education. My fey lanterns came with a magic off switch and glowed in a variety of colors, while most people's fey lanterns were blue and glowed continuously when the magic was up. I wasn't a fan of blue light, except as a rare accent here and there. Too harsh.

I walked to my desk and sat in my chair.

So far, this murder was all questions and no answers.

I reached for the familiar connection in my mind, looking for Turgan. A light shone in my mind and unfolded into a view of a house with brightly lit windows. Nick Feldman sat at a kitchen table, by the first-floor window, eating a sandwich and reading a thick book. The view tilted slightly as Turgan readjusted his grip on the branch.

"Stay on him," I whispered.

The raptor clicked his beak in acknowledgement.

I let go, and the image faded.

The eagle would call to me if anything happened. As long as the magic stayed up, I would know every move Nick made.

Tomorrow I would dig deeper, but before I could do that, I needed to figure out where to start.

I pulled a big stack of papers toward me. I had picked them up on my way home, three months' worth of the Atlanta Journal-Constitution. Let's see if anyone announced their discovery of new Christian relics.

[6]

I rode out into the city at eight a.m., unsupervised. Ascanio hadn't left anyone to babysit me. Maybe he decided I wasn't worth keeping an eye on. Maybe it slipped his mind. Both possibilities were equally unlikely, which meant whoever followed me was staying way back, tracking my trail. By the time I stopped by the blue house to hide the care package for Marten, I'd sprinkled wolfsbane on my tracks twice. It wouldn't stop my tail, but why make it easy for them?

Twenty minutes later, I rode up to St. Luke's Methodist Church on the edge of Tuxedo Park.

In the wake of the destruction brought about by the slow-motion magic apocalypse, the affluent of Atlanta fled north. Neighborhoods like Tuxedo Park had the bonus of being older, with historic mansions that fared much better than modern office towers and high-rises. While the skyscrapers fell and crashed, places like Villa Juanita, the ten-thousand-square-foot signature Tuxedo estate, suffered no damage, still as opulent as they had been a century and a half ago.

St. Luke's Church straddled the divide between the wealthy of Tuxedo Park and the new business center that had sprung up along Peachtree Road. Calling it a church was a bit of an understatement. The massive cathedral, built with brick and white concrete, occupied five acres with its grounds and auxiliary buildings. A testament to the stoic values of the Gothic Revival, the entire complex was a fortress: a hospital, a school, and an administrative center all arranged into a single neat rectangle with the cathedral front and center, looking like a smaller cousin of Notre Dame.

A stretch of lawn bordered the cathedral, the killing ground, another fun real estate peculiarity of our apocalypse. A long walkway cut through the lawn, leading to a wide terrace before the stairway to the church. The terrace was filled with cut flowers. Roses, lilies, and wildflowers rested on the pavement, with candles burning between the blooms and small wooden crosses. The city had turned this space into a memorial to Pastor Haywood. A few mourners still remained, three days later, sitting on the low stone wall bordering the terrace and praying.

I rode to the side parking lot, dismounted, tethered Tulip, and walked up to the doors on foot.

A middle-aged white man with a receding hairline and wire-rimmed glasses met me at the entrance and gave my tattered cloak a long glance. Under the cloak, I wore a green t-shirt, a pair of comfortable brown pants secured by a belt holding pouches of herbs, silver dust, and other useful things, and a pair of running shoes. Nothing special.

This morning I had opened the smaller weapons crate and pulled out two knives identical to the one I lost yesterday. I also carried a leaf short sword, with a twenty-two-inch-long blade that was about two point one inches across in the widest part. At a pound and eleven ounces, it ran on the heavy side, and the weight and the leaf profile made it a good slasher. The cloak hid all that, but it couldn't hide Dakkan, my spear. My grandmother had a huge problem with that name, because the closest translation of it to English would be "Stabby." She claimed it wasn't a proper name for a weapon, so after the first Dakkan broke, I offered to name the new one Sharpy McStabbison, the Son of Stabby, after which she groaned and left my quarters, followed by a throng of her advisors all giving me reproachful looks.

Dakkan rested in two parts in the sheath on my back. When screwed together, it reached six feet. The two shafts protruded over my right shoulder, easy to grab, and the sentry at the church door clearly had trouble figuring out why I was carrying two metal sticks on my back.

After a few awkward seconds, he decided to stop pondering my weapon choice. "How may I help you?"

I took out my Order ID. "My name is Aurelia Ryder. I'm investigating Pastor Haywood's murder."

The man flinched slightly. "It's awful. It feels like a nightmare…" He caught himself. "Would you mind waiting? The bishop is in residence and she may want to speak with you."

"I don't mind."

"Please follow me."

The inside of the church was ten degrees cooler. Soothing light streamed into the reception area through the stained-glass windows tinted in a dozen shades of blue and red. Through the open doors, I could see the inside of the church, rows and rows of wooden pews with cobalt cushions, the raised pulpit, and the simple wooden lectern upon it. There was no opulence in this church; everything was well made but restrained.

I had done some reading on the topic of Methodists while riding the ley line to the city. The Methodists had always viewed healing as an important theological theme, and after magic had wrecked the world, they focused on it with even greater intensity. As a result, the Methodist congregations swelled, and there came a need to have a point person for large geographical areas, usually a bishop, sometimes elected, sometimes appointed. The bishop I was about to meet was responsible for the entirety of North Georgia. She could open many doors. She could also slam them shut.

A side door opened, and a middle-aged woman in a beige business suit walked in, the man who had met me following close behind. The woman was in her mid-fifties, with straight black hair cut in a flattering bob and features that hinted at East Asian heritage.

The woman held her hand out. "Hazel Chao. I'm the Methodist Bishop of North Georgia."

I shook her hand. She had a firm, dry handshake. "Aurelia Ryder, knight of the Order."

"A pleasure to meet you, although I wish it was under better circumstances. Why don't we talk in the garden?"

I followed her through the side door, down a hallway, and through another door that led outside. We emerged into a large courtyard garden, with the cathedral directly behind us and auxiliary buildings on the three sides, each rising three stories high and topped by turrets on the corners.

"A good place to weather a siege," I noted.

"'The old world is dying, and the new world struggles to be born: now is the time of monsters,'" she quoted.

"And monsters necessitate castles," I said. "Although I doubt Antonio Gramsci had our kind of monsters in mind."

There were two translations of that quote, and as it often was, the least accurate one sounded the best.

She gave me a surprised look and smiled. "And I just showed my own bias. I didn't expect you to be well-read."

"My family emphasizes education. Between stabbing people, of course."

"Of course." She glanced at the man. "It's okay, Gerald. I don't believe the knight will harm me, and if she tries, I'm not sure you could stop her anyway."

Gerald gave me a suspicious look and went inside.

The bishop and I strolled down the path. On the right bees

buzzed around delicate pink flowers of mountain laurel. On the left, rhododendron bushes were ablaze with bunches of raspberry-red blossoms. Blue-eyed grass and bluestar bordered the path, offering purple and blue flowers. They must've had beehives somewhere on the premises.

"I will be blunt," Bishop Chao said. "The death of Pastor Haywood was a devastating blow. On a personal level, he was one of my dearest friends. His contribution to the Church and to the people of Atlanta cannot be overstated. Whoever killed him tore a gaping hole in our city. I will help you in any way I can."

"Thank you."

"In seeking answers, I have a responsibility to his congregation and to the city at large. He meant a great deal to a great many people. He was beloved, yet he was murdered with such shocking violence and for unknown reasons."

She had put a lot of emphasis on that "unknown." Atlanta viewed Pastor Haywood as a saint. She had just warned me that if I found out any unsavory secrets that led to his murder, the responsibility for ruining the memory of the holy man would rest on my shoulders. Interesting.

I had to stay in character, so it was my turn to reach for fancy quotes. "'For each one will bear his own load.'"

Bishop Chao glanced at me. "Galatians 6:5."

"My load is to discover who killed Pastor Haywood. His sins, whatever they were, are his load. Your load is to deal with the consequences of his loss. Think of me as a tool. I do not take sides. It's not up to me what people do with my findings."

"I see," Bishop Chao said. "Perhaps this is a conversation I should have with the Knight-Protector."

Oh, Nick would just love that. "Perhaps."

If Pastor Haywood had done something sordid, the blow to the Church would be devastating. Questions would be asked. Did the bishop know, and if she didn't, why not?

Bishop Chao sighed. "So how can I help you, Knight Ryder?"

"Shortly before his death, Pastor Haywood was approached by a man about a 'holy artifact.'"

The bishop frowned. "Really? What kind of holy artifact?"

"My source isn't sure. They were preoccupied with cookies at the time. I do know that Pastor Haywood left in a car the next day and returned several hours later."

"Nathan?" Bishop Chao asked. "Are you sure?"

"Why is that unusual?"

"He got carsick. He preferred to walk or ride a horse. Also, many of the people he ministered to didn't have a vehicle. He didn't want to set himself apart." She smiled a sad little smile. "He really did get terrible motion sickness though. He vomited twice on the way to his own ordination. We had to coax him back onto the bus, because he declared that since Jesus walked, so would he. And that was thirty years ago."

Magic fell. Both of us paused, adjusting to the sudden absence of power. Technology had temporarily gained the upper hand. It wouldn't last, but meanwhile I had fewer tools at my disposal.

"So this artifact must've been very important to him?"

"Yes. I can't imagine what would make him get into a car, especially with someone he didn't know. I don't understand why he didn't call me. He always called me about things like that."

"Was it common for Pastor Haywood to authenticate artifacts?"

Bishop Chao sighed again. "It happened. Nobody likes to talk about it, but holy items are a big business. Especially Christian relics. Ninety nine percent of them are fake, but that one percent can perform miracles."

Not all miracles were benign. A few years ago, the rod of Aaron was found in Egypt. When cast down, it created an enormous unkillable serpent that devoured several dozen people before the army finally managed to drown it.

"Nathan had the gift of discernment," the bishop continued. "But he was selective with his expertise. Five years ago, the Catholics asked him to authenticate nail clippings from a saint, because they wanted an independent expert. Unfortunately, the clippings didn't belong to a saint. They don't know where they came from, but they induced madness in the devout. Nathan lost three days to delirium. After that, he was very careful."

"And you're sure the request didn't come through the Church?"

"Absolutely. I will check, but since the clipping episode, all such requests are forwarded directly to me."

So, either they approached him on their own or she was lying. If she was lying, she was an incredible actress, because she seemed genuinely surprised.

"You have to understand," she said. "Nathan didn't care about money or prestige. Whatever they showed him had to be truly extraordinary."

"Who are the most prominent relic hunters in the region? Who would have the kind of reputation that would lure a man like Pastor Haywood away from his church?"

Her face twisted with disdain. I might as well have asked her who were the best pimps in the neighborhood.

"I would have said Waylon Billiot, but he died three or four years ago. Besides him Darryl Knox and Dakota Mooney. Darryl and Dakota used to be married. They had some kind of falling out, and rumors say Dakota shot him in the a... upper posterior. Now they can't stand each other. There is also Mark Rudolph, who is extremely unpleasant. I'll ask Gerald to give you a list. It may take him a couple of hours."

"Thank you," I told her. "I'll come by later in the day and pick it up."

"These are not nice, reasonable people, Knight Ryder. They

are the kind of people who cross an ocean filled with monsters, climb into dark tombs filled with horrors, and then sell what they find to the highest bidder. They will shoot you for a dollar. If they decide that you are interfering with their business, they will retaliate."

"Thank you for your advice."

"Keep me in the loop," Bishop Chao asked. "Please."

"I will," I promised.

TULIP TROTTED DOWN THE DESERTED STREET. BEHIND ME towering poplars and oaks shielded the tall walls that guarded the houses of Tuxedo Park. Ahead lay urban ruins. After leaving St. Luke's, I'd turned south and then east, on West Paces Ferry Road. Soon it would cross the New Peachtree Road, and I would turn right again, heading south to Jesus Junction.

Jesus Junction, otherwise known as the safest place in Atlanta, sat at the intersection of three roads, Peachtree, East Wesley, and West Wesley. It was a place where three churches formed a rough triangle: the Cathedral of Christ the King, the mother-church of Catholic Archdiocese of Atlanta, Second Ponce de Leon Baptist Church, and the Cathedral of St. Phillip, home to one of the largest Episcopalian congregations in the country. A good chunk of Buckhead lay in ruins, but Jesus Junction stood untouched, a beacon of safety among the chaos, the houses of worship protected from magic's teeth by the faith of its congregants.

Pastor Haywood had worked with the Catholics before, and among all the Christian denominations, the Catholic church bought the most relics and offered the highest prices. If I were selling holy artifacts, I'd tap the Catholics first.

I had just passed the Atlanta History Center when I heard the jingling. It was an odd, disconcerting sound, as if someone had sharpened some metal coins and was now shaking them in a sack. I'd heard this before.

Tulip flicked her ears.

The jingling came again, insistent. *Jingle. Jingle.* Scrape of metal on metal, sharp enough to make you cringe.

Interesting. I brought Tulip to a halt. Let's see what happens.

Two men stepped out into the road from behind the ruins of Regions Bank. The one on the left, six feet tall, with a beefy build and a gold chain around his tan neck, looked like a typical street tough guy, the kind who made his money collecting debts and carried brass knuckles in his pocket. He wore jeans, a tank top, and a custom pair of tennis shoes, handmade. A rifle hung off his shoulder. He was a large man, but next to the other guy, he looked like a child.

The second man towered over the first by a good foot and a half. Huge shoulders, barrel chest, weirdly long arms bulging with muscle. He wore stained camo pants tucked into giant yellow boots and a brown tank top that left his shoulders bare. A three-and-a-half-foot wooden club hung from his belt. Every inch of his visible skin was covered with dense red body hair, matching the greasy mane hanging from his head. His brutish face sported a permanent sunburn, except for the spots covered by his beard.

The two men strode to the middle of the street and stopped, blocking my way. The goon on the left wouldn't be a problem. His swagger told me he was strong and likely relied on brute force and his mass rather than speed and training. The giant next to him was another story. He moved like a man half his size, with a kind of animalistic smoothness. Like a bear, seemingly lumbering but big and fast, and hard to stop once he charged. Not good. With a club, his reach was longer than mine by half a foot. With magic up, he wouldn't have been a problem. But magic was down, and he outweighed me by at least a hundred and seventy-five pounds.

Jingle, jingle. Getting closer.

The smaller man unslung his rifle and pointed it at me. "Don't move."

I'd picked this road to avoid traffic. Buckhead used to be an edge city, an uptown anchored by a cluster of high-rise hotels, offices, condominiums, and restaurants, none of which had fared well since the Shift. It also spawned some nasty magic hazmat during magic waves. Like downtown and midtown, the area was a treasure trove for the reclamation crews, but downtown was safer, and so far, the city mostly left Buckhead to its own devices.

These two weren't run of the mill bandits. This road wasn't well used, and the persistent jingling told me they were a good way from home. Were they waiting for me? Why?

I could shoot them now with my bow, but there was a good chance I'd kill them, and any answers would die with them.

A huge dog trotted into view from behind the Regions building, thirty-five inches at the shoulder and slabbed with monstrous muscle. His chest was so deep and broad that his hindquarters looked like an afterthought. He gripped the ground with paws the size of melons. A single hit would crush a human skull. His head with wide oversized jaws sat on a neck thicker than my thigh. Long metal spikes thrust from his skull, running all the way down his spine to the long tail. His fur was a forest of blueish metal needles.

An iron hound. There was only one place in Atlanta it could have come from.

The beast saw me. His turquoise eyes focused on my face. He opened his cavernous mouth, flashing four-inch fangs, and snarled. The spikes snapped erect with a metallic screech. The dog took a step toward me and halted, brought up short by a thick chain wrapped around his throat.

A moment later its handler waddled into view. He was the smaller man's height, but the giant's weight, and he carried most of it in a beer gut. White, hairy, wearing denim overalls with no shirt. A machete hung in a sheath on his hip. He held the dog's chain in his left hand, and a second chain, stretching behind the building, in his right.

The handler anchored himself, pulling the hound short, and yanked the other chain. A small body flew into view and landed at the handler's feet.

Dougie.

His face was a puffy bruise, his lips split, his right eye swollen shut. His hair was caked with blood. His jeans were shredded, and bloody flesh gaped through the holes. They had dragged him, scrapping his knees raw. The chain was wrapped around his narrow waist, and it had worn the skin way from his ribs and stomach. He hadn't fallen the way a person would normally fall. He had collapsed like a rag doll, boneless and making no effort to catch himself.

The world turned red in a single furious second. They'd beaten a child. They'd broken his bones. They put him on a chain. They dragged him across the city. The rage burned in me like a firestorm.

The handler yanked the chain, lifting the child three feet off the ground. "This her?"

No answer.

The asshole shook the chain. The boy dangled like a broken doll.

I would kill him slowly.

"Is this her?"

Dougie opened one eye to a mere slit. His voice was little more than a whisper. "No."

The handler dropped him and looked at the giant. "It's her."

If I showed the slightest interest or concern, they'd torture him to get me to behave. I had to shift their priorities.

"Wow, the hills really do have eyes," I called out. "And greasy hair."

The giant peered at me. "You look like a good breeder."

"You look like your parents met at a family reunion."

His sidekick with the rifle frowned.

"Keep thinking. It will come to you."

The handler bared yellowed teeth at me. "Mouthy bitch."

My middle name. "Did you finally get it? Don't be ashamed. It's hard to be the son of Sasquatch."

Dougie crumpled, forgotten on the ground. *That's right, focus on me.*

"Get off the horse and lie down on the ground," the asshole with the gun ordered.

I needed to get them away from the boy. I raised my arm and pointed at the gunman.

"What's that? You gonna shoot me with your finger, you dumb bitch? Get off the horse and lie down on the ground. I'm not gonna tell you again."

I got off Tulip and tapped her with my hand. She trotted off to the side, out of the way. The three men watched me. Dougie lay still.

I whistled once, a short, harsh note, and dropped to the ground.

Turgan dropped from the sky like a stone, raking the gunman's face with his talons. The man shrieked. A shot rang out. I jumped up, dashed left, behind the Regions building, and whistled again. The eagle streaked across the sky, soaring clear. The whole thing took less than two seconds.

I pulled Dakkan out and screwed the spear together. The building blocked the street. I couldn't see them, but they couldn't see me either.

The gunman was still screaming.

"Shut up," the giant snarled, his voice cold and vicious.

"It took my fucking eye!"

A wet thud announced a punch landing. "Shut up or I'll crush your head."

The screams died. I moved east, circling the building, moving silently along the wall.

"Larry, loose the fucking dog on her."

The chain clanked on the ground.

I waited.

The dog came around the corner, following my scent, his massive paws scraping the stone in a shower of sparks. Fangs flung spit into the air. The cavernous mouth opened wide...

I stabbed Dakkan into that gaping maw. The spear bit into the soft tissue inside the throat, slicing through muscle, cartilage, and bone into the brain. I jerked the spear free. The dog stumbled, his charge suddenly aborted. Blood gurgled, gushing from his mouth.

I withdrew and drove the spear into its neck, cleaving the spinal column. The hound collapsed, its needles jingling like a sack of coins spilled on the ground. One down. I turned and kept circling the building.

"Charger?" Larry called out.

I rounded the corner and pressed myself against the wall. He was out in the street, just a few feet away. Dougie curled into a ball to Larry's right.

Hold on. I'm coming.

Twenty yards down the street, in the direction I had been coming from, the shooter stared at the ruins. He gripped his rifle with his right hand. His left pressed some cloth against his injured eye. The giant was gone.

"Charger! Get back here, boy."

I lunged from behind the building and thrust the spear into the handler's back. The metal blade slid into flesh, ripping the kidney and liver on its way up. Larry gasped. I twisted the spear in the wound. He moaned in an oddly high voice. It would take him a long time to bleed out, and it would hurt every moment. He would never put another child on a chain.

Larry's body jerked on my spear. A bullet bit into his stomach. The sound of the rifle was like the popping of a firecracker. Sudden lack of depth perception was hell on aiming.

"Larry, get out of the way!" the shooter yelled.

I spun Larry to my left, using his bulk as a shield, pulled the spear free and sprinted back to the ruin. Behind me the rifle cracked again, the bullet whizzing by to ricochet off a brick wall half a foot away. I ducked around the corner and kept moving, to the spot where two rectangular columns had once framed the entrance. I hid behind the first column and waited.

The handler whimpered, fragments of incoherent words slipping out between his sobs.

"Fuck you," the shooter muttered from my right. "Fuck you, bitch, fuck you..."

That's right. Come closer.

"I'll fucking find you. I'll blow your head off."

A boot came into view.

"I'll shoot you in both eyes and—"

He gurgled as Dakkan's blade slid though his neck. His remaining eye bulged, his mouth opened... He tried to say something, but blood was gushing from his throat, staining his skin bright red.

A dark shape swung off the roof and dropped on top of me. There was no time to free the spear. I dodged left, desperately trying to get clear. A boot landed on my thigh. Pain exploded all the way to the bone. The glancing blow tossed me into the air like a ragdoll. I flew, curling into a ball, straight into the soft embrace of a brick pile, and landed on my side. Ow.

The world swam. I clawed through the fog of blurry vision. The giant was stomping toward me, brandishing his club. If I had been a touch slower, he would have broken my femur. I couldn't afford to be hit again.

I jumped to my feet. The giant bore down on me, swinging the club, eyes cold. I shied left, then right, the club whistling inches from my face. He was between me and my spear, pushing me against the brick heap. If even a single blow connected, I was dead.

He struck again and again. Left, right, left...

I ducked, avoiding a blow, grabbed a brick off the pile, and hurled it at his face. It hit him square between the eyes and bounced off. He roared, the red brick dust raining off his forehead.

Fuck.

He swept the club right to left. I dropped under his swing and ran right, the only way I could, leaping over refuse toward a side street. My leg screamed in protest. Every step hammered a hot spike of pain into my thigh.

I reached the side street and glanced back.

He hung the club back on his hip. Slowly, casually, the giant leaned forward onto his arms. Something in his pelvis shifted with a crack. The line of his spine realigned. He sprinted toward me on all fours.

What the hell...

He loped toward me in a familiar disjointed gait, the kind of stride that the human body wasn't made for but was unnaturally fast. In a fraction of a second my mind crunched the numbers. He would catch me. I couldn't outrun him even if my leg wasn't on fire with pain. He gave me a head start because he knew it.

He ran like a vampire.

I would treat him like one. I pulled a knife from the sheath on my belt. My uncle's voice echoed in my head. *Wait for it. Breathe.*

Twenty yards.

Fifteen.

Eight.

Three.

Now, Hugh's voice commanded.

I sidestepped. The giant's momentum carried him past and I swung my knife, straight down on the back of his neck. The blade bit into his vertebrae, slicing deep into cartilage. He rolled forward, blood drenching his shoulders and back, came up into a crouch, and leaped at me.

Son of a bitch. He should have dropped like a stone. He should have been paralyzed.

I dodged but not far enough. A huge arm swept me into a bear hug. I jerked my right arm up to keep it clear. He reared, yanking me off the ground, his arms crushing me. My ribs screeched with agony. The world turned black and fuzzy at the edges.

I sank my knife into his eye. He howled, and I stabbed him in the ear. He flung me aside like a feral cat. I rolled clear and came onto my feet. Suddenly there was air. My lungs hurt with every breath.

The giant rushed at me, flailing wildly, kicking, swinging, a bloody hole where his eye used to be. His neck gushed blood. I backed away toward the main street. He chased me, but his movements grew sluggish. Dodging him now was child's play. I walked him all the way to where the boy still lay on the pavement.

The giant was breathing heavily now, each exhale a tortured gasp.

I crouched by Larry's body and came up with his machete.

A sudden realization flared in the giant's remaining eye. He turned.

"No," I told him.

The giant stumbled away on shaking legs. I let him take two steps and sliced the back of his knees. Good machete. Sharp.

The giant toppled like a felled tree.

I walked in front of him. He was trying to crawl forward. I grabbed his hair and spun him around so he could see Dougie. The effort sent a blinding flash of pain through me, but I didn't care.

I gripped the giant's hair and forced his head up. "Tell me who hired you and the pain will end."

He growled. There was nothing human in the sound. His face was a mask of rage, but there was no power in it. His mouth drooped, his eye stared, unfocused.

"Tell me who hired you."

"Fuck you."

I wouldn't get anything from him.

Dougie was looking at us with one eye.

"Look at the boy," I told the giant.

His hands were trembling. I yanked his head up, forcing him to look. Their stares connected.

I brought the machete down on the giant's neck. This time the blade cut clean through the flesh and bone. The giant's head rolled clear. His eye was still blinking. His mouth moved trying to shape words, but without lungs, nothing came out.

I whistled for Tulip and scooped the boy off the ground. He was so light and limp.

"I didn't tell them," he whispered. "I didn't tell about you and Marten."

"I know."

"It hurts."

"I'm sorry. I've got you."

"Don't let them hurt me anymore," he whispered.

"They're all dead. I've got you."

Tulip ran over. I draped him over her saddle on his stomach. It was the least jostling position. He moaned softly.

"Stay with me, Douglas."

He shivered.

"Stay with me."

"Okay..."

I grabbed the giant's head, shoved it into the saddlebag, ran to get my spear, and patted Tulip's cheek. "Smooth."

Tulip started off. Most people were aware of four horse

gaits, walk, trot, canter, and gallop. Those more familiar with horses knew about pace and amble, a four-beat intermediate gait between a walk and a canter. Tulip had her own amble, fast and smooth as silk. I had ridden dozens of horses, and none of them could match her.

"Stay with me, Douglas."

I ran next to her, trying to block out the pain and failing. The jolts of pain became a tortured cadence to my run. I sank into it, into a weird place where the hurt was background to the thing I had to do. Getting back to St. Luke's was the only thing that mattered, and when the church finally loomed in front of me, I was almost surprised.

I pulled Dougie off the saddle and carried him up the steps to the doors. People came running out. Someone waved me to the right. "This way."

I followed them thought the church, through the garden, to the hospital, where people in scrubs took the boy out of my arms and carried him off.

I waited on the bench by the reception area. Minutes ticked by.

Bishop Chao came rushing through the doors past me and down the hall. A woman in scrubs came out to talk to her. A moment later a door opened and a tall black man in scrubs walked out into the hallway. He and the bishop approached me.

"He's alive," the doctor said. "A broken leg, two broken arms, internal injuries. We will know more once we run the scans."

"Will he survive?"

"There are no guarantees. If we get a magic wave in the next few hours, his chances will improve."

"I will pay all the charges, whatever he needs."

"No need," the bishop said.

The doctor turned and hurried away.

Bishop Chao sat next to me. "What happened?"

"A crew out of the Honeycomb." Only Honeycombers had

iron hounds. "They were after me specifically. Yesterday I talked to some street kids that witnessed Pastor Haywood leaving his church in a car to identify the artifact. The boy was one of them. Kind of their leader. They beat him, chained him, and dragged him around the city, trying to find me."

They must've used the hound to track me to the church and then either made a good guess as to which road I'd take out of it or saw me leave and got ahead of me.

Bishop Chao closed her eyes for a long moment. "We will do everything we can."

"Thank you. And if anyone comes asking, call the Order. Please."

"You look like you might need to be checked out."

I rose. "Thank you again, but I have somewhere to be."

I started toward the doors. He didn't tell them about Marten, but that didn't mean they were the only people looking for her. I had to find her.

"Ms. Ryder," she called after me. "Do be careful."

[7]

I walked into the Order's chapter carrying my saddlebag.

The female knight who had originally escorted me walked out of the nearest office. A slow smile stretched her lips.

"What truck ran you over?"

"Did a child come here looking for me?"

The female knight nodded. "Follow me."

I followed her into her office. Marten sat in a chair, munching away on chocolate chip cookies and drinking from a large mug. She saw me and grinned, presenting me with chocolate-stained teeth.

I slumped against the doorway. It had taken me almost thirty minutes to get to the chapter, and the entire time I was picturing Marten's broken body discarded like garbage in some ruin.

"Your bag is dripping," the female knight observed.

I held the bloody bag up. She reached to the side, pulled a metal pan from a drawer, and placed it on her desk. I set the bloody bag into it. She sat behind the desk. The plaque on it said "Stella Davis."

I leaned against the wall and looked at Marten. "What

happened?"

She swallowed. "I went to get cookies." She gave Stella a suspicious side-eye. "In that place you told me about."

Clearly the knight of the Order couldn't be trusted with sensitive information like the location of the cookie stash. Stella rolled her eyes.

"I ate a cookie, and I hid the rest. Then I went back to the Mouse House. There were two scary guys there and a taker there. They had a dog with iron fur."

The taker meant the highest level of danger, someone to run away from, someone who took the kids and they would never be seen again.

"What were the scary people doing?"

"Talking to Dougie." Marten took another small bite from her cookie.

Talking to this kid was like pulling teeth. "Could you hear what they were saying?"

She nodded.

Stella growled. "What did you hear?"

"They were asking about the Order woman. Dougie lied and said he would show them where you went. And then he went the wrong way and they followed him."

"What did you do next?"

"I went to the secret place, got the cookies, and came here. Like you told me to."

Stella glanced at me. "She showed up here about two hours ago. She's eaten three giant cookies and drank almost a quart of milk." She looked at Marten. "Where is it all going?"

"In my tummy." Marten rubbed her bloated stomach and smiled. Then her smile fell. "Is Dougie okay?"

"Dougie got hurt," I told her. "He is in the hospital now."

"Can I see him?"

I shook my head. "I will take you later, when he is feeling better."

Nick Feldman loomed in the doorway. "What's going on here? Who is this child?"

"She's a material witness," I said.

Nick pointed at my bag. "And what is this?"

"Evidence."

He squinted at the bag. "Well now I feel bad. I didn't get you anything. Why is your evidence bleeding all over Knight Davis' desk?"

I stepped to the desk, opened the bag, and pulled it down. The two knights and Marten stared at the Honeycomber's head.

"The taker!" Marten said.

All humor evaporated from Nick's face. "Pick that up and bring it into my office."

He turned and marched down the hallway.

Stella leaned forward and whispered, "Oooh, you're in trouble."

Marten made big eyes. "Oooh."

I picked up the tray and followed the Knight-Protector.

"Close the door," Nick ordered, sitting down behind his desk.

I shut the door and put the tray in front of him.

"Explain."

I brought him up to speed.

Nick pondered the head, thinking.

I tapped the greasy head in front of me. "Who is he?"

"Jasper. No last name. Rapist, kidnapper, slaver. Do you know about Honeycomb?"

"I know they don't like outsiders."

"It used to be a trailer park for retirees. Now it's a place that scrambles reality."

Honeycomb sat deep inside Honeycomb Gap, a fissure that cleaved the southeast of Atlanta. According to the city archives, before the Shift, it was a nice place with pretty, white mobile homes and manicured landscaping. I had only seen it after the

Shift when it turned into a nightmare. Magic warped the trailer homes and splintered reality into pieces. The double- and single-wides multiplied, growing on top of each other like grapes in a bunch. Outsiders never went into the Honeycomb without a guide. It was a place where people accidentally walked through walls and never came out. One wrong step, and you were gone forever.

"Nobody goes into Honeycomb, and the Honeycombers venture out into the city only when they need money," Nick continued. "They're not picky. They'll do any shitty job that will pay cash. We don't even know how many of them are in there. Could be ten, could be a hundred."

"What about Jasper?"

"Until this morning Jasper ran it." Nick leaned back. "Congratulations. You killed the king of Honeycomb."

"Think he will be missed?"

"I doubt it. But I can't discount the possibility that you've just made yourself a target for revenge by a gang of deranged assholes. Low profile isn't really your thing, Ms. Ryder, is it?"

"Jasper didn't just happen to meet me, Knight-Protector. He tracked me down. Nobody knows me in the city, which means someone hired him to either look into the Haywood murder or make sure I didn't."

Nick grimaced. "Probably the second. He was cunning in a way, but he wasn't the sharpest tool in the shed."

He also wasn't fully human in the strict definition of that word. "Do you know who usually hires him?"

"He was what you might call an independent contractor. I'll tell Knight Davis to get you the list of known associates. Don't get your hopes up."

Nick fixed me with his stare again. "Do not go into Honeycomb. That's an order. You won't find any witnesses, and you won't get any information. Nobody will talk to you. They will walk you into a wall and you'll disappear."

On that we agreed. Going into the Honeycomb was point-less. I was much better off trying to find out who hired Jasper. I didn't know what his employer's goal was, but I had a long bill to settle for Dougie's broken bones.

I realized Nick was waiting for confirmation.

"I promise to not enter the Honeycomb. But if I were to hire someone from the Honeycomb, how would I go about it?"

Nick sighed. "Which part of not going into the Honeycomb was unclear?"

"I said I wouldn't. But they must hire them somehow. Do they just stand at the edge of Honeycomb Gap and scream at the top of their lungs?"

Nick shook his head. "There is a phone line."

"Into the Honeycomb? How?"

"Nobody knows. Rumor says it works, and if you know the number, you can dial it, and someone will pick up."

I stared at him.

Nick shrugged. "You asked."

"Do you know the number?"

"No. And if I did, I wouldn't tell you."

A faint idea began to form in my head.

"Whatever you're thinking, I don't approve," he said.

"Do you ever approve of anything?"

"Yes. Right now, I approve of you getting the hell out of my office. I will handle the Jasper fallout if any occurs. Do what you need to do and don't get killed."

And here I was, planning to die a gruesome death. "You've said that to me before."

"I want you to really listen to me this time." He dug into the drawer of his desk, took out a plastic jar, and shook two pills out onto his palm. "Here."

I held my hand out, and he dropped the pills into it.

"Take this and get out."

I walked out. Nick Feldman had just gifted me prescription-strength ibuprofen. In post-Shift world, the stuff was worth its weight in silver. Aww. I swallowed the pills and walked back to Stella's office.

Marten crouched on the chair, crestfallen.

"What is it?"

"She's eaten all the cookies," Stella said dryly. "Now she has a tummy ache."

"The Knight-Protector told me to ask you for a list of Jasper's known associates."

Stella heaved a sigh and got up. "Wait here. Don't touch anything."

She left. I looked at Marten. She looked back at me.

"Do you have a mom?" I asked.

"No."

"A dad?"

"No."

"Aunt, uncle, cousins? Any living relatives?"

She shook her head.

I had to keep her safe and off the streets. What was I going to do with her? I needed to find a secure place with someone who would watch her twenty-four-seven, because left to her own devices, she would take off. Someone strong enough to protect her from another Jasper.

Stella returned with a single piece of paper. I glanced at it. Four names. An impressive file. A veritable cornucopia of information.

I kept my voice casual. "Thanks. Also, the phone line into the Honeycomb, is it more on the east or the west side of the Gap?"

"West. Just past Martha Street."

I nodded to her and held my hand out to Marten. "Come on."

She hopped off the chair. "Where are we going?"

"To see some nice people. They will keep an eye on you until it's safe." And they would also keep her from running away.

She glanced up at me. "Will they feed me?"

"Absolutely."

"Okay." She took my hand, and we walked out of the chapter.

THE CLERK OF THE MERCENARY GUILD WAVED ME OVER TO HIS counter. Eight years had passed, and he looked exactly the same, as if I had seen him yesterday. Average height, average build, tan skin, brown hair, perpetually around forty-five. He looked like a seasoned bartender, calm, reserved, and ready to whip out the shotgun from under the counter and blast whatever broke through the Guild's giant metal doors.

Nobody remembered his name. He was just the Clerk, in charge of assigning gigs, tracking down mercs when special jobs came in for them, and handling other mundane admin tasks. He had always been there, and I suspected he always would be.

The Clerk saw Marten holding my hand and smiled. Marten smiled back. For a little kid, Marten was very aware of her cuteness, and she weaponized it. On our way here, I'd stopped at the 75 Market and bought her three changes of clothes, toiletries, and a backpack. Somehow, she had ended up with a small bag of candy, a strip of jerky, and a peach, all freely gifted by the stall keepers. If she'd been allowed access to the market, she wouldn't be this thin, but normally the market security chased street kids out. My presence validated hers, and my face smoothed away any doubts anyone might have had. People treated you differently when you were beautiful. Fucked up, but true.

"How can we help you?" the Clerk asked.

"I'd like to see Barabas Gilliam."

"Do you have an appointment?"

"No, but I have money."

The Clerk nodded. "Let me see what I can do."

I stepped back a bit. The Clerk lifted the phone, spoke into it, and waved us over again.

"He'll see you in about fifteen minutes, if you don't mind waiting."

"We don't mind."

Marten and I walked to a client reception area to the left and slightly in front of the Clerk's counter, where several padded chairs were arranged in a horseshoe around a coffee table. From his counter, the Clerk could keep an eye on us and on the front doors.

In its previous incarnation, the Guild used to be a luxury Buckhead hotel, a hollow tower with an atrium in its center. The top of the tower had broken off long ago, gnawed to a nub by magic and then pummeled by a giant. The renovations had stabilized the building, but the height was capped at five floors. Anything taller and you risked magic erosion. Now the former hotel served as a base for about three hundred mercenaries, housing an armory, containment cells, storage, barracks, a sick bay, and everything else muscle-for-hire might need.

Behind us, a food court occupied a good chunk of the floor. Several rough-looking people ate at the tables, some alone, some in groups. The air smelled like fresh bread, cooked meat, and strong coffee. After Curran gave up being Beast Lord, he found himself the majority owner of the Mercenary Guild. His first act was to fix the food. Shapeshifters ate a lot and often.

Marten sniffed. "Smells yummy."

"I thought your tummy hurt?"

"It's all better now."

Stella was right. This girl was a bottomless pit.

We waited. Barabas occupied a large office on our left, behind a glass wall. Normally the door was open, and you could see him working at his desk through the glass. Today the plantation shutters behind the glass blocked the view and his door was closed. He must have wanted privacy.

Nobody bothered us. The mercs kept to themselves. They teamed up for larger jobs, but most of them were lone-wolf types. They handled jobs the cops wouldn't or couldn't, anything from hostile magic hazmat removal to bodyguard detail and armed escort. They drew the line at assault- and murder-for-hire and generally tended to stay on the good side of the law, but aside from that, any job was fair game if it paid enough.

I casually glanced at the exposed ceiling beams high above us. Empty.

The door of Barabas' office swung open slightly, as someone paused with one hand on the door handle. A low male laugh, a deep rumble, came from the gap.

Curran.

I swept Marten into my arms and made a beeline for the women's restroom. Behind me the door swung open with a faint creak. *Don't run, don't run, don't run...* Curran was a cat. If I ran, he would notice.

I pushed the restroom door open, and we ducked inside. I leaned against the door and braced myself. A long moment passed. Another...

Marten blinked at me and said in a hushed voice, "Why are we hiding in the bathroom?"

"We are not hiding. We're executing an evasive maneuver."

"Why?"

"Because it's to our strategic advantage."

Marten nodded.

Excited voices came muffled through the door. Curran laughed again. It was taking every iota of my willpower to keep the door closed. He wouldn't recognize me. Of course, he wouldn't. But if he did, I would have a lot of questions to answer. I wasn't sure I could lie to Curran, and if I tried, he would probably know.

The voices receded. Someone yelled, "And stay out, you beach bum!" More laughter followed. Finally, it died down.

I waited another half a minute and came out of the bathroom. Barabas' door was open. The shutters were up, and I saw him sitting at his desk, his blazing red hair standing on end like hedgehog needles.

"He'll see you now," the Clerk called.

I walked into Barabas' office, set Marten into one of the two client chairs, and took the other.

Barabas looked up. He had an agile face with angular features and smart green eyes. His skin, so pale it was a wonder he didn't glow at night, resisted a sunburn with the power only Lyc-V could muster. He wore a suit despite the heat, but he'd taken the jacket off and rolled up the sleeves of his blue dress shirt, exposing lean muscular forearms. Everything about him seemed quick and sharp.

Don't hold your breath. Act natural. You don't smell the same.

Barabas studied me and Marten. "What can I do for you?"

I put a narrow gold bar on his desk. It was about the length of my finger, half an inch wide and half an inch tall.

Barabas' eyebrows crept up. He picked up his phone. "Charles, I need you for a second."

A moment later, an older Hispanic man walked through the door. He picked up the bar, looked closely at it, and put it down. "Real."

Barabas nodded, and Charles left without another word.

The guildmaster steepled his fingers in front of him. "The Guild is at your disposal."

For twenty grand, it better be. "This is Marten."

Barabas held out his hand. "A pleasure to meet you, Marten. I'm Barabas Gilliam. I run the Guild."

Marten gave him a little wave but kept her hands to herself.

"Marten is a street kid," I told him. "She doesn't trust anyone, especially adult males."

"A good policy." Barabas leaned back in his chair.

"I need you to guard her."

"Do you have any legal authority over this child?"

I knew this was coming. Before taking charge of the Guild, Barabas had been a Pack lawyer. "No. However, she has no living relatives. She is an orphan living on the street. I didn't kidnap her."

Barabas turned to Marten. "Are you an orphan?"

"Yes."

"She's a witness to a murder." Technically that wasn't true but explaining the details would take a while, and Barabas didn't need to know them. "Violent people are looking for her."

"How long do you expect her to require protection?"

"A week."

Barabas glanced at the gold bar. "You're overpaying by at least half, possibly more."

"I think you misunderstood. I want *you* to guard her. You, personally, or…"

Crap. I wasn't supposed to be on a first-name basis with either of them, and Barabas and Christopher had gotten married after I left. Who took whose last name? Was it Christopher Gilliam, Christopher Steed, or Christopher Gilliam-Steed? Or Christopher Steed-Gilliam? If I said the wrong thing, it would mean I knew them from before they had gotten married. Barabas would never let that slide.

"…a member of your family." Yes! Dodged that bullet. "Hence, the higher fee. Should she require protection after one week, I'll return with a similar payment."

It would put a dent in my immediate funds, but it was worth it.

"What if you don't come back?"

"Then I expect you to do what you feel is right. You have a reputation as an ethical man."

Barabas pondered the gold, glanced at Marten, and looked back at me. "Very well. I have just the person." He raised his voice slightly. "Sophia!"

Marten eyed him.

The door swung open, and a teenage girl walked in, with a backpack hanging off one shoulder. She looked about fourteen, athletic build, dressed in shorts and a tank top. A pair of ruby red sunglasses perched on her head. Her hair, pulled back into a short ponytail, was the lightest shade of platinum blonde. Barabas was pale, but she was porcelain-white, and her eyes, fringed by white eyelashes, had an odd lavender tint. An albino.

"Father?"

"This is my daughter, Sophia," Barabas said.

Barabas had a daughter? And Conlan hadn't told me?

"Pleased to meet you," Sophia said.

"She is a member of my family and she is uniquely qualified for this assignment."

A red sheen rolled over Sophia's eyes, and for a second, I saw the outline of a long horizontal pupil before it contracted into a human round shape. A weremongoose. Like Barabas.

Albinism in humans was rare, roughly one in seventeen thousand. In mammals it occurred slightly more often, about one in ten thousand. Albinism in shapeshifters didn't exist. Albinos carried a higher risk of sunburn and skin cancer, and the lack of eye pigmentation sometimes caused vision problems that required corrective surgery. It was theorized that Lyc-V removed albinism in the womb, though there was no consensus on how exactly it did that. I had seen thousands of shapeshifters. Not a single albino among them.

There was only one way for Sophia to exist, and that way was very illegal. Barabas knew that better than anyone. *What did you and Christopher do, and how in the world did you get away with it?*

"Qualified for what?" Sophia asked.

"Bodyguard detail, twenty-four-seven, one week," Barabas said.

"Overtime?"

"Pay and a half."

"Hazard bonus?"

"Situational, depending on the level of the threat."

Sophia narrowed her eyes. "I want it in writing, with the hazard bonus scale specified."

"Done," Barabas said.

Dear gods, he'd made a small female version of himself.

Sophia smiled. "Who will I be guarding?"

"Me," Marten said.

"Hi. I'm Sophia." Barabas' daughter held out her hand.

Marten shook it. "Hi. I'm Marten. What's in your bag?"

"Nagaina."

Like father, like daughter.

"What's a nagaina?" Marten asked.

Sophia slid her hand into the backpack and pulled out a cobra. Big and black, it wrapped around her arm and reared up, displaying a bright yellow chest. Marten froze.

"Sophia, you're scaring the client," Barabas said.

"Don't worry. She's an Egyptian cobra. They're pretty docile and they don't spit venom." Sophia smiled. "And they don't eat pine martens." She slid the snake back into the bag.

"Are you sure about this?" I asked Barabas.

"Quite. Sophia has a lot of experience despite her age, and Marten will be more comfortable with her."

"This won't be a peaceful assignment. They will both be in danger."

"And that's precisely why Sophia would be an excellent fit." Barabas smiled, a sharp, controlled baring of his teeth. "She can dedicate herself to this assignment completely. During the day, they will be here, at the Guild. During the night, they will be at our home. If problems arise, my husband and I will handle them. Additionally, we live in a unique community. I assure you, it's quite safe."

I bet. "It's essential that nobody interrogates her about the murder, including Ascanio Ferara."

Sophia cracked her knuckles. "Oh, that won't be a problem."

Conlan clearly had something against Ascanio, and apparently Sophia wasn't a fan either. He sure had a way with children.

"Does the Pack have an interest in this case?" Barabas asked.

"I don't know yet. However, Mr. Ferara definitely does. Does that complicate things?"

"Not at all," Barabas said. "We do not fall under the Pack's authority."

Like everyone who left the Pack with Curran and Kate, Barabas enjoyed a special status, and I counted on it.

"Great. Here's her clothes and toiletries." I passed the bag to Barabas. "The fee should cover her food, but please make sure she eats something besides cookies."

Barabas nodded. "Of course."

"Do you like honey muffins?" Sophia asked Marten.

I loved honey muffins. Curran's adoptive mother made them. I would kill for one of Martha's honey muffins right now. I would eat it and cry right here in the office.

Marten's eyes lit up. "Are they yummy?"

"Very yummy."

"Then I like them."

"I have some in my office." Sophia held out her hand.

Marten jumped off her chair, winked at me, and took Sophia's hand. They walked out of the office.

That wink spelled trouble.

"She is very good at escaping," I said.

"Sophia is very good at preventing escapes. I promise you, Ms. Ryder, she will be treated well; she will be bathed, fed, and tucked into bed at night, and most of all, she will be under constant supervision."

I had a nagging feeling he would eat those words, but there was nothing else I could do. I had given all the warnings I could give. I hired them to do a job and I had to let them do it.

[8]

The phone line was nowhere near Martha Street.

I figured on about a fifty/fifty chance of Stella sending me on a wild goose chase. Clearly, she either didn't trust me or decided to get payback for me ditching her. Fair enough, a point for her. I respected both her being cautious and trying to get even. In her place, I'd do the same thing.

The Honeycomb sat deep inside a gorge, a crack in the ground about three miles long and a quarter of a mile deep called the Honeycomb Gap. The Gap pulled iron into itself, gathering it from junkyards and the abandoned Ford Motor plant. The area around it lay in ruins, and climbing back and forth over the rubble with an injured leg and a bruised shoulder was all kinds of fun.

If the magic had been up, I could have just called Turgan and had him scout the Gap. The eagle would have spotted the cable in seconds. But with magic down, looking through Turgan's eyes wasn't an option. Turgan was an intelligent bird, but he was just a bird. Telling him to find the cable on his own was like asking Lassie if Timmy was stuck in a well. Words like "cable" had no meaning to an eagle.

Instead I picked my way through the debris and abandoned buildings for over an hour before I finally found it, a single phone line diving into the Gap from a pole that rose at the top of a ruined three-story building. The structure's roof was gone, leaving the inside exposed, and the tall wooden pole had been anchored to the remains of the top floor with a mound of concrete. Climbing said pole with my hurt thigh proved to be about as fun as cuddling a feral cat, but after sliding down a couple of times and cursing in half a dozen languages, I finally cut the line, climbed down, and sat on the edge of the crumbling top floor, dangling my feet over the chasm.

The Gap stretched in front of me, plunging deep below, narrow in this spot, only a couple hundred feet across. A forest of curved metal spikes grew on its bottom, climbing up the sides. Piles of refuse, scrap metal mixed with trash, rose here and there between the skeletal husks of abandoned cars slowly melting into the Gap. Fog slivered between the spikes and heaps of junk, curling in long tendrils, trying to reach up to the edge and the abandoned buildings rising on the other side. Far to the left, a bird glided above the Gap. From here it looked like a stork. Looks were deceiving. Honeycomb spawned Stymphalian birds with iron feathers that cut like razorblades.

My leg hurt. Other parts of me hurt too, but the leg would need attention once I got home. Nick's pills had shaved a slight edge off the pain, but not enough to dull it. Sitting still felt like a sinful luxury.

I had been sloppy. I should've anticipated Jasper's pounce from above. I hadn't because I'd been focused on saving the boy. Now I was paying for it.

Douglas' face flashed before me. Worth it.

When I was a teenager, I would've just shot Jasper. Back then using a shotgun or a rifle wasn't a problem. I used to be a good shot. Not Andrea Medrano good, but decent enough. I could hit a target with a bow on horseback at full gallop. Now guns were no longer an option for me.

All living beings generated magic. Some stored it, like shapeshifters, which enabled them to still transform during tech. Others, like me, emanated it. Over the years, I'd learned to transform these emanations into a cloak, hiding my power during magic, but without it I was a miniature magic generator, and these emanations short-circuited tech in my immediate vicinity. Guns didn't work for me. Gasoline cars were a gamble. Sometimes I could drive one, sometimes it wouldn't start.

Grandma warned me it would happen if I claimed my magic heritage. Kate used to have the same problem, and I used to snicker about it. Her magic short-circuited phones and guns. She'd try to make a call, hang up the phone in disgust, and stomp away, and then I'd pick it up and it worked perfectly. Now I had it worse than her. At least she could fire a gun. She couldn't hit water if she shot it from a boat in the middle of a lake, but the gun would discharge. I just got a smug click when I pulled a trigger.

Still, trading proficiency in tech for one in magic was an easy choice at the time. I wanted to know where I came from and what my bloodline was capable of. I didn't regret it, but I kept paying for it. It was still the wiser option. Magic would win, eventually.

I sat quietly, enjoying not moving. The Honeycombers seemed in no hurry to fix their phone. They probably wouldn't even notice for a few hours, until one of them picked up the phone and the line was dead.

I needed a phone at my place. Phones worked for me about half of the time, and fifty percent was better than zero.

I'd been in the city for over twenty-four hours and so far made no progress. I killed a lesser ma'avir, an insignificant victory. I found out that Pastor Haywood's murder was connected to some unknown magical artifact. I killed the king of Honeycomb. None of that brought me closer to stopping Moloch.

It felt as if a huge doom clock hung over my head, counting off each second.

I leaned back. No, I couldn't think like that. If I let myself run down that road, it would make me sloppy and desperate. I had to take my time, no matter how precious it was.

A high-pitched shriek rolled through the Gap. Yep, a Stymphalian bird. Derek and I used to come here for the feathers once or twice a year. They made good knives that never needed sharpening. We'd pack a lunch and make a day of it, combing the Gap for the fallen feathers, then eating in one of the ruins just like this one.

When we met, I was thirteen. He was eighteen. At that point, I'd only had one boyfriend in my short life, a slimy little weasel called Red who wanted to steal my magic. I thought he was amazing until he sold me out to the sea demons. Then Derek walked onto the scene, like a blazing sun, and the sad puddle of scum that was Red evaporated.

If I closed my eyes, I could picture Derek sitting next to me, long legs stretched over the edge, scarred face turned up to the sun, his eyes shut.

An eerie feeling washed over me. The tiny hairs on the back of my neck rose.

Something was watching me from across the Gap. I scanned the ruins.

Nothing.

Whoever it was, they were well hidden. But they were there.

The weight of the watcher's gaze pressed on me. Like being sighted by a large predator ready to pounce. Every nerve in my body went on guard. I'd felt this before, when I'd arrived in the city. Something had watched me from the darkness as I rode across that bridge, something dangerous and frightening, and here it was again. Was it tracking me? Why?

I raised my hand, smiled, and waved.

That's right. I know you're there. Come out to play.

Nothing. The ruins lay still.

It was still there, watching me. All my instincts warned me it was a threat, the kind of threat I didn't want to face with a busted leg. The simple animal part of me wanted to sit very still and hope that the thing that watched me would forget I was there. The crazy human part wanted to laugh in its face until the fear vanished in a flash of adrenaline.

I made myself heave an exaggerated sigh, got up, and walked away, trying not to limp. I would come back to the Gap later. Hopefully magic would be up. If my silent watcher decided to approach for a closer look, they would be in for a fun surprise.

MAGIC FLOODED THE WORLD IN A BLINK. THE PAIN IN MY THIGH flashed with heat and melted into a tolerable hurt. I shifted on the chunk of the concrete and squinted at the setting sun. I had taken one of my aunt Elara's herbal concoctions when I got home. The wave had activated its magic. If I managed not to strain the leg too much, I'd be almost at full power by tomorrow.

After the Honeycomb Gap, I had gone to Jesus Junction and talked to the representatives of all three churches. None of them owned up to hiring Pastor Haywood or referring anyone to him in the past six months. Another dead end.

Then I made my way to the municipal utility office, flashed my badge and a few hundred-dollar bills, and asked them to string a phone line to my house. The money gave them incentive and the badge offered a convenient excuse to drop everything else and bump me to the front of the line as law enforcement, so they sent a technician out with me despite the end of the business day. To say he wasn't a fan of my house or the location would be an understatement, which was why I had to park myself outside between him and Unicorn Lane to officially "guard him from that cursed place."

The phone tech came striding up. He was short and broad, not fat but solid, with a mop of curly dark hair and olive skin, and he spoke with a mild accent. He might have been Moroccan, but I wasn't sure and not rude enough to ask.

"Well, I hooked it up, but we won't know if it works until magic falls again."

Story of my life. When I needed magic to fight oversized Honeycombers, there was none to be had. But when I wanted a phone, suddenly I got all the magic ever.

"Thanks," I told him. "I'll walk you out."

He eyed Unicorn Lane. About three blocks down, a former skyscraper had sprung a small waterfall. A bluish liquid, shimmering with swirls of lavender, spilled over the top of the ruin and slowly slid down its side in a three-foot-wide stream. It looked viscous.

"Yeah," the tech said. "I'll get my tools. If it doesn't work tomorrow, let us know."

The tech came back with his toolbox, and we walked down Peachtree Circle, heading south, toward civilization. My leg started hurting again. When I got home, I'd chant it into regeneration.

Peachtree Circle ran into 15th street. It used to be a three-way intersection, and now it was more like a small roundabout, with the west end of 15th cut off by heaps of debris from fallen condominiums. The only way out was down the other end of 15th, southeast.

A small shopping plaza had sprouted in the round intersection, only two shops: a pirogi stand manned by a smiling blond man and a convenience bus operated by an older, brown-skinned woman. The bus sold first-aid supplies and necessities: salt, toiletries, bandages, and so on. The pirogi stall sold delicious pirogi. I had sampled them this morning on the way to St. Luke's. The intersection was (now) deserted, except for a lone beggar sitting on a ratty blanket by the debris.

The tech waved at me and headed to his van, sitting by the pirogi stand. The beggar eyed me. Thin, old, with skin the color of dark chestnut creased by wrinkles, he hugged his knees on his blanket. His thin greasy hair hung in long strands over his face. His shoes, beat-up old boots, waited next to him. Grime stained his bare feet. He held himself in that careful way people do when moving meant pain.

He looked so alone.

Wind fanned me, bringing with it a hint of stale urine and the thick scent of a human body that hadn't been washed for far too long.

I walked up to the bus. The old lady was packing up for the day and pretended not to see me. I refused to move. Finally, she squinted at me. I pulled out forty bucks and put it on the counter. "Men's socks and aspirin."

She looked past me at the beggar, then at me, sighed, put two pairs of socks on the fold-out shelf and added a small bottle of aspirin, twenty pills.

"Thanks." I took myself to the pirogi stall, bought the mushroom flavor—less chance of rat meat that way, and took it and my bus purchases over to the beggar.

He shied away from me, scrambling backward. I left the stuff and twenty bucks on the edge of his blanket and walked away.

By the time I got home, less than a mile away, my leg was in full protest mode. I walked into the house, locked the door behind me, and headed into my sanctuary. I reached the door and stopped.

Someone was inside.

I didn't hear anyone, I didn't see anyone, but I knew with absolute certainty that someone had broken into my home.

I walked through the doorway, shut the door behind me, and slid the heavy bar in place, trapping the intruder inside with me.

Quiet. Water gurgled in the stream bed. Plants spread their leaves, eager for the light.

I cracked my knuckles.

A dark shape lunged at me from the left, flying through the air as if he had wings. I sidestepped, gripping the intruder by the arm, and flipped him in midair, using my entire weight to drive him down. His back slapped the limestone. He flipped, legs over shoulders, bounced up like he was made of rubber, and crouched ten feet away, a big grin on his face.

Damn it, Conlan. "You need to work on your pouncing."

Grey eyes laughed at me. "You need to work on your hearing. I stood five feet behind you for a whole minute before I walked into your house. You never turned around."

So he'd snuck in before the magic hit. Explained how he got past my wards. "Remind me, what did I say about not blowing my cover?"

He shrugged. "Who's here to see us? I don't see anybody." He made a show of looking through the plants. "Are you hiding witnesses in your pretty shrubs?"

The problem with Conlan was that he had his father's unshakeable confidence and his mother's mouth. He was also Roland's grandson. He'd spoken in complete sentences when he was eighteen months old, and he cracked complex incantations like they were sunflowers seeds when he was five. Math was child's play, engineering was a fun amusement, chemistry was a hobby, and he took none of it seriously.

His eyes shone. "Do you have food?"

And he was a nine-year-old werelion. "Maybe."

I headed to my fridge. Tamyra Miller had stocked it to my specifications. Let's see. What could I make that would be fast and filling?

"Ham, chicken, venison?"

"Yes!"

"Normally I charge one hug per meal, but for you it's free."

I wasn't a fan of forcing hugs on children. If he wanted to give me a hug, he knew I would welcome one.

He pretended to sigh, came over, and hugged me. He did it very carefully, using a fraction of his strength, aware that he was hugging a human. I'd finally seen my brother in person after eight long years.

"Hey," I told him.

He grinned at me and broke free.

I pulled out a chunk of salted smoked ham, wild mushrooms, four slices of bacon, and some cheddar and mozzarella, got a cutting board and my cleaver, and stocked the fire in the stove. Conlan settled into a chair by the kitchen table.

"You really aren't glad to see me?"

"Of course I'm glad to see you. But now your scent is everywhere and Ascanio knows where I live."

Conlan wrinkled his face, showing me a hint of a fang.

I set the pan onto the fire, tossed bacon into it, and started dicing ham into bite-sized chunks.

Conlan spun around on his chair, leaned to the side until he was nearly horizontal, and plucked a metal sphere from the nearest pedestal. It was about the size of a basketball, a ball of delicate metal lace and gears. I had placed six of them around the sanctuary.

Conlan tossed it up over his head, sending a spark of magic through it. The sphere unfolded into a monstrous metal spider above his head, razor mandibles out, metal claws poised for a kill. For a fraction of a second it hovered above him, looking ready to devour his head, then the tiny drop of magic powering it ran out, and it fell, rolling back into a ball. Conlan caught it with his other hand. The control required to achieve this would make the sages back at New Shinar giddy with joy. Conlan spun the sphere in his fingers and tossed it back up.

Sphere, spider, sphere, spider, sphere...

I finished with the ham, flipped the bacon, and moved on to slicing the mushrooms. "What's the deal with you and Ascanio?"

"I don't like him."

I cut the cheese into thin slices. "Did he do something?"

Conlan shrugged. "That's not important."

"Okay, I'll bite. What is important?"

I took the bacon out, drained most of the fat into a jar, and tossed mushrooms and ham into the pan.

"I want to help."

"Help with what?"

"Help with the secret thing that you talk to grandfather about when I'm not there. The secret thing that makes you stay here and prevents you from coming home."

"Ah. That secret thing."

I took out six eggs, cracked them into the pan, and moved them back and forth with my spatula. Conlan, like his dad, couldn't stand runny eggs. He'd complained about them before when discussing school meals. And like his dad and most shapeshifters, his tolerance for heat in his food was almost nonexistent. If I'd been cooking for me, I would've been throwing jalapenos into the pan.

I salted the scramble and reached for the cheese.

My cutting board wasn't there. Conlan sat on the table, holding the cutting board with the neat stack of cheese slices out of my reach.

"Really?"

"You're avoiding the answer."

"Give me the cheese and we'll talk about it."

He handed the cheese over. I tossed it onto the eggs, stirred it a bit and took the pan off the fire. He watched me. I took a fork out of the drawer, added a big plate, slid the eggs and melted cheese onto it, and pushed it toward him.

He tried it. "Tastes like Mom's."

Well, of course. "Who do you think taught me to cook?"

"Do you remember when I was seven and I had a problem with the druid clique at school?"

"What about it?" Druids had a lot of magic that directly affected animals. He had been seven and the group of kids that tried to torment him were twice his age. He'd refused to tell Kate or Curran about it, and if he'd resorted to violence, he would've been expelled.

"You remember what you said to me? You said, 'You have to tell me these things. I'm your sister.' And the next day, when we went on a lunch break, Roman was waiting for me in the yard in his black and silver robe. He had his staff with the bird head that screeched at people, and when I got near, it started purring. He gave me a big hug and announced he'd brought me pirogi his mother had specially made for me. We had lunch and talked about family and what to get people for Koliada and Christmas. Never had a problem after that."

Roman was a black volhv, a Slavic pagan priest. He served Chernobog, the god of decay, war, and darkness. All Neo-Pagans were taught from an early age about other Neo-Pagans, and Roman was officially listed in their registry under the heading of "Do not fuck with." His mother, Evdokia, was one of the witches of the Witch Oracle. I took lessons from her when I was young, which was how Sienna and I became friends. Calling Roman for a minor favor was no trouble. The priest of the God of All Evil loved helping people. It was his chance to shine, and he made the most of it. Kate had done something similar for me when I was a teenager.

"Your point?"

He raised his head from the food. There was barely half left on his plate. "You have to tell me these things. I am your brother."

Aw.

But he was only nine. The ma'avirim were dangerous as hell.

Conlan leaned forward, his gaze unblinking and direct. "I'm not a baby."

It's like he was telepathic sometimes.

"You're not a baby, but you often act like one. You don't like to study, you don't apply yourself, and you squeak by doing the bare minimum to keep Grandfather from losing his temper..."

Conlan raised his hand. Claws burst from his flesh. The hand stretched, fingers elongating into monstrous digits. Coal-black fur sheathed the new hand. He sliced at his forearm. Thin threads of blood stretched from his wounds, wound about his hand, and snapped into a gauntlet.

Someone had been practicing.

"Let me see the range of motion."

He moved his fingers, bending them toward his palm, pinkie to thumb. Blood armored claws cut through the air. The hair on the back of my neck rose.

Making blood weapons and armor was one of the two most important skills to the Shinar bloodline. Dealing with the *shar*, an irresistible urge to claim land and defend it from all threats, was the other. Blood armor had its limits and blood weapons broke after a few hours of use, their magic exhausted, but while they lasted, they made you practically invulnerable. A blood blade cut through solid steel like it was nothing.

It was a skill that would've been out of my reach if it wasn't for Kate.

Years ago, I was bitten by a shapeshifter and my body rebelled against me. I would've gone loup, but the Pack's chief physician, Dr. Doolittle, had sedated me, delaying the inevitable to allow Kate and Curran to come to terms with it. I was going to be put down. In a last-ditch effort to save me, Kate pulled the blood out of my body with magic and washed it with hers, purging the Lyc-V from me.

Her blood coursed through me, and it gave me the powers of her bloodline. Even after my transformation forever altered me,

I had retained the power of blood magic. After Erra and I had awakened her people, Erra named me her formal heir. Some of the advisors raised concerns about whether or not I was suitable. I walked into the session of the council, dumped a gallon of vampire blood at my feet, cut my arm, and clothed myself in blood armor. Nobody ever questioned my right to rule again.

Conlan rotated his wrist. The gauntlet fit him like second skin. The construction was perfect. A year ago, he could only coat his claws. It must've taken him months of intense work. I wondered why he spent so much time with Grandfather. Every time I popped in, he was there.

"I've applied myself," my brother said. "I want in."

He was looking at me with that single-minded determination I often saw on Kate's face. Conlan had made up his mind. He would find out what was going on. My choices had shrunk to two options: tell him myself and control the narrative, or let him figure it out on his own and kiss the chances of reining him in goodbye.

"I'm trusting you with something important."

"I know."

"One careless word, and we'll end up with the kind of disaster nobody can fix."

"I understand."

"What do you know?"

"If you go home, Mom dies."

Ah. "Grandfather?"

He nodded. "He told me eight months ago. I haven't told anyone. I understand the gravity of the situation. Let me help."

"It's imperative that your parents don't know."

"I understand."

"You must learn everything you can about Moloch."

"Who is he?"

"The enemy. An ancient god has been reborn as an avatar. The Witch Oracle foretold that in the future he will kill your mother. We've been trying to alter that future, but so far we've failed. If your mother finds out about the prophecy, she will die."

He sat very still. Fear flickered in his grey eyes. That's how I reacted the first time the meaning of the prophecy had really sank in.

"The eye you took, did it belong to Moloch?" he asked.

"Yes."

"Is that why you look different?"

"Yes."

I pulled an unmarked book off the shelf and put it in front of him. He opened it and stared at the pages lined with my handwriting and illustrations of sigils.

"This is everything I know about Moloch right now. This book doesn't leave this house. Read it here, commit it to memory. Once you're done, you must go to Grandfather and get as many details about Moloch as you can. Moloch attempted to invade Shinar in the past. Grandfather can tell you more. I need you to figure out what to watch out for. I need you to guard your mother. If you spot any signs of Moloch or his shithead priests, you must tell me immediately. Do everything you can to keep Kate and them from interacting."

The distant cry of an eagle echoed through my mind. Turgan.

I let the eagle's sight unfold in my mind. Nick's house came into focus, like a vision woven in a net of glowing threads. Turgan turned his head. A large lupine shape was coming toward us, running at full speed down the dark street.

What in the world?

The wolf stopped by Nick's front door. It was massive, bigger than any wild wolf I'd seen that wasn't dire. A shapeshifter. Their beast forms ran larger than their animal counterparts.

The wolf sat on its haunches and gently scratched the door.

A moment and the door swung open. The wolf's body surged up, a controlled whirlwind of flesh and bone, and a nude woman rose on Nick's doorstep, long blond hair falling down to her waist.

Ummm...

The woman threw her arms around Nick. The eagle caught a glimpse of her face, and I almost fell out of my chair. What?

He scooped her up, carried her inside, and kicked the door closed behind him.

Nikolas Feldman, the Knight-Protector of Atlanta's chapter of the Order, the paragon of knightly virtue, was having a torrid affair with Desandra Kral, the alpha of Clan Wolf.

I got the hell out of the chair. This I had to see.

"Earth to Julie?" Conlan said.

"I have to go."

"I'll come with."

"Not this time. But there is something you can do for me tonight. Read the book first. Then go to Shriker Boulevard on the edge of the Honeycomb Gap. One of the ruins has a wooden pole with a phone line going from it. I cut it this afternoon. If they repaired it, cut it again. Don't let yourself be seen."

My brother smiled. "Done."

I told him my phone number. "Don't write it down anywhere. Call me tomorrow when tech hits and tell me how it went."

I was almost to the sanctuary doorway when he called out, "Julie..."

"Yes?"

"Do you blame Mom for that time?"

I stopped and turned around. When Kate washed my blood with hers, she created a magic bond between us. That bond gave her the ability to suppress my will. For the next few years, I was magically tethered to Kate. I was aware of her at all times. I couldn't pinpoint her exact location, but I knew in which direction to go to find her from miles away. I sensed when she was hurt, and if she gave me a direct order, I was compelled to obey.

She had only given me that kind of order once and for the best of reasons. The shock of having my will crushed haunted me for years. It was the deepest violation of me I'd ever experienced.

The bond was no more. Kate's death had severed it. She had died for mere seconds, but it set me free. The freedom was agony. The severed bond left behind a gaping raw wound that burned and gnawed on my soul. It took me a long time to heal. My Uncle Hugh and I had that in common. He too had been once bound to Grandfather. If it hadn't been for him, I would've suffered more.

I'd rather die than experience that again. It wasn't just an empty turn of phrase. If anyone ever attempted to bind me again, I'd slit my own throat.

Conlan was waiting for an answer.

"I don't blame her. She was trying to save my life. I love Kate very much, Conlan. She, Curran, you, and Grandmother, you are the people I treasure most. You are my family. In this wide world, with all its knowledge, riches, and pleasures, only the people you love matter most. Read the book. Call me tomorrow."

I walked out.

———

THE FULL MOON SHONE IN THE NIGHT SKY LIKE A COIN OF WHITE gold, sliding in and out of ragged clouds. I sat on Tulip's back, in the shadow of a large dogwood on the edge of what used to be West End Park. Decades ago, the trees inside the park had rioted, fed by magic. They grew at a shocking rate, spreading their branches, stretching their roots until the park became a forest.

Across from me, on the other side of Lucile Avenue, a solid two-story building rose in the middle of a lot. Built like a fortress, with thick stone walls and windows shielded by steel and silver grates, it sat alone, the nearest neighbor five hundred yards away. Nick liked his privacy.

A lone oak spread thick branches near the house. Technically, it presented a security issue since someone could hide in its branches, like Turgan was doing right now, but Nick clearly didn't care. Anything that could climb that oak could likely climb the building, and the tree shaded the house. In a time when air conditioning was an unbelievable luxury, a shady spot was worth its weight in gold.

It took me about thirty minutes to get here through the deserted streets, and I had disconnected from Turgan for most of it. Eavesdropping on Nick and Desandra's private time was close to dead last on the list of things I wanted to do.

The night breeze fanned my face. So nice after the heat of the day. The city around me lay empty. Anyone with a crumb of sense hid indoors at night, behind thick walls and sturdy doors.

Why Desandra? I wouldn't have imagined those two being together in a million years. Nick was a rock in a storm, calm, steady, unmovable, never losing his temper until the very end. His was a cold kind of crazy. Desandra was a hot whirlwind, funny, unpredictable, and often wildly inappropriate. She said things that made boudas blush.

She was also deadly.

Years ago, Kate and Curran went to the Mediterranean with some heavy hitters from the Pack to get panacea, an herbal remedy that reduces the occurrence of loupism. They came back with Christopher, who was now Barabas' husband, along with Desandra and her twin newborn sons. She made her first kill on US soil two days after she joined the Pack and within a year clawed her way to becoming the wolf alpha.

Was she using him? I couldn't imagine what for. Well, I could imagine, but I didn't want to.

If I delayed any longer, they might fall asleep. I shut my eyes and gingerly tried to listen through Turgan's ears.

"...Haywood murder," Nick said.

Oh good, good, good. Talking. Talking was great.

"Good people don't last, but assholes live forever," Desandra murmured.

I sank into the glowing web of Turgan's sight and saw them through the window. They were lying in bed, Desandra's head resting on Nick's arm, her golden hair spilling over the pillow in a tangled curtain.

"Where was Desimir last Thursday night?" Nick asked.

"Where he usually is, home."

"Are you sure?"

Desandra turned, leaning her head on her bent elbow so she could look at him. "Do you think my son murdered Haywood?" Her tone wasn't hostile, just softly chiding.

"The killer flew in through the skylight, ripped the body to shreds with its claws, then went back out through the skylight. It was a cat kill."

Desandra sighed.

"He's going through puberty," Nick said.

"Yes. Between him and Miladin I knock before I open any door in the house. Every sock is a possible landmine. I make them do their own laundry."

Was there something wrong with Desimir? Desandra'd had a weird pregnancy; her two sons were born at the same time but had different fathers. Miladin was a wolf, and Desimir was a lynx. I'd babysat both when they were toddlers a dozen times. They were normal shapeshifter babies. Their magic was identical hunter green. Why would Nick think that Desimir could fly? Weirder and weirder.

"You see him every weekend," Desandra said. "Why don't

you ask him?"

"Because I don't want him to think I suspect him."

"But you do."

"No, I don't. But other people might and if it ever comes up, I want to have all my facts ready. If I have to defend him, I need to be able to honestly say where he was at the time of the murder. If you tell me he was home, I believe you. I just need you to be sure we can prove it."

Desandra sighed again. "Was it eaten? Haywood's body?"

"They took his heart, but no."

"Well, there's your answer. We both know what my son is. He also knows what he is. We raised him well. He's a smart kid. He has no interest in power or turning into a monster. He spent Thursday at home doing what he usually does, which is reading old comic books and listening to music. There are half a dozen people besides me and Miladin who can confirm this."

"Good."

Desimir had nothing to do with it. No matter what he turned into, his primary magic was that of a shapeshifter. Lyc-V left a magic trail a mile long, and it colored all other magic a person might have. Years ago, before I left, Curran fed on divine beasts to gain more power and save Kate from death. He'd been a hair away from true divinity and his magic was still green. The creature that killed Pastor Haywood was golden silver.

"I know mothers don't know everything, but I don't see him doing this. He is a thirteen-year-old boy. Can you picture him smashing through a skylight, ripping apart a holy man he'd never met, and digging out his heart?"

"No," Nick said. "Even if he turned, there are easier targets. He could hunt homeless in the Warren and nobody would know for years."

Desandra traced his jaw with her fingertips. "Then why did you ask?"

"Ferara is sniffing around this case."

Desandra collapsed onto a pillow, her arms in the air. "Of course he is."

"Do you think he knows about Desimir?"

"If he does, Andrea or Raphael told him. Kate would never. Neither would Doolittle or the bears."

She was right. Besides Curran, I was the closest person to Kate, and I had no idea what the hell they were talking about. This was clearly Pack business, and at least a dozen people knew, but somehow everyone who came back from that trip managed to keep this secret. Curiosity was killing me.

"Does Jim know?" Nick asked.

"I imagine he does." A low snarl reverberated in Desandra's throat. "He was the chief of security at the time. Curran would have told him."

"So, this could be coming from the top or from the boudas."

"Jim and I have never had a problem. We have our disagreements, but he isn't petty. If he suspected something, he would've given it to the rats."

Clan Rat ran the Pack's security.

"You know Jim," Desandra continued. "He does everything by the book, with a paper trail and receipts. No, this is coming from the boudas."

"Ascanio could be acting on his own. He's ambitious," Nick mused.

Desandra grimaced. "There's the understatement of the year."

"If Desimir was responsible and Ascanio found the proof, would he try blackmail, or would he bring it to Jim and try to remove you?"

A golden sheen rolled over Desandra's irises. Her hand flexed on the pillow as if it had claws. "I don't know exactly what his game is, but I'll find out."

A chill dashed down my spine. Nope, she hadn't mellowed.

Not even a bit. Ascanio wasn't stupid. Why would he screw with her?

Nick leaned to the side, pulled a piece of paper out of something I couldn't see, and held it out to Desandra. "Smell this."

She grinned. "Oh baby, such inventive come-ons you have."

Nick rolled his eyes.

Desandra plucked the paper from his fingers and sniffed it. "Why am I smelling this?"

"A woman showed up at my office. This is a form she filled out. She has a badge that dictates that I assist her in every way possible."

"Mmmm, kinky. How do I get one of those?"

"You have to render a great service to the Order."

Desandra grinned and smelled the paper again. "Oh, I've done that. Many, many times."

Nick smiled. Oh my gods.

"Have you smelled this scent before?"

Desandra shook her head. "No. I would remember. Why?"

Nick frowned. "There's something familiar about her. I can't put my finger on it but..."

"Keep your finger and everything else away from her." Desandra's eyes flashed again. She toyed with the paper. "Is she pretty?"

"Pretty is the wrong word."

Desandra's voice dropped into dangerous territory. "What is the right word?"

"Regal." Nick grimaced and held out his hand. "I need the paper back."

"No." Desandra held the paper out of his reach and sniffed it again. "I like smelling it."

My magic gave me an affinity to horses, birds of prey, and wolves. They liked my scent.

"Seriously." Nick reached for the paper.

"You can't have it. Mine." Desandra waved the paper and

stopped abruptly, her eyes looking straight at me like two shiny moons. "Honey, where is your crossbow?"

"By the bed. Why?"

"There is an eagle in your tree."

"So?"

"I grew up in the Carpathian Mountains. We had many eagles. They sleep at night."

Busted. I sent a mental push to Turgan. *Go!*

The eagle took off. I tossed a handful of wolfsbane into the air, spun Tulip around, and urged her into a canter. She flew through the night-soaked streets like a ghost. Wind tugged at my hair. Even if Desandra chased me, she'd have a hard time catching up, and the wolfsbane would leave her nose-blind for a couple of hours.

Ahead, Lucile Avenue dead-ended into Abernathy Boulevard. We made a right and headed northwest.

An eerie howl floated on the night wind. The hair on the back of my neck stood on end, an instinctual reaction coded in my genes from when humans were food and feared being eaten.

It had come from the left. If Desandra had chased me and howled, it would've come from the right or behind us. Were there wolves guarding her? She could've brought a team with her. Had I blundered into a trap?

I sent my magic out in a pulse. It splayed out, searching, collided with bodies, and I felt wolves, running fast through the wrecked houses on my right. One, two...

A second group, on the left, gliding through the overgrown wood that used to be Westview Cemetery. Three more, all larger than a wild wolf had a right to be.

Shit.

Another howl rose, a vicious song of hunt, a promise of sharp fangs and a swift death. A second howl answered. The pack was closing in.

Tulip neighed, more outrage than fear, and broke into a

gallop. We thundered up the deserted street past the husks of abandoned homes. The wolves sang again. Ice rolled down my spine. This wasn't a pretend chase. I was being hunted.

A new presence came in from the right, moving fast on the edge of my magic. It lashed my senses like a knife, emanating power. Not Desandra. Something else. Something savage, something more... Moving way too fast.

Tulip screamed in alarm.

We rounded the curve. Ahead, something blocked the road. The moon peeked through the clouds. An overturned semi, flanked by a bunch of smashed cars.

Wolves burst from the woods behind me.

Forest on the left, semi in front. Turning right, toward East I-20, was my only option. I swung Tulip onto MLK Drive.

The overpass in front of me had crumbled. A hill of debris blocked the road.

A dead end. They'd ran me to ground.

I let the reins go slack, so Tulip could stop on her own. She made a wide arc by the rubble, slowing, and I turned her toward the road and the cemetery on the other side, our backs to the overpass. I was done running.

No more howling. It was quiet now. The only sound was Tulip breathing hard.

Shadows congealed from the gloom between the trees on the other side. Slowly, paw over paw, the wolves padded out into the open. Three from the woods, two from the right, coming from Abernathy. Two grey Eurasians, one white Arctic, and the other two grey sprinkled with cinnamon—Timbers. Every single one was over two hundred pounds. Five pairs of glowing eyes stared at me.

Tulip bared her teeth.

The odds weren't in my favor. With the magic up, I could take them, but then the Pack would come after me in force.

A huge shape leaped from the roof of a brick building on the left and landed in front of the pack. Magic screamed a warning in my head.

The grey monster, bigger than any lupine shapeshifter I had ever seen, raised his head. He was almost as big as Curran and Curran was a fucking prehistoric lion.

Two golden eyes focused on me, their gaze pinning me in place. Suddenly it was hard to breathe. My body locked up, convinced that I was prey. The alpha stare.

He *dared*.

I stared right back. Holding his gaze was like trying to lift a car.

The moon tore through the clouds, spilling pale light onto the intersection. It slid over the giant wolf's fur, setting it aglow. He wasn't grey. He was silver. Unnaturally silver.

I blinked, bringing my magic vision up. A faint mint green rippled over his coat. Fuck.

The wolf took a step forward, bathed in moonlight.

My hands went cold. A bitter metallic taste coated my tongue. I blinked the magic colors away and reached for my bow, attached to Tulip's saddle.

Step.

Another.

I raised my bow. Everything came into crystal-clear focus. My breathing was deep and even. The world shrank down to three things: the wolf, my bow, and the distance between us.

A third step.

I plucked an arrow from the quiver.

His black lips stretched, showing me a forest of fangs.

Keep smiling. You'll look really funny with an arrow sticking out of your mouth.

His silver fur tore. In an instant, bone melted like wax, reshaping itself, muscles stretched, snapping over the new frame, and human skin sheathed the new form. A man with golden eyes stared at me, tall, broad-shouldered, corded with muscle. The moonlight played over his face, highlighting the network of thin scars.

Derek.

My heart stopped. It couldn't have, because I would've died, but it felt like it had.

His eyes were ice-cold. He looked at me as if this was his land and I'd trespassed.

Derek opened his mouth.

I had to run. Now. Before I heard his voice.

I sent a mental scream to Tulip. *Go!*

The magic command whipped Tulip into motion. She reared, pawing the air. The faint outline of a horn shimmered on her forehead. Tulip spun, surged toward the rubble, leaped, landing on the broken concrete like a gazelle, and dashed over the fallen overpass. For a moment we went airborne, and then we were galloping down the road at a breakneck speed into the night.

[9]

I paced back and forth inside my sanctuary.

Why did I run? I'd been in battles that had lasted days. I had dived into Eagle's Nest Sink, a cave so dangerous, it had a sign with a grim reaper on it and a warning "There is nothing in this cave worth dying for," because I had to talk to a mermaid. I visited my grandfather every couple of weeks, for crying out loud. And the moment Derek opened his mouth, I turned tail and ran.

All the fights I'd been in, all the torture I'd braved, all the magic I'd learned, and that's what undid me. Meeting the guy who used to be the center of my universe until I turned eighteen.

Stupid. So stupid. Was I thirteen again? What the hell had happened?

He hadn't recognized me. The look he gave me was so cold.

It hurt.

Some fragile part of me must have been convinced that the moment he saw me he would magically know who I was. But he didn't.

It wasn't him. It was me. I made myself run away.

I thought I'd buried that crush. I was no longer an adolescent who kept hoping Derek would realize I was growing up and fall in love with me. I didn't say goodbye to him before I left because I was too chicken to chance it. If he'd asked me to stay, I might not have gone through with it, and if he hadn't, it would've crushed me. None of that was his fault. He had to know how I felt. He never took advantage of it. He never even gave me a hint that he was waiting for me. In all the time I was gone, he hadn't tried to find me. After that initial phone call, I called home every week when I could. Kate and Curran knew where I was. If Derek wanted to see me, all he had to do was ask them. For the first couple of years I had held on to a fragile hope that one day he would just show up unannounced, but he never had. And then Kate told me he left Atlanta.

I waited. I was so sure he would make his way to me in California. He hadn't.

I gave up. It hurt too much, so I let it go. Atlanta had stirred up memories, and I had thought of him more than once in the last couple of days, but prior to that I made myself abandon him. *Sah akin tonar erani es. His shadow didn't darken my mind.*

Eight years had passed. Everything about me had changed, but I was still in love with Derek Gaunt. How was this possible?

I sat on a plush azure divan. In front of me, a bronze statue shimmered softly with reflected light. A winged serpent winding around a slender pole, her swan-like wings spread wide, as if she were about to take flight above the white gardenia blossoms and burgundy star-shaped hoyas dripping from their trellises. At once delicate and ferocious.

One of Erra's artists had created this statue and offered it to me as tribute. That's how she'd seen me, the princess of this new age always ready to spill blood in defense of the new kingdom's people, beautiful and deadly.

Thank you for the reminder, Gemeti.

I was no longer Julie. These feelings were a ghostly echo

from someone else, and that girl was gone. Derek didn't know the new me. There was no connection between us.

I didn't know the new him either.

The Derek I knew had been born into a religious household deep in the mountains of Appalachia, where families were money poor but land rich. They guarded their land and their independence with "Trespassers will be shot" signs and meant it.

When Derek was fourteen, his father caught Lyc-V at a tent revival. He went loup fast, drowning in the brew of runaway hormones. Loupism had no cure. It turned shapeshifters into psychotic, sadistic spree killers. Derek's father was no exception. Every repressed urge, every dark desire forbidden by religion and law, bubbled up to the surface and exploded.

The neighbors and authorities minded their own business. Nobody had helped. Derek's mother and sisters became his father's hostages and slaves. His mother caught the virus from his father and killed herself, leaving Derek, his brother, and his five sisters alone with a loup.

The nightmare lasted almost two years. Everyone became infected within months. They tried to fight their father, but loups were freakishly strong. Two of Derek's siblings died from starvation, chained by their father in the basement. Three of his sisters died from their injuries. One went loup and turned on her brothers and sisters, reveling in their father's demented cruelty. The day Derek found the half-eaten body of his youngest sister, he couldn't take it anymore.

The local authorities finally took notice when a column of smoke rose from the top of the mountain and called in the Pack. When Curran arrived with a group of shapeshifters, they found Derek sitting by the burned-out husk of his house, his father's blood on his hands. He'd finally stopped the nightmare, but it was too late for everyone else.

Derek didn't resist. He made no effort to explain what

happened. He didn't speak at all. He'd ripped his father apart and that's all he cared about. Jim, the current Beast Lord, thought Derek would go loup and wanted to kill him. Curran forbade it. He took Derek with him to the Pack and slowly coaxed him back to life.

That was my Derek, and he held himself in a steel grip. Everything that influenced shapeshifters affected him stronger than normal. The moon made him half-crazy. When he locked onto a scent, nothing else mattered. And when he fought... Derek had a hard time sparring. He was worried that if he let go of his control by a hair, he would fall off the same cliff his father had.

He never felt comfortable around other shapeshifters; their presence made his struggle for control worse. But he was fanatically loyal to Curran and Kate. He stayed in the Pack for their sake, and when Curran stepped down, Derek was right behind him. He didn't hesitate for a second.

After the separation from the Pack, Derek fully embraced his Lone Wolf of Atlanta status. He worked for Cutting Edge, but he seemed most content when he was working on his own.

Old Derek was a loner. The new Derek had a pack. He had landed with his back to them, and they had positioned themselves to protect him. I had no doubt that if he growled a command, they would have tried to tear me apart. That was his pack. Not Desandra's, not a Pack crew. His.

Old Derek was grey. Large, by shapeshifter standards, but still within normal range for a lupine shapeshifter. The new Derek was silver, bright uniform silver, without any black or brown, and he was huge. I'd never seen a werewolf that large before.

Old Derek emanated strong hunter green, right in line with the rest of the Pack. The new Derek left a trail of mint-green magic.

Old Derek's eyes glowed amber. The man I saw tonight had

eyes that shone with gold. And it wasn't just the shine. It was the way he looked at me. He'd stared at me as if I had intruded into his territory and he had the right to punish me. He'd given me the alpha stare. You couldn't buy one of those. You couldn't steal or borrow it. You could learn to imitate it, but most natural leaders were born with it. It was one of the most effective means of control for a pack leader. Curran had raised it to the level of art, and Conlan was doing his best to catch up.

In all of our years together, I had never seen Derek give someone the alpha stare. He focused on them and he had what I used to call his "death glare," but it wasn't an alpha stare.

What the hell had happened?

It was Derek. The scars were unmistakable.

Perhaps that was all that was left of the Derek I used to know.

Ascanio must've realized Derek was back in the city. That time when he had tried to take the cookie from me, a shapeshifter, one of his people, had run up and reported that she saw "him" and then she waved her hand in front of her face. She must have been indicating the scars. Besides our family and the Medranos, Derek would be just about the only person for whom Ascanio would drop everything and go chasing into the night. The rivalry between them started the day Ascanio tried to put his hands on me, and Derek had shown him the error of his ways. It never got better, only worse.

Derek had returned to Atlanta, and now he and Ascanio both were somehow tangled up in Pastor Haywood's murder. Why had he left in the first place? Something had occurred, some seismic shift must have taken place for him to abandon Kate and Curran and disappear.

Maybe it wasn't Derek at all. Maybe something was just wearing his body. The thought brought me up short.

If something dared to take his body, I would kill it.

Magic flashed in my mind. Someone had just crossed my

outer ward. I jumped off the divan, picked up my spear, and marched to the front door.

It couldn't be him. I had used wolfsbane, and then Tulip and I swam through Lake Adair for half a mile, dodging water snakes and snapping turtles living on the drowned trees left over from when the lake had been Adair Park. It would take him and his people ages to find my scent, if they ever did.

Someone knocked on my door. I flung it open.

Knight Stella Davis took a step back. "Easy now. I just came to borrow a cup of sugar."

The tension went out of me. "White or brown?"

"I don't know. I don't really bake." Stella looked over my shoulder. "That's a textbook shithole you're living in. I admire your commitment, but just so you know, we don't take a vow of poverty in the Order. You can live somewhere nice. With furniture that hasn't been gnawed on."

Ha. Ha. "It's after midnight. Did you need something, or did you just come over to insult my house?"

Stella narrowed her eyes. "Aren't you curious how I found you?"

"Let me guess, someone from the city called you about the phone service?"

A little of the excitement went out of her. "Yep. Funny thing, when you wave around an Order badge and a wad of cash, people still want to check you out and see if you're legit. Great job staying off the grid. You should teach covert work at the academy."

"Would that be before or after your class on surveillance, with an emphasis on how to lose a suspect on your home turf? That really pissed you off, didn't it?"

"Yes. Yes, it did. But now I found you."

"Congratulations. You're the best that's ever been."

Stella grinned. "Thank you." She raised a piece of paper and waved it at me.

Fine. I made my tone flat and disinterested. "What's that?"

"This is a murder. I think it's connected to yours."

I opened the ward. "Come in."

"Is it safe? Will the germs get me?"

"Poverty isn't contagious. You'll be fine."

Stella entered and followed me to the kitchen.

"Beer, coffee, tea?"

"From this kitchen? No thanks." She passed me the paper.

I read it. A name and an address. "Alycia Walton. Why do you think she's connected?"

"She is, well, she was, a historian specializing in early Christianity."

If you had some Christian relics and they had real power, the next step to selling would be to establish their history and provenance. Stella knew about the relics.

"How?"

Stella grinned. "I would imagine she went to college, maybe for many years."

"How did you know about the connection to the Christian relics?"

"Alleged Christian relics. The Christian relics Pastor Haywood may have authenticated, those Christian relics?"

I would strangle her in a minute. I sat down at the table and smiled at her. "My patience is an infinite lake. Feel free to drown yourself." There were times when ancient proverbs came in handy.

"You are no fun. I'm here to help. Like a colleague or a partner."

"You screwed up and got sent to Atlanta, because that's where the Order dumps troublemakers with potential, those who don't follow orders. This is the end of the line if Nick can't"—I paused, looking for the right word—"rehabilitate you. Except both times I came to the Order, you were there, in the middle of the day, at your desk, instead of being out working a case and making a difference. Nick is keeping you on a short leash. It's killing you, and here is a high-profile murder that none of the other knights are working. You saw it and you jumped on it. So, you didn't come to help me. You came to help yourself."

Stella looked at me for a long moment. "That, and I don't trust you. Also, I'm bored."

"How did you find out about the relics?"

"Nick sent me to the Methodists to check on the boy. While I was there, one of them handed me a list of relic hunters to pass on to my 'colleague.' He also mentioned that there were two historians in north Georgia who specialized in consulting on relics and Alycia Walton was one of them."

And Stella had put the rest of it together. Smart. She would be all over this murder, except Nick had surrendered this case to me, and she probably didn't have authorization to investigate things on her own. She needed me.

"Can I have that list?"

She passed me another folded piece of paper. I opened it and scanned the six names. None of them looked familiar.

"How is Douglas?"

"Who's Douglas?"

"The little boy."

Stella grimaced. "They said they are doing all they can."

Whenever I heard that, things turned out for the worse.

"Do you want to see this crime scene or not?" Stella asked. "I'd love to waste more time, but if we don't hurry, the cops will cart the body off."

"You mean this is a recent murder? When exactly did this happen?"

"It was reported about an hour ago."

"Were you going to tell me this at some point?"

"I just did, but if you want, we can keep trading barbs in your charming kitchen."

"Wait for me outside, please." I got out of my chair and went to get my horse.

THIRTY MINUTES LATER, STELLA AND I STOOD IN FRONT OF HENRY L. Bowden Hall in the heart of Emory University. The three-story building loomed in the dark, dimly illuminated by a row of fey lantern streetlamps, and the ghostly blue light gave it a foreboding air. When we arrived, two policemen, armed with shotguns and swords, guarded the entrance. We had shown them our badges, and one of them went inside to let the lead detective know that we were there.

We'd been standing around for twenty minutes, waiting for the PAD to finish processing the scene. Supposedly, we'd be allowed in once Biohazard said it was safe.

The building was older, pre-Shift, with the first floor sheathed in pale stucco and the two upper ones inlaid with polished stone tiles, marble or granite; I couldn't tell in the dark. All three floors sported rows of rectangular windows, three feet wide and six feet tall, shielded by thin metal grates. Half inch steel bars, only two cross bars, cheap-looking steel without any trace of silver. Protection on a budget. To make things worse, the grates opened like shutters, so the top and bottom edges of the grate weren't anchored. The entire mess was secured by four bolts on each side, driven into the wall.

Do you want magic monsters in your office? Because this is how you get monsters in your office.

I was pretty sure Alycia Walton hadn't wanted monsters.

"The grates aren't properly anchored," Stella said quietly.

"It's a college."

"So?"

"They have a limited budget."

Stella rolled her eyes. "The Academy is a college and it has proper grates."

She wasn't wrong. "Let's take a walk around the building."

We turned left and followed a paved path around the corner, rounding the building. The Woodruff Library sprawled to the left of us, cushioned in trees and steeped in deep, night shadows. You could hide a dozen wolves in those shadows, and using my magic to send out a pulse and check if they were there was out of the question. I didn't know what Stella's special tricks were. The less she knew about me, the better.

Moonlight cascaded from the dark sky, illuminating the side of Bowden Hall. A hole gaped in the top row of windows, second from the left, emanating a faint cerulean glow. The steel grate that used to shield it stuck out of the hedge bordering the path. The corner of it jutted up, with the bolts still attached to the hinge. You get what you pay for.

Deep gashes marred both sides of the window.

"Those are claw marks," Stella said. She held her hand up, sizing them up. "Big boy."

"It had trouble fitting through," I murmured.

We stared at the window. There were no claw marks on the wall. No tracks on the lawn on the other side of the path either. It didn't run up and climb the building. It had to have flown. A manticore checked some of the boxes: winged, large, carnivorous, fangs. You could probably train one to attack on command. But they were smaller, and they hunted in packs at dusk, swooping down onto the running prey. They rarely attacked humans. Their preferred targets were deer and herds of feral cattle.

"There's one thing I don't understand," Stella said.

"Yes?"

"Why did you decide to live in that deathtrap?"

Really? "Here we are at a murder scene, examining the claw marks of the perpetrator, three stories up and in poor lighting, and your mind is laser-focused on the mystery of my house. Truly, Knight Davis, no detail escapes your notice."

"I like to know things. It doesn't make sense."

"I like to know things too, like what did you do to get shipped off to Atlanta?"

Stella raised her chin. "I punched a superior."

Somehow it didn't surprise me. "How superior?"

Stella pondered the question. "In terms of rank or morality?"

"Hey!" the cop called from the entrance. "You can go up."

We went up the marble staircase to the third floor where a hallway stretched, interrupted by doors on both sides. Brighter fey lanterns, fastened to the walls, bathed the corridor in sharper light. At least I could see where I was putting my feet.

One of the doors on the left, almost at the end of the hallway, stood wide open. Two people waited by it, a middle-aged white woman in a PAD uniform and a black man in his mid-thirties in a suit and tie. Two others, wearing white coveralls with PAD Biohazard Unit stenciled in red on the back, crouched on the floor by a portable M-scanner.

Biohazard's official name was the Center for Magical Containment and Disease Prevention, but it was confusing, while "Biohazard" was clear and familiar. Whenever someone reported a freaky life-threatening magic incident, Biohazard would race there, secure the remains, process the scene, and sterilize the site. They were the city's magical CSI and the first line of defense between it and magical hazmat.

The detective waved us over. He had one of those weary faces that told me he was used to being woken up in the middle of the night to examine the bloody end of someone's life. For the survivors, the murder of a loved one was the worst thing that ever happened to them. For him, it was early Tuesday morning. Veteran mercenaries and soldiers sometimes looked like that after decades of fighting, except he was barely in his thirties.

He gave us a quick look. "Badges."

Stella and I held them out.

"What's the Order's interest in this case?"

"We believe it's connected to an ongoing investigation," I said.

"Which one?"

Telling him about Pastor Haywood would catapult this into high-profile territory. Two things could happen. First, they could hand this murder off to us, the way they gave us Pastor Haywood. Second, far more likely, the PAD would want to hold on to this murder and request any findings from us, because the two cases were connected. That would allow them to benefit from my investigation, while keeping an eye on the Order. There would be a lot of red tape, meetings, and, in the worst-case scenario, a joint task force, which I needed like a hole in the head.

"I'm not at liberty to say. Our findings are not conclusive at this time."

The detective's look communicated that he wasn't born yesterday, that he knew I was dodging, and that he wasn't impressed.

"I'll allow you into my crime scene as a courtesy. Don't cross the chalk line. Don't touch anything. You have five minutes."

"Before we go in and the countdown starts," Stella said, "who found the body?"

"The cleaning crew," the detective answered. "They work nights because of the heat. The custodian was taking out the trash around ten thirty, noticed the broken window, and came to check. He knocked, Professor Walton didn't answer, he unlocked the office, and here we are."

"Any witnesses?" Stella asked.

"No. Graduation was on May 11th, and the summer session doesn't start until June 1st. The campus is deserted."

"Thank you." I stepped into the room. Stella came in right behind me.

The office was a rectangle, and if it were drawn on paper, the door would be in the right bottom corner, by the wall lined with bookcases brimming with volumes and binders. Next to them, a man in his early twenties waited with a bored expression. Bronze-skinned, with big brown eyes and short black hair, he wore the white Biohazard coveralls. A patch with stylized flames marked his left sleeve. A firebug, a pyromage, in case the body rose, grew fangs the size of steak knives, and expressed a desire to eat human faces.

The broken window was in the wall opposite the door, about mid-way, its frame scarred by deep claw gashes and stained with smudges of blood. Something had really dug into the wood, trying to squeeze inside, and then left the same way it came in, smearing the blood of its victim in its wake. Shards of glass from the window littered the floor and the imitation Moroccan rug. In the center of the rug, Alycia Walton's corpse lay in a crumpled heap, staining the beige carpet fibers a gory burgundy.

Her head, a wet red mess, rested against her right shoulder. The killer had bitten through her neck from the left, nearly severing it in one bite and leaving the head attached only by a narrow strip of skin and flesh. Her white blouse and shreds of her bra hung off her body, blood-soaked and torn, and her chest cavity gaped open, the broken shards of ribs slick with dark blood. More blood colored her khaki capris.

Someone, probably Biohazard, had drawn a protective chalk circle around the rug and the body. Standard procedure. The chalk would delay the reanimated corpse long enough for the firebug to torch it.

I approached the circle to get a better look at the body. No heart. Only a puddle of dark blood pooling inside. The blood was still liquid. Once the heart stopped pumping, the blood settled within the lowest points of the body due to gravity, turning the skin an ugly mauve. The process was called livor mortis, and it started anywhere from thirty minutes to four hours after death, reaching its most pronounced stage in about twelve hours. Alycia's body showed no signs of it.

She was killed a couple of hours ago, at most. The creature had come through the window and attacked her right there on the rug—all the blood was confined to it. It likely bit her neck first, knocking her down, then straddled her and broke open her chest to get at the heart.

Past the body, almost all the way at the other wall, a large desk waited, with an office chair pushed back from it, but still upright. Two smaller chairs lay overturned against the desk.

I blinked and the office blossomed into colors. Gossamer tendrils of the palest gold bordered the window, stretched in thin lines across the floor, then exploded over the body into a familiar cascade. No other strong magic signatures. Just assorted blue traces, old and faded, likely left by students or other visitors to the office days ago.

I blinked it off.

The same creature that killed Pastor Haywood murdered Alycia Walton. Both of them likely handled the same item. The "Christian" artifact had a guardian. It was an established practice in the ancient kingdoms. I'd come across it once before, and I had been taught how to do it in case I ever needed to protect something of significance. If you had enough power, you could bind a magical beast to an object you wanted guarded. Once bound, the object emitted magic that only the beast could feel, and anyone who touched it would be stained by it. The guardian would track that stain until it killed the thieves and retrieved the object or died trying.

The old myths were full of such stories. The dragon watching over the Golden Fleece, the spriggans guarding fae treasure, the Pixiu who craved the smell of gold and secured it in the homes of their masters. Both Pastor Haywood and Professor Walton had touched the artifact, and the guardian had punished them for it.

It probably couldn't get to the artifact itself or the thief who owned it now. Whoever it was either knew about the curse or was very lucky.

Now the ma'avir's confession made sense. He'd said that Moloch wanted Pastor Haywood's killer. The artifact wasn't important to Moloch. The divine beast guarding it was. Why?

If I got my hands on the artifact, the beast would come for me. I had to find this magical trinket.

Selling an artifact required three people, an expert to assess its magic, a historian to trace its provenance, and a broker to calculate its value and facilitate the sale. The magic expert and the historian were dead. I had to find the broker. As long as I had the broker, the guardian would come to find them, and the ma'avirim would follow.

"Why was she here late at night alone?" Stella wondered.

"Working on a book, apparently," the firebug said.

Steps echoed down the hall—someone walking toward us, briskly.

I surveyed the scene again. The more I could figure out about the artifact's guardian, the better.

"How old was Professor Walton?" I asked.

"Forties," the firebug said.

"No cane, no mobility problems?"

"If she had a cane, we didn't find it."

"What are you thinking?" Stella asked.

I carefully walked around the circle to the desk and stood behind it. I could see both the door and window. The desk had been positioned to enjoy the view of the woods. "About twelve feet to the door?"

Stella nodded. "Give or take."

I pointed at the window. "A giant flying creature tears the

grate out of the wall and tries to force its way inside. It's too big, so it claws at the window frame, trying to wedge its way in. You're a forty-year-old college professor sitting behind this desk. Your next move?"

"Run for the door," the firebug said.

"Twelve feet." Stella's eyes narrowed. "She should've made it."

"She jumped out of the chair," the firebug added. "It's pushed back. But then she didn't run."

"Why wait?" I thought out loud.

"Maybe the creature has some sort of hypnotic magic gaze?" Stella said.

"But she jumped out of her chair and came around the desk," the firebug said. "If there was some sort of hypnotic gaze, she would have stayed seated. If it was me, I would come around the desk so I could fry its ass without damaging the furniture."

"Maybe Professor Walton had some sort of offensive magic we don't know about," I said.

"She didn't," a new voice said.

A stocky, white man stepped into the office. He appeared to be in his early forties. His tousled dark hair stuck out from his head in all directions, as if he'd rolled out of bed and hadn't even bothered to drag a comb or even his hand through it. A pair of wire-rimmed glasses perched on his nose. He wore khaki shorts, work boots and a blue T-shirt with a pointy hat printed in white ink. The words below the hat said KEEP CALM, I'M A WIZARD.

The firebug stopped slouching and stood straight, suddenly looking alert and professional.

"Crap," Stella muttered.

Luther Dillon. When I left, he was a higher-up in Biohazard. Whenever Kate had to report something to them, she called him first. I'd met him a handful of times, twice because Kate asked for my help with a crime scene and on a few occasions at family gatherings, like Kate and Curran's wedding. All I remembered about him was that he called Kate a heathen and pretended she bothered him, while helping her in every way he could, and he was brilliant. On the recognition danger scale, he ranked pretty low.

Luther gave me a cursory glance and focused on Stella. "Knight Davis."

"Assistant Director Dillon," Stella squeezed through clenched teeth. "I didn't know you would be here."

She winced as soon as she said it.

"I'm a wizard, Knight Davis. We are always exactly where we're supposed to be. You, however, are not where you're supposed to be. I was wondering who was cavorting around my crime scene, asking smart questions, and imagine my surprise when it turned out to be you."

Uh-oh.

Luther crossed his arms. "Do you remember the song I taught you last time you interfered with one of my crime scenes?"

Stella looked like she'd swallowed spoiled milk. "Yes."

"Splendid. Let's sing it together. I'll start. Biohazard is a law enforcement agency, yes, yes, yes. Your turn."

Stella unlocked her teeth. "The Order is not a law enforcement agency, no, no, no."

"All the crime scenes in Atlanta Metro are mine, mine, mine."

"All the crime scenes in Atlanta Metro are yours, yours, yours," Stella intoned.

"When are you allowed into one of my crime scenes?" Luther continued.

"When I'm personally invited, invited, invited."

Wow. What did she do to make him that mad? I'd never seen him like this.

"Knight Davis," Luther said without any trace of humor. "Were you invited to this crime scene?"

"No."

"Begone, ye unfortunate." Luther pointed at the door. Stella headed straight for it without another word, and I followed.

We walked down the hallway with Luther about twenty feet behind.

"What did you do?" I whispered.

"Later," Stella ground out.

"No, no, Knight Davis," Luther called. "Don't be shy."

Stella shut her eyes for a second. "We were working a murder case jointly. Several people died standing up with strange bulbs growing out of the bodies. One of them came to life."

"And in blatant violation of the safety procedures established over the last four decades, Knight Davis didn't give way to the pyrokinetic specialists. Instead, she had a lapse in judgement."

We turned onto the staircase and headed down.

"I hit the corpse with a sword," Stella said, her tone resigned. "It exploded."

"And because Knight Davis was in the way, the explosion couldn't be contained in time."

"What do you mean, exploded?" I asked.

Stella grimaced. "I mean its insides, suddenly and with great force, became its outsides. People got splattered, nobody died."

Luther's voice held no mercy. "Nobody died because they were in the ICU for five days receiving cutting-edge medical care. Many of them wished, loudly, that they had died, and some even asked us to kill them. And this is why this particular Feldman minion is not permitted at any of my crime scenes."

Okay then.

"Stella, did you get sick?" I asked.

"I don't get sick. Ever."

"Accurate," Luther called out. "She was covered in gore. Some of it even made it into her mouth. She didn't have a single symptom. No agonizing pain, no projectile vomiting, no bloody diarrhea. Fresh as a daisy."

"You really don't have to walk us out," Stella said.

"On the contrary, I really do."

We ran out of stairs, and the big double doors loomed in front of us. Stella and I opened them at the same time, she on the left and I on the right.

Ten feet away, in a pool of light from the nearest fey lantern streetlamp, stood Nick Feldman.

Oh shit.

Nick looked like a statue from Easter Island, whose eyes were on fire with ice-cold fury.

Stella turned and tried to go back inside. Luther blocked the doorway and shook his head.

Nick's voice was ice-cold. "Knight Davis."

Stella turned and faced him. "Yes, sir."

"Follow me."

He turned and marched down the path. Stella sprinted after him.

I halted. Nick was having a terrible night. I wasn't sure if Stella would survive.

Should I go and try to explain? I could lie and say I dragged Stella here. But then he might get angrier that a complete stranger somehow convinced her to disregard his orders. That would make it even worse.

Luther came to stand next to me. "Well, someone is in trouble."

I didn't answer. It wasn't a question, and sometimes silence was the best strategy.

"Ms. Ryder, if I could borrow you for a moment."

I pivoted to him. "Of course."

Luther glanced at a red-haired woman holding a set of keys, who stood by the door. "Could you please open the library for us?"

The woman nodded, her expression shell-shocked.

Luther waved at one of the uniformed officers and started

down the path toward the library. The three of us trailed him. The woman unlocked the library, Luther thanked her, and she rushed back to Bowden Hall.

Luther looked at the cop. "Stand by the door. Nobody comes in. If an emergency happens, they wait outside, you come and get me."

"Yes, sir."

Luther turned to me. "Okay then. Let's find a comfy spot and chat."

We headed deeper into the library. The moonlight spilled through towering floor-to-ceiling windows, and our steps sounded too loud in the empty building. The campus clearly didn't take security too seriously. You could drive a pack of manticores through those windows.

Luther found a group of couches by the window and landed on one of them, indicating another with his hand. I sat.

He studied me for a long moment and smiled. "Love the new face. Have you told the Lennarts that you're in the city or should I be the one to break the happy news?"

I OPENED MY MOUTH. NOTHING CAME OUT. OF ALL THE potholes to walk into.

Luther chuckled. "Take your time."

"How?"

"As a sensate, you see the nature of magic and the traces living beings leave in their environment. I perceive the specifics of one's magic, but only when I meet them face-to-face. To me, everyone's power has a unique signature."

He had remembered me. I must have been special enough to commit to memory. When we'd first met, he'd accused Kate of holding out on him because she had a sensate all this time. I should've asked myself how he'd identified me. I shouldn't have forgotten this. A blunder.

"I never forget a magic 'face.'" He tapped his temple. "You've evolved. There are layers and layers of power wrapped around your core, but that core remains the same. I remember it from years ago when I first met you. You are still you."

He had no idea what those words meant to me.

"Did I say something wrong?" he asked gently.

"I have lived through so many versions of me. I don't even know who I am anymore."

"This is life," Luther said. "We change, we alter ourselves, we grow or shrink. It's part of the human condition. You might have altered your identity, but when I heard you think through the scene, you sounded just like Kate. She always had good instincts and so do you. Hold on to that."

Huh. I was still me, and "me" sounded like Kate. "Thanks."

"You're welcome."

I would need to watch my speech patterns around people who used to know me.

"Would you mind letting me see your full power for a moment? The cloak is obscuring things."

The cloak was supposed to obscure things. That's why I had painstakingly crafted it and practiced maintaining it until it became second nature. If I let him see my magic, he would learn way too much about me. If I kept hiding, I would shatter any hope of him trusting me. I needed his trust. I had to convince him to keep my secret.

I met his gaze. "There is a reason I haven't told my family I'm here. I'll explain why, but you have to promise not to tell them."

"So I would know something the Lennarts don't?" Luther smiled. "My lips are sealed, pending the explanation."

I dropped the cloak.

Luther became completely still.

We sat quietly, looking at each other. When Erra helped me

to unlock the reservoir of magic inside myself, she told me I shone like a star. And then she made me promise I would never show it to my grandfather.

Luther came to, as if waking up, cleared his throat, and reached for me. "May I?"

"Yes."

He gently took me by the chin, leaned forward, and examined my face. "Fascinating. What happened?"

"Transmogrification through magic assimilation. I took someone else's body part and had to incorporate it."

"Incredibly risky, but it clearly paid off. Was it an eye?"

"Yes."

"Physically they look identical, but the concentration of magic in the left eye is much higher." Luther nodded and sat back. "Beautiful shade of green. The pain must've been excruciating."

"It was."

"How long?"

"About two months and then I went into a magically induced coma for another nine."

"I'm amazed you survived." Luther leaned forward, his eyes alert. "What possessed you to do a thing like that?"

"Fear." I reinstated my cloak.

"An excellent motivator. Tell me more."

"Are you familiar with Moloch?"

"A Canaanite god, the unpleasant kind. Famous for his dominion over fire and a fondness for child sacrifice. As I recall, he prefers his offerings to be burned alive. There is some murky water around the interpretation of the name."

"It's not a name. It's a title. It means god-king. It was used by hereditary rulers who descended from Saidoune ibn Canaan, who founded the city of Sidon over seven thousand years ago. They ruled the people who later became known as the Phoenicians, and their kingdom stretched over modern Israel all the way to southern Jerusalem."

"Roland's contemporaries." Luther grimaced.

"Not exactly. Moloch's reign officially ended during the time of Roland's grandfather. He was the last of his line."

In the ancient age, wars could be decided by a single duel between powerful magic users. The rulers of the countries were expected to take the field and defend their land and their people. They went to great lengths to augment their powers. For my adoptive family, that meant dealing with *shar*, an irresistible urge to claim and protect land. Moloch paid a different price.

"Moloch's family feared death," I told Luther, "so they focused on regeneration. They wanted to become unkillable, and when their natural magic wasn't enough, they reached for divine power. They allowed themselves to be worshiped as gods."

Luther frowned. "Divinity comes with a big price tag."

All living things generated magic, but humans with our intelligence and emotions were particularly adept at directing it. Human thoughts carried power, especially when blended with emotion, and few things were more emotional than a prayer. Each plea to a god sent him a portion of the human's power, especially when it was spoken aloud. Together, the faithful powered up their deities like charging up a battery. The bigger the congregation, the greater the power. In theory, it was limitless. But Luther was right. The arrangement came at a heavy cost.

"And that's why Moloch's kingdom fell," I said. "He became a god, obsessed with accumulating power through sacrifice and prayer. He lost his grip on the physical world. Normal human needs and urges no longer troubled him. He let his ancestral kingdom be conquered and carved into pieces. As long as the invaders worshipped him, he didn't care."

"Abandoning humanity wouldn't have been much of a stretch for him," Luther said. "Once you decide that burning tiny humans alive is a perfectly acceptable method of upgrading, you stop being human. Made the transition to godhood that much easier."

I nodded. I'd seen the inside of Moloch's citadel up close. There were no words to describe that kind of suffering. I hadn't known human beings could endure that much pain and despair.

"After the magic civilization collapsed and tech flooded the world in waves, Moloch should have faded away like other ancient gods without a persistent mythos. But he got a boost from the Old Testament. He's mentioned five times in Leviticus, once in Second Kings, and once in Jeremiah, not counting the allusions in Deuteronomy and Ezekiel. Sometime during the Middle Ages Christians became a bit obsessed with him and he made the transition to demonhood."

Luther sighed. "Christianity, the most composite of all religions. Why let a rival god, even a small one, die when you can turn him into a demon and rummage through his rites and holidays for the bits you can scavenge to attract his worshippers?"

"Exactly."

After the first Shift, magic hadn't disappeared completely. It dropped too low to be useful, but it was still there. Every time Moloch's name was mentioned, he got a crumb of power. That trickle kept him alive like an IV drip to a coma patient. Then the second Shift flooded the world with magic and delivered a shot of adrenaline to Moloch's power reserve. He hoarded it, biding his time, until he had accumulated just enough.

"Four flares ago, Moloch chose to be reborn."

Luther leaned back. "An avatar?"

"Yes."

"Flares drop every seven years, which would make him in his mid-thirties. Plenty of time to build a power base."

"He has a citadel in Arizona. He is practically indestructible.

I dismembered him, cut off his head, and threw his body into his forge, and he popped right back up in less than two years. Near perfect regeneration isn't his only trick. He is almost impervious to fire. He wields it like a weapon and he's highly skilled in metallurgy. He overlaps with Hephaestus in powers, and he is taking full advantage of any stray Greek Neo-Pagans that come his way looking to serve a god with a forge."

A shadow passed over Luther's eyes. "Why Arizona?"

"Metallic mineralization belt. He mines copper, gold, silver, lead, and zinc. It gives him access to some iron, but also tungsten, peridot, and azurite, which he uses to create enchanted weapons. He's building an army. Also, the area he's in is mostly empty and hot as hell."

"Ha-ha. I get it. Hell as in Tophet," Luther said. "The Levant is a rather crowded place right now. You can't swing a sacrificial lamb without hitting some old god."

He wasn't wrong. Any of the fertile regions where ancient civilizations had flourished were becoming hotly contested territories when it came to deities. By contrast, the continental US was a vast and relatively sparsely populated area, especially since the Shift had decimated the population across the board. A lot of areas had fallen to the wilderness. A perfect place for an avatar to hide and quietly grow his power.

Luther rubbed his chin, thinking. "So, Moloch has free reign in Arizona? None of this is giving me the warm fuzzies, but so far all the bad things you're describing are over there." He pointed vaguely to the west. "I imagine you're about to tell me something that will make it relevant and so much worse."

"The Witch Oracle had a vision."

"Oh goodie. They always have visions. It's always vague and it's always bad. Just once I'd like a prophecy proclaiming that, without a doubt, everything is going to be fine."

I waited for him to get it off his chest. When I was in school, I was taught about Heisenberg's uncertainty principle, which in essence stated that the only way to determine the position and velocity of a subatomic particle was to hit it with another particle. You would know where the target particle was at the moment of collision, but the impact would change the course and speed of that target particle, and its new parameters would be unknown again.

Prophecies functioned just like that. The very act of knowing what might happen altered the future in complex ways. That's why everything Sienna revealed was carefully calculated. Luther knew all that. He was just delaying the inevitable.

Luther sighed dramatically and motioned to me. "Lay it on me. I have braced myself."

"When magic crests at its peak, the King of Fire will leave his citadel of misery in the Western Desert and travel east to devour the queen who doesn't rule and sever bloodline reborn. Only the one who shares his power may oppose him."

Luther blinked. "Moloch is going to kill Kate during a flare."

"Yes. They meet. Kate dies. The world burns and becomes darkness."

"That is…oddly specific for Sienna."

"It was a very vivid vision. She had to be sedated afterward."

"The future isn't definite, and Sienna sees the most likely probability," Luther thought out loud. "Are there are other probabilities where Kate survives?"

"So far all of her visions have been the same. If Kate comes into contact with Moloch in any way, they fight, she loses, he kills her. If I come into direct contact with Kate, the vision becomes sharper and clearer."

"You meeting Kate in person makes her death more likely."

"Yes."

Luther pondered me. A long moment passed.

"How old is this prophecy?"

"Four years."

"And you've been trying to fight it and failed?"

I nodded.

"Moloch's former divine nature is a significant factor, isn't it?"

I nodded again.

"That's what I thought." Luther's gaze turned dark. "If he were just a human, there would be wiggle room, but he is an avatar, a god made flesh. This isn't just the most likely version of the future; this is a deity communicating its will and intent through time. This future is incredibly resistant to the change."

"Yes."

Luther looked at the ceiling. I could practically feel the gears turning in his mind.

"Does he know of the prophecy?"

"He does. Sienna has touched his mind."

"Risky. Why Kate?"

"He fears the Shinar. The family has repelled his invasions in the past. He worries about the reunification of Kate and Erra. To his mind, each is a kingdom unto herself and their reach will grow until he is trapped between them. Kate is an easier target than my grandmother."

"A follow-up question: why you?"

"I don't know. According to Sienna, I'm the wild card. Perhaps it's because I'm educated by Shinar but the power of my bloodline is fundamentally different from theirs. He hasn't fought my ancestors. He doesn't know what I can do."

"That seems thin to me." Luther frowned. He drummed his fingers on the armrest of his chair and seemed to come to a decision. "So, you can't go home."

"No."

He leaned back and steepled the fingers of his hands. "Tell me how I can help you."

I explained the magical artifact, the guardian, and the

ma'avirim. "This murder has the same MO as Pastor Haywood's. I need access and support."

"That I can do. I will also keep this conversation to myself. Who else knows you are you?"

"My grandmother and Conlan. Kate and Curran haven't seen me since my face changed."

"Good," he said. "Let's try to keep it that way."

[10]

I sat inside Alycia Walton's office behind her desk. The door was open, and the light from the fey lanterns in the hallway drew a long rectangle across the floor. The rest of the room lay shrouded in gloom, and I sank into it, wrapping myself in it like it was a blanket.

Luther and I had formed an alliance. I would keep him in the loop, and he would allow me unsupervised access to crime scenes I believed were connected. Then a woman from Biohazard had arrived and Luther had to go. PAD and Biohazard finished processing the scene and left too, taking the body with them. Only I remained, waiting.

Moloch's priests would come. The ma'avirim were fanatically single-minded. It was just a matter of time.

I had to get answers this time. The longer I spun my wheels, the greater was the likelihood that Moloch would murder Kate. Every time I thought about it, my throat tried to clench itself into a fist.

Magic tugged on me, and I sank into Turgan's vision. The eagle perched at the top of the oak across from the entrance to Bowden Hall. Three people ran across the lawn toward the building, low and fast. One dashed to the entrance, and the two others rounded the corner.

I disconnected. Just what I needed right now.

Faint sounds came from beyond the broken window. A light rustling of the hedge, a scrape against the stone. Three, two, one...

Ascanio jumped through the open window and landed by the rug.

"What, no combat roll?" I asked.

He pivoted to me, his eyes flashing with a ruby glow as they caught the light from the hallway. For a moment he looked ready to pounce, then he straightened, his expression nonchalant.

"You again. We keep meeting like this. It must be fate."

Oh no, the return of Mr. Smooth. "What is your interest in Pastor Haywood's murder?"

Ascanio picked up a chair, set it before the desk, flipping it around, and saddled it, his arms resting on the chair's back. "My interest is private. I may be persuaded to exchange information, but you don't have the authority to question me."

"And you don't have the authority to be here."

"Neither do you."

I gave him a small smile. "Actually, I do."

Ascanio smiled back. "Fine, I'll play. Says who?"

"Luther Dillion, the Assistant Director of Biohazard."

Ascanio rested his chin on his arms. "If that's true, I'm intruding on your crime scene. What's your plan for removing me?"

Somehow, he managed to make it sound suggestive. "You're being tiresome."

"It's a personal failing. I was told I can also be invigorating under the right circumstances."

I bet. "Does the Beast Lord know you're here?"

"This is a clan matter."

He had Andrea's and Raphael's blessing and was confident that they would back him up if things went bad. "Why does Clan Bouda care about these murders?"

"You're still not trading. How about this, I'll tell you mine, if you tell me yours?"

I gave him a theatrical sigh. "You must think that your smile is charming."

"Is it not?"

"You know what I see when you smile? Teeth. Teeth that can grow into big, scary fangs. We both know it's a threat."

He pushed from the floor, and the chair rolled back with him in it. "Do you feel less threatened now?"

"Not really. Keep rolling. Out the door, down the hall, down the steps..."

He tilted his head to the side. He really was stunning, especially when he smiled like right now.

"Why don't you like me?" he asked.

"You menaced me on the bridge, showed up uninvited to my house, made veiled threats, tried to bribe me, and now you are contaminating my crime scene."

"The bridge was a misunderstanding. I came to your house to apologize and offer help, and as for the crime scene, I was on this case before you were." He spread his arms, a picture of innocence. "I'm blameless."

I laughed. I couldn't help myself; it just came out.

Ascanio leaned forward, feigning concern. "You stopped scowling for a second there. Are you alright?"

"Pe..." I caught myself. I was about to say "peachy," and the moment he heard it, the game would be up. It was my mom's favorite phrase. "Perfectly fine."

A warm sensation washed over me. My ears heard a phantom lamentation, offered in an eager voice. My nostrils caught the scent of burning herbs and human flesh. It should have been revolting, and intellectually it was, but there was a part of me that found it comforting. A very small, faint voice whispered in my mind, *"This is right, you should be offered this, this is your due."*

The ma'avirim had arrived.

The lament echoed in my mind. My pulse sped up. I couldn't even sense the ma'avir at the first murder scene until I had concentrated on the glyph. This one radiated magic. It pressed on me, like a heated wall, sucking out the air and making it hard to breathe.

This would be an entirely different fight. I had to get Ascanio out of here. I couldn't let him get hurt.

"We are getting nowhere," he said. "How about this? Each of us asks one question, and the other gives an honest answer?"

"And then you leave."

"Deal. Ladies first."

I leaned back in the chair. "What advantage would you personally and/or Clan Bouda gain if you tie this murder to Desandra Kral?"

The charming smile vanished. The man who rose smoothly out of the chair was lethal and dangerous. He stalked across the room, put both hands on the desk, and leaned forward. He glared at me, his eyes like two bloody rubies lit up by fire from within. It was a stare that said I was food.

A cold shiver dashed down my spine. Ascanio was right before. When he threatened someone, they didn't have to ask. Suddenly the office was too small, and I was acutely aware that I would have to get past him to reach the door.

"You made a deal." I kept my tone cold. "Pay up or leave."

The red light in his eyes grew brighter. His stare was difficult to hold. That's twice in one night. First Derek, now him. This time, I wouldn't be running.

Seconds ticked past.

Ascanio opened his mouth. His diction was perfect, but his

voice was knitted from a growl. "Be very careful. You're playing a dangerous game."

"That's not an answer."

"It's free advice. You had trouble with one overgrown human. I won't go down that easy."

That was about enough. Any longer, and he would get dragged into the fight. I had to get him gone. "That's not what I heard."

He whipped around and leapt out of the window. The sudden emptiness was startling.

I raised my chin. Showtime. "We're alone now. Show yourself, worm. I don't have all night."

The darkness pooling in the corner of the room moved.

It flowed from the ceiling, from the floor, to its center, as if a large piece of the thinnest black gauze had been spread over the far wall and the floor and now someone caught it with a hook and was pulling it to me. I forced myself to sit still, my hand on the shaft of my spear.

The darkness coalesced into a human shape, tall, lean, male, and woven of fire. Smoke swirled around him, transforming into a voluminous black robe and a long cloak. Human skin the color of alabaster sheathed him, obscuring the fire, but failing to hide it completely. It was still there, licking his skin from the inside and warming it with a soft peach glow here and there.

Not just a ma'avir. One of the high priests. Shit. At least I'd gotten Ascanio out of here.

The ma'avir folded his hands in front of him, left palm up, right resting on top of it. He was hairless. No stubble, no eyebrows, no eyelashes. Just smooth skin stretched tight over angular features. His eyes, a light bluish green, fixed me. There was no surprise in them, only recognition. He came here especially for me.

The amount of magic he required to maintain a human form had to be staggering. I wasn't sure I would win this fight.

The high priest gave me a shallow bow, little more than a nod. "We finally meet, Dananu."

"What reason would I have to meet with a child killer?"

Leviticus 18:21 prohibited the faithful from sacrificing their children. The specific line stated, "And thou shalt not let any of thy seed pass through the fire to Molech." The ma'avirim received their name from that act. They were the ones who took living children and "passed them through the fire" to their god. One didn't become a high priest until he had murdered hundreds.

"I've hidden well, yet you knew I was there. Tell me, Dananu, does my magic call to you? Does the sacrificial fire smell sweet? Does its power tempt you?"

"No. It sickens me."

"Really?" He tilted his head like a puzzled dog. "I think it beckons you. It's a craving, a gnawing need that only sacrifice can satisfy. Imagine tasting it. Imagine the rush of power flooding through your throbbing veins."

"Veins don't throb. Arteries do."

"Why deny yourself the ecstasy?"

"I don't know, the burning babies alive part probably has something to do with it."

"Life is pain and suffering. A nasty and brutish journey of toil and regret." His magic pressed on me like a heavy weight.

"Thomas Hobbes called. He wants his thesis back."

"Children are innocent and pure. We spare them a lifetime of misery. In a brief flash of pain, their souls join our god in the glorious eternity of the afterlife."

"How very noble. Your god feeds on suffering."

The ma'avir gave me a condescending smile. "All gods feed

on suffering. Without it, there are no prayers or offerings. Mankind is selfish. They give only when they have to. If this world was idyllic and life was just, what need would there be for gods?"

The more he talked, the higher the chance I had of learning why he was in Atlanta. But he was too high up on the food chain to let something slip unless I got him agitated. I had to bait him.

"The Christian God doesn't require blood sacrifice."

The ma'avir laughed softly. "Oh, but he did. Their god thirsted for blood, he demanded it, and when his ratings slipped, he hid behind a kinder, softer version of himself. How many died in that humble god's name? How many killed for the martyr? Firstborn sons were his favorite."

That's right. Keep ranting. "And yet his followers flourish."

The ma'avir sneered. "The gullible who willingly swallow lies and the blind who shut their own eyes for the fear they will see the truth. The cults of Abraham. The biggest con of the modern world."

How to insult Judaism, Christianity, and Islam in three sentences or less. "Tell me, when I kill you, will you pass into the glorious eternity of the afterlife and bask in the love of your god?"

He smiled. "Eventually when I die, yes. But it won't be today, and it won't be by your hand."

He was very sure of that. I leaned forward. "One thing puzzles me. Perhaps you can clear it up, given your vast knowledge."

"I shall do my best."

"Those Abrahamic religions you sneer at chased your god out of the world, because nobody wants to sacrifice their children and their future to a rabid glutton eager for the next hit off the sacrificial altar. Since nobody knows who he is, Moloch is starving for followers and he had to be reborn. He became flesh."

The ma'avir stared at me. Hold on, I'm getting to it.

"So, answer me this, high priest. If I kill you now, and you pass through the mortal veil, what will you find on the other side? Your glorious eternity is empty. Your god isn't there. He is in Arizona digging in the dirt. Your soul will float in nothing, lost and alone. Do you know what hell is? Hell is the absence of god."

His face rippled. Ha! Direct hit. I sank his battleship.

The ma'avir opened his mouth. "Say what you wish. Fight with everything you have. Struggle, kick, bite, none of it matters. He wants you and you will come to him. You will dedicate yourself to him, and when that moment comes, you will beg to bring him your mother's head on a silver platter. You will weep tears of gratitude when he devours her eyes."

"That's beautiful. You should write that down. If my journey is so inevitable, what are you doing here in Atlanta? Why not just wait for me?"

He leaned forward, the flames inside him flaring. "I will carve you into pieces and bring them to my god. The drop of power you stole will keep you alive, and when you awaken half a century from now in his fiery embrace, we will speak again."

Fear hammered a cold spike through my heart. I could see it in my head, my body in pieces, clinging to life, aware, watching, but powerless as everyone I cared about died one by one. I had to kill him. If he won, what kind of world would I wake up to?

The high priest showed me his teeth, blood-red fangs made of fire. "I can hear your heart flutter. I watched you walk around this city you used to call home, wearing pretend arrogance like armor. Now you understand. He is a god and you are still an abandoned child craving approval and shivering in the dark."

The fear crystalized into a new emotion and I let it fuel me. "Fear isn't the only thing that can make a heart flutter."

"What else is in your heart, orphan child?"

"Rage."

I spat power words, a command from a language so old, it shaped magic itself. *"Sert ranam girreh!" Bar the city gates.*

Magic pulsed from me in a flash of blinding pain, splashing against the boundaries of the room, and burst into an invisible wall, cutting us off from reality. My grandmother used this spell millennia ago when enemy armies besieged Shinar cities.

The ma'avir recoiled.

I leapt over the desk, Dakkan in my hands, and stabbed at the priest, aiming just under the breastbone. The spearhead shone with red as it sliced the air. I had brought two canteens full of vampire blood primed with my own. An hour ago, when I took up my post behind the desk, I had coated Dakkan in the blood mix and solidified it, turning the metal spearhead into a razor-sharp blood weapon.

The ma'avir turned to smoke. The spear pierced him and passed through with no resistance.

The swirl of smoke surged to the window and rammed the invisible magic wall, turning solid for a micro-second. The magic tolled in my head like a giant bell being struck with a hammer.

I stabbed at him and he went ethereal again. My spearhead shredded smoke.

The high priest streamed toward the door and slammed into my wall again. I thrust at him before the sound of the impact rolled through me. Dakkan met only air. Missed again. Damn it. I couldn't stab smoke, and he couldn't break the wall unless he turned solid. Fine. I could keep this up until he got tired or I got lucky.

We danced across the room, him throwing himself at the boundary and me trying to nail him with my spear to it. The world shrank to the clump of smoke and the tip of my spear.

Where was the fire? Absorbing Moloch's eye granted me some immunity, but it had limits, and a high priest would burn through them in a single blast. Why wasn't this room a sea of fire?

Using the language of power took a hefty chunk of my magic. I could hit him with another one—I had a whole arsenal at my disposal—but there was no guarantee it would work. He was holding back, and until I knew the full extent of his power, so would I. The blood spear would work just fine.

Stab. Stab. Stab.

My spear sliced through solid flesh. Fire splashed the magic wall, and then the ma'avir was smoke again. Nicked him. I just had to be a hair faster.

The smoke turned into fire. A glowing nebula of light and heat splayed out near the ceiling and contracted, like a star collapsing into a tiny white-hot spark. It shot across the room like a bullet, shrinking into a blinding mote of light, and bit into my wall.

A scalding hot needle of pain punctured my skull from one temple to the other and vanished. He was through. Shit.

The fire exploded outside the window, snapping into the ma'avir. I spun to the desk, dropping the wall as I moved, grabbed my bow, turned, and fired. It took less than half a second. The arrow tore through the ma'avir and streaked into the night.

No damage.

The high priest laughed. "Chase me, daughter of Shinar. Catch me. Drive me from your city. Try to take my life before I feast on the eyes of your loved ones. Show me what you can do."

I let out a shrill whistle, swiped my spear off the desk, and ran downstairs. He dared me to chase him, which meant he had a trap prepared and would lead me to it. That was the plan all along, and I would follow him into the trap. I had no choice. He had seen Ascanio and probably Luther. If his rant wasn't a bluff, he might have seen others. Stella. Marten. Nick. My family.

I had to kill him no matter what it took.

I burst out of the front doors. The ma'avir hung above the lawn, fifty feet in the air. Too high. I unscrewed Dakkan and slid its halves into its sheath on my back.

Tulip came running, and I sprinted to her and jumped into the saddle. Above us, the ma'avir surged across the sky, an ink-black swirl of magic that blotted out the stars as it passed. Turgan took to the air, and I sent him high, out of the reach of the priest. I chased the shadow in the sky heading west.

Tulip dashed through the deserted pre-dawn streets. The priest turned north. I made a left on Clifton. Tulip broke into a gallop. Buildings rushed past us. The smoke veered right, to the northeast. Woods loomed in front of me, the entrance to the trail cutting through them illuminated by a single fey lantern streetlamp. I steered Tulip onto it.

The trail shied left, then right. Tulip took a turn too fast. Tree branches slapped me.

I couldn't see him, but my magic told me he was still there, trailing spicy smoke and echoes of human weeping.

The trees on the right ended, as if jerked out of sight. Asphalt replaced packed dirt. We galloped along a lake, Tulip's hoofbeats too loud on the paved ground.

A shred of darkness streaked on the edge of my vision and disappeared beyond the trees ahead. I would kill him tonight. It was that or my people would start dying.

We reached a bridge and tore across it. The trail turned right, the trees parting like opened hands. A huge ruin loomed ahead, pale grey in the light of the dying moon. A sign flashed by. Atlanta VA Medical Center.

The thing I was chasing hovered above it and dove down. This was it.

I blinked into Turgan's vision. It was fuzzy and dark, but I saw the ruin from above. The roof was gone, but the outer walls and some of the inner ones still stood, jutting into the sky anywhere from fifty to seventy feet high, turning the abandoned building into an unpredictable labyrinth. The inside of the medical center had collapsed and was cleared, probably looted or salvaged.

A spark ignited in the heart of the ruin. The ma'avir making sure I didn't get lost.

I dismounted. Tulip stared at me, wild-eyed, and I hugged her to me. "If I don't come back, go to your mother."

She knocked me with her head. I grabbed my bow off her saddle and ducked into the building.

The air smelled of concrete powder, a dry chalky scent that lingered in buildings chewed up by magic. Weeds grew through the crumbled floor, widening the cracks. Here and there, walls rose, distorted by the remnants of wiring and plumbing. I glided through it, quiet and fast.

A slight breeze fanned my face, bringing a hint of smoke. Close now.

I walked through an arched doorway. A big square room lay in front of me under the open sky. The floor was a memory, all grass punctuated by a tiled chunk here and there, but the walls were solid, without breaks. At the other end, the ma'avir waited, poised against the pale backdrop.

Too far for an arrow. At this range he would dodge.

I took a step. Another.

The ma'avir waited.

This was a killing box and he wanted me to get deep enough for him to slam the trap door shut.

"You're making me do all the work," I told him. "Come. Show me the might of Moloch's chosen."

"You're right. You've come all this way. Let me show you the hospitality we reserve for the royalty of Shinar."

The ma'avir spread his arms. The world ignited.

Fire rose like a monstrous dust storm and rolled toward me. I shut my eyes. It singed my skin and kept going. I opened my eyes. The walls were on fire. They shouldn't have been, but they blazed so bright, they looked white. Heat assaulted me, unbearable and dense. This was nothing like the weak attacks the other priest had tried. This was like standing in the heart of the sun. Or hell.

At the other end of the room, the priest was a living flame, a simulacrum of a human-made inferno.

The heat burned my back. I took a step forward. The room was shrinking, or rather the fire was moving. He was herding me toward him.

"Ranar kair!" Come before me.

Agony sank its fangs into me and ripped me apart. For a terrifying second, I thought it killed me.

The torrent of power shot from me to the priest. The fire flashed...and nothing.

I had pulled fifty enemy troops to me with that one command before. He didn't even waver.

It didn't work. He had no body. He was Moloch's sacred fire, and that placed him beyond my power. I could alter the environment around him, I could lock him in a spell, but a direct attack would fail.

The heat licked my back again. The stone walls sagged, melting.

Another step.

The scorched ground twenty feet in front of me burst into flame. The thin layer of soil burned off, revealing a gaping pit. Four-foot-tall spikes bristled at the bottom. Not steel, tungsten, just beginning to glow with heat. Burning me would consume my flesh. It would take me longer to regenerate. It might even kill me. The high priest didn't want to take the chance. He had prepared a tiger trap for me instead.

I had a choice: I could burn to death, or I could be impaled and cut to pieces. How considerate.

Heat scalded me. I took another small step.

The pit was at least thirty-five feet across. Even if I were an Olympic champion, I wouldn't clear it.

The air felt thick like soup. It was getting harder to breathe.

I could not die here. I would not die here. I'd come too far.

The fire wall behind me moved another six inches.

I had one shot. One chance to get close enough. If I failed, if it didn't hold...

Another half a foot. I took another step. This would be my last one.

I ripped the canteens of blood from my belt and squeezed their caps. Two small blades popped up. I stabbed them into my shoulders. The magic shivering in my blood broke free, ready to go. I pulled on it and it shot out of me in twin streams, turning into crimson mist. I hurled the contents of the canteens into the air, mixing it with my undiluted blood, and sprinted to the pit, bow in hand.

The ma'avir's fire flared, and I saw his face within it, lips spread in a wide smile. He knew he had me. He thought I had chosen the easier death.

The blood mist rushed to me, coating me, sheathing my skin and my hair. I had clothed myself in blood armor just like this hundreds of times. It was as easy as breathing now. I just hoped it was strong enough.

I leaped into the pit. For an instant, I flew, weightless, as my blood and magic combined on my body. Then gravity hit, and I plunged like a rock, the ma'avir vanishing from view. A low laugh rolled through the room.

The blood armor snapped together, covering me from head to toe. Only my eyes and nostrils remained uncovered. I needed sight and air for the next few seconds.

My feet touched the spikes, heat burned me, but I kept running, my blood boots blunting the sharp points, shaping an arrow out of my blood as I ran. The edge loomed in front of me. I wasted a precious half-second to crouch and jumped straight up. The priest's shocked face flashed before me, only twenty-five feet away.

A cone of fire roared toward me, impossibly hot.

I shut my eyes, letting the blood armor flow over my entire face. Deaf and blind, I took the shot.

I landed badly. My left ankle rolled under me, heat burning the soles of my feet through the armor.

There was no air. I held my breath and waited. It felt like I was being cooked alive. I had sprinted so hard. My body screamed for air.

I staggered forward. The few precious moments of oxygen my movement cost me would make no difference.

Twenty seconds.

Thirty.

Fuck it.

I let the armor slide off my face. It fell off in black chunks, crumbling in midair, its magic exhausted.

The ma'avir hung from the wall in front of me, no longer fire, but pale flesh. My arrow had pierced through his heart, or through the place it used to be.

Got him. I got him. "Why are you here? Why do you want the divine beast who killed the priest? Tell me!"

His light eyes focused on me. "I can see now. I understand why he wants you."

"Why does he want the beast?"

"He who consumes the heart of the beast will be given a brief glimpse of the true future. Once seen, that future will not change." The priest's voice faded. "Forgive me. When you ascend to his side, I will serve you in the afterlife."

His eyes rolled back in his head. I dropped to the ground, building a new face shield from what little blood I could still take.

The high priest detonated.

[11]

Tulip moved through the streets at a steady, even pace. The sky had lightened to a luminescent pre-dawn grey, and the ruined Midtown slid by on my left, dark against the pearlescent backdrop. My blood armor had turned coal-black, its magic gone. It crumbled away at the joints with the motions of the horse, breaking into black dust. The wind caught it and carried it off.

Everything hurt. I floated in a sea of pain, anchored by it to reality. The ride would end eventually. I just had to wait it out.

Tulip turned onto our street. Familiar landmarks crept by. The heap of rubble with a chunk of a wall tiled in bright turquoise sticking out of it. The tall oak tree where Turgan liked to sit. The edge of the yard. The front door.

I slipped off Tulip's back in a shower of black specks. Untacking her took superhuman effort, but it had to be done. I settled her into the stable, made sure there was clean water, and willed myself to walk to the front door. I passed through the two outer wards, entered the house, and locked the door behind me. The air smelled of herbs, a thick pungent aroma. Conlan had found my aunt's purification bundle and burned it in the brazier to cover up his scent. If any shapeshifters showed up, the smell would make them nose blind.

My brother was amazing.

I dragged myself to my sanctuary.

Turning the key in the lock hurt.

The door slid open, revealing the familiar limestone floor and columns. Water murmured in the channel, flowing slowly.

I shut the door of the sanctuary behind me, heard the thick metal bar of the lock slide into place, and finally let go. The blood armor cracked, losing what little integrity it had left. I walked down the path slowly, and as I moved, the last chunks of my armor fell off me, shattering on the floor into clouds of dark dust.

I zeroed in on the metal rose on my desk. Almost there. Just a few more steps.

Almost.

My fingers closed about the cold stem. I plucked the flower from the vase with my ruined fingers. Made it.

The sack of herbs was next, an ordinary bag with five pounds' worth of a priceless herbal mix, tucked away into the corner of the third shelf. When you want to hide something precious, put it in plain sight.

I carried the bag and the rose into my bedroom. The water in the bath lay placid. The stream kept it filled, and the magic coils buried under it made sure the water stayed warm when the magic was up.

I put the rose on the edge of the tub and emptied the contents of the sack into the bath. Herbs, flowers, and powders tumbled into the water, releasing swirls of blue, then red. Dried leaves and blossoms unfurled slowly. Ground blue thistle, shaved mandrake, Solomon's seal, pasqueflower, goldenseal, sage, ginseng, lavender, valerian, French mallow... All treated with magic, carefully processed, and prepared for me by my aunt. I had just dumped twenty-five thousand dollars' worth into the tub.

The mirror on the side wall had no mercy. The entire front of me was fire-engine-red. The armor had kept the damage contained, but now blisters broke open all over my face and neck.

I pulled a knife off my belt and cut through my T-shirt. My chest and stomach were a constellation of blisters. The heat had cooked me like a lobster in the shell.

I sliced through my bra. It came apart. Pain jolted me, and I whimpered. I just had to hold on long enough to get out of my clothes.

The boots were the worst. The soles of my feet were gaping raw sores with charred edges, all skin gone. I pulled the tie out of my hair, releasing the bun. My hair fell around me. The armor had protected it from direct fire, but even if it hadn't, I wouldn't be bald for long.

The water in the bath had foamed and turned a nearly opaque eggplant-purple. Petals and leaves covered the surface. I dipped my foot into the liquid. I knew it was just warm enough to let the herbs steep faster, but it felt scalding hot. I grit my teeth and forced myself into it, sinking onto the small shelf. The heat was unbearable. I submerged, again and again, soaking my face in the mix.

Slowly, the pain grew dull, blunted by the analgesic herbs. I wanted my rose, but I had left it at the other side of the tub, far out of reach, and getting there right now was beyond me. I'd dropped the cut T-shirt on it accidentally, and I could just make out the hint of metal petals peeking out from under the lymph-soaked cloth. Good enough.

A rush of agony twisted through me, the magic I stole from Moloch and made my own eager to repair the damage. It hurt now, but I knew it would hurt more before my body was fully healed. I rested my head on the smooth edge, the water just below my lips, inhaled the aromatic mist rising from the medicinal bath, and let saffron, lemon balm, and valerian soothe me into sleep.

I wasn't alone.

The realization filtered in through my drowsiness, triggering an internal alarm. Someone was with me in the room. I reached for magic and found nothing. The tech was up.

Nobody should have been here. I had locked both doors behind me. I was absolutely sure.

Tepid water brushed against my neck. I was still sitting on the shelf of my tub.

I tried to open my eyes. I managed a tiny sliver of light, blocked by some sort of translucent curtain. What the hell? Had I gone blind?

I sat up. Something ripped with a dry crunch, and the curtain fell away. A thin, almost transparent layer of my skin peeled off my face and fell into the water. Ewww.

Across from me, past the other side of the bath, Derek sat on the floor.

My heart hammered in my chest, as my brain grappled with what I saw, trying to make sense of it in a feverish rush. I was awake and lucid. He wasn't a dream. He wasn't a hallucination either. First, everything else looked normal, and second, if my medicine-addled brain were to serve me a version of Derek, it wouldn't have dressed him in a modern ninja suit stained with blotches and dots of black and grey. I had never seen him wear anything like this in my whole life.

No, it was him. In the flesh. Sitting on the floor of my bedroom and staring at me with fiery eyes, while I shed dead skin like a snake.

I stared back. He looked hard and cold, sharper, more awake

somehow than I remembered. The thin network of scars criss-crossed his face. Years ago, some creatures poured molten silver on his face. He should've died. He had survived against all odds, and the scars were the price he paid. Before the scars, people used to describe him as handsome. Now they used other words. Dangerous. Scary. Lethal.

He sat relaxed, as if finding a camouflaged fortress filled with strange magical artifacts and weapons in the middle of Atlanta was just one of the things he'd done today. He wasn't bothered by it. He wasn't bothered by me sitting naked in the dark water or my healing rituals. He just watched, his headlights stuck on bright. Dad's gold was like the sun, hot and yellow. Derek's glow was icy golden moonlight.

I forced myself to not hold my breath and searched his eyes for recognition.

No trace of the Julie he knew remained. The moment I slid the Eye of Moloch into the empty orbit in my head, it began assessing my body and set about fixing its flaws. It tore my muscle and reshaped my bones. It wasn't gentle. It was relentless. Nothing could make it stop.

Unlike shapeshifters, who benefited from a cocktail of biological endorphins and painkillers when they changed shape, I had to endure my transformation slowly and in a great deal of pain. I had asked my grandmother about it between the bouts of agony, and she'd told me that many features we considered beautiful were simply signs of health and beneficial adaptations. The bloodline of Moloch had focused on survival for generations, and the Eye was trying to improve my chances of not dying.

It started by making my face perfectly symmetrical, enlarging my eyes, streamlining my nose, giving me a longer neck and elegant fingers. It didn't like the texture of my hair, so it made it thicker, wavier, and gave it a darker golden tint. It turned both of my eyes a matching light green, the same as

Moloch's. I was always frustrated with being short, and it stretched me, gifting me three inches of height, bigger lungs, and larger heart. Growing pains was an understatement.

The strain proved unbearable. My mind unraveled. With each new torturous improvement, I slipped closer to madness.

When the pain had become too much, Erra forged a pocket realm for me, woven of her memories. It was the only way to keep me sane. She and a dozen of her retainers went into the magically induced coma with me, so I wouldn't be alone. My grandmother loved me so much. She had risked her own safety for my sake. She went into the dream, allowing her body to lay helplessly next to mine, vulnerable and easy to kill.

My aunt and uncle guarded us for nine months. To me, in the dream, four years had passed.

My grandmother dedicated that time to educating me. I lived as a princess of Shinar, the way Shinar used to be. I had lessons in magic, combat, politics, and history. I learned to speak the old language, and by the time I woke up, English was a memory and I'd picked up a slight trace of an accent. I studied, I improved, I learned the ancient magic skills I required to survive. I had dedicated myself to becoming worthy of my grandmother's sacrifice. She believed in me.

The Eye had picked up on my determination and once again decided to help me against my will. Even as my body assimilated its magic, it changed my appearance one more time. I wanted to be like Erra and like Kate. I wanted to belong to their family. I wanted to be strong like them.

The Eye had found Kate's blood in me and used it. It made me into the princess of Shinar I had imagined. When I woke up, I looked like Kate's daughter.

Nobody would confuse us. Our faces were too different. But if you put my grandmother, Kate, and me together, you would see the three generations of Shinar. You would see the same eye shape, the same eyebrows, and the same jawline. I was paler, blonder, with green eyes that matched Moloch's, and sharper features, but the progression of the bloodline was plain for all to see.

When I saw my face for the first time, I thought I'd gone mad and screamed. When my grandfather saw the new me, he stared at me in silence for several minutes while his magic pierced me until he finally said, "Well, you are truly your mother's scion."

I had been examined by the best experts my grandmother could find. They concluded that the changes were permanent. If I had children, they would look like the new me. The Eye could no longer change me back. It had become a part of me and lost that power.

The old me had been erased forever. Derek would never recognize me. He would never know why my heart was trying to jump out of my chest.

My heart. Right. I had to find calm. If he focused, he could hear my heartbeat.

We'd been looking at each other in silence for five minutes. One of us had to say something.

"It's you," I said. Brilliant opening.

"It's me," he said.

"You found my house." I kept my voice casual and calm. No loud noises. No quick movements.

He nodded. He seemed comfortable, wrapped in a kind of casual arrogance that came from killing a lot of scary shit. His presence filled the room. He was impossible to ignore.

"I tried to talk to you before, but you left in a hurry." His voice still sounded the same, a kind of gravely rasp, the result of permanent damage to the vocal cords not even Lyc-V managed to fully heal. It made him sound like a wolf in the flesh.

"I'm a busy woman."

"That's why I decided to visit you at home."

"Very prudent of you."

"I like to plan ahead."

His shoulders were broader than I remembered. His body bigger, harder. His clothes weren't skintight, but I could see definition on the arm he rested on his knee and a hard contour of muscle on his thigh. With magic down, my arsenal had shrunk, while he still had the benefit of superior speed, strength, and regeneration. The old Derek would never attack a human woman without provocation. This new Derek was an unknown commodity. If he decided to fight me, my odds were crap.

But shapeshifters were still human, and their regeneration wasn't instant. I knew where to strike and how to cut to incapacitate a shapeshifter. The real question was, could I bring myself to cut Derek's throat if he forced me?

I had to avoid this fight at all cost.

"So you tracked me down and let yourself into my home. How can I help you?" I asked.

"Do you need a medic?"

My mind tried to make a ninety-degree turn with him and failed. "What?"

"Last night someone set the old VA hospital on fire. It's still burning. Metal melted. Concrete walls cracked from thermal shock. Your scent is all over the street leading to it, and your yard reeks of charred human flesh. So I'll ask again, do you need a medic? I know a good one."

"No."

We stared at each other.

"Stop wasting our time and tell me what you want," I said.

"I'd like you to tell me about Pastor Haywood's murder."

"Why do you want to know?"

"I have a personal interest in the matter."

"And that personal interest caused you to break into my house and intimidate me while I sit naked in my bathtub? Do you think Pastor Haywood would approve?"

He hit me with his alpha stare. "I broke into your house because you hold crucial information and I thought you might be dying. If I were you, I'd focus on answering my questions."

His gaze pressed on me like a physical weight. I wanted to either explode out of the bath, slicing at him, or jump out and run for my life.

So that's how it is? Okay, buddy. I'll play.

I stared back at him with disdain, the way I looked at those who threatened the New Kingdom when I wanted them to back away with tail between their legs. *I am Shinar reborn, shapeshifter. I do not submit.*

Silence filled the chamber, cold and oppressive. Why did I keep goading him? If he was anybody else, I would've maneuvered the conversation where I wanted it to go by now. Instead I turned it into a standoff.

He hadn't looked for me. He hadn't called. He hadn't written. Gods, I was so angry at him. I hadn't realized how much until this moment. It burned my common sense to ashes.

Emotion boiled in Derek's eyes. I couldn't place it. Frustration, rage? A bit of both? Not, that wasn't quite it. Whatever it was, it was clearly driving him nuts. He looked at me like I was everything that was wrong in his life.

A faint sound came from the other room. A man walked in and halted in the arched entrance to the bedroom. In his early twenties, tan, with a mane of soft reddish-brown hair he had tied back from his freckled face. He wore a similar grey outfit, and when he moved, he walked with the fluid grace of a shapeshifter. Not a wolf. Something else. Something smaller.

Derek kept looking at me. "Yes?"

"The hyenas found Jerome. He is leading them on a merry chase."

A slight trace of a Slavic accent.

The shapeshifter hesitated. "Perhaps I could help you communicate…"

"No," Derek and I said at the same time.

"Okaaay. I'll just go away then."

The shapeshifter retreated.

"I'm not leaving until I get some answers," Derek said.

"Then you'll die of old age at my house."

"I thought you were severely burned, but maybe I'm wrong. Perhaps you hit your head instead and can't see this situation clearly."

"Enlighten me. What is it I'm failing to see?"

He took a deep breath and let it out slowly. "I'm hungry. I'm going to get up and find something to eat, so you can get out in privacy. Use this opportunity to think about..."

I stood up. The last shreds of my discarded skin fell into the bath.

Derek stared at me, caught mid-word.

I tossed my hair out of my face, flinging water and loose petals back into the tub, stepped out, and walked past him to my closet to get dressed.

WHEN I CAME OUT OF THE BEDROOM, DEREK WAS SITTING IN MY sanctuary at my kitchen table spreading a thin layer of honey mustard on a slice of bread with a wicked-looking knife. Another slice with an inch-thick slab of smoked ham waited on his plate. He put the top slice on top of the ham.

He'd made himself a sandwich. Maybe I'd get lucky, and the son of a bitch would choke on it.

"You don't have any iced tea," he said.

I would strangle him. "That's just one of the things I don't have."

Derek sliced the sandwich in half. "Oh?"

"I also don't have any patience for people stealing my food."

Derek picked up half of the sandwich, bit into it, and

chewed.

Food held a special significance to the shapeshifters. When a shapeshifter offered to feed someone, he communicated willingness to protect and take care of them. A shapeshifter who couldn't protect his meat was weak. Derek broke into my house and ate my ham, and now he was rubbing my face in it.

Just you wait. You'll regret it.

I sat across from him. "Is it good?"

He licked his lips. "Delicious."

I'd negotiated peace agreements with people I hated. I would not give him the satisfaction of slapping the rest of the sandwich out of his hand. No matter how satisfying that would feel.

I pulled a pad of paper toward me, wrote $20 on it, and passed it to him.

"What's this?"

"The bill for the sandwich."

"A twenty-dollar ham sandwich?"

"You chose to eat here. You should've asked about prices in advance." I pointed at the doorway. "The door is that way. This restaurant is closed. Take the rest of your meal to go."

He finished the first half of the sandwich and leaned back with a kind of languid grace, a wolf in repose. "Let's be adults about this."

"That would be a refreshing change."

"Several years ago, I was in a bad place in my life. I came to Pastor Haywood for guidance. He helped me."

When did that happen? What bad place? I opened my mouth to ask and clamped it shut. He was a stranger, and I had to treat him like one.

"I told him that if he ever needed help, I would return the favor. He called me on the night before he died. He told me that he was worried and asked for my help. He sounded scared. I left an hour after that phone call, but unfortunately, I was across the country. I didn't make it in time."

Oh damn.

"I'm here to find out who killed him." Moonglow flashed in his eyes and died. "We're on the same side."

"I doubt that."

"Tell me why you're investigating this murder and what you found, and I will tell you why Pastor Haywood was scared that night."

Every crumb of information could mean the difference between Kate dying and living. Was there any harm in sharing with him? I searched for the downside and didn't see one. After all, I didn't have to tell him everything.

"Deal. You go first."

"No."

I narrowed my eyes at him. "You don't trust me?"

"I don't. You're a liar." He picked up the rest of the sandwich and took a nice big bite.

"How am I a liar?"

"You pretend to be a knight of the Order."

I took the badge out of my pocket and put it on the table. "Feel free to clear it with Nick Feldman."

"Your badge is real. Your knighthood isn't. I've got two words for you. Jaiden Higgs."

"Is that supposed to mean something?"

"Seven years ago Knight-Defender Jaiden Higgs suffered a psychotic break. He thought he was possessed, and demons were talking to him. He took three people hostage and barricaded himself in an elementary school on Jefferson Street. Jaiden was sent to Atlanta after he had some issues, and Nick Feldman took him under his wing."

I could guess where this story was going, and the end wouldn't be happy.

"Nick did everything he could to get Jaiden out, and when that didn't work, he called Pastor Haywood. The pastor went into that elementary school and came out sixteen hours later with Jaiden and the hostages unharmed."

"Was Jaiden possessed?"

"Nobody knows. He hung himself a month later in the psychiatric ward."

Yes, just another sunshine and rainbows fable of post-Shift Atlanta.

Derek pointed the remainder of his sandwich at me. "Nick Feldman owed Pastor Haywood. He held him in the highest regard. Right now, Feldman should be tearing this city apart looking for his killer. Even if he received a direct order from the Preceptor himself, he wouldn't let this go. Instead he gave it to you, a knight nobody knows who's been in the city for five minutes."

Two could play this game. "You seem to know a lot about me. Here is what I know about you. You're an alpha. You have your own pack. You aren't a member of the Atlanta Pack, nor are you affiliated with them in any way. If the Beast Lord finds out a foreign shapeshifter is running around in his territory, the entire Pack will hunt you down. You seem to already have some kind of beef with Ascanio Ferara, whose boudas your people are right now trying to evade. Why hasn't he turned you in? Do the two of you have some sort of history?"

Derek raised his eyebrows half a millimeter.

"Maybe we should stick to the facts of the murder," I suggested.

"Yes. That would be best."

"Tell me about the artifact," I said.

If Derek was surprised, he didn't show it. "It's a box of some strange material, two feet long, one foot wide, and about one foot deep. It has a cross engraved into its lid."

"What kind of cross? A Christian cross?"

Derek shook his head. "Pastor didn't think so. He said it emanated magic. Trying to probe it was like holding your hand to a spraying fire hydrant. The magic felt old. He said pre-Hellenistic. It disturbed him."

"In what way?"

Derek frowned. "He said it was like looking at a radiant diamond. It had complexity and facets on a level he hadn't encountered before."

Sounded like an object from the old ages. Never good. "Did he say who hired him to authenticate it?"

"No. Your turn."

"Someone hired Pastor Haywood to authenticate a magical artifact. The next night the pastor was murdered. The killer broke through the skylight, ripped out his heart, and left the same way. Last night Professor Walton, an expert in early Christian history, was also murdered. The killer came through the third-floor window, ripped out her heart, and left through the same window."

He focused on me with single-minded intensity. It was slightly unnerving. "It's a creature."

"I believe so. It's highly likely the artifact is bound to a guardian. That guardian can track anyone who touches the artifact and will continue killing until it's able to regain its treasure."

"What are you thinking?" he asked.

My heart squeezed itself into a tight, painful ball. This was us. This is how we used to do it when we were solving a thorny problem together: we would sit down some place with food and bat theories back and forth until we decided what to do next. Dear gods, it hurt. Oh wow.

I made my mouth move. "Something with wings and claws. Any beast with sufficient magical power can be bound. Could be a griffin. A manticore. A zilant..."

"Not a griffin. They have a distinctive stink."

That's right. I was sitting across from one of the best trackers in the entire Pack. "What did it smell like?"

He shook his head. "Not anything I've come across."

Derek remembered thousands of scents. Worse and worse.

"What's the deal with fire?" he asked.

"That's a personal matter. It doesn't concern you."

"I'll decide what concerns me."

I burst out laughing. He looked just like Conlan when he'd said that, too.

"Did I say something funny?"

I waved my hand at him. "No."

The other shapeshifter reappeared, hovering in the doorway. I turned and looked at him.

The other shapeshifter raised his hand and gave me a small wave. "Hello. I'm Zahar."

"A stoat?" I guessed.

Zahar shook his head.

"What is it?" Derek asked.

"He's brought in a second crew. Females."

The bouda females were larger and stronger than the males.

"Looks like our charming chat is coming to an end," I said. "You're clearly needed elsewhere. Let's not do this again."

Derek reached into a hidden pocket, pulled out a twenty-dollar bill, and put it on the table.

Zahar's eyes widened.

"The sandwich bill," I told him. "One last question. Why is Ferara chasing you anyway?"

Derek rose smoothly and came around the table. "He has a score he wants to settle."

"What kind of score? Why?"

He took a step toward me, leaned forward, and smiled at me. It was a sharp wolf smile, and the impact of that smile resonated through me. For a second, I forgot I could move.

"That's a personal matter. It doesn't concern you," he murmured close to my ear, turned, and walked out.

That bastard.

189

Regeneration made me hungry. I had to regrow several pounds of skin, as creepy as it sounded, and my stomach was screaming for calories. If I didn't give it some, it would shut me down.

I ate the rest of the ham with the bread I made last night. The clock told me I had slept till noon, almost six hours. It cost me a good chunk of time, but it couldn't be helped. My body ached now, the familiar post-healing pain that felt a little like waves of shallow muscle spasms rolling through me. They would stop once I got moving.

The herb mix was an emergency measure. It was expensive and took a long time to produce. I'd had one bag, and that was it.

He who consumes the heart of the beast will be given a brief glimpse of the true future. No wonder Moloch had dispatched a high priest to handle it. Now that his attack dog was dead, Moloch would send another heavy hitter, if one wasn't in Atlanta already. If I were him, I'd send more than one. I couldn't let myself be caught again. I didn't have another herb bag handy.

The examination of my doors didn't yield any clues as to how Derek had gotten inside. None of the locks showed any sign of tampering. If he had tried to break through my wards, the impact would've woken me up. He must've done it during tech, but how remained a mystery. That was an unpleasant development. From now on I would have to engage the siege bar on the door every time I locked it from the inside.

While the food settled, I needed to make some calls. The phone worked, which was a minor miracle, or as my grandfather would explain, the direct result of all my magic having been drained below any reasonable threshold by the process of regeneration. I was so tired and sleepy, I needed little toothpicks to hold my eyes open. Too bad I wasn't a cartoon cat.

I called to the Methodist hospital first.

"My name is Aurelia Ryder. I'm calling about Douglas."

"Please hold."

I held. Please be alive. Please be alive...

A different female voice came on the line. "This is Carol Wood. I'm the ICU nurse. The medmage team worked on him during the wave. He is hanging in there."

Hanging in there wasn't "making progress" or "feeling better." A slick nauseating worry squirmed through me.

"Can I see him?"

"Yes, but he is heavily sedated."

"Thank you."

The Order was next. Stella answered on the second ring. "Atlanta Chapter of the Order of Merciful Aid."

"I see you survived."

"That's still in doubt."

"Did anything from Biohazard come for me? Paperwork, a file?"

"Big ass envelope?"

"Yep, that's it. I'll come and get it."

"I'll be here."

I bet she would. "See you in a few."

If a magical artifact with that amount of power had gone on the market, people would know about it. I called to Nader Youseff, who acted as New Shinar's buying agent when we wanted to purchase something magic-related. I explained what I wanted, and he told me to sit tight.

Next, I took out the list of Jasper's known associates and compared it to the list of the relic hunters the bishop's people had passed to me through Stella. No matches.

Someone had sent Jasper hunting for Marten and me. That someone had deep pockets.

I called to PAD, used my badge and Luther's name, and got contact info for the four people on Jasper's list. Four calls later, I learned that of the Jasper-connected associates, two were dead, one was incarcerated, and the fourth had moved out of state, abandoning his spouse and three children. I got a five-minute rant from his wife detailing the shortcomings of the relevant parts of his anatomy and his moral character.

A dead end.

The phone rang. I picked up.

"They'd fixed the line and put traps around it," Conlan said quietly. "I cut it again last night and threw the traps into the Gap."

He hung up. Conlan Lennart, master of covert ops. I laughed a little and made myself a venison sandwich.

Once the sandwich was gone, I pulled up a piece of paper, wrote *Potential employers,* and underlined it.

First, the current owner of the box. Perhaps they got alarmed when Pastor Haywood was murdered and hired Jasper to clean up any loose ends that could lead the investigation back to them.

Second, the original owner of the box. If the box was stolen, the old owner might have been looking for clues of who had taken it.

Third, someone who wanted the box for themselves.

So far all of my suspects pointed back to relic hunters or collectors. Anyone working for any of the churches was out. They had their own way of dealing with things, and they kept that sort of thing in house. If they wanted the box, they wouldn't have hired Jasper.

The phone sat in front of me. It had been almost a month since I last talked to Kate. I really wanted to call home.

No.

The phone company assured me that reverse dialing no longer was an option, but the risk was too great.

I had to go back to Honeycomb. Jasper had taken two people with him on his little outing. He would've told them about the job. Someone in the Gap knew something about it.

Getting dressed was an effort. I powered through it on sheer will and went to the stables. Thick clouds pregnant with rain crowded the sky. The air was still and humid, baked in oppressive heat. It would storm before long.

Tulip was in her stall, but her mouth was bloody again, so she had clearly gone out this morning.

"See this? This is perfectly fine feed. Premium quality oats. Delicious hay. Would it have killed you to stay put?"

Tulip snorted at me. I cleaned her up, saddled her, and we were off.

My buddy the homeless man was back at his post at the intersection, looking starved and pitiful. I rode by him, bought two oversized kolaches from a stall again, and brought one to him. He eyed me as if I were Sophia's cobra but took the hot pastry.

"It's going to rain," I told him. "You might want to get inside."

He ignored me.

The Methodist hospital was my first stop. I sat by Douglas's bed, held his limp hand, and watched the liquid slowly drip from his IV bag.

He was a good kid. Brave. Kind. He tried to protect someone who was smaller and weaker than him even knowing he would get hurt. He tried to protect me, even though he didn't know me, and he owed me nothing. He had so little in life.

I wanted him to survive. But all I could do was sit by his bed and stare in helpless rage. I remembered sitting just like this behind the bars of Moloch's cages inside his citadel and watching people around me rot slowly. Beaten, exhausted, filthy, they had given up. They had no names. They had let go of their memories. They didn't live, they existed in agony waiting to die.

It was almost impossible to pummel hope out of human beings. It was an irrepressible part of our spirit. Hope kept us going, but as I'd sat in the middle of that sea of human bodies, I knew with absolute certainty that their hope was dead. I'd watched them suffer, and I'd cried to keep the helpless blinding fury from tearing me apart.

It didn't matter how powerful you were. Life always found ways to stab you and twist the knife in the wound. Nobody was immune.

I CHOSE THE LONG ROUTE TO THE HONEYCOMB GAP. IT TOOK AN extra ten minutes, but it let me ride by Galina's Bakery. The little shop was still there after all these years. I bought a strawberry hand pie, munched on it while Tulip carried me through the streets, and thought about the box, the divine beast, the weird color of yellow that someone had painted the car forcing its way down the street in front of me... Anything to avoid thinking about Derek.

I had many failings, and the overwhelming need to be in control of myself was one of them. I didn't care about controlling other people. I didn't micromanage, and I delegated when someone else was better suited for the task, but I had to maintain an iron grip over myself at all times. There was probably a host of deep-seated psychological issues behind that urge that would take a dozen psychiatrists ages to sort out, but it boiled down to one thing: I kept my emotions divorced from my actions. I hid my weaknesses. Even when anger crested in me in a hot, red wave, I surfed it to my goal. I never lost my hold in front of other people unless they were family. If I screamed, it was calculated. If I wept, I did it for impact.

Derek made me lose it. I kept going over our conversation in my head. It was the way he had looked at me. The way he sat, the way he smiled, the way he spoke. Everything he did reminded me of what I'd left behind. Somehow, he bypassed my armor and got an honest, instinctual response out of me. I hated that so much.

He was one of the reasons I'd learned to control myself. Not the main one, not even close to the most important, but still one of them. Even as a kid, I recognized that if I openly threw myself at him and told him how much I loved him, how happy I was to see him every day, it would make things irreparably awkward. I didn't want him to avoid me.

Now I would give anything to avoid him.

There was no reason for us to interact again. Sooner or later Ascanio would catch up to him and his motley crew of shapeshifter badasses. Derek would have other things to worry about and leave me in peace.

We had arrived at the building with the phone line. I finished my pie in one bite, jumped off Tulip's back, and headed up the ruined stairs. The phone line was back on the pole. They had repaired it again. I loved it when a plan came together.

I took off my cloak and climbed the pole. I was two-thirds up, when a familiar raspy voice asked, "What are you doing?"

I had excellent reflexes, which was why I didn't fall off the pole and land on my ass.

Son of a bitch. Fuck, shit, fuck.

Derek leaned against a crumbling wall. He wore khaki work pants, stained with cement dust and rust, a green long-sleeve Henley, and a robin-hood, a hood that fit over the shoulders and came with a face mask that covered the nose and mouth. The reclamation crews wore them to keep the dust out of their lungs and sun out of their face. He looked like he had just walked off one of the salvage crews from Ted Turner Drive. I couldn't even see his face, let alone his scars.

Why was he here? Why, why, why, why…

"What are you doing here?" I asked.

"You haven't finished sharing. You seem like the kind of person who will be bothered by leaving things unfinished, so I saved you the trouble of tracking me down."

Stay civil. "How magnanimous of you."

"I can be. I can be a good friend or a terrible enemy."

"So, you're saying you're not very good at being an enemy?"

He shrugged. "Well, you could ask my opponents for references, but none of them are around anymore."

Right. I resumed my climb, keeping my face calm. "We had a deal. We traded information. You got yours. Go away."

"You kept things from me. Important things."

"Like what?"

"Like the boy in the St. Luke's hospital and the girl the Gilliams are guarding."

And how the hell did he find this out? "That's none of your business."

His eyes flashed. "That's very much my business."

He didn't snarl, his tone was calm, but his voice had an undercurrent of menace that wasn't wholly human. You could feel the wolf in him, watching, waiting, biding his time, separated from the world only by a thin layer of human skin.

My hands slid. They had greased the top third of the pole with WD-40. Assholes.

He watched me trying to scramble up. "Every time we meet, Ms. Ryder, you try to get away from me. Is there something about me that makes you uncomfortable?"

Everything about him made me uncomfortable.

I slid again. Damn it.

Derek jumped up fifteen feet in the air and sliced through the phone line in a blur.

I slid off the pole and landed by it, turning so my back was to the wood. And he was right there, a foot away. His hood was down, and his eyes were on fire.

"What's the deal with the pole?"

"I like climbing poles in my spare time."

"Yesterday someone killed an iron hound a mile and a half from St. Luke's Church and called it into Biohazard."

If you killed a weird magical thing in Atlanta's city limits, you had to let Biohazard know so they could pick up the corpse and quarantine it on the off-chance it decided to sprout twelve legs and a mouth lined with teeth and went off looking for human snacks. I had called it in from the hospital's reception desk.

"The Honeycomb is the only place near Atlanta that spawns iron hounds." Derek's voice was dangerously intimate. If he really hated someone, he would speak to them in that tone just before he killed them. "Now you're here, cutting a cable leading into the Honeycomb. Is that a phone line?"

I didn't answer.

"I'm waiting," he prompted.

"For what?"

"A confirmation."

"Do you really need me to add anything? You're doing well on your own."

His flat demeanor broke and frustration spilled forth. "Damn, you test my patience."

Alarm shot my senses into hyperdrive. "You gave me a vague description of a box. You didn't tell me what the box does, what it's made of, or who has it. Considering how little you offered me, what I told you is more than fair. Stop following me around. Can't you take a hint?"

His eyes ignited. "Not this time!"

A vibration pulsed into my back through the pole. Another. A little aftershock shivered through my feet. Something shook the building.

Derek clamped his mouth shut.

I held still, listening.

A deep rumble announced rocks falling to the right, where the Honeycomb Gap dropped off into a chasm.

He pulled off his hood. I grabbed Dakkan out of my sheath and screwed it together.

A thick pungent stench rolled over us in a viscous cloud. It smelled like wet fur, swamp, and rotten fish, perfumed with a spritz of skunk.

I gagged.

Next to me Derek locked his teeth, making the muscles in his jaw stand out. Strong smells and sounds hit shapeshifters much harder, and this reek was beyond revolting. It stuck to you, coating the inside of your mouth.

The building trembled slightly. A dry scratching noise came from the wall that faced the Gap, a crunching of weakened concrete under claws. The dry sound moved to the left and we pivoted with it.

Crunch.

Crunch. Like some enormous lizard crawling around the building, climbing the walls in a lazy spiral.

Crunch. Tiny chunks of concrete shivered on the floor. We'd made a hundred-and-eighty-degree turn, following it. Now we faced the street.

Crunch.

Silence.

We waited.

Above, ragged clouds crept across the sky. A Stymphalian bird shrieked, gliding on the air currents. A wasp landed on the concrete next to me and crawled around on segmented legs.

Derek looked up.

A frog-like head, five feet wide and shaggy with long dark green fur, stared at us from above the wall with big red eyes. Two yellowed horns, stained with dried blood, curved from the sides of its head, pointing up. Two saber fangs, almost the same size, protruded from the enormous maw studded with conical teeth. The teeth fit together with unnatural precision, like a bear trap. If this thing caught you in its mouth, it would cut you in two.

Thank the universe I brought lemon juice. The next time I saw Sienna, I would bring her all the marzipan ever.

The hodag sniffed the air with a flat, black dog nose the size of a basketball. A gob of mucus slid out of his left nostril. Ewww. I had seen one of these before, years ago. They were native to Wisconsin. The Honeycomb was the last place I would've expected to find it. And such a big one too. There was only one way for a hodag to grow that big.

Derek shifted his weight.

"Don't bite it," I murmured. "It's poisonous, even to you."

The hodag leaned forward. The wall shook as it dug into it from the outside. It arched its back, showing off a crest of horns protruding from its spine. Its thick body rode low on four powerful legs, each armed with absurdly long claws. A long dinosaur tail swung to the right, giving it leverage for a leap.

The world slowed down, turning sharp and clear.

The hodag sprung from the wall, aiming straight for us.

Derek leaped to the side. I jumped back, stabbing with Dakkan, and the beast went after me, swiping at the spear with its claws. Fast bastard. I whipped Dakkan around and smashed it on the creature's nose. It bellowed like an angry bull gator and charged me.

On the left, Derek pulled off his shirt.

I dodged left. The hodag spun about, lashing its fat tail. The spikes rent the air six inches from my stomach.

Derek pulled off his boots. You've got to be kidding me.

I dashed left and leaped over the hole in the floor. The concrete gave under my feet, and I almost fell through the floor. Behind me the hodag pitched into the hole, caught itself, jerked back, and came after me like some giant mutant gecko chasing after a cricket. I leaped back and forth, dodging its swipes.

Derek had removed his jeans, folded them in half, and was carefully placing them on top of his boots.

I would strangle him. I would hit him in that smug handsome face with a brick. You think you got scars, buddy? Just you wait.

The hodag reared, trying to pin me with its bulk. I threw myself into a roll, sprang to my feet, and stabbed Dakkan between the beast's fat toes. The hodag howled.

Derek gave me a thumbs-up.

"Dead!" I danced back, avoiding the hodag's strikes.

"What?"

"You're a dead man!"

He held out his hand. "Tag me in."

"Eat dirt."

I raced around the gap, hodag on my heels, and threw myself left, toward Derek. The enraged beast barreled past us.

Derek waved his hand at me. "Anytime."

The hodag braked and turned, impossibly limber. Red eyes

locked on me. A deep rumble gurgled in its throat. Oh please no.

The beast inhaled, sucking in the mucus.

I dashed to the side.

The hodag spat. A gob of mucus the size of a basketball flew through the air. Derek jumped straight up. The poisonous spit-ball splattered under him, splashing on concrete. He landed next to the puddle and glanced at his clothes. A fat drop of hodag spit rolled off his folded jeans and dripped to the floor.

I gave Derek a thumbs-up.

A hot werewolf glow sparked in his eyes. He opened his mouth and growled. It began as a human sound, and as it left his mouth, his body exploded. Bones grew in a blink, building a new oversized frame. Muscle spiraled up the new skeleton, and dense silver fur chased it, covering the monstrous body. Claws the size of my fingers burst from his new hands. Long lupine jaws jutted from his head, filled with fangs, and the final notes of that eerie growl announced an apex predator entering the field.

The hodag opened its huge maw and roared.

Derek's black lips rose, and he snarled, wrinkling his muzzle, like a wolf in the woods defending its kill.

The hodag charged. Time stretched, impossibly slow, and I saw it all in excruciating detail: the hodag barreling forward, mouth gaping, eyes bulging, claws ready to tear and rip and Derek making no effort to move aside.

I moved without realizing it. I was five feet too far when the hodag reached him. Smoothly, almost casually, Derek swayed out of the beast's path and thrust his left hand out. The awful claws ripped through the matted fur like it was tissue paper. Blood and alien guts spilled through the ragged wound. He'd split it from front shoulder to groin.

The hodag kept running, unable to stop, trailing its insides, and smashed into the wall. Chunks of concrete flew. The wall quaked, wobbling like a loose tooth, and collapsed, taking the hodag with it.

Derek sprinted past me and jumped after it.

I leaned over the edge and looked down. The broken body of the hodag sprawled on the rubble three floors below, where a ruined house was slowly sliding into the Gap. The nightmarish blend of human and wolf that was Derek crouched by its head, methodically carving through the hodag's neck.

He had killed the hodag with one swipe of his claws. Even if it hadn't fallen, it would be dead. The hodag had bigger teeth and longer claws and outweighed him ten to one, and none of it mattered. Of the two, Derek was the better monster.

There was something so beautiful in that combination of precision, speed, and strength. When I saw that strike, it shot electric needles through my skin. For a brief moment, I was both terrified and caught in admiration.

Derek grasped the hodag's head and tore it free with a wet crunch. It was the size of a truck cab, and he was holding it with one hand.

What in the world happened to you, Derek?

He looked up. Our gazes met.

"What are you doing?" I called down.

He opened his mouth. Most shapeshifters had trouble maintaining their warrior form, and fewer still could speak in it. Their jaws didn't fit together quite right, or their tongues were too long. Derek could speak, but his words sounded ragged. Combined with his permanently damaged vocal cords, he sounded like gravel being crushed, but he had no trouble carrying on a conversation.

"Making things clear."

I almost did a double take. The voice that came out was deep and powerful, and his diction was perfect.

"To whom?"

"To anyone who's watching."

He took a running start, leaped, and climbed the wall, dragging the head with him. In a moment, he made it over the edge and landed next to me. He walked over to the pole, jumped up, caught it with his free hand, pulled himself up, and impaled the hodag head on top of it. Gore dripped down, falling on his fur.

Above us, thunder rumbled. I looked up. The sky churned with thick dark clouds.

Derek hopped down to the floor. He was the biggest werewolf I had ever seen. I stood five feet six inches tall, and he had two feet on me, at least. He was almost as tall as Curran in warrior form, but leaner, with longer limbs, powerful but not quite as bulky. Curran was stronger, but Derek would be faster.

He walked toward me, flinging hodag blood off his clawed hands. Oh joy.

"It smells worse dead than alive."

"Did any of the blood get in your mouth?"

He was standing way too close, and I had to look up.

"Why?"

"It's highly poisonous. Even to shapeshifters. I have the antidote." I lifted a small vial I had fished out from the pocket on my belt.

He raised his bloody hand to his snout, sniffed the blood, grimaced, and gave it a long lick.

"Are you out of your mind?" I thrust the vial into his hand. "Drink this!"

"It's fine," he said. "Tingles a bit."

Argh.

"Tastes like shit, too. Like a pig crossed with a gator."

"Drink the antidote."

He flicked his ears. "Or what?"

"Or I use the Order to file a formal complaint with the Pack."

He pried the cork off with the tips of his claws and gulped the contents. "Lemon juice?"

"Lemon juice is the only known hodag antidote."

"You do realize that makes no sense?"

"Nothing about the hodag makes sense."

"Why?"

"Because they are modern Americana mythos. In the 1890's Eugene Shepard, who was a land surveyor from Rhinelander, a town in Wisconsin, claimed to have caught a hodag. He described a ferocious battle with a fearsome beast with the head of a frog, the face of an elephant, the back of a dinosaur, and the tail of a gator. It had horns on its head and along its spine, sabretooth fangs, and improbably long claws. He claimed the hodags prowled the swamps of upper Wisconsin, feeding on mud turtles, water snakes, and oxen, but their favorite food was white bulldogs. It could be killed only with dynamite, chloroform, or lemons."

He reached out and put his fingers on my forehead. I jerked back.

"You don't feel warm," he said. "Did you get any of the blood in your mouth?"

"Why am I even talking to you?"

I turned, and he moved to block my way.

"How did it go from Eugene Shepard to that?" He pointed at the head.

"Shepard paid a taxidermist to stuff the 'hodag' and paraded it at county fairs for the next several decades. The Smithsonian scientists called him on it, and he had to admit that the whole thing was a hoax, but he didn't stop displaying it, and people didn't stop paying to see it."

"Aha. What was he displaying exactly?"

"I have no idea. I saw a picture of it, and it looked like a large bulldog with horns glued to its head."

I walked to the edge of the building and looked down at the hodag corpse.

"So it was a fun local legend. Then what?"

Why did he keep asking me about the stupid hodag? "Then the logging business died out, and the town shifted to hodag tourism instead. A hundred years later, they had a Hodag Country Festival, Hodag Park, Hodag BMX Club, Hodag Honda... The high school mascot was a hodag. They even built a giant statue of the creature in front of city hall. Tourists used to take pictures with it."

"Let me guess, the Shift hit, and the creature came to life."

"Something like that. Locals might not have believed in the hodag, but the kids did, and some of the tourists too. At some point, all that accumulated faith gained critical mass, and a pack of hodags ran out of the woods and came after the crowd at the Hodag County Fair. Rhinelander is a walled town now. Bad news, hodags lay twenty-five eggs at a time. Good news, their leather and fur fetch a good price. So, the woods are back, but they're full of hodags."

"Someone sold the Honeycombers a black-market hodag egg," he said.

"Probably."

"Why would Honeycombers send a hodag after you?"

"Because that's the third time I cut their phone line. I need to find out who hired Jasper..."

I stopped and pivoted to him.

He smiled, showing me a forest of fangs that would give any sane person nightmares for life.

"Nice," I told him.

"Who's Jasper?"

"Nobody."

I pulled a rag from my pocket and wiped Dakkan's blade. The stench made my eyes water.

"Let's work together."

"Let's not."

He moved to stand in front of me again. "You and I carried on a civil adult conversation for the last five minutes."

I blinked at him. "I fail to see your point."

"You were distracted, and amazingly you didn't demand that I leave, and you didn't try to run away from me. Clearly, you can control yourself in my presence."

"Trust me, I'm doing a superb job controlling myself right now. When I lose control, you'll know about it."

"Let's join forces. The faster we find Pastor Haywood's killer, the sooner I will leave this city, and your life again will be blissfully free of me, just as you like it."

He planned to leave again. "Where will you go?" Why did I ask that?

The werewolf shrugged. "Home."

"Where is home?"

"Not here."

It was like a stab to the heart. Atlanta used to be his home. Kate, Curran, and Conlan were still here. I was... Right. I wasn't.

I recognized the look in his eyes. Derek had locked onto a target. It would be impossible to avoid him. I had exhausted all of my emotional reserves trying to shove him out of my orbit. He was powerful. He was an asset. We would help each other, and then he would leave.

"Jasper was the self-proclaimed king of the Honeycomb," I told him. "A little girl, a street kid, witnessed Pastor Haywood getting into a car with a fatso who took him to identify the artifact. Someone hired Jasper to find her, so he got two of his flunkies and crawled out into the city. I got to the girl first. When Jasper couldn't find her, he caught one of the other street kids instead. The child wouldn't tell him anything about the girl or me, so Jasper and his two assholes beat him to within an inch of his life."

Derek's hackles rose.

"Jasper had an iron hound and tracked me to St. Luke's Cathedral. When I came across the three of them, they were dragging the boy on a chain with him. He was black and blue. He couldn't stand. They broke his leg. They snapped his arm. They shattered his ribs…"

My voice was about to quiver. No. Not happening. I scrambled to maintain some semblance of control. Derek took a step forward.

A bullet dug into the concrete inches from my foot. I threw myself left and ducked behind a wall.

Derek swore and jumped over the edge.

I STUDIED THE TWO PEOPLE DEREK DROPPED ON THE CONCRETE. He'd come up the stairs, carrying them by the back of their pants and dumped them in front of me. They seemed slightly rumpled, but their guts were still inside their bodies, which was a huge plus.

The younger one had short chestnut hair and bronze skin and was probably a young girl in her mid-teens dressed in oversized men's clothes. The older one, about my age, had lighter skin, dark hair, a dark beard, and the kind of look in his eyes that told me he expected to be beaten and had come to terms with it.

"You sent a hodag after us."

The man spread his arms. "You cut the cable three times. Honestly lady, what do you have against us? Do you cut other people's phone lines or is it just ours?"

"Just yours."

He leaned back. "What did we ever do to you? I don't know you." He turned to the girl. "Do you know her?"

The girl shook her head.

He turned back to me. "See? We don't know you. We need that line to survive. We need food, we need clothes, we need ammo, and backyard gardening only gets you so far."

"Gardening, huh?"

"Yes. We grow things, tomatoes, cucumbers. We're peaceful folks. We mind our own business."

I pointed at the hodag's head. "To grow a hodag to that size, you have to feed it human meat."

The girl looked freaked out.

Surprise flashed in the man's eyes, but he recovered quickly. "So, he ate a few corpses. They would have rotted anyway. It's a circle-of-life thing, lady."

Uh huh. Circle of life. "What's your name?"

"Don't tell her, Cephus," the girl whispered and clamped her hand over her mouth.

Cephus just looked at her for a second.

"I want to know about Jasper," I said.

"We don't know Jasper," Cephus said.

Derek loomed above him. "Answer her or I'll put your head in my mouth."

Cephus swallowed. "Oh Jasper? That Jasper. Yeah, okay. We do know Jasper. What about him?"

"Yesterday he took two of you and left to do a job. I need to know who hired him."

Cephus spread his arms to the sky. "Who knows? Jasper isn't the sharing type. He isn't exactly beloved. He had a hard childhood. The man has trouble processing his feelings, so when he has them, they make him angry. And when he gets angry, he lashes out."

"The last time I lashed out, Jasper lost his head. It's sitting on a metal tray in the Order's morgue."

The girl clutched onto Cephus. He put his arm around her and rearranged his expression, looking hurt. "No need for threats. We're all friends here. The phone line is for everyone's use. You pay into the jar per phone call. Sometimes money goes to buy medicine. Sometimes Jasper takes it. He has poor leadership skills. I don't know who hired Jasper. I do know some people he worked with."

"Give me some names."

He looked at the sky. "Christi Constanza, Dallas Karen, Bambi Nolastname, Mark Rudolph, Felix Goswin..."

"Okay," I told him. "You can go."

Cephus eyed me, glanced at Derek over his shoulder, looked at me again, grabbed the girl's hand, and took off. We heard them stomping down the stairs all the way to the bottom.

"They're really broken up about Jasper," Derek said. "I can feel their grief."

"You heard them. The man had trouble processing his feelings. Probably kept most people at a distance. Never formed strong bonds with his peers. His inner core wasn't vibrating in tune to the celestial heartbeat."

A gust of wind tore at my hair. The world turned dark. The storm was almost on top of us.

"How is the boy?" the massive werewolf next to me asked.

"I don't know. They told me he is hanging in there. I saw him this morning. He looked like he was dying." I really had to shut up.

"The offer of a good medmage still stands."

"Thank you. If it's possible, the Methodists will heal him. It bothers me. There are at least thirty minutes between White Street and St. Luke's. They dragged a boy on a chain, and nobody fucking did anything about it. Why? Did the city go blind?"

"The city was always blind," he said, his voice hard. "People don't want to get involved. As long as it doesn't touch them, they can pretend it's not happening."

People knew about his family and didn't help. People saw me in the streets every day and didn't help either.

We stood next to each other. The wind pulled at his fur.

"What happens when we find Pastor Haywood's killer?" I asked.

"I'll rip his heart out."

It wasn't a turn of phrase. He meant it.

"It won't bring him back," Derek continued. "It probably won't make me feel better. But it must be done."

"This is nasty and complicated," I told him.

"My favorite."

"There is an avatar involved."

"I've met a few gods."

"Not like this one. If I tell you to sit a fight out, will you do it?"

"Sure."

Too easy. Sitting anything out wasn't in his nature. "Promise me."

"I promise."

"I'll hold you to it." I held my hand out. "Aurelia Ryder."

Clawed fingers swallowed my hand. "Darren Argent."

It sounded familiar. "Argent" meant silver. Many shapeshifters took new names when joining a new pack, and I knew several who chose "Argent" as a last name. Silver killed Lyc-V, the virus responsible for their existence, and they considered the name ironic. Not a name I would expect him to pick for himself.

Then again, "Aurelia" meant gold, and I chose it without considering its meaning. I wanted a name that reminded me of Julie, so one day I just looked at a list of Roman names and picked one that sounded pretty. Maybe I was reading too much into it.

We shook and let go.

"So, which of the four names Cephus mentioned rang a bell?" he asked.

"Mark Rudolph. He's on the list of relic hunters Bishop Chao gave me."

"Then we should pay him a visit."

"Yes, we should. I'll head down to the street," I told him.

"Don't want to stay and watch me change?" There was a hint of humor in his inhuman voice.

"No."

"What if something attacks me while I'm getting dressed?"

I looked at the hodag head and then back at him. "Throw the head at them and scream for help. I'll see you downstairs."

I limped out of the building and whistled for Tulip.

Someone had turned the muscles of my legs into wet cotton. I had expended way too much energy dodging the hodag, and now my freshly regenerated body was making me pay for it. My thigh hurt like hell.

A wind gust hit me, tearing at my hair. Thunder rocked the world, the clouds broke open and rain drenched me, warm and heavy. I raised my arms, closed my eyes, and let it wash over me, wishing all my troubles would drain away with the water.

I could've stood under the rain forever.

The sound of Tulip's hooves drew close and stopped.

According to his address, Mark Rudolph had done quite well for himself. He lived all the way in Mt. Paran-Northside, an affluent neighborhood with ten-thousand-square-foot mansions and home prices in the millions. If things had stayed the same since I left, that neighborhood was protected better than the White House. They hired off-duty PAD officers to patrol it and had their own private security force manning the perimeter wall and towers. Trying to get to the northern edge of Buckhead from here and then gain entry in this deluge was all but impossible.

I had to go home and try tomorrow.

At least I had a lead. My first real lead.

I opened my eyes. A fully human Derek stood right in front

of me. His eyes were aglow, and he looked at me as if I were the thing he wanted most in the entire world.

I turned away from him and mounted. "The rain is too heavy. I'm going home."

"Tomorrow then."

"Tomorrow." I gave him my phone number. "Call me if anything serious happens."

As I rode away, he was still standing in the rain, watching me. Then I blinked, and he was gone.

[13]

Marten waved at me from my couch.

I paused with my keys in my hand. I had put up Tulip, walked in, and there she was. If it weren't for her expression, I wouldn't have recognized her. The layer of grime covering her face and hair was gone, revealing a cute seven year old with big eyes and delicate features. Shoulder-length, copper brown hair fell in soft ringlets around her adorable tan face. But her eyes were exactly the same, a light golden hazel full of mischief.

How did people keep finding me? I spent all this time and money making a secret hideout and literally everyone I've met in the last two days now knew where it was.

Marten grinned at me. "I found you."

"I see that. Where is Sophia?"

Marten giggled.

"You didn't lead her into quicksand and leave her trapped somewhere, did you?"

She shook her head. "She had homework. I executed an evasive maneuver."

Right. How in the world had she snuck out past a

shapeshifter? They could hear a fly buzz two hundred yards away. "How did you know where I live?"

"I'm smart."

She was not going to answer. As soon as the magic came back, I'd scan her.

I shut the door. It was raining cats and dogs, and by now Sophia was probably going out of her mind.

I pulled off my boots and took my dripping self to the kitchen. Here's hoping Barabas still had the same number.

Sophia picked up on the first ring. "Gilliam residence. How may I help you?"

"Have you misplaced a small child?"

"Ms. Ryder, I'm so, so sorry. I left her playing video games for twenty minutes and she was gone. I tried to track her, but the rain is too heavy."

"So she bolted just before the rain started?"

"Yes."

It would take at least thirty minutes for a normal human child to get to my house from Kate and Curran's "gated community." Marten's hair was dry.

"I'll come and get her right away," Sophia promised.

"Don't worry about it. It's flooding, so you can get her when the rain stops."

"Thank you."

I gave her directions and hung up.

Marten slunk into the kitchen and climbed onto a chair. "I saw a boy here."

Don't tell me. "What did he look like?"

"He was pretty. He had dark hair and big grey eyes."

Conlan.

"Was he in the house or outside of it?"

"Outside."

Oh good. The rain would've washed away his scent trail by now. "Did you talk to the pretty boy?"

Marten nodded. "Yes."

"What did he say?"

"He said to tell you that Grandma called the house."

What did that mean? "Was there anything else?"

"That was it."

There had to be more to it. Erra called to talk to Kate as often as I did, usually through the fire, because phones rarely worked for her. Conlan must've decided Marten wasn't completely trustworthy. I was somehow supposed to infer some deeper meaning from "Grandma called."

Marten pulled her knees up to her chest on the chair. "Can I stay with you until the rain stops?"

"Of course. Are you hungry?"

She nodded.

My phone rang. Probably Barabas or Christopher.

"Hold that thought." I picked it up.

"You haven't spoken to your grandmother in six days," my uncle said.

How did Hugh get my number? He wasn't even in the same state. "Does everybody know where I live?"

"Everybody who cares about your safety. Do you know how I know that it's been six days? Ask me."

Oy. "How do you know?"

"I'm so glad you asked. Your grandmother mentioned it to me five times in the last forty-eight hours. She called me twice through the fire and three times on the phone. Hold on a second. PUT DOWN THAT COW!"

I held the phone away from my ear.

"Sorry about that."

"How did she call you? Phones don't work for her."

"Apparently, someone dials the number for her, and she stands across the room and screams at it. Your grandmother has no trouble making herself heard. Boy! Yes, I'm talking to you. What did I say?"

I shook my head trying to get the ringing to stop. The two of them could roar loud enough to be heard all the way across a battlefield. I've heard them do it.

"You seem pretty busy, Uncle."

"Call your grandmother. She's worried about you, and she'll keep calling me until she hears from you. Otherwise, I'll be forced to come to Atlanta in person to verify that your arms and legs are still attached, and you have not lost the ability to speak. And we both know how much I enjoy visiting Atlanta."

Oh gods. "That won't be necessary. I'll call her as soon as the magic is up."

"Are you doing okay? Do you need anything?"

"I'm fine."

"If you do need anything, you tell me. If you need backup, you tell me. I'll come down and smash some heads for you."

Aww. "Thank you."

"Gotta go. OR WHAT? I WILL SHOW YOU WHAT. YOU'RE ABOUT TO FIND OUT, AND YOU WILL TELL YOUR MOTHER THAT YOU BROUGHT THIS ON YOURSELF."

I hung up.

"Was that your daddy?" Marten asked.

"No, that was my uncle. Cu... My dad doesn't yell. He mostly roars."

"My daddy is nice."

I thought she was an orphan.

She smiled. "He brings me treats and presents. But he can't be with me right now."

What kind of father let his daughter live on the street? I got this really sick feeling. "What does he do when he sees you?"

"He tells me stories, and he does magic tricks."

"Does he ever touch you anywhere?"

Marten scrunched her face at me. "He gives me hugs. He's not a creep."

216

Creep was street slang for child molester. For a seven year old, Marten was really sharp.

"What happened to your mommy?"

"I killed her," Marten said. "When I was born."

"Would you like a hug?" I held out my arms. "It's okay if you don't."

"I want a hug." She slid off the chair and hugged me.

I patted her hair. "You didn't kill her. Sometimes things like that just happen."

She snuggled closer.

"Let me make another phone call and we'll cook dinner."

Marten gave my kitchen a suspicious look. "I looked in your fridge and there was nothing there."

"I have a secret fridge."

Her eyes lit up.

I picked up the phone. It was half an hour before five. I bet that Stella was still in the office, and I was right.

"I thought you were coming by. What happened?"

"A hodag."

"In Atlanta? Are you shitting me?"

"Nope. Big one too."

"Do you need me to bring you some lemons?"

"No, I'm good. Could you check on a name for me?"

She sighed. "What am I, your secretary?"

"I'll owe you one."

"Fine, fine. What's the name?"

"Darren Argent."

"Sounds odd enough. At least it's not John Smith. Who is he?"

"Someone I ran into."

"Okay. I'll check it out."

I said thank you and hung up.

Marten jumped up and down. "Secret fridge?"

"Secret fridge."

The rain stopped at about nine, and fifteen minutes till ten someone knocked on my door and then rang the bell.

Marten looked up from her spot on the divan. She had eaten an entire steak by herself and two helpings of roasted potatoes. I still couldn't figure out where it all went. Afterward she settled on the plush cushions. I gave her a book with illustrations of dinosaurs, which didn't seem to hold her interest. Next was a book about cats, then dogs, and finally we settled on the Encyclopedia of the Ancient World. It had tons of pictures, and she sank right into it.

"I don't want to go. I want to stay in your secret garden house."

"It's not safe for you here."

Marten flopped on her back and put the book on her face.

"I still see you," I told her.

"I like you better," she said.

"I like you, too. When things calm down, you can come and stay with me."

She lifted the book and gave me a squinty stare. "You promise?"

"I promise."

The doorbell rang again.

"Come on," I told her.

She sighed and crawled off the couch, slow enough to make a sloth look like a sprinter. I followed. With great hesitation, Marten meandered down the path heading to the door. One of my ornate metal spheres waited on a narrow pedestal to the right of the path. She reached for it in passing.

"Don't," I warned her.

"Why?"

"It's dangerous."

She sighed.

"You know this is a secret place," I told her on the way to the front door. "Don't tell anyone about it."

She gave me the side-eye. "I'm not a dummy."

I opened the door to Sophia dressed in pink bike shorts and a matching pink tank top. Her pale hair was damp, her glasses foggy. I didn't see a vehicle, so she probably ran here on foot. There were times when being a shapeshifter came in handy.

"Once again, I'm dreadfully sorry."

"Once again, don't worry about it. How are the two of you going to get back?"

"My other father is coming to pick us up. Can we wait here? He shouldn't be long."

"Of course."

Sophia came in, demurely sat down in a kitchen chair, and took in my kitchen. Clearly, certain calculations were taking place in her head. I had paid with gold, which didn't line up with my shabby house.

I waited. She just sat there with a small smile on her face, offering no information and waiting for me to say something. Pure Barabas.

I set the tea to boil and set out three teacups. "I'm curious about something. What do you have against Ascanio Ferara? You had a strong reaction when I said his name."

Sophia flushed. Embarrassment or crush?

"I didn't realize. Thank you for making me aware of it. I'll make a better effort to hide my disgust in the future."

She was the most serious kid I'd ever met. "But why the disgust?"

"Ascanio Ferara is the devil," Sophia announced. "One day he'll get what's coming to him, and I hope to be there."

A shadow swooped down on my lawn. I caught a glimpse of crazily large red wings, just before they vanished, and a tall man strode to my front door. Marten sat up and smiled.

A careful knock sounded. I opened the door. Christopher

Steed stood outside. He wore a light grey suit that fit him like a glove. Tall, pale, with platinum blond hair, he had one of those refined faces that looked elegant no matter his expression. His sharp eyes locked on me.

You don't know me. We've never met.

He stared at me for five long seconds. "We lost your child. My apologies."

"Marten is resourceful."

"I suspect she's much more than that."

That made two of us. "Please come in."

I added another cup to the table. Christopher took the chair next to Marten. She gave him an angelic smile.

"We were talking about Sophia's disdain for Mr. Ferara."

"Ah." Christopher allowed himself a small smile. "By all means, continue."

"It's like this," Sophia said, as I poured tea into the cups. "I have a group of friends."

I put a jar of honey in front of Christopher and set a small bottle of cream next to it.

"We are a very capable group."

Christopher hid a smile and added honey to Marten's tea. She gazed at him like he was the most wonderful person in the world.

"Most of my friends live in the same neighborhood, but one of them, Bea, lives with the Pack, in a Clan House."

Baby B, Raphael and Andrea's daughter.

"Her parents are what you might call overprotective."

Andrea and Raphael? Overprotective? Raphael gave Baby B a dagger for her second birthday and then laughed when she tried to stab him with it.

"When Bea doesn't return to her Clan House on time or when she forgets to tell them where she's going, they send Ascanio to fetch her. And since we're usually together, he takes it upon himself to fetch us as well."

"For which your parents are deeply grateful," Christopher said.

"That's beside the point, Father. The point is, he isn't my babysitter, or Conlan's, or Mahon's and Ricardo's. He isn't in a position of authority over me. He simply decided to be insufferable."

"The tea is exquisite," Christopher said.

"I'm glad you like it," I told him.

Sophia took a sip. Marten got a hold of the honey jar and was busily spooning honey into her cup. At this rate, she'd end up with honey tea syrup.

"You'll have to drink some of the tea to make space," I told her.

"For example," Sophia said. "One time we went to play in the sewers."

Marten stopped with her spoon in midair. "The Impala Worm is in the sewer."

"We were being very quiet. It was perfectly safe until Ascanio found us and yelled at us, and of course, the Impala Worm showed up. He didn't have to fight it for half an hour, and he didn't have to almost drown. He created this situation and then chose to be dramatic about it."

I stared at her. "How old were you?"

"Nine."

Conlan would have been six. Mahon and Ricardo would have been five. Oh my gods.

"Then there was another time we wanted to go to Savannah for the pirate festival. We would have been back by morning. And all of us could swim. The boat was sinking very slowly, so there was no reason to panic."

"I feel like you skipped a part. How did you get on a boat?" I asked.

"We took a ley line to Savannah, but it doesn't go straight to the city."

Ley lines were persistent magic currents. They lasted even during tech, although they lost a lot of their speed. The ley line was like a train track with a continuous train running at high speed.

To travel on a ley line you had to have some kind of platform, a raft of metal, plastic, or wood. I'd ridden ley lines on old doors and one time in a very large Styrofoam cooler. Anything worked as long as it separated you from the current. The magic of ley lines sheared anything living, and walking into one would leave you without your legs. That's why the government put up billboards with graphic pictures of bodies cut into pieces by ley points.

The points were another fun ley line feature. The current wasn't continuous. It had breaks called ley points, and when you reached one, the current ended abruptly and jettisoned you out. You had no choice about it.

"I know that ley point," I said. "It dumps you in a salt marsh."

Which was why most people shipped goods from Atlanta to Savannah by cart or car. The ley line that led from Savannah to Atlanta was just fine, but that was the post-Shift world for you.

"We didn't know that bit," Sophia said.

"So, it dumped you in the middle of the marsh. Was it dark?"

"There was some light."

"Was it moonlight?"

"Possibly."

Christopher smiled into his tea.

"We were fine until the tide started coming in."

I stared at her.

She shrugged. "There were no signs telling us where to go and the scent trails were confusing. We found a boat. It was leaking only a little bit, so we were completely fine. It was fun. We were going to paddle to the coast. Except Ascanio showed up and made us go back."

"Then there was the minotaur," Christopher said quietly.

Sophia sighed.

"I don't understand how the kids keep escaping," I said. "Was nobody watching them?"

"Shapeshifter children come with unique challenges," Christopher said. "A certain degree of independence is highly encouraged."

It made sense to some degree. An average shapeshifter toddler was stronger and faster than most human adults, and their regeneration kept them relatively intact. But they were still kids.

"Unfortunately," Christopher continued, "when these six get together, they seem to develop an unshakeable confidence in their own abilities to handle things regardless of the reality of the situation."

Sophia glanced at him. "Five, Father. JJ is too young. We don't always invite him."

JJ? "Tell me about the minotaur."

"It wasn't an actual minotaur, which was a huge letdown," Sophia volunteered.

"No, it was worse," her father said. "Most minotaurs are calm until they're provoked. This was a buffalo shapeshifter gone loup. He'd taken off into the North Forest after massacring his entire family. The Pack's herd leader was away at the time, and the decision was made to wait until Eduardo returned to avoid unnecessary loss of life."

Dad would have gone in there by himself and killed it. I opened my mouth to ask why he didn't and caught myself. Oops. Eh... "Why didn't the Beast Lord take care of it?"

"His predecessor would have. However, Shrapshire is not that hands-on. The Pack has developed procedures and protocols to handle a variety of situations, like this one, and he doesn't get involved until all other avenues have been exhausted."

Interesting. That was always the problem with the Pack and

Dad. He'd made the Pack, or rather it accreted around him, and he was the answer to all their problems. It wore him down. There were days when all he did was run around putting out Pack fires. It looked like Jim had installed a structure that had been missing. And this type of incident could get ugly fast. If the wolves or the cats killed a bovine shapeshifter, even one gone loup, it could open a big can of worms.

"One of my friends wanted to hunt the minotaur," Sophia said.

I choked on my tea. I knew exactly which friend that was.

"When was this?"

"A year ago."

Damn it, Conlan. "Sophia, how old were you? You should have known better."

"It was perfectly safe."

Clearly, that was her battle cry. Everything was on fire, and sharks and dragons were circling us, but it was perfectly safe. "How?"

"We hid in the brambles, the black kind with red thorns. He was circling around the bramble bushes, but he couldn't get to us, because he was too big. He would have gotten bored and gone away, but Ascanio showed up. Again."

I put my hands over my face.

"As I have pointed out before," Christopher said, "this was less about hunting a minotaur and more about hiding from a minotaur, trapped, with no escape route, while your parents frantically searched the entire city for you since the lot of you left a note that said, 'Gone on a monster hunt.'"

"Did he kill the loup?" I asked.

"Yes," Christopher said. "Eventually. Ascanio suffered a broken femur in his left leg, two broken ribs, and a collapsed lung, but he did kill the loup. My guess is, he thought the children would die if he failed."

"We helped! Towards the end. Well, Conlan helped the

most." Sophia grit her teeth. "Do you know what he did after? He cursed at us. An adult man. And then, when I told him that we could run away from him because of his broken leg and he should be nicer, he put us in loup manacles."

"He what?"

"He's part of the Pack's loup rapid response unit. He always has loup manacles in his SUV," Christopher said. "He manacled the children to one another and led them out of the woods like that."

Sophia flushed. "Everybody saw. Everybody. I'll never forgive him. He'll get what's coming to him."

Oh my gods. He had to walk them out on a broken leg. And the ribs. Every breath would be fire.

"And now you know why my daughter isn't a fan of the man who constantly saves her and her friends from themselves."

Sophia opened her mouth.

Christopher looked at her. "It's time for you to return home. Be careful, the roads are muddy."

"Yes, Father." Sophia rose. "Thank you for the tea. And for giving me another chance with Marten. I promise there won't be any more escapes."

"You're welcome."

She left.

"Ms. Ryder, if I could offer a word of advice?"

"Of course."

"The situation in the Pack is delicate. Jim Shrapshire, the current Beast Lord, wants to retire. Leading the Pack is an exhausting, high-pressure position, and he gets little thanks but shoulders all the blame. He's missing the childhood of his children and it's wearing on him. He will, however, continue until a worthy successor presents themselves. Such a successor must have support from the majority of the clans. Ascanio Ferara is sizing up the Beast Lord's throne, and he thinks it will fit him. He may be right, but he has a long way to go. He has the brains, money, and the drive, but he lacks experience and the sheer physicality required for the role."

"He took on a loup buffalo."

"He's a superb fighter. The question is, can he inspire people to follow him? Can he walk onto a battlefield and lead the charge? That remains to be seen. Whatever you and he are involved in, and I'm not insinuating anything by that remark, keep in mind that if you put yourself in the path of his ambition, he will bulldoze over you."

"Thank you."

He turned to Marten. "Ready?"

She gazed at him, her face serene. "Are we going to fly?"

"We are. The only question is, how high would you like to go?"

"Wait." I ran to the back of the house and came back with a thick sweatshirt and pulled it over Marten. It swallowed her. "It will be cold up there."

Marten hugged me and held out her arms to Christopher. He picked her up and carried her out the front door. For a moment they stood poised in the moonlight. Then two enormous blood-red wings burst from Christopher's back, beat once, and he streaked into the sky, taking Marten with him. The theophage who had devoured Deimos, the Greek god of terror, was flying away with the little girl I cared about, and I was totally okay with that.

A pair of ruby eyes caught the light in the shadows across the street. A bouda. Ascanio must have left someone to watch my house, and they had just given themselves away. Sloppy. Or they wanted me to know I was being watched.

My phone rang. Looked like my night wasn't over yet.

I went inside and picked it up.

"I found Darren Argent." All humor was gone from Stella's voice.

"I have a feeling I'm not going to like this."

"Do you know what Ice Fury is?"

"The largest shapeshifter pack in the United States. They're based in Alaska, half of them have gone wild, and they don't like outsiders."

"Darren Argent is the beta of Ice Fury."

Cold washed over me. I remembered where I had heard the name.

There was no way. It couldn't be Derek.

"There are more warnings on his file than I have ever seen. This guy is death on legs."

"Is there a description?" Maybe he just used the name.

"Male, white, early thirties, dark hair. He's kind of hard to misidentify. He's got scars all over his face."

The world stood on its hands and kicked me in the face.

"You said you ran into him." Urgency vibrated in Stella's voice. "Tell me he isn't in Atlanta right now. Because if he is, the Knight-Protector has to know. I can't know this and not tell him."

Of course. A prominent member of the largest shapeshifter pack entered Atlanta's Pack territory and didn't announce himself. Nick would expect a shapeshifter war.

"Go ahead and tell him."

"I already did."

"Then why the hell did you ask me?"

"I wanted to know what you would say."

"Stella!"

"Feldman wasn't happy. He wants you to come in."

"Let him know I'll be there first thing in the morning."

"No, he wants you to come in right now."

Right now wouldn't be happening. I had to figure out how to handle this situation, and I was so exhausted, I could barely stand. "I'll be there in the morning. Tell him that it's not a shapeshifter war."

Stella exhaled into the phone. "Aurelia..."

"In the morning. I have to go."

I hung up.

A few years ago, a family of wererats joined the New Shinar, husband, wife, and their two children. They were originally from California but had had a falling out with the rest of their extended family and had gone up to Alaska to join Ice Fury. Things didn't work out, and once the husband's father died, they packed up and moved back south to take care of the husband's mother.

At the time, Erra had wanted as much information about Ice Fury as she could get, and the family spent several days telling us about their former pack. Some of it we already knew, a lot of it we didn't.

Ice Fury consisted mostly of wolves and bears. At least one-third of the pack had gone wild, meaning they spent more time in fur than in human skin. Atlanta's Pack was forced to interact with human society. Ice Fury made sure they didn't have to.

About ten years ago, Mihail Kamenov, an enormous Kodiak from Siberia, took over as Ice Fury Alpha. He favored a hands-off style of leadership. From what the rats had said, he spent most of his time in the woods, coming out only when there was a problem that needed to be crushed with his giant paw. Ice Fury was run by a series of betas. The latest beta and the one who'd lasted the longest was Darren Argent.

The wererats couldn't really tell us what was so special about Darren, but when they described him, their eyes glazed over. He had some sort of pull, some kind of magnetic thing about him that other shapeshifters, wolves especially, instantly recognized. Shapeshifters flocked to him. According to the father of the family, Darren could have taken the pack away from Mihail whenever he felt like it, and Ice Fury would back him up.

At the time, I'd guessed that Darren was a First. The legend said that during prehistoric times some humans made bargains with animal deities, and that's how the first shapeshifters came about. Descendants of those bloodlines were very rare, even during the time of the Old Shinar. I only knew of one—Curran.

The Firsts were capable of remarkable things. Other shapeshifters sensed them somehow and would follow them through fire.

Derek wasn't a First. Someone would have recognized it by now. It wasn't a thing one could hide. His dad had gone loup, and the Firsts had the highest loup resistance. According to Erra, they were practically loup-proof. And if his mother had been a First, she would have squashed his dad like a bug the first time he raised his hand to her. Whatever that magnetic thing was, the old Derek didn't have it.

Becoming a beta of anything was a hundred-and-eighty-degree turn for him. Derek hadn't just shown zero interest in climbing the shapeshifter leadership ladder, he actively avoided it. Desandra had offered him the beta position repeatedly and he'd declined every time. So, he left Atlanta for no apparent reason, went up to Alaska, and became the de facto ruler of Ice Fury. Why?

I could just imagine Curran's reaction to it. *Why did you have to go across the country to be a beta there? What's wrong with the Pack I built? Is it not to your liking? What was so bad about it that you had to move to a frozen hellhole and run around the woods with a bunch of crazy people who don't want to be people anymore?*

I dragged my hand across my face. I would not want to be there for that conversation.

When Curran retired from being Beast Lord, a group of people from his immediate circle separated with him. Like Curran, they enjoyed immunity. They had a right to be in the Pack's territory without being subject to Jim's authority.

Derek was one of those people. But now he was also the beta of a rival pack.

If he truly was the beta of Ice Fury, his presence in Atlanta was a catastrophe. Shapeshifters, especially high-ranking shapeshifters, didn't just enter other packs' territory. There were protocols in place, and Derek hadn't followed any of them, or Ascanio wouldn't be chasing him all around the city.

It looked bad. It looked like Derek had snuck into the city to assess the Atlanta Pack for a possible attack. Although Ice Fury was far away, rival shapeshifter packs were known to stage raids. On the surface the idea was absurd because of the distances involved, but shapeshifters were a paranoid lot.

The very act of him entering Atlanta could be taken as a declaration of war. And yet the Pack probably couldn't do much to him personally because of his immunity. This was a diplomatic nightmare.

I stared at the wall, trying to sort through this tangled mess in my head. Now would be the perfect moment for some wise wizard or a messenger of some god to pop in and explain it all to me.

Derek was in Atlanta illegally, and Ascanio was chasing him all around the city. Most likely, Ascanio hadn't reported it to anyone because, according to Derek, he had a mysterious score to settle.

Ascanio always had an angle, and for the life of me, I couldn't figure out what it was. How did this benefit him? Was he planning to subdue Derek and bring him in, pulling him out like a rabbit from a hat? *Look at who I found!*

He probably had no idea Derek was Darren Argent.

It would backfire. Oh dear gods, it would so backfire. If Ascanio somehow succeeded, he would assault and drag a foreign beta before the Beast Lord. If he failed and got hurt, a foreign beta would have injured the beta of Clan Bouda.

The two of them were idiots. What were they even doing? They hadn't seen each other in years. They were two grown men. There had to be more to this than some teenage feud. I felt like I was looking at a heap of puzzle pieces with all of the corners missing.

And now Nick knew. Nick, who was in love with Desandra and who was the stepfather to her two boys. In a shapeshifter war, Desandra would be on the front lines, and unless the Order gave him their blessing, Nick wouldn't be able to fight beside her. He would react. I had no idea how, but it would be bad. Really, really bad.

I had to contain Nick. I'd bought myself a little bit of time, but I couldn't dodge him forever.

If Curran were still the Beast Lord, Derek would have been given about six hours of freedom, and then he would get a formal invitation. Something along the lines of, "We're delighted that the beta of Ice Fury has graced us with his presence and anxiously await his arrival at the Keep. We're dying to meet him face to face." It would have been delivered by Clan Rat, and knowing them, it would just magically appear on Derek's pillow while he took a shower.

Where were the rats? Clan Rat handled the Pack's security. I hadn't seen a single rat operative in the city. They were very good, so I might not have noticed them, but still, they would keep an eye on Ascanio.

What in the bloody hell was going on with Atlanta's Pack?

Argh. I didn't have time for any of this. I needed to get to Mark Rudolph and squeeze the information out of him before any more people got murdered or the ma'avirim made their next move.

My head was killing me. I desperately needed rest. Either I went to bed now or my body would shut me down and I'd fall asleep right here, on the floor.

Maybe I would get a flash of brilliance in the morning.

I locked my doors, both of them, and dragged myself to bed.

[14]

The morning brought a fresh magic wave, and a strong one too. The lotuses in the basin bloomed in seconds, and now their petals glowed gently above the water.

I brewed a fresh pot of tea and built a fire in the cauldron. The flames licked the dry wood, it caught, and I tossed a handful of herbs into the fire. They ignited in a flash, turning the flames blood-red. Magic splayed from the cauldron. I grasped it and reached through it to my grandmother.

Her voice came through first.

"Seven days! How very modern of you."

The flames snapped into the image of my grandmother. Tall and broad-shouldered, in real life she towered over me. Like Kate, she was stunning. Powerful face, beautiful features, bronze skin, and a wealth of black hair streaming down over her shoulders. I'd seen her in armor and in formal gowns, with gold jewelry tracing her brow and neck. Seeing her in a tank top and sweatpants never failed to crack me up.

"Ungrateful child. I see you smirking. Was my worrying funny to you?"

"No, ma'am."

"Ugh." Erra shook her head. "Tell me everything that's happened."

By the time I brought her up to speed, I was on my second cup of tea.

"What a damn mess."

Don't I know it.

"What are you going to do about Feldman?"

"Depends on where his mind is when I meet him this morning. I must contain him at all costs, or he might mobilize the Chapter and start a manhunt to find Derek. Or worse, he might rope the Pack into it."

"That man is good at keeping secrets. Use it."

"I'll do my best."

Erra frowned. "Tell me about this divine beast."

"I have no idea what it is. I have never seen that magic signature before. I've never heard of anyone eating some creature's heart to see the future. There are legends of people eating mystical birds' hearts and gaining magic powers, but nothing that fits."

My grandmother tapped her fingernails on something, thinking. "You said the historian had a chance to flee, but she didn't take it."

"Yes. It looked like she started to but stopped."

"It must have spoken to her."

"Why?"

Erra drained her cup. "An academic like her would be trained to keep an open mind. Something made her more curious than frightened, and as a teacher, she would place great value on communication. If the beast spoke, she would stop and listen to it. She would reason and ask questions."

How did I not see it before? "That makes perfect sense."

The list of creatures that could speak was short. The general rule was if the creature was depicted with a human head, it had the power of speech, provided it reached a high level of magic or the right age. Lamassu was one. The manticore was one, too, although the manticores I'd run across were beast-like and never spoke. Sphinxes. Nagas. Harpies.

"An idiot would have run away and kept running. Sometimes our intelligence is to our detriment." Erra sighed. "There has been a development. If you hear about any incidents related to the Casino and necromancers, try to avoid that area."

"Why?"

Erra hesitated.

"Grandmother?"

"Namtur is in Atlanta."

I choked on my tea. "What is the High Sakkan doing here?"

"Damned if I know. He said he wanted a 'respite.' I gave him a month, and what does that ingrate do with his vacation? He goes to Atlanta and gets himself captured by the necromancers."

Now her frantic attempts to reach me made sense. Namtur was a ticking time bomb. She didn't even trust Hugh enough to tell him about it. Probably because he would've dropped everything and come to drag Namtur out of Atlanta before he caused a massive incident.

"He let the People capture him? How are they still alive?"

"They're alive because he has some kind of scheme."

"That's what I am afraid of." When Namtur schemed, streets ran red with blood. Literally. "I thought we agreed that I would handle Atlanta on my own."

Erra raised her hands. "I didn't send him there! I didn't even know where he was until Ghastek called us two days ago."

Ghastek, the head of the People, now EIN, in Atlanta, was trouble. He was calculating and ruthless. A navigator armed with a single vampire could wipe out a SWAT team in seconds. Ghastek could easily pilot two at a time and had enough navigators under his command to massacre everyone in the city in twenty-four hours. I couldn't afford him as an enemy. Not right now.

"What did Ghastek want?"

"He wanted me to send someone to escort Namtur back. He's worried about Namtur's safety because he is elderly."

I opened my mouth. Nothing came out.

"That was my reaction, too."

"Could he know who Namtur is?"

Erra grimaced. "I doubt it. That old fox can look so decrepit, you'd think he couldn't make it up a flight of stairs."

"Ghastek is a lot of things, but he isn't an idiot. If he has even an inkling of what Namtur is, he wouldn't have detained him."

"I honestly don't think he knows." Erra shook her head. "None of this is your problem. I just wanted to warn you, so if something happens, you don't run headfirst into the Casino and get exposed."

If Namtur started killing the EIN personnel, Kate would get involved. Kate and Ghastek had a complicated relationship. When Grandfather attacked the city to subdue Kate, Ghastek had thrown his lot in with Kate. For a short time, he became her Legatus, the head of the navigators under her banner. When Kate gave up her claim to the city, he had argued against it. I remembered hearing that conversation. He'd actually raised his voice. For some reason, he desperately needed her to remain in power, but she had no interest in ruling anyone or anything. They had had a falling out over it, but Kate considered him a friend. If Namtur caused trouble, she would come to Ghastek's defense.

That was the last thing I needed. "I'll go and get him."

"He can handle himself. He made that mess. He can get himself out of it."

"Grandmother, he is your blood brother. He can't be allowed

to run around unsupervised in the city with the ma'avirim sniffing all over the place, Ghastek plotting gods know what and me trying to hide. I'll go and get him right now. He likes me. He will come with me."

"If you pick him up, you won't be able to get rid of him."

"I'll find him something to do. I love you. I have to go now."

"I love you, too. Be careful."

"Always."

Of all the places in Atlanta, the EIN Casino was my least favorite. Cavernous and devoid of windows, the main floor resembled a luxurious cave decorated in rich purple and gold hues and filled with rows and rows of slot machines. Entering through the main gate put you straight in the middle of it. The slot machines, rigged to work during magic or tech, flashed with bright lights and played jarring music, keeping the patrons awake. The people in front of them stared at the screens with vacant eyes, while waiters glided between them, offering alcohol and caffeinated drinks. There was something infantile about the bright lights, oversaturated colors, and treats delivered on demand, and the chaos of it unraveled you, until you lost yourself to ringing tunes and spinning screens and became one of the anonymous gamblers.

I turned left, where two journeywomen in identical purple blouses and black pencil skirts waited behind a marble counter. The path from sensing an undead to becoming a full-fledged navigator and earning the coveted Master of the Dead title was long and took years. Those who embarked on it became journeymen. Most of them never made it.

I flashed my Order ID. "Please let Mr. Stefanoff know that I'm here to pick up Mr. Sakkan."

When talking to non-Shinar people, Namtur used his title as his last name.

"Please wait," the shorter journeywoman told me.

I parked myself in the lounge area, a soft shadowy spot, tucked away into an alcove and furnished with overstuffed purple couches. Below the floor, underneath the slot machines, the gamblers, and the gaudy carpet, vampire minds glowed like angry smears of foul magic.

Ugh.

They glowed in my mind, evenly spaced, each undead confined to its own stall in the stables under the building, twenty per column. One, two, three…ten… At least six hundred. Probably more, the dots were beginning to blend in the distance. Kate would've known precisely how many. She could also pilot them all at once. I used vampire blood, molded it, and worked with it, but piloting was forever beyond me, and I wouldn't have it any other way. I would not share my mind with one of those things.

A male journeyman in his late teens stopped by me. "The Director will see you now."

I followed him deeper into the bowels of the Casino.

Director. That was something new. I supposed it went well with their new name, the Eastern Institute of Necromancy. Why Eastern? Was there a Western Institute?

In the next few hours, I needed to get Namtur, somehow convince Nick to stand down, do something with Namtur to keep him occupied and out of trouble, and then go see Mark Rudolph. There were too many fires to put out, and if I didn't do it fast enough, Moloch's priests would set the kind of fire I couldn't deal with.

We reached the back wall and walked through a hallway past a velvet rope, into a wide room ending in a spectacular staircase. Ghastek came down the steps, a tall, gaunt figure in a black suit and charcoal dress shirt. He'd been balding as long as I could remember, but the receding hairline only accentuated his high forehead. His features were narrow, and he looked at the world with piercing dark eyes.

Usually Ghastek wore a turtleneck or a Henley, sometimes a sweater. His clothes were simple, but expensive. He dressed like a busy CEO who had too much on his plate to worry about dressing up. Why the suit? It couldn't be for me. I was an anonymous Order knight.

His gaze fastened on me. "Ms. Ryder, I presume."

"Knight Ryder."

He smiled.

"Did I say something funny?"

"Not at all. You're too young to get the reference and it would take too long to explain. What's your relationship to Namtur?"

Direct and to the point. No pleasantries. My disguise was holding. "I don't have one. I was told to escort him to the chapter."

Ghastek studied me. I had made a reasonable effort to look as normal as possible and hid most of myself with my ragged cloak. People in cloaks were a common sight in the city, and he could see my face well enough.

"You're not one of Feldman's regulars."

"I've been recently assigned to the chapter. If you contact the Order, they will confirm my credentials."

Ghastek looked at me for another long moment and said under his breath, "Bring him."

Somewhere in the depths of the Casino a vampire had just spoken in Ghastek's voice.

We waited. Ghastek stared at me. Most people would at least try to pretend to look elsewhere out of politeness. Ghastek openly scrutinized me.

Two journeymen appeared at the top of the stairs. A short elderly man walked between them. He wore a dark brown tunic that was two sizes too big and hung around him like a sheet on a clothesline. Age had stolen his hair and cut wrinkles into his walnut-brown skin, but his eyes, the color of clover honey, were alert and bright.

He saw me. His eyes sparkled, and he straightened up and picked up speed, sandals flashing under the hem of the tunic. The journeymen struggled to keep up. Ghastek turned to look at him, taking his eyes off me for a second, and I put two fingers on my lips and touched the outer corner of my right eye in a single quick motion. *You do not know me.*

A small smile flickered on Namtur's lips and vanished. He was the one who'd taught me the language of thieves.

Ghastek turned back to me. I presented him with a blank, almost bored expression. Just a knight preparing to escort a senior citizen. Nothing to see here.

Namtur stopped about two feet away and gave Ghastek a withering look. "What is it now? Are you offering me this pretty child? What is an old man like me supposed to do with her?"

Ghastek looked offended. "A knight has come to escort you to the Order. I didn't realize Eahrratim and the Order had such close ties."

Using my grandmother's full name wouldn't score him any brownie points.

Namtur stuck his chin in the air. "The things you don't know or realize are an ocean, and your mind is a tiny boat upon its waves."

Ancient disses were the best.

"Delightful," Ghastek said dryly.

I needed to move this along. "Do I need to sign anything?"

A group of people came around the corner, from my left, led by a woman in a light green dress that did wonders for her already spectacular figure. Her long red hair dripped on her shoulders. Rowena, one of the Masters of the Dead, the second most powerful necromancer in Atlanta. She had to be in her fifties, and she was still gorgeous. I always suspected that she and Ghastek were an item, but nobody could ever prove it.

The three men behind her wore identical outfits: dark pants, dark tunics, and heavy ceremonial cloaks, artfully draped over their shoulders. The leading man, older, with white hair and bronze skin, wore a cloak the color of jade, and the two younger men trailing him had cloaks the color of turquoise. People of the Sun.

There goes the neighborhood...

Among the Aztec cults, the People of the Sun were the strongest. Even before the Shift, twelve million Mexicans spoke the Aztec language. After magic had flooded the world, the Aztec mythology and religion came back full force. Some of it was good and some of it was horrifying.

The People of the Sun worshiped Huitzilopochtli, the god of war, sun, and sacrifice, and they controlled random spots all over the Southwest. Anyone could join. They didn't discriminate by national origin, gender, sexual orientation, or magical abilities, as long as you prayed to their god and no other.

So far, the People of the Sun stayed away from mass human sacrifice, probably because they were powerful enough without it. We had run up against them during our time in LA, and they had been one of the factors that prompted our move to San Diego.

Rowena's group headed straight for us.

This was planned. Ghastek meant for us to see each other. It couldn't be for me, so it had to be for Namtur.

Rowena moved slightly to the side, and I saw the older man's face. Tizoc. One of the tecuhtli, the lords, old, powerful, dangerous as hell. His real name was Luke O'Sullivan. Most of his family still lived in Boston, and he occasionally made trips up there for Thanksgiving. The two guys behind him were likely Jaguar warriors, elite fighters who served as tecuhtli personal bodyguards.

I turned away, so my hood blocked my face. Tizoc and Namtur had tried to negotiate before, and it was hate at first sight. Could this get any worse?

The two old men saw each other. For an instant, nobody moved.

Tizoc recovered first. "Namtur, you geriatric desert snake. I thought I smelled something foul, and there you are."

Namtur ignored him. "We shall leave now."

All around us, the smears of undead magic moved closer. There were six vampires right above, ready to fall through the ceiling, and more were coming. Ghastek expected a confrontation. He'd arranged it and now he was preparing to contain it.

"Running?" Tizoc mocked.

Namtur made no indication that he'd heard him. The ultimate insult—he'd decided that Tizoc was so insignificant, he was beneath notice.

"Knight woman, I do not have time to stand around."

"Looks like we'll be going now," I said to Ghastek.

Tizoc flicked his fingers and the two guards moved to block the exit.

"Who is the errand girl? The best your bitch queen could send for you, a child in rags?" Tizoc reached for me.

Namtur moved so fast, he blurred. His hand knocked Tizoc's fingers away. "You dare?"

Turquoise mist boiled out of Tizoc, like two glowing wings. His eyes shone with green.

I had to stop this, or people would die.

I put my hand on Namtur's shoulder and moved so Tizoc could see my face. He jerked as if shocked with a live wire. Behind him, his bodyguards unsheathed their swords in unison.

"We should go, Great Uncle," I said softly in the old language. *"We aren't among friends."*

Namtur patted my hand solemnly and turned toward the exit. The guards stepped aside, giving us a lot of room. We walked between them and kept going, through the Casino, out the doors, across the plaza. Two vampires covered in lime green sunblock discreetly followed us. I turned and looked at them to make sure the navigator knew they had been seen.

"Great Uncle," I murmured. "How could you ruin it? You were supposed to not know me."

He harrumphed. "Filthy dog. His hands are unworthy. If he'd sullied you with his bloodstained fingers, I'd have cut them off."

Bloodstained? Pot, kettle. "Thank you for caring, Great Uncle. What were you doing in the Casino?"

"I've heard that the thin man is looking to make an alliance. I wanted to know to whom he was offering his pitiful wares."

He'd made Ghastek sound like some peddler on the street.

"And now we know," Namtur said.

"Did he mention why he wanted an alliance?"

"No, but he asked many questions about the Kingdom."

Interesting.

We reached the side lot where I'd left Tulip and Lady, the horse I'd rented this morning. The vampires halted at the curb.

Namtur spun around and waved at them. "Shoo! Go home, you unnatural creatures!"

The vampires remained where they were. "We will escort you to the chapter."

"That won't be necessary," I told them. "Mr. Sakkan is in the Order's custody. I will consider any further interference from the Institute as a sign of aggression. This is your official warning."

The vampires froze as the two navigators piloting them waited for orders. A moment passed. The undead turned and loped back toward the Casino in their odd, disjointed gait.

Namtur jumped and landed in Lady's saddle. The hired horse startled. "Are we going home now?"

"No, Great Uncle. We're going to the Order of Merciful Aid."

Namtur nodded. "I see. And why would we do that?"

"Two reasons. First, your former host will have us followed. I'm posing as a knight, so I'll need to take you where the knights are."

"And the second?"

"I have to convince a paranoid man prone to spree-killing and snap judgements that someone isn't a threat."

"He's right to be paranoid. This is a city of fools, incompetents, and madmen. I haven't felt this young in centuries."

"And if things don't go well, you'll probably get to kill a great many of them."

"You and your enticing promises. It's been eight months since I wet my blades. I will kill something before my respite ends."

Not if I could help it.

STELLA PONDERED NAMTUR'S FACE. "I DON'T SEE THE resemblance."

"'Great Uncle' is an honorary title." Explaining that he was my near-immortal grandmother's sworn blood brother would only complicate things.

Namtur gave Stella his best smile. His eyes crinkled into tiny slits and he looked as sweet as could be. "I won't be any trouble."

Stella got up. "Please sit down. Would you like some tea?"

Namtur smiled even wider and took his time to waddle to the seat and gingerly lower himself into it. "Oh no, no. You're very busy, and I don't want to be a bother."

I really wanted to clap in appreciation of his fine performance, but that would ruin things.

"It's no trouble; I was going to make a cup for myself anyway."

She reached into her desk and took out a small flag made out of a rag tied to a chopstick and a tiny pitcher. She thrust the flag at me.

I took it. "What's this?"

"That's your war banner. He has been in his office with his butt glued to his chair since this morning. He canceled all his meetings. Nobody can go in. He's waiting for you. Wave your banner."

I waved the banner. "Why?"

Stella picked up the small pitcher. "I'm going to sprinkle milk on it like the Mongols did before battle. That's all I can do to help."

"That's so nice," Namtur said. "You're such a thoughtful friend."

I held the war banner out, and Stella sprinkled some milk on it. Then I turned around and marched to Nick Feldman's office.

I knocked on the door.

"Come in."

I entered and shut the door behind me.

Nick Feldman looked like a human thundercloud.

I walked to his desk and sat in the chair.

He picked up a small glass tube from his desk. White powder floated inside it. Nick snapped it in half and tossed the powder on the floor. Orange lines ignited in the floorboards, forming a complex spell, and vanished. He'd sealed the room.

Seals like this came in several varieties. Some blocked sound, others blocked sight, a third type did both. This one was a trap. It had sealed us inside the room, blocking all sight, sound, and magic, and I would have to break it to get out.

Nick Feldman was going to kill me.

I didn't want to hurt him. He was always kind to me. Once Nick started, he wouldn't stop. I would have to cripple him.

He looked at Stella's war banner. I put it on his desk and sat back.

"Ms. Ryder, do you know what happens when a foreign shapeshifter enters Pack territory?"

He wasn't just calm. He'd turned into an icicle.

"They must present themselves to the Beast Lord in twenty-four hours."

Nick fixed me with his stare. His eyes were filled with lead. "Do you know what happens if the visitor fails to observe the proprieties?"

"The Pack finds them and brings them in?"

"Yes. They are not always gentle about it."

I waited. He was going somewhere with this.

"An average shapeshifter is at least three times stronger than the average human and twice as fast. Throw in the claws, the fangs, the accelerated healing, the hunting instinct, and what you have is an overpowered apex predator, armed with the intelligence of a human and the strength of a monster."

None of this seemed to require a response on my part. If this was anyone else, I'd ask if I should be taking notes or if this was going to be on the final. But the main objective here was to keep him calm.

"Shapeshifters are insular, distrustful of outsiders, and deeply paranoid."

Pot, kettle.

"Their humanity is often hanging by a thread," Nick continued. "It takes very little prompting for that thread to snap. When they encounter a foreign shapeshifter in their territory and are met with resistance, they assume that that shapeshifter is up to no good. They will attempt to apprehend this invader. They may get excited and even kill them. When that happens, the pack this visitor belongs to retaliates. This is the point where rational thought and logic goes out the window and we have a shapeshifter war."

He was working up to something. There was an explosion coming, I could feel it.

Nick crossed his arms. "What we have here, right now, is a foreign shapeshifter who happens to be the beta of the largest shapeshifter pack in North America. His mere presence in the Pack's territory is an insult. If they find out he's here and he escapes, the Pack loses face, and they will retaliate. If they apprehend him and he's injured, Ice Fury will retaliate. Either way, this is a declaration of war. We are watching the beginning of a massacre. And that massacre won't be fought in Alaska; it will be fought here, in this city."

He pointed to the window.

"On those streets. Right out there."

I sat very still. This conversation was like crossing an iced-over lake. One wrong step and I'd plunge into frigid water.

"Hundreds of shapeshifters will die. Thousands of innocent bystanders will be murdered. These are not some hypothetical statistics. This country has seen shapeshifter wars before. We know in gruesome detail what kind of casualties result from it. And those were small packs. Can you even imagine the scale of the slaughter when the two largest packs rip into each other?"

I opened my mouth to answer.

"I think you can," he said.

The ice under my feet just cracked.

"I think you're counting on it. To the people you serve, humans have no more value than mosquitoes."

He picked up a folder from the corner of his desk and dropped it in front of me. It fell open. Pictures fanned out over the desk. A photograph of Erra on a horse, my uncle on her left and me on her right. Another image, me in a royal gown of Shinar, receiving a group of businesspeople, half of them glaring, the other half awkwardly trying to bow, on the sunlit terrace of Dosari, Erra's California palace. The pale green gown hugged my body. My hair, caught by a golden circlet, cascaded down in a waterfall of golden waves. Gold bracelets, identifying me as the Heir, glinted on my wrists. A third image, a painting, so lifelike it was almost a photograph—me in blood armor and on a horse, splattered with gore and screaming.

Great. Fantastic. He'd given me the case way too easily. I knew he would dig into my background, but I'd hoped all the roadblocks I had set up in the last few months would delay him long enough for me to stop the ma'avirim.

Damn this fucking face.

"I have a theory." Nick's voice cut like a knife. "Would you like to hear it, Dananu?"

"Do I have a choice?"

"No. There are four and a half thousand miles separating Atlanta's Pack and Ice Fury. So, I asked myself, what would the beta of Ice Fury, the guy who runs things on a day-to-day basis, be doing in Atlanta? They call him the wolf who rules in all but name. The Silver Wolf, the guy who managed to wrangle over five thousand separatists and misfits, half of whom have gone wild, into an actual working society, everything they had rejected, and they love him for it. Why would he come here? Why now?"

Oh dear gods. Here we go.

"He has to realize raiding the Pack is a logistical nightmare. They can't possibly sustain a prolonged conflict. The Pack has the Keep and it's a fucking fortress. They would know Ice Fury was coming, because Argent would have to move thousands of shapeshifters all the way through Canada and the Midwest to here. He must want something. The Pack has exclusive rights to panacea, which helps prevent loupism. They have a vault full of magical artifacts. Maybe he wants one of those. Or he wants to crush the Pack and take over. Maybe his people are tired of the north and the cold."

"Can I say something?"

"No. I'm not done." Anger flashed in Nick's eyes. "Argent isn't stupid. He wouldn't be who he is otherwise. He knows all of this, but he's here stirring the pot. He must be sure that he can get what he wants to risk it. That means he has a powerful backer. You."

And now we had paranoia on parade with floats and marching bands.

Nick leaned forward. His eyes locked on me.

"You're going to back his play. It's a good plan. He has brawn and you have magic. A one-two punch. There was a time when Atlanta would have come together to stop you, but now is not that time. You and Argent, you must've hoped that the Pack would notice him by now. You need an excuse to start this war. Except, for some bizarre reason, the Pack hasn't reacted the way you anticipated, so you leaked his name to Stella. You know of my connection to the Pack. You counted on me sounding the alarm to save the woman I love and our children."

Oh Uncle Stupidhead...

"Tell me, what do you get out of it? What does Erra want? Is this about Kate? Do you think if you wreck the Pack, Curran will step in, and you and Argent can kill him? And then Kate, alone and grieving, will pick up her orphan son and return to her aunt like a good little prodigal daughter? Did you honestly think you people could hide your involvement in this? Or did you simply not care? Is this revenge for Roland?"

I opened my mouth again.

"I won't allow it. This scheme ends here, with me. There won't be a war."

"Argent doesn't want a war." Yes! Finally got a word in.

Nick focused on me. He looked slightly deranged, and his icy voice just made it worse. "Enlighten me. What does Argent want?"

"He wants to find out who killed Pastor Haywood."

Nick laughed. "You're here for the same thing. How convenient."

Strange bulges slid under his skin, like golf balls rolling

along the muscles. The secret weapon my grandfather had grafted onto him.

Nick's eyes told me I was about to die. Except it wouldn't go the way he thought it would.

I couldn't kill Nick to save Kate. It went against everything I stood for. Everything she stood for. She wouldn't want that. If she knew I killed him on her account...

I'm so sorry, Kate.

"It's Derek."

Nick blinked.

"Darren Argent is Derek Gaunt. He's here because Pastor Haywood asked for his help, but he arrived too late. He won't do anything to endanger the Pack Curran built. As to nobody knowing about him, Ascanio has been chasing him around the city for the past three days. He probably doesn't know Derek is Argent, but he must have recognized the scent."

The words lay between us like heavy bricks.

Nick stared at me, speechless.

"You don't have to kill anybody. There won't be a war. There is no takeover. Desandra is safe. The kids are safe. Everything is okay. I won't let anyone hurt Kate."

Silence stretched.

"Julie?"

"Yes?"

Nick Feldman opened his mouth. "What in the fucking hell have you done to yourself?"

"You drank their Kool-Aid. You let them change you and twist you, and why? What was wrong with you before?"

I sighed. Nick hadn't taken the whole Princess of Shinar thing well.

"I told you, I didn't have a choice. The Eye changed me. I

hadn't realized the changes had happened until I woke up with a new face. All I wanted was to be like Kate and like Erra. I wanted to belong and to be strong."

"That entire family is poison."

That again. "There is nothing poisonous about Kate. Kate spent most of her adult life protecting this city and the people in it. If there is any kind of trouble, she runs into it, no questions asked. She cares. She always does."

"Caring isn't enough."

Aha. "You worked for Roland. You let him change you. Your tentacles aren't clean. Who are you to pass judgement on her?"

His face turned white. "I was undercover."

"And she is Roland's daughter. He loved her and he offered her everything, power, wealth, the family she desperately wanted, and she rejected all of it because it was the right thing to do. She's the kind of person who lets the man she considers her brother call her an abomination to her face."

"I have not done that in years."

"You don't get credit for not being an asshole, Uncle."

"Fine," Nick growled. "I don't have that big of a problem with your face. You wanted to look like Kate, and I can understand that. I can even understand why you put the eye in. What I don't understand is why you allowed Erra to indoctrinate you into being her puppet."

"She didn't indoctrinate me. I chose New Shinar on my own. I have my reasons."

"The Old Shinar was a tyranny, and you're trying to resurrect it."

I leaned forward. I'd had this argument before. "You are judging an ancient civilization you know nothing about by applying the modern political structure to it. Shinar was never an absolute monarchy. The power of the royal bloodline was limited. It had three branches of government: executive, legislative, and judicial. That idea is much older than the United

States. To come here, I had to convince the council of New Shinar that it was ultimately in their best interests for Kate to survive."

They hadn't needed much convincing. Kate was Erra's beloved niece and a princess of Shinar, whether she saw herself as such or not. Also, everyone pretty much knew that if they tried to keep me from protecting the woman who raised me as her own daughter, I'd abdicate on the spot.

"I had to stand before twenty people and present the best- and worst-case scenarios. They deliberated and voted. They had the power to prevent me from going."

Nick threw his hands in the air. "I don't understand you. You grew up in a democracy."

"No, I grew up in a federal republic. In a true democracy, the vote of majority is absolute and has the power to override the interests of minority. In a republic, the individual rights of a citizen are absolute, and the vote of majority cannot infringe upon them."

He stared at me.

"In terms of individual rights, the Old Shinar wasn't that different from the current system. It had its problems, but it guaranteed citizen freedoms. It offered a path of advancement based on merit. Anyone could run for office after the required period of military or civil service. The man in Stella's office was born a commoner. He begged on the streets until he was ten years old. Before Shinar fell, he had become a High Sakkan, the highest level of minister one could attain."

Nick held up his hand. "It's still a monarchy."

"So is the United Kingdom."

"Look at this picture. You're wearing gold. People are bowing to you. Does that make you happy? Is that how you see yourself?"

I sighed. "Before the magic Shift, major world powers had nuclear weapons. Everybody understood that as long as these bombs existed, another world war was out of the question or life on the planet would end. Thousands of years ago, before the technology Shift when magic reigned supreme, one didn't become a king or a general, unless they possessed great magic power. As the Heir of Shinar, I'm my people's sword and shield. If a threat arises, I will be the first and sometimes the only one to respond to it. I am their atomic bomb. It is my duty to put myself between the kingdom and its enemies. When I wear gold at a formal function, it's because I'm signaling to others that Shinar is prosperous and strong enough to keep its wealth. When the council members wear identical green and white robes, it's because their uniform signals that all of them are equal. Appearances matter."

"Roland was a tyrant."

"And the council of New Shinar passed an official resolution stripping him of his Shinar citizenship. If he ever gets out of his prison, the New Shinar will put him back in."

Nick laughed.

"This federal republic that you so love is unraveling at the seams," I told him. "It worked before the Shift. It doesn't now. Yesterday in this republic, a man broke a child's bones and dragged him on a chain in plain view through the streets and not one person did anything about it."

Nick's face darkened. "That's a punch below the belt. Any of the knights from this chapter would have stepped in. Any PAD officer would have intervened."

"But they didn't. The law enforcement is too few and stretched too thin. Jasper wasn't being covert about it. He felt sure that his act would go unpunished. The system failed. It failed two decades ago when I became a street kid. I know exactly how ugly those streets are. It wasn't the republic that saved me. It was Kate."

He grimaced. "Fair enough."

"The old system will collapse eventually, and sooner rather

than later. LA is practically a city-state. So is Atlanta. I don't want to live in a time when the strongest rise to the top and carve the country into tiny fiefdoms. I want to build a new nation where people are safe."

"By claiming land and imposing your rule on others."

He was like a dog with a bone. "The territory of New Shinar currently includes San Diego. Do you know why?"

"I'm sure you'll tell me."

"Because San Diego held a referendum within its borders and their citizens voted to join us. We don't tell the city how to govern itself. We respect its lawfully elected municipal government."

"No, you just expect them to bow and scrape." He tapped the photograph with the businesspeople. "Just like this."

"That's La Mesa's Chamber of Commerce. Nobody asked them to bow. They came to meet with us because they had a death cult stealing children for human sacrifices and they had already tried a couple of other powers in the area and they thought scraping was expected." I dug through the file. "I remember when this happened. I bet there is another picture... Here it is."

I pulled it out and put it in front of him. On it, I, still dressed in the same getup, was helping an older businesswoman up the steps while the other businesspeople hovered nearby, not sure what to do with themselves.

"The New Shinar isn't a tyranny, Uncle. No matter how much you want it to be. But since we're on the subject, were you elected to your current position? How about Desandra? Was she elected to be the alpha of the Wolf Clan?"

"That's different and you know it."

"No, it's exactly the same. Desandra could've left Atlanta and gone to Kentucky, where shapeshifter packs are outlawed, and raised her kids quietly. Instead she carved her way to the top with her claws."

He shook his head. "It's like talking to a wall."

I sighed. "Let me ask you this, do you think Atlanta is safer now than it was ten years ago when Kate defended it?"

He didn't answer.

"I'm not blind. I'm not peddling oppression. I'm doing my best to make sure that the ideals of individual freedom and rights don't disappear. But I didn't come here to convince or recruit you. I'm here because Kate is in danger. Moloch burns babies alive to power up. Can we agree that it's bad? Will you help me stop him?"

He shook his head.

"Is that a no?"

"I'm shaking my head at myself. Because I am an idiot. Who else knows?"

"Luther."

"You told Luther, but you didn't tell me?"

I grimaced. "I didn't have to tell him. He figured it out."

Nick pondered me. "I will help you with Kate. And it's the only thing I will assist you with. I'm watching you. Every step. Every breath."

"Deal."

I unloaded. I told him everything I'd learned about the murders, Derek, Ascanio, the ma'avirim, and relics.

He took it all in. "Ferara is getting worse."

"I heard that he is aiming for the Beast Lord's throne, but I have a hard time seeing it."

Nick sighed again. "It's complicated. Jim's tired. You know he has children?"

"A boy and a girl."

"He's missed milestones with JJ and he doesn't want to miss Diana's childhood. He also restructured the Pack, pushing a lot of the burden for day-to-day functions onto the Clans. Nobody disputes that this had to be done, but the process gave the Clans a lot of autonomy. Desandra thinks too much. It will take someone as exceptional as Jim to hold them together after he retires."

If Jim picked the wrong person, the Pack would fracture. A divided Pack would be bad for everyone.

"The alphas respect Jim," Nick continued. "He earned their trust. Ascanio, not so much."

"Why?"

"Part of the reason was the way he went about it. There are two paths to the top in the Pack: strategic alliances and physical power. One could say they are the sides of the same coin."

Pack politics were a quagmire. The conflicts between individual clans could get hellishly complicated.

"Raphael made the boudas into a financial powerhouse. Both he and Andrea recognize that Ascanio is ambitious. They're not ready to step down and make way for him, and they don't want to fight him. Together they might win, but there is a good chance he would kill at least one of them."

"So, they redirected his ambition away from themselves?"

"Exactly. They are advising him and plotting on his behalf. Ascanio is trying to build a coalition through money. Right now, both Clan Nimble and Clan Jackal are in the boudas' pocket because they have joint financial ventures. Clan Heavy and Clan Cat oppose Ascanio. He tried to get a foothold in and was rebuffed."

That made sense. Clan Heavy was still led by Mahon, who had raised Curran like his own son. In Mahon's mind, only Curran was the proper Beast Lord. Clan Cat belonged to Jim. Cats were independent and infuriating in their stubbornness, but Jim had been their alpha before becoming Beast Lord and they would follow whoever he endorsed.

"What about the rats?"

Nick frowned. "It's murky. They made some money off him, and they must've reached some sort of understanding, but rats always look out for rats. You can't count on their support unless

255

you get a definite yes from Thomas and Robert Lonesco, and so far Ascanio hasn't gotten one."

So that's why he was running around the city unsupervised. The rats took the "wait and see" position. They observed him, they let him scheme, but they didn't aid him. The fact that they didn't interfere meant they thought he might succeed. Nobody would know where they stood until five minutes to midnight.

"I will say that for him, he's gone further than anyone expected," Nick said. "He's good at observing people and using their weaknesses to his advantage. He doesn't lose his temper like a typical bouda and he uses his head. Except when it comes to your boyfriend."

"Derek Gaunt is *not* my boyfriend."

"Does he know who you are?"

"No, and I plan to keep it that way. What happened between him and Ascanio?"

"This was just before Derek left, about six years ago. Ascanio needed to establish himself in Clan Bouda, so he could claim the beta spot. He tried to pull off a scheme in the city. It wasn't exactly shady, but it was borderline." Nick raised his hand and moved it side to side. "I don't know all the details, but Derek got involved in it and told him to knock it off."

That fit the pattern. As long as I'd known them, Ascanio had tried to prove that he was awesome, and Derek had showed him the error of his ways. When we were kids, Ascanio was younger and had less training. Ascanio's own clan gave him to Kate to keep him breathing, while Derek had Curran, who treated him like a younger brother, something Ascanio envied. They were never friends.

"Things didn't go well?" I guessed.

"Derek beat his ass in front of Ascanio's bouda crew. They decided to jump in, and he beat them into submission. There were witnesses. People saw them cringing."

And now everything made sense. Ascanio got his ass handed

to him in public. Derek embarrassed Ascanio and then left before Ascanio could get a rematch. No matter what Ascanio did, his crew would always wonder if Derek was the better shapeshifter.

He had to fight Derek to keep his authority.

"So Ascanio has Clan Bouda, Clan Jackal, and Clan Nimble," I thought out loud. "Clan Cat and Clan Heavy are in opposition. Clan Rat is sitting on the sidelines. Ascanio needs Clan Wolf. They are the largest clan. All of them are solid fighters, and they work well together. If he gets the wolves, he could tip the balance in his favor."

"That's right," Nick said.

"What does Desandra think about him?"

"He irritates her." Nick smiled. "Desandra is an alpha before all else. For her to bow her head, you would have to be stronger, smarter, and more skilled. Someone who would make her feel secure. Ascanio isn't trustworthy. In her eyes, the very fact that he is resorting to money instead of making alliances or just challenging Jim makes him unfit."

"That's why he went after Pastor Haywood's killer. Tying Desandra's children to it would give him leverage."

The muscles on Nick's jaw bulged. "That's what he thinks."

I really wanted to ask what was wrong with Desimir that Nick would suspect him of flying around and murdering people, but he wouldn't tell me in a million years.

"It's not Desimir," I told him. "I'm absolutely sure. The magic signatures don't lie. Your stepson isn't involved in this at all."

Some of the tension went out of Nick's shoulders. Despite everything, he still worried.

We looked at each other.

"You almost killed me."

"I didn't know who you were."

"You made up this huge crazy theory and nearly started a war. I thought you were better, Uncle. You seemed so sane until this morning, but you're worse now than when I left eight years ago."

A slow, crooked smile stretched his lips. "Insanity works for me."

Eventually the Order and the Pack would come into conflict. It was inevitable. I didn't know what he would do then, and I had a feeling neither did he.

"What's your next step?" Nick asked.

"I'm going to drop my great uncle off at my house and then I'll go after Mark Rudolph."

"Use the badge," he told me.

"I'm planning on it."

"I want updates. Every day."

"I'll do my best."

"Don't die."

"Yes, Uncle."

He waved his hand. The magic slithering along the floorboards died. I was free to go.

I was almost to the door when he asked, "The old man in Stella's office, you said he was the highest-ranking minister."

"Yes."

"Minister of what?"

"Internal security."

"He is a counter-spy?"

"He's a royal assassin. The best in the Old Kingdom."

Nick stared at me.

"Like I said, Shinar had its issues." I smiled and escaped.

When I walked through the door of Stella's office, she was on the phone. She had this flat expression on her face. Namtur watched her quietly.

Stella saw me. "She is right here."

She held the phone out to me. I took it. Miraculously, the connection held.

"Knight Ryder?" Bishop Chao said into the phone.

"Yes?"

"Douglas had a stroke. I'm so sorry."

Cold rolled over me. The world slid sideways. The memory of Douglas on the ground, his small, battered body smeared with blood. *Don't let them hurt me anymore...* The words blended with a hoarse whisper from all those years ago that didn't even sound like Kate. *Want to...die...at home...*

I heard myself say, "I thought he was improving."

"So did we. They are working on him now. I will let you know if there is any change."

"Thank you for everything you've done," I said.

"We will pray for him," she said.

I handed the phone to Stella. She carefully hung it up and looked at me.

"You should sit down," she said.

"I have things to do." My voice sounded light, almost carefree.

"Whatever you're thinking, it's not good," she said. "I think you should sit down, take a breath, and reevaluate."

I didn't need to reevaluate anything. I was crystal clear on what I needed to do. "Thank you for your advice, Knight Davis. We will be going now."

I walked out of the office with Namtur next to me. The groom was walking Tulip and Lady toward us.

"Who was he?" Namtur asked.

"A street child."

"There will always be street children," he said gently. "They will always get hurt. Some will die too early. You and I know this better than anyone."

"This one was different."

"How?"

"I saved him. He is supposed to survive."

I took the reins from the Order's groom and swung into Tulip's saddle. She sensed my mood. Her ears went flat back.

Namtur mounted, and we rode down the street.

"You smell of murder," the old assassin said. "It's in your eyes."

"I'll take you to my home now, Great Uncle. I have something I must do this morning. Please wait for me in my house."

He bowed to me slightly. "Yes, Sharratum."

[15]

The guard stared at my badge and chewed the toothpick in his mouth. Middle-aged, but hard and fit, he didn't look like your typical private security. Higher priced private guards made efforts to appear clean-cut. This man looked like he just came out of a rough bar—long, greasy hair tied back into a ponytail, old jeans, black shirt stained with sweat, and a jaw that had a one-night stand with a razor a week ago and hadn't liked it.

Mark Rudolph didn't just live in Mt. Paran, he lived in the Enclave, an area to the west, where individual houses sat on ten acre lots, each with its own fence and gate. My badge got me into the Northside, and now I was stuck at Rudolph's private gate trying to deal with his hired muscle.

Ponytail had sent a younger guard "up to the house" to find out if they should let me in. That was fifteen minutes ago. Rudolph was likely running a background check.

Ponytail was staring at Tulip a little too hard. She stared back at him. He thought he spotted a horse he'd like to have if I didn't come out of Rudolph's house, and Tulip thought his face

261

was nasty, but if he got close enough, she would bite him anyway.

A short dark-haired man came trotting down the driveway. With a sallow tint to his skin and heavy bags under sunken brown eyes, he had the dashing looks of a man fresh off a drunken binge. "Let her in."

Ponytail stepped back into the guardhouse. Metal clanged, and the heavy wrought-iron gate slid aside about four feet, just wide enough for me to pass through.

"Leave the horse here," Ponytail said.

I dismounted. He held out his hand for the reins. I snapped my fingers. Tulip took off down the road.

Ponytail gave me an ugly look. "You shouldn't have done that. Not a safe place for horses here."

"Don't look for her if you want to keep breathing."

Ponytail waved his fingers at me. "Ooo. Spooky."

"Your funeral."

I walked up the driveway toward the house.

On second thought, house was the wrong word. It was a mansion, one of those pseudo-Colonials one finds sprinkled in affluent neighborhoods all over the South. Two stories tall, red brick, white grout, a row of columns up front, and two rows of rectangular windows, shielded by bars.

The dark-haired man and I walked up the circular driveway, up the white stairs, and to the front door. He opened the door for me and leered as I went in. Inside, a double staircase curved upward from a round foyer. A tall blond man in his thirties waited for me between the staircases. He was built like a bear, with a thick, short beard and hair shaved to almost nothing on the sides and back of the head. He'd braided the hair on top into a skinny plait, and it hung over his shoulder, secured with a leather cord. A ragged scar carved the left side of his face, reaching up into his hairline. Something had clawed him. A large predator or, more likely, a shapeshifter. A modern gladius hung in a scabbard on his belt.

Big, strong, intimidating. A good choice for a bodyguard. Rudolph didn't rent his guards. Everyone I'd seen so far was likely a relic hunter. This one was no exception.

He gave me a slow, heavy look and pointed to the weapons rack against the wall. I pulled out Dakkan and slid it into the rack. My knife followed.

I held out my arms. He patted me down. He was heavy-handed, but quick and thorough. I wasn't the first person he'd frisked.

"This way."

I followed him to the left, through a sitting room, into an office. Walking into the room was like stepping through a portal into some British lord's 19th century study. Heavy, ornate book-cases of dark walnut wood lined the walls. The light from the windows, draped with thick green and gold brocade, reflected in the shiny dark parquet and drew bright rectangles on a bear's pelt stretched like a rug over the floor. A massive stone fireplace rose on the left. Above it a manticore head glared at the world with glass eyes, its fangs bared.

An oversized baroque desk sat directly opposite the door. Behind it, an older man lounged in a chair. In his sixties, he must have been beefy when he was younger, but now his skin sagged, giving him prominent jowls. His longish grey hair was pulled back into a ponytail, mirroring the guard at the gate. It must have been in fashion among relic hunters, and it clashed with his white and blue polo shirt. His skin had the ruddy tint of someone naturally pale, who'd spent a lifetime broiled by the sun. His thick features and the heavy jaw combined into a brutish face, not stupid, but mean and short-tempered.

Mark Rudolph. The man who hired violent thugs who tortured little boys.

He pointed at an elaborately carved chair in front of his desk. "Sit."

I sat. The bodyguard shut the double doors and stood in front of them, facing us, his arms crossed.

"What do you want?" Rudolph asked.

"Someone hired Pastor Haywood to authenticate some Christian artifacts. Now the pastor is dead, and you're looking for the guy that hired him. Why?"

Rudolph leaned back, took a decanter from the corner of the desk, and splashed some amber-colored liquor into his glass. The smell of alcohol floated across the desk.

He didn't offer me any. Aww, where was that famed Southern hospitality?

"Eighteen years ago, an asshole by the name of Waylon Billiot invited me to do a job with him. Normally I don't work with those Creole motherfuckers out of Louisiana, but he'd been in Atlanta for years and the prospect was good, a buried temple on Mykonos. That's a Greek island."

I nodded. So considerate of him to educate me.

"He'd done his research; he had a guy who actually had seen the landmarks with his own eyes, so all he needed was extra money and muscle. We got ourselves a ship and crossed the Atlantic. It's a pretty trip, the Mediterranean. With all the weird shit that's breeding under the waves, you never know if you'll make it. Was part of the appeal."

He refilled his glass and took another swallow. Looked like that ruddy color wasn't all sun.

He was talking and taking his time. Stalling. That was fine. I wasn't in a rush.

"We got to the island. Took us a month to find the right cave and another two weeks for the divers to empty it. They pulled a lot of weird shit out of that cave. We had boxes of crap. But, the most valuable find, the real good stuff, was this chest, about this big, with a cross on the lid. We found it on the last day."

He held his hands eighteen inches apart. "Solid white. Not plastic, not ceramic, not metal. Looked like wood but didn't feel like it. They found it underwater, and as soon as they set it on the deck, the damn thing was dry. We poured some water on it, and it just rolled off. We tried to scrape it for sampling, couldn't scratch it with a drill. Wanna guess what it was?"

"No." Just because he was buying time didn't mean I had to sell it cheap.

"We never figured it out. But during magic, the damn thing radiated power. Nicolson, he was our mage, tried to touch it and it knocked him the hell out. Haven't seen anything like that since."

He waited. I didn't say anything.

"The market for Christian relics was hot. People realized faith had real power and they were buying artifacts left and right. You had your collectors, your investors planning to sit on it and resell it later, and your denominations, trying to purchase proof of their god."

"Not a believer, yourself?"

"Can't go to hell if you don't believe in it. Besides, I like things I can touch, things I can own." He raised his glass, letting the sun play on the cut crystal. "This glass is real, the bourbon in it is real. Faith didn't buy this glass, or the bourbon, or this house."

"Spoken like a true hedonist. That's a Greek word."

Anger flashed in his heavy-lidded eyes. Rudolph didn't like to be mocked. No surprise there.

"We both knew that white chest was retirement money. We sailed home. Stopped in the Azores. Stopped again in Bermuda, spent a few days celebrating. Left port. And a mile from the fucking Port of Savannah the ship sank. No storm. No critters. Something blew a hole in the hull. I went to get the box. It wasn't there."

A shadow crossed his face. His eyebrows came together, his

upper lip rose in a grimace, his hands curled into fists, and an instant later it was all gone, and he was back to drinking bourbon.

It still ate at him all these years later.

"The cargo went down with the boat. We spent a month combing the seabed. Pulled out everything else except for that box."

"So you got conned by the Cajun. Did you still make a profit?"

He looked at me like I was an idiot. "Sure. And Billiot gave me two-thirds of his earnings to compensate me for my boat. But it wasn't about money. It was about respect. Nobody fucks with me like that. Nobody."

"Nobody except Waylon Billiot."

His eyes narrowed. "You got a mouth on you."

You have no idea. "He never did admit to stealing the artifact, did he?"

"No. He was real smart about it. Never heard a peep about the box or him trying to sell it. He died about four years back. I opened a good bottle when I heard. For six years his snot-nosed kid kept his head down. See, the son is like his father. Billiot had a nose for magic, and so does Junior. He's been digging in South America. But something happened on the last trip. Word on the street is, he's damn near wiped out. He's looking for a buyer for the box. He had the pastor to authenticate it, and he had a historian to establish where and when it popped up through history."

"How do you know?"

"Billiot's sources said there was a curse attached to the temple. If you messed with it, a monster would come and eat your heart. Now you've got a dead pastor and…" he tapped the newspaper on his desk. "… a dead professor who's known to trace Christian artifacts for the right price. And you in my office."

Rudolph smiled, showing yellowed teeth. Like looking into

the mouth of a shark. He was telling me all this because he thought I wouldn't be leaving. At least not while still breathing.

The doors behind us swung open. Two men walked in, the hungover guy who came down to bring me up to the house and a tall black man in his twenties with the misshapen nose and mangled ears of a street fighter. Between them they dragged a limp body. Behind them a third man came in, pale, red-haired, carrying a machete. The Viking-wannabe moved to my right and parked himself there.

Showtime.

They dumped the body on the floor. A girl, fifteen, maybe sixteen, tan skin, dark hair, jean shorts and a tank top. Her breath came in hoarse gasps, as if she couldn't get enough air into her lungs.

The fighter grabbed her by the hair and tilted her head back. She spasmed. A strangled cough tore out of her and a trickle of dark grey slid from her mouth. A shapeshifter with a lung full of silver dust. They must've thrown powdered silver at her and she breathed it in. Silver killed Lyc-V, turning the blood grey.

She had to be one of Raphael's boudas. She'd followed me and now she was half dead. Without medical attention from a Pack mage, she wouldn't last long. I'd planned to take my time, but my revenge didn't matter anymore.

Rudolph had an ugly look on his face. You fucking shithead. You want to kill another child? One wasn't enough for you?

"I went to Billiot's funeral," Rudolph said. "I left that part out."

The moment I got up off the chair, they would slit the girl's throat. I pulled my magic to me. This would require specific targeting and I needed to concentrate.

"His widow and his kid were standing next to his casket, both dressed real nice. I walked up real close, looked straight into Junior's eyes, and said, 'Your daddy owes me a box. But don't you worry. I always get what's mine.'"

My magic splayed out, washing against the three relic hunters behind me and the gasping shapeshifter on the floor. I discarded her, focusing on the three upright humans, forcing them to glow brighter in my mind's eye.

"Brave man," I said. "Threatening a widow and an orphan at a funeral."

Rage flared up in Rudolph's eyes again, and this time it stayed there. "I've been in this business longer than you've been alive. Junior has gone into hiding. Three weeks ago, he was running around the city looking to raise money, then he fell off the face of the Earth. My guys can find a virgin in a whorehouse, but they can't find Junior or his family. That tells me he is about to put that box on the market."

The shapeshifter wheezed behind me.

"In a week or two, that box will be sitting right on that shelf. Where it belongs." Rudolph pointed to the shelf behind him. "Eventually Junior will crawl out from under whatever rock he's hiding under and I'll send him on a short trip to say hi to his daddy. Maybe I'll keep a piece of him on the same shelf."

"You're a real charmer."

"Don't you get it yet? Nothing comes between me and what's mine..."

The three relic hunters congealed into clearly defined silhouettes, while the girl faded to a transparent shadow. Targets acquired.

"...not Billiot, not his punk kid, not some blond bitch with a badge."

"Drop the shapeshifter and walk away, and you'll live," I said. "Stay and you'll die."

"Dumb bitch." Rudolph nodded to his thugs. "Kill the shapeshifter first."

The red-haired man raised his machete.

"*Arrat dar non karsaran.*" The power words burst from me

like a magic cannonball. I was so angry, the pain was a mere sting. *Those behind me, break.*

A sickening wet crunch announced multiple bones snapping. Three people howled in agony.

The Viking unsheathed his gladius and lunged at me. I jumped to my feet, leaned out of the way, gripped his wrist, and twisted hard. His fingers opened. I caught the short sword and slashed his throat with it. He stumbled back, his hands on his neck, blood leaking out between his fingers.

On the edge of my vision, Rudolph aimed a crossbow at me. *"Artum."* Shield.

The bolt sliced through the air with a twang and froze three feet from me, vibrating slightly as it tried to burrow into the invisible wall of magic. Pain of the magic feedback punched the bundle of nerves in my solar plexus and faded.

Rudolph scrambled to reload.

I plucked the bolt from the air with my left hand and jumped onto his desk.

Rudolph swung the crossbow like a club.

I kicked him in the face. His head snapped back. The crossbow clattered to the floor. The chair kept Rudolph from falling, and he righted himself. Blood poured from his nose. I'd broken it.

I crouched on the desk, put the gladius down, and toyed with the crossbow bolt.

"Reggie! Hunter!" Rudolph screeched.

"Reggie and Hunter are indisposed," I told him.

"You fucking…"

I snapped a quick punch to his ruined nose. He pitched back again, wheezing.

The howls of pain behind me were too loud, and my time was short.

I raised my voice. "Be quiet and still, and I might forget you're there."

The moans died.

I kept my gaze on Rudolph. "How is it going, bouda?"

"I'll...live." She sounded like her throat was full of sand and jagged glass. I needed to wrap this up.

Rudolph managed to sit back up. "What the fuck do you want?"

"Who would Billiot hire as the broker?"

"How the fuck would I know?"

"Is it hurting time again?" I asked.

"Fuck you."

I stabbed the bolt into his eye. If you were careful, you could stab a human in the eye without injuring the brain. And I was very careful.

Rudolph screamed and clamped his hand over his eye.

"You're one 'fuck you' away from being blind. Billiot isn't stupid. He must have a plan. He'd hire a broker you can't touch. Who is it?"

"Okay," he gasped. "There is a woman. I don't know her name. She's fucking choosy. She doesn't just sell everything, only high-priced shit."

"How do I find her?"

"You go to 15th street, just on the edge of Unicorn Lane. There is a pirogi shop there."

Yes, and their mushroom pirogi were to die for. Small world.

"You leave your number with the stall owner. If the broker's interested, she'll call you."

He was sliding his chair to his left, ever so slowly. The only thing within reach was the bookcase filled with his trophies.

"That's it?"

"That's it. The shop owner doesn't know anything. He just keeps the number in a bucket on the side and eventually it disappears."

I blinked at the bookcase. Inert junk, more junk. On the fourth shelf, a small adder stone, about the size of my fist with a two-inch hole in its center, emitted a dense yellow knot. Animal magic. Got you.

Rudolph kept talking and sliding. "I tried to find the broker before when she wouldn't take one of my jobs. I had her followed before and she just disappears. She's there and then she's not. Nobody can find her. I leaned on the shop owner and got nowhere."

He was almost close enough.

"She didn't like that. She hasn't touched my shit since."

Rudolph lunged for the adder stone. I dropped the crossbow bolt, grabbed the gladius, and drove it into his right side, just as he turned, reaching for the stone. The blade slid between his third and fourth rib and into his liver.

Rudolph collapsed into his chair. Dark blood drenched his side. He let out a long hoarse breath.

"It's over," I told him quietly. "A kindness you don't deserve. I'd come here to kill you and planned to take my time, but you brought the shapeshifter in, so now it has to be quick."

"Why are doing this? Why me?"

"You hired Jasper."

"So what?"

"He was looking for the child that witnessed Pastor Haywood leaving with Billiot's people and couldn't find her. Instead he found a boy named Douglas. He beat him. He put him on a chain. He dragged him through the city. Today Douglas had a stroke. The medmages are working on him now."

"What boy? Was he your brother? Is that why…?"

"Just a street boy. I didn't know him well."

"For a homeless kid? All this for a homeless kid?"

I slid off the desk and leaned forward, so my eyes were even with his. "He was a beggar without a family. Half-starved and alone. He had so little, and you took it away from him. Now I took everything from you."

"I'm worth more…"

I turned, took the adder stone off the shelf, and slipped it into my pocket.

"Did you hear me?" His voice trailed off, weak, sliding into a whisper. "I'm worth more..."

I walked to the shapeshifter. She lay on the floor facedown. I flipped her over. A mottled grey patina climbed up her neck. She had minutes. Fuck.

"Why didn't you tell me?" I asked.

"Didn't matter," she breathed. "I was dead already."

Damn it.

I heaved her onto my back and ran to the front door, grabbing Dakkan on the way. She was trembling like a leaf. Lyc-V generated a lot of heat. Her body should've been burning up, but it was cold and clammy. The virus was losing the battle.

"Where is the closest safe house? Is it still on Durham Street?"

"Too far." She clutched my arm with her hand. There was no strength in her fingers. "Just take me out of here. Don't want to die in this shithole."

I reached the front door and almost collided with Derek. He saw the shapeshifter on my shoulders.

"Put her down."

There was an unmistakable authority in his voice. I dropped my spear and swung the girl to the floor.

Derek knelt by her and looked into her eyes. "Look at me."

She did. Her tremors stopped. Suddenly she was completely focused on him.

Derek pulled out a knife. "I'm going to flood your lungs with blood. It will pick up the dust. You'll need to push it out."

All of the Pack's shapeshifters went through silver-extraction training. Their flesh shrank from it, and it required a great effort of will to force it out of their bodies. But that training was designed for bullets and arrowheads, not silver dust.

"It will hurt," Derek said. "It will be hard to breathe. Listen to my voice. Look at me. Don't be scared."

"I'm not," she squeezed out.

"Good." He split her shirt down the middle and stabbed between her ribs, once, twice, a third time. Oh gods. She shuddered, but her gaze never left his face. Five, six.

"You're going to kill her."

He ignored me. "Push," he ordered.

The girl strained. Black blood oozed from the wounds in her chest. Convulsions gripped her.

"Hold her down," he told me.

I pinned her shoulders to the floor.

"Push." His voice turned deep, commanding, as if woven from pure magic. There was something primal about it, not primitive but ancient. It caught the girl like a lasso and anchored her to life. He ordered her to live, and she obeyed.

"Push."

The girl gasped. Dark blood poured out of her.

"Good," he told her. "Push harder."

More blood, thick like tar.

The girl's feet drummed the ground. She shuddered and went still.

We'd lost her. We'd lost her, and she'd died right here in my arms.

It felt like I'd fallen off a cliff. I was falling and falling and couldn't find the bottom.

Derek gripped the girl's sides. I felt magic move and slid into my sensate vision. Derek's hands glowed with mint green.

"You need to breathe for her," he told me. "Start CPR."

I put my hands on her bloody chest and pushed. More blood poured out, drenching my fingers. I counted to thirty and breathed two slow breaths into her mouth.

She didn't move. Nothing. The mint green wrapped her whole body now.

One, two, three, four… Thirty.

Two more breaths.

The girl jerked. Blood spilled out of her chest wounds, black, then grey, then red. She sucked in a deep breath and coughed, spraying grey blood on my face. Awareness came back into her eyes. She saw Derek and smiled. Her voice was a soft whisper.

"Did I make it?"

"Yes." Derek let go of her.

"Oh good. I'm so happy right now."

Her eyes closed. Shit.

I shook her. Derek caught my wrist.

"It's fine now. Let her sleep."

He'd saved her. She was going to die right here, in my hands, and he'd saved her.

I sat on my ass and looked at my hands, stained with dark blood. It smelled like rust. Across from me, Derek wiped his knife on the shreds of the girl's shirt. He looked haggard, as if he'd packed an entire rough night into the last five minutes.

Shapeshifters didn't do magic. They were magic. The few exceptions I'd met had magic abilities because of their origin, like Dali Shrapshire, the Beast Lord's mate, who was a mystical white tiger.

I pointed to the girl. "What was that?"

"An acute case of silver dust poisoning."

"I know that…"

He shrugged, his face impassive. "Congratulations, Ms. Ryder. She was dying, and you saved her life through the wonder of CPR."

What?

Derek straightened.

From the corner of my eye, I saw a shadow move in the hallway, a crossbow in their hands. I swiped Dakkan off the floor and hurled it. The spear punched the shadow in the chest. The crossbow bolt went wide, sinking into the wall three feet to Derek's right. A woman. Her crossbow clattered to the ground.

"Look at you. Two for two. Saving lives left and right." Derek turned and walked deeper into the house.

"Where are you going?"

"To wash my hands. They itch."

Thirty seconds later he was back, and ten seconds after that I was in the bathroom lathering up my fingers with lavender-scented soap. My brain finally processed what I'd seen and decided it made no sense. I wiped my hands on a towel and went back into the hallway.

Derek had the girl in his arms and was waiting for me by the door. We walked out of the house. He strode down the driveway, carrying her like she weighed less than a feather pillow. His jaw muscles were locked. Derek was pissed off.

"You didn't wait for me," he said, his voice casual. "We had a deal."

"Douglas had a stroke. He might not make it."

"I'm sorry."

He sounded like he really was. We walked down in silence.

He had magic. It was mint green.

"This one will make it," Derek said.

No thanks to me.

We reached the end of the driveway. The gate was open, and Ponytail sprawled on the ground. A hoof-sized hole gaped in his skull, and black flies crawled on his bloody hair. Next to him Tulip waited with a docile expression, looking like the picture of equine innocence.

Derek raised his eyebrows.

Tulip saw us and started forward.

"We both know it wasn't CPR," I said.

He ignored me and loaded the girl onto Tulip's saddle.

"Did you get anything useful from Rudolph?" he asked.

"Yes. He—"

Rudolph's house exploded. A ball of fire bulged and roared upward, blooming like a mushroom cloud. Heat smashed us with a scorching fist. A meteor shower of burning debris shot into the air and rained down all around us.

Derek snarled.

I yanked Dakkan out.

Zahar leaped out of the tree to the right and dropped by Derek.

A chunk of the roof landed in front of me, sending sparks skittering over the pavement. Fire shot out of it and snapped into a familiar tattered wraith. The ma'avir spread his hands, tipped with fiery claws.

The sound of ritual drums echoed through my mind, faint and weaker than before, when the high priest came to me in Professor Walton's office. The enticing scent of the sacrificial smoke was a mere hint. This was a messenger, a lesser.

"We know where you have been." His voice was like the hissing of wet wood in a fire. "We know where you are going. Nothing you do is secret from us. We could have burned you inside that dwelling, yet we have spared you to remind you that he is waiting. Cease your pitiful attempts to prevent the inevitable. Accept your fate. Go to him now and all will be forgiven..."

I stabbed Dakkan into his chest. Bones broke with a dry crunch like twigs. The ma'avir shrieked and flailed, fire raging around him. I thrust the spear deeper, carving through him.

"Die, worm."

He howled, trying to form a prayer. I heaved the spear and drove him in an arc over my head into the ground. His robes tore, flames spiraling out, revealing the burned, desiccated husk that was his body. I yanked Dakkan free, reversed it, and drove the butt of the spear into the priest's skull. Bone crunched. I hammered his ugly face again and again, pounding his skull with the butt of the spear into dust.

"Die and tell your god I sent you to the afterlife!"

The flames wailed like a living creature. The ma'avir jerked and exploded.

Soot drifted through the air. I took a deep breath and looked up.

Derek rose from the ground. Next to him, Zahar, still prone, stared at me with eyes as big as saucers. In the distance, all the way across the road, Tulip pinched some grass off the ground and chewed, unconcerned, while the bouda girl lay limp across her saddle.

Derek's eyes went gold. "Is there something you need to tell me?"

"We need to go to the pirogi stand. Right now."

He stared at me.

"We need to get there before they do!"

"Zahar," Derek said. "Take the girl to the Pack safe house. There is one on Durham Street. Leave her there. If they try to detain you, use my old name. Pull everyone in. Where is this pirogi stand?"

"On the corner of 15th and Peachtree, by my house."

"Bring everyone there."

"Yes, Alpha." Zahar took off at a run, swept the girl into his arms, and dashed up the street.

Derek turned to me. "Get on your horse. You will explain this to me on the way. *All* of it."

16

The pirogi stall was on fire.

I swung off Tulip's back and sprinted to it. Pieces of the stall smoldered, sending greasy smoke into the air. I tried to peer inside the gutted structure. Behind me Derek inhaled.

I had told him the bare minimum about Moloch. Mentioning Kate would give me away, so I explained that a person close to me was Moloch's target, and that he and I "had a score to settle." I also told him that Moloch wanted the divine beast's heart so he could glimpse the future.

I wasn't sure if he bought it, but for now it would have to do.

"I don't smell any burned corpses," Derek said. "Did they take the owner hostage?"

"It's not their style. They must've missed him and burned the stall to make sure I miss him, too."

Come to think of it, it was a weird location for the stall. Too close to Unicorn Lane. The area was poor, the foot traffic light. I had never seen any other customers there. I was keeping them afloat all by my lonesome.

Derek stopped and inhaled. He was staring at the raggedy blanket where my friend the beggar spent his days.

Derek shook his head and inhaled again.

"What is it?"

"There is no fucking way."

"What does that mean?"

For a second his flat expression slipped. "I smell a dead man."

"I don't see a corpse..."

"I saw the corpse. I saw it eight years ago. I carried his coffin at his funeral."

The fractured pieces in front of me snapped together. A female broker who disappears into thin air and whom nobody can find. A pirogi stall on the edge of Unicorn Lane that isn't doing any business except collecting the phone numbers for the broker. The beggar who watches it.

I blinked. The magic trails blossomed in front of me. The filthy blanket where the beggar had sat turned into a dazzling mix of clear human blue and silver shot through with gold.

Son of a bitch.

"Can you track him?"

Derek started forward. "Oh yes. And when I get my hands on him, he'll wish he fucking stayed dead."

We jogged down Peachtree Circle, Tulip gleefully keeping pace with us.

"Did other shapeshifters know him?"

"Everyone knew him," Derek growled.

"Ascanio Ferara had to have walked by his blanket when he came to see me."

"His blanket is soaked in piss. When you get close, all you can smell is ammonia and mothballs. Most people will take a whiff and give him all the space he needs."

We rounded a collapsed building and emerged onto my street. My house was a hundred yards ahead.

"He went into Unicorn Lane," Derek growled.

I slipped back into the sensate vision. The beggar's trail was a mere wisp, dissipating with every second. Beyond it, Unicorn

Lane was a psychedelic rainbow soup of magic, clashing, mixing, boiling.

Derek stopped. I stopped too.

Ahead of us Ascanio walked out from behind my house and gave us a friendly wave.

Oh, for fuck's sake.

"Wait here," Derek said. "I'll handle this."

"Will you?" Ascanio asked. "Is that a fact?"

He strolled toward us, leisurely, one foot in front of the other. You could almost see the hyena in his movement. Behind him, shapeshifters stepped into the open, from behind my house, from the abandoned building across the street on our right, from the fallen ruin on our left. Nine boudas total, with Ascanio. Crap.

"Mr. Gaunt and I are old friends," Ascanio purred.

"You don't have friends, Ascanio," Derek said. "You have people who are useful to you and people who are not."

"Awww. You're trying to hurt my feelings." A ruby light rolled over Ascanio's irises. "And I was so looking forward to our reunion."

Derek raised his hand and flicked his fingers. Five shapeshifters materialized from the buildings on the right, three men and two women. Wolves, all of them, except Zahar, who perched on the heap of rubble directly behind us. Our eyes met, and he winked at me. With Derek, that made six against Ascanio's nine.

"You're outnumbered," Derek said.

Ascanio laughed. "You haven't changed."

The two groups fanned out behind their leaders, each shapeshifter sizing up their opponents and picking out targets. This was now bigger than the two of them. If they fought, it would be a bloodbath.

"Walk away, both of you," I said. "This accomplishes nothing. What are you hoping to win?"

"This isn't about winning," Ascanio said. His face took on a savage edge. A deranged light played in his eyes, the bouda crazy spilling out. "You should have stayed gone."

Derek looked impassive, as if he were attending a boring lecture and couldn't wait for it to be over.

No intelligent life on either side. I tried again. "You do this, and the Pack goes to war."

"Cherry," Ascanio said. "Remove the knight and keep her safe."

A larger female bouda on the right stepped toward me.

Right. "Cherry, I am a Knight of the Order. Put your hands on me, and you'll be hauling rocks for weeks."

Cherry halted, unsure. The Pack was a big believer in redemption through hard labor.

I turned to Ascanio. "If you give them an illegal order, they will still be punished. Your authority won't shield them. Is that the kind of beta you are?"

"This doesn't concern you," Ascanio snapped. "Stay out of Pack business, human."

The front door of my house burst open, and Namtur stormed out in all his tunic and sandals glory. "What is the meaning of this?"

Behind him Marten snuck out onto the porch and gave me a little wave.

I slapped my hand over my face. Why, Fate? Why? What did I do?

The shapeshifters froze, momentarily perplexed by the appearance of an indignant old man in their midst. Ascanio blinked. Derek raised his eyebrows.

Namtur pointed at the two boudas standing too close to my house. "You there! Get off this land."

One of the boudas cackled.

"Great Uncle," I growled.

He stabbed his finger at me. "You! You come over here. It is unseemly! It is beneath you to brawl in the street."

Ascanio shook his head. "Somebody, pick up grandpa and put him back in the house before he gets hurt."

Namtur's eyes bulged.

"Uh oh," Marten said.

"Insolent worm," the Royal Assassin hissed. "I'll skin you, weakling, and wear shoes made of your mangy pelt."

Derek looked at me. "Interesting relatives you have."

Ascanio pivoted to Namtur. "Mangy?"

Of all the things he could have taken offense to.

"Yes, carrion-eater. Slink away. It's what your kind does best."

Ascanio sighed and waved his hand. The female bouda on his left started toward Namtur.

Namtur smiled. There was no warmth in it.

"No killing!" I called out. "No—"

Namtur bent his right leg and raised it up, resting his ankle on his left leg, toes flexed out. His left arm came up to his chest, bent at the elbow. His right elbow rested on his left wrist, the forearm pointing straight up, his palm parallel to the ground, fingers pointing at the female bouda. Python's coil.

Well, it could've been worse.

The female bouda covered the last six feet and reached for him.

Magic struck out of Namtur in a purple cloud filled with the coils of a phantom serpent. It splayed through the street, like a blast wave, and vanished. Translucent purple chains gripped every shapeshifter, locking them in place. The top ring of the chain clamped their mouths, gagging them.

The shapeshifters strained. Muscles bulged. Faces turned red. Nobody moved. Ascanio's eyes burned with murderous fire. If looks could kill, Namtur would have two smoking holes in his head.

"Ooh," Marten said. "You could steal all their things."

Namtur smiled at the child. "I told you, there is no thief in this world equal to me."

My life was a circus. A circus full of thieves, and stupid shapeshifters, and small children executing evasive maneuvers.

"How long will it last?" Marten asked.

Namtur shrugged. "In my day, the People of the Fur were valiant and mighty. Great men and terrible beasts, a wonder to behold and a challenge to fight." He waved his hand. "These... Meh."

Derek flexed his shoulders. The chains shattered and melted into thin air.

Wow. He hadn't even strained.

Namtur's eyes narrowed. "Except that one. Go inside, child." He pulled a long, curved knife out of his robes.

Okay, that was enough. The words of the old language came naturally, as if I was born to it. *"Release them and take the child inside. Please."*

"You will be safe?"

"I'll call for your aid if I need it."

Ascanio snapped his chains with a guttural snarl. Namtur rolled his eyes, ran up to the porch, swept Marten into his arms, and disappeared into the house. The door clanged shut.

The chains vanished. Shapeshifters stumbled and a couple fell, suddenly free.

Ascanio's face was pure rage. Things just weren't going his way. He started forward. I moved between him and Derek.

"No."

"Step aside." The menace in his voice shot alarms through me.

"Or what?"

"Or I'll move you." Ascanio looked at Derek over my shoulder. "Hiding behind a human?"

Derek smiled. "Idiot."

A shiver dashed through Ascanio. He was a hair from shifting.

"Well, that was very informative," a familiar voice said. "But playtime is over."

I turned my head. Robert Lonesco crouched on top of the debris pile blocking the side street. Lean, dark-haired, with eyes like chocolate and bronze skin, Robert looked almost pretty. Until he switched to his warrior form, and then he looked like your worst nightmare.

Zahar gaped at him. Apparently, like everyone else, he hadn't heard or smelled Robert, and having him materialize twenty feet away was probably extremely upsetting. That's why Robert was the alpha of the Rats and the Pack's Chief of Security.

Marten and Namtur popped their heads out the door.

Ascanio kept walking toward us. Behind him the boudas started forward.

Robert shook his head.

Three dozen shapeshifters rose from nearby roofs.

"When I said the party was over, kids, I meant it."

Ascanio halted. His people stopped too. The wolves moved closer to Derek.

"We had an understanding," Ascanio said to Robert.

"Our understanding hinged on you being discreet." Robert waved his hand to indicate the scene. "This is not discreet. The venerable gentleman was correct. This is unseemly."

"I'm handling this. My people will clean it up," Ascanio said.

"No need. This is done."

"No."

"Beta Ferara." Robert's voice turned ice-cold. "Do you know where Abigail Lewis is?"

Ascanio glanced at me, as if looking for someone. "No. Not at the moment."

"I do. She's being transported to the Keep from the safehouse on Durham Street. She inhaled a pound of silver dust. She should be dead."

Ascanio's face blanched.

"Instead, she is in stable condition. They were able to wake her up with an adrenaline shot and she stayed conscious long enough to tell everyone in the safehouse that a pretty human knight and a magic werewolf with scars on his face saved her life. The man who dropped her off told them that Derek Gaunt said 'hi.' Doolittle is standing by in the Keep's clinic. He says it's a miracle and can't wait to examine her."

All the fight went out of Ascanio. They called it into the Keep. The cat was out of the bag, and now Robert would do things by the book.

Robert looked at Derek. "You have some choices to make. Are you here as Gaunt or are you here as Argent? Think carefully before you answer."

A brilliant move. Robert had just solved the dilemma of Derek's identity by pushing the burden onto Derek's shoulders. Most of Derek's people were right here with him. If he said he was Gaunt, Robert would let him walk away. If he said he was Argent, he would be given an invitation to the Keep he couldn't refuse. His people would go to the Keep regardless. He had the immunity that belonging to Curran provided. They did not. He wouldn't abandon them.

Derek opened his mouth. "Greetings to the alpha of Clan Rat. Thank you for your hospitality."

"Greetings to the beta of Ice Fury," Robert replied.

Ascanio looked like somebody had slapped him with a fish.

"The Beast Lord is eager to meet with you," Robert said.

"Why make him wait any longer?" Derek said.

Robert smiled. "Excellent answer. You were always good at thinking on your feet." He looked to Ascanio. "The Beast Lord will see you as well. When the call came into the Keep, the Beast

Lord was in a meeting with your alpha and the alpha of Clan Wolf."

Oh no. Nick told Desandra. The two of them knew about Ascanio and Derek's incident, realized that a confrontation was inevitable, and so Desandra must've positioned herself in the Keep waiting for Ascanio to fuck up.

Robert's face softened. "If I were you, I'd use this time to think of answers to some pressing questions. Such as why you assigned a bouda to follow a Knight of the Order without authorization. Why you inserted yourself into the investigation of Pastor Haywood's murder. Why you failed to report the presence of foreign shapeshifters in the Pack's territory. Most important of all, why you picked a fight with the beta of the largest shapeshifter pack on the continent. Bear in mind that ignorance won't be an effective defense."

Ascanio's expression went blank. Derek's status had set the situation on its ears, and now he was rapidly recalculating. Judging by the look on his face, his brain had to be shifting through the possibilities so fast, I half expected smoke to come out of his ears.

Robert turned to me. "Our apologies to the Order for any inconvenience."

"No need. As you said, this is done."

Robert nodded and looked at Ascanio and Derek. "Gentlemen, shall we?"

"Wait for me," Derek murmured under his breath.

"I will," I promised. I didn't have a choice.

He walked to join Robert. Ascanio did the same. The two groups formed two columns behind their leaders. The rats fanned out around them, and they walked away. In a few breaths the street lay empty.

I sighed and headed into the house.

Marten was curled up on the divan, hugging a pillow. I'd covered her with a soft throw, and from my spot at the table, she looked like a little lump.

I poured more wine for Namtur. He sipped it from a small cup. The old man loved sangria and, given a chance, drank it like water, but today he was pacing himself. The assassin was expecting a fight.

I sipped my tea. Wine and I didn't agree. It made me sad and gave me nightmares.

Three hours had passed since the shapeshifter standoff. Three hours for the ma'avirim to do whatever they wanted.

I wanted to pace around like a caged tiger. Instead, I made myself be calm.

Sophia showed up at my door minutes after the shapeshifters left. She apologized profusely. I told her that I had Marten and there was no further need to guard her. It wasn't strictly true. Rudolph's death eliminated most of the risk to Marten, but the ma'avirim could still come for her to get to me. However, I had thought of a more permanent solution to her safety.

Despite my best assurances that she wasn't fired, Sophia seemed crestfallen. According to her, if I ever needed anything done in Atlanta, there would be a teenage weremongoose on standby. I had her call the Methodist hospital for me because I couldn't get a dial tone. Douglas had survived. He was still in ICU. He would likely live, but they couldn't tell us how much of his mobility or brain function he would regain. I'd thanked Sophia and she left.

Then I'd packed my bag with weapons, so I'd be ready to go the moment Derek showed up. Then I made a big meal, which Namtur and Marten devoured. Then Namtur told her stories of his exploits until finally she fell asleep. Then I poured him wine and made tea.

No word from Derek. Just waiting.

Every minute we delayed ate at me. I felt like a woman trying to run a race with my feet tied together.

"Smart child," Namtur murmured, looking over Marten. "She eats when there is food. She sleeps when she's safe."

"She's a survivor. I paid some strong shapeshifters to keep an eye on her, but she keeps escaping."

Namtur smiled, then his expression turned serious. "That shapeshifter who shrugged off my chains, what is your connection to him?"

"We're working together."

He shook his head. "Ah, the arrogance of youth. You seek to avoid the question, and you think I won't notice. Tell me about this scarred man."

"He's someone I used to know."

"Ah." Namtur smiled without showing his teeth. "A person from your childhood."

"Sort of. What do you think of him?"

"I have known many warriors among the People of the Fur. Their kind seeks to intimidate. They snarl and flaunt their strength and speed. In this way they seek to avoid unnecessary combat. It is the way of animals—make yourself larger, make yourself scarier, puff out your fur, and show your teeth." Namtur took a swallow of his wine. "This man is different. He could have broken my chains at any time, yet he waited to see what I would do. He thinks. He has patience. And that makes him dangerous. If I had to kill him, surprise would be best."

On that we could agree. Fighting Derek one-on-one would be a monumental challenge.

The old man nodded. "Were you friends in your old life?"

"Yes."

"Are you friends still?"

"I don't know," I answered honestly. "Many things have changed."

"That they have."

Namtur fell silent. His eyes clouded with memories. I finished my cup and still he didn't speak.

"Why are you here, Great Uncle?" I asked gently.

He looked into the distance. "This is the place she chose to die."

When Roland woke up in the new age, he was filled with hope and possibilities. When Erra came to, she awoke to despair and pain. Something she cherished most in the world had been torn from her. She saw no point in living.

By that point Roland must have begun to suspect that his daughter was in Atlanta, and he had decided to send Erra to the city to draw Kate out. Grandmother had recognized Kate instantly. The two of them looked so alike, nobody could deny the resemblance.

They had fought, and Erra let Kate kill her. Oh, she'd made Kate work for it. It was one of the hardest fights of Kate's life. But in the end Grandmother let go and let herself slip into oblivion. Except with our family, nothing was ever that simple.

"I wanted to see it for myself. To think that this is the place where she had drowned in despair beyond all hope..."

Namtur let it drop and wiped the moisture from his eyes. "I've known her since she was fifteen years old. She was so strong, so full of life, a glittering jewel suffused with light. How could we let her become a listless shadow of herself? How could we have failed her so completely? Her own brother..."

He clenched his fist, his voice choked up.

"Her own brother." Rage bubbled in his voice. "He should have waited patiently by her resting place. He should have built a residence, he should've trained retainers for her, and when she awoke, he should have gently ushered her into this new world. Instead he sent his servants to fetch her like some freight. Because of him, she thought that precious gift had been lost. He let her think that. And then..."

Namtur's face turned savage. If Namtur ever got his hands

on Roland, my grandfather would die. His great cosmic powers wouldn't matter.

I reached out and touched his hand with my fingers to bring him back to reality. "What he did was unforgivable. I understand it better than anyone. I've heard his explanations. They rang hollow because I've seen what he has done to my uncle."

Of all the people besides Kate and Erra, I was closest to my uncle. He understood me in a way nobody else could. We both had stared into the burning void left behind when the binding shattered. We'd both overcome it. We'd both pledged to never be bound again.

"It wasn't just Nimrod." Namtur's face turned dark. "We all used her. The entire kingdom stood by as she became the Plague Maker. She sacrificed herself for us in the worst way possible. We all allowed it. I allowed it."

I laughed.

He glanced at me, startled.

"How brazen of you. My grandmother is the Queen of Shinar. Nobody allows her to do anything. She did what she did because she judged it necessary."

"There were times when I could have pulled her back. Instead, I urged her on." Namtur shook his head. "I will not make the same mistake again. I have aged, but I will not die until I am sure she will not succumb to darkness. She deserves all the happiness."

Erra's death must have shaken him to his core. The raw emotion in his voice and the naked regret in his eyes made me want to turn away. I was witnessing his grief. It felt intensely private, and I was intruding.

I had to bring him out of it. "So, does my grandmother know you love her?"

He blinked, taken aback. "Of course I love her. We all love her."

"I'm not talking about the love of a friend or a loyal subject."

Namtur stared at me for a second, grabbed a newspaper from the desk, squeezed it into a tube, and hit my head with it. "Evil child!"

Wap!

"Shameful!"

Wap!

"How do such ideas even enter your mind? Must your mouth speak every stray thought that flitters through your head?"

I laughed and leaned out of the way. "You protest too much, Great Uncle."

"Your grandmother is my sworn sister!"

"But not blood sister."

Namtur waved his newspaper. "Not another word!"

I held up my hands. "I'll stop if you do me a favor."

"You dare? After the inanity you blabbered?" He tossed the newspaper onto the table. "What is it?"

"When you go back to the new kingdom, will you take the child with you?"

Namtur pivoted in his chair and looked at Marten.

"She has no future here," I said. "She will die in the streets."

"You can stop pretending," Namtur called.

Marten opened one eye.

"The princess asks me to take you with me."

Marten opened both eyes. "Is she a real princess? Like in fairy tales?"

"Yes," Namtur said with great gravity. "If you are willing, I will take you with me to her kingdom. It is a land of food and wonders. I will give you food."

Good.

"I will give you clothes and teach you to read ancient books."

Also good.

"I will make you my apprentice."

Good... Wait, what?

"Umm... That's not what I asked," I said.

Namtur ignored me. "Do you understand what that means?"

Marten sat up. "There will be no thief in this world equal to me?"

"Great Uncle, let's talk about his..."

Namtur's eyes shone. "Yes. And so much more. It won't be easy. You will weep, you will fail often, and you will want to quit. Your body will have to endure great hardship to grow strong, and your mind will do the same."

"I won't fail," Marten said. "And I won't cry."

Namtur rose. "Come here, child."

Marten hopped off the couch and approached.

"Do you have a name?" he asked.

"This is a terrible idea," I said.

"Deira. Nobody calls me that, though."

"It's a good name," Namtur said. "Kneel."

Marten knelt. Namtur reached out and put his hand on her head.

"Deira of Atlanta, do you accept me as your master?" the Royal Assassin asked.

"Think very carefully," I warned.

"Yes," Deira said. "I accept."

Magic punched them, surging from Namtur's hand. In my mind's eye, they glowed with brilliant intense blue, Namtur darker, closer to indigo, and Deira, a light cerulean shade. The two blues collided, mixed, and flowed back, binding the old man and the little girl.

Well, that hadn't gone the way I wanted.

"You can get up now."

"Thank you, master."

Deira jumped up.

"Why?"

Namtur spared me a look. "I am old and tired."

Yeah right.

"Who will take care of you when I'm gone?"

"She's a little girl."

"She named herself Marten after a small vicious killer. She didn't name herself after a meek rabbit."

Magic pulsed through me. Someone was at my front door. I dissolved the outer ward. A moment later Derek walked into the inner chamber. Finally.

I grabbed Dakkan, my bag, and my bow and quiver.

"I will raise the Enki shield," I told Namtur. "Should the ma'avirim arrive, use the tunnel. Everything here can be replaced except you and Deira."

"Should they break through, I will bring this place down on their heads. It shall become their tomb. If that happens, the child and I will wait for you where your grandmother gave up her life. Make your kingdom proud."

"I will, Great Uncle."

"I'll keep her safe, old man," Derek said.

Namtur fixed Derek with his stare. It was cold and dark, and it promised death. "Pah. Keep yourself safe, Shepherd of the Wolves. And if the danger is too great, hide behind her. Dananu Edes-Shinar has no need of your puny protection."

Derek's eyes shone with gold. He looked like he wanted to say something. The last thing I needed right now was the two of them getting into it.

"Let's go." I marched to the door.

Derek followed me. We exited into the hallway, crossed the house, and went out the front door.

Six shapeshifters waited by my porch, four men and two women. Zahar I already knew. The rest I had seen on the street when Derek and Ascanio had almost had their idiotic show-down, but aside from that, none of them looked familiar.

I turned around and strained. Magic broke free of me, pulsing through the wall of my house and sparking on the tappum, the clay tablets with ancient cuneiform I had affixed around the inner chamber. The Enki shield snapped into being with an audible thrum, and for a second the translucent dome towered over the house. It faded almost instantly, an invisible, impenetrable barrier.

"Cool alarm system," Zahar said. "Where can I buy one?"

We turned down 17th street, heading straight into Unicorn Lane.

"What happened with the Beast Lord?" I asked.

"The usual," Derek said.

Derek Gaunt, chatty Cathy. "Could you elaborate?"

"We have three days to conclude our business in the city," Zahar told me. "If we overstay our welcome, there will be consequences nobody will like."

If we survived, Derek would leave in three days.

"Not a lot of time," someone said behind me.

"It's enough," Derek said.

We were a hundred feet into Unicorn Lane when Derek picked up the beggar's scent and the nearest lamppost sprouted teeth and claws and tried to eat his face.

17

The portal measured about six feet wide and ten feet tall. It wavered, its edges ragged and glowing softly, hidden deep inside a ruined parking garage. Inside the portal a wide plain stretched, awash with green grasses, and in the middle of it, a good couple of miles off, a house rose on a low hill.

Around me the shapeshifters formed a circle, all still human. It had taken us half an hour to get to this spot, and they paid for it with blood. Their flesh wounds knitted closed, but one of the men had a broken arm, and one of the women, a tall redhead, had taken a giant insect pincher to the abdomen. She was breathing in short, shallow gasps. I was pretty sure her intestines were lacerated.

"What is this?" the other woman asked. "Is this an illusion? It doesn't smell like an illusion."

It smelled like the steppe, of grass, and wind, and water meandering from a hidden stream.

"It's the home of the man we're looking for," Derek said. "It's his refuge. He always was a coward."

"I don't understand," a short male shapeshifter said. "If we go through this, where are we going to end up? Is this someplace far away but on this planet?"

They looked at me. Apparently, I was the designated tear-in-the-fabric-of-reality expert.

"I don't know," I told them. "It could be. It could also be a naturally occurring pocket of deep magic or a crafted realm, something a powerful being made for themselves."

"He isn't that powerful," Derek said. "Most likely he found it, and he's squatting there."

"Or," I told him, "he may have made a deal with whoever crafted it, and the moment we go through it, they'll dump a meteor shower on our heads."

"Are we going in?" Zahar asked.

"I'm going in," I told them. "I can better protect myself from magic. I'll tell you if it's safe."

They would follow me. The ma'avirim hadn't found this hidey hole, because the house wasn't on fire, but Derek knew they would be coming. If we could find it, they could too, and leaving shapeshifters by the entrance to face Moloch's priests alone would be stupid.

"Single file," Derek said. "Once we're through, we may have to run. Nia, how's the stomach?"

"Could be better," the injured shapeshifter said.

"Krish," Derek said to the man next to her, "if she slows down, pick her up and carry her."

Krish nodded.

The shapeshifters formed a column behind Derek, and I had a vision of a wolf pack padding one after another through the wilderness.

I blinked my sensate vision on. A ward surrounded the gap, a narrow column of tense magic. No surprise there.

I stepped forward into the magic field. Pressure clamped me, piercing my eyes with painful needles. The spell crunched me, trying to break my defenses. I concentrated, pushing outward.

Using a power word would crack it like a hammer hitting a walnut, but I had no idea what the day would bring and my magic barely had four hours to recover.

"Do you need help?" Derek asked.

"No."

The ward chewed on me. Thin veins of dim green light formed in the empty air—the spell trying to expel me. I held my magic shield. Defensive wards came in different flavors. Some were walls, barriers you had to break through with sheer force. Some, like this one, were designed to cause pain and squeeze the intruder until they retreated. This wall type had to be shattered. Most people thought that the squeezing type couldn't be broken. Most people were wrong.

"What are we waiting for?" someone asked behind me.

"Quiet," Derek ordered.

The ward squeezed and squeezed, the pressure grinding on me. It would keep squeezing until it broke me or ran out of power. Pain was temporary. It would pass like the water of a moving river.

The green veins flashed with white. With a sharp clap, the ward crumbled around me, its magic exhausted. The pain vanished.

"I just broke his ward. If he didn't know we were here before, he knows now."

Derek nodded.

I jumped through the gap and landed in the grass. The soft stalks reached just above my knees. Sunshine spilled from an impossibly high sky. The air carried scents of herbs and grass. A bee flew by me.

I waited to see if the ground under my feet would open up and swallow me whole. It didn't.

Ten seconds. Fifteen. Long enough.

I jogged toward the house. Behind me, Derek leaped through the gap. In a few breaths, his wolves overtook me, fanning out in front of me. Nia caught up to me, her face flushed.

"Do you need me to slow down?"

"I need you to speed up," she said. "At this rate, I'll be old by the time we get there."

I picked up the pace. We ran through the plain unhindered.

We were a hundred and fifty yards from the house when my sensate vision picked up another ward, a translucent dome of green, sheathing the structure and the hill it sat on. Dense currents of magic swirled on its surface like colors on a soap bubble. This one wouldn't be that easy to break. Letting it chew on me this close to the house would also make me an excellent target.

I pulled Dakkan out and sliced across my left forearm. A few drops of blood coated the spear's tip. The Shinar wasn't the only family who used blood as a catalyst, so I wouldn't be giving myself away.

Ahead of me, Derek halted. The ward should have been invisible to him, so he must've sensed its magic. The two werewolves on his left and right missed their cue and ran headfirst into the spell. Green pulsed from the impacts. I ran past Derek without altering my pace and stabbed Dakkan into the ward. My blood sliced through the magic like a knife through warm butter. The ward shattered. I kept running.

A hundred yards to the house.

The grasses in front of me rippled.

Derek sprinted. One second he was behind me, the next he picked me up and charged ahead.

"What..."

Derek leaped. Below us an emerald green serpent the size of a fire hose reared from the grass.

"I'm sensing a theme here," I told him.

"Mhm. He likes green."

Behind us, wolves howled. Derek ran so fast, it felt like we were flying. I wanted out of his arms. Out.

"Should we help?"

"No. They're having fun."

His definition of fun needed some work.

He leapt left, right, dashed up the hill in a dizzying sprint, and set me down in front of the enormous double doors. A stone hall rose in front of us, its grey walls thick and towering.

Derek pounded his fist on the wood.

Below, Derek's wolves, all in warrior forms, attacked the serpents. As I watched, a huge reddish beast jerked a coiling green body into the air and tore it in two.

"I know you're in there," Derek bellowed, "Open these damn doors or I'll break them."

The doors swung open with a soft creak. A man stepped forward. He was perfectly average; average height, average build, neither pale nor tan, with non-descript features and a bald head. Only his eyes were remarkable, filled with intelligence and slight contempt, as if he were the only genius in a world full of idiots and he had come to terms with his fate.

"Well," Saiman said. "I suppose it had to happen sooner or later."

I SAT ON AN OVERSIZED ERGONOMIC COUCH THAT CURVED AROUND a glass coffee table. The glass was thick and cut in a sinuous curve. The base of the table was an S of black steel set on its side. Saiman sat on an identical white couch across the coffee table. Derek parked himself behind me with his arms crossed. His crew had taken positions throughout the cavernous stone hall, some by the front doors, some by the two hallways leading deeper into the keep, and a couple by the floor-to-ceiling windows rising to the high ceilings. Above us, a circular chandelier of plain white metal paid homage to its medieval origins.

The building was pure castle, with stone walls, an enormous fireplace, and massive beams of aged wood. The furnishings were the epitome of pre-Shift ultra-modern luxury. The duality that was Saiman.

Saiman studied me. "Fascinating bone structure..."

His face rippled, the bones shifting and reforming, stretching his skin like it was a rubber mask. When shapeshifters changed forms, it was nearly instant. Saiman took his time, reshaping and fine-tuning. The whole thing was revolting. I'd seen him do it before, so I knew it was coming, but it still made me want to vomit.

"I saw you die," Derek said. "I was at your funeral. I watched them close the casket and lower you into the ground. Why aren't you dead?"

"You don't have to sound so disappointed." His face was still crawling, and his voice sounded distorted.

"Kate mourned for you," Derek continued.

"I cannot be responsible for her emotional attachment."

Asshole. He hadn't changed a bit.

Derek leaned forward, menace rolling off him in a heavy wave. "You let her think you were dead. She saved you."

"And for that, I am eternally grateful. However, I repaid that favor. I settled my debts before my carefully arranged demise. I don't owe anything to anyone."

"They should have put that on your tombstone," Derek said.

"No, I rather like my stele as it is."

Saiman's features finally stopped moving. A close facsimile of me sat on the other couch, wearing my face and Saiman's clothes. He took a mirror off the coffee table, checked his reflection, and frowned. It didn't quite match.

"Why did you fake your death?" Derek asked.

"Because there is a great difference between being renowned

and notorious. Prior to Roland's involvement, I was respected for my expertise. I was a businessman."

A businessman who had charged exorbitant fees for his magic expertise and amassed a fortune in currency and magical items. None of it had helped him in the end.

"After Roland took an interest in my blood, I became a victim, someone to be pitied and rescued. My credibility plummeted. I have no desire to remain a man who couldn't protect himself, yet I have too many contacts here to pick up and start over. This was a perfect compromise."

Saiman was an egotist of the highest order, someone who detested altruism in all its forms. He maintained that friendship was a weakness and love was a delusion, a view that let him justify the utterly selfish way in which he lived his life.

The realization that he survived the encounter with my grandfather only because Kate took pity on him was simply too much for him to deal with. Instead of adjusting or altering his philosophy, he had faked his death, run away, and hid here, in this pocket of separate reality.

"I will see the box now," I said.

The fake me tilted her head, trying to mirror my movements. He liked to shock and keep his opponents off balance. Most people would be uneasy when confronted with an exact replica of themselves, but there were things about me he could never duplicate. No matter how much he tried, he would always be a pale imitation.

"And who do I have the pleasure of addressing?" he asked.

"Someone who broke all of your wards."

"Touché." Saiman smiled with my lips. "Beauty and power. An attractive combination. Do you have a preference in your partners? A type?"

Ugh.

Derek leaned forward, about to jump over the couch, and I put my hand over his forearm. I had to cut Saiman off at the knees, or this would degenerate fast. My expression snapped into my hard Dananu mask.

Saiman shifted, thrown off balance. It wasn't my expression alone, it was the transformation from a normal person to Princess of Shinar. It was in my eyes, in the lines of my body, in the authority written on my face.

My voice went cold, suffused with magic. "You forget yourself, jotunn."

He tried to match my gaze and squirmed. *That's right. I know your true form. I've seen it.*

I held my stare. Silence filled the room.

"You mentioned a box?" Saiman raised his eyebrows.

"Time is short, jotunn."

"I have a name," he said pointedly. "And I'm a businessman. If, hypothetically, a valued client entrusted me with an item they wanted sold ..."

I tossed a small bag onto the coffee table. It made a clinking sound as it landed.

Saiman reached for it, pulled the drawstrings open, and gently shook the contents out onto the table. Five blood-red rubies as big as my thumbnail clattered onto the glass, each with a six-rayed pale star shimmering on the surface.

"Natural stones mined in Burma."

Star gemstones took enchantment much better than regular gems. Their magic reserve was significantly larger, and the enchantments lasted longer.

Saiman stared at the two-hundred and fifty thousand dollars on his table. Money was the fastest way to cut through his bullshit, and time was short.

"I'll see the box now," I repeated.

He picked up a ruby, looked at in the light, set it down, and walked deeper into the house.

Derek leaned toward me. "You *paid* him?"

"It's faster."

"Or I can put his head into my mouth."

"That doesn't seem sanitary. Wouldn't you taste their hair? Is that just a thing you do because you get bored in Alaska?"

Saiman returned carrying a parcel wrapped in purple velvet. He set it on the table with a flourish.

I pulled the velvet free. A small box rested within its folds, shaped like a classic treasure chest. It was opaque and blueish white, with a cross embossed on its lid. The surface of the box appeared soft, almost ivory like, but the sheen that played on its walls was distinctly metallic.

My heart skipped a beat. I had seen this hybrid of bone and metal before. I passed my hand over the lid. Magic nipped at my fingers. Not human. Metal fed with magically grown animal bone.

Derek stared at the box, his face unreadable. Kate's sword looked very similar to this. It was made from her grandmother's bones. Telling him this wasn't carved from one of Kate's relatives would blow my cover.

It wasn't made from the bones of my family, but I would recognize the workmanship anywhere. I had to have this box.

I reached into my bag, pulled a gold bar out, and set it on the table, raising the stakes to three hundred grand. I carried more rubies on me, but there was no reason to give them to Saiman. Adding the gold bar indicated that I had appraised the box, decided its worth, and was willing to pay a fair price. Billiot was hard-pressed for money. Saiman would take it.

Saiman studied the table. "Triple it."

"It's not worth that."

"Then I regretfully decline."

"This box has a guardian. The guardian has killed Pastor Haywood and Professor Walton. It would have killed Billiot himself, if he hadn't found a way to hide from it."

Saiman shrugged. "My defenses are regenerating as we speak."

I looked at Derek. "Is the offer to put his head in your mouth still open?"

"Always." Derek's voice told me that he would really enjoy it.

Saiman rolled his eyes.

I leaned forward. "I was told you were a smart man. I see the rumors were wrong. I'll explain slowly. Try to follow. You have the magic box. It's guarded by a divine beast. The beast is ancient and tireless. It exists for a single purpose: to punish the thieves of its treasure and restore it to its rightful place. It will find this place, it will shred your pitiful wards like tissue paper, and then it will carve your heart out of your chest."

Saiman sat up straighter.

I pointed at Derek. "He doesn't like you. He has six shapeshifters with him, and he is now in your house. He wants to kill the guardian of the box. If he takes the box from you, the guardian will come to him."

Saiman glanced at Derek.

"Moloch has been reborn in Arizona. He also wants this box, and he has sent his ma'avirim into the city. They're currently scouring Atlanta looking for you."

Saiman startled. He'd heard of the ma'avirim, and they had made an impression.

"I don't have the time to draw you a chart, so just imagine all the intersecting lines and realize where they intersect. Sell the box to me and solve all of your problems."

The veneer of arrogance was gone. "How much time do I have?"

"I think the answer to that question is none," Zahar said, looking out the window.

I got up and went to the window. A thundercloud boiled through the portal, an angry black mass backlit with red. It churned and roiled, and within its depths raged a brilliant white fire. The Ma'avirim Firestorm. My heart sank.

This wasn't a single priest. This was much worse. I'd underestimated Moloch, and now everyone with me would pay for it.

I had to stop them at any cost. If I let them through, they would incinerate the house and everyone inside. Nobody, not even Derek, would survive that fire.

"Stay inside," I said. "All of you."

I headed to the door, digging in my bag just in case. *Don't follow me, don't follow me...*

Derek murmured a few words to the shapeshifters and followed.

I turned around and walked backwards, facing him but still moving towards the door. "Remember that promise you made? About sitting it out when an elder power shows up?"

"Sure." He showed no signs of slowing down.

I couldn't let him get into this fight. The fire would be too hot. If he failed to dodge even a single fireball, he'd go up like a candle. I would not allow him to become a pile of ashes. "Stay here."

He pretended to think it over. "I don't believe I will."

"So, the beta of Ice Fury is a liar?"

"Yes."

I reached the door. There were ten feet between us. I had to do this fast. "You're shameless."

He grinned. It was the kind of smile that promised blood. "Yes, and many other things."

"It's not your fight."

"I decide which fights are mine."

His gaze caught on my bag. He would never let me get my hand out of it.

I yanked my magic to me.

"Don't do it," he snarled, reaching for me.

"Aarh!" Freeze.

The blast of magic tore through the house, freezing the shapeshifters in mid-move. Saiman halted, halfway off the couch. In front of me, Derek stopped, standing on the toes of his left foot, reaching for me like an ice skater about to leap.

The power word would buy me five seconds. More than enough.

I stepped outside and pulled a glass apple out.

The skin on Derek's face wrinkled. Oh crap.

I threw the apple on the stone floor of the courtyard. It shattered, spilling my blood, primed with magic.

A muscle on Derek's shoulders flexed. His body trembled, straining.

I punched a stream of power into the blood. It snapped into a hair-thin line, glowing with red, and circled the house. A wall of red shot up. Derek crashed into it at full speed and bounced off. The ward tolled like a giant gong.

His human body tore, and the terrifying silver beast spilled out. His eyes were on fire. "Open it!"

"Not your fight." I turned.

The Firestorm splayed across the sky. It would be on us in half a minute.

The blood ward boomed behind me.

I glanced over my shoulder. Derek ripped into the wall of magic. He wouldn't break through. It took an insane amount of power to pierce a blood ward.

I pulled a golden sphere out of my bag and hurled it into the air. Of the six in my sanctuary, I had taken this one because Grandfather had made it especially for a fight like this. The complex metal filigree unfolded like a flower, sliding and moving into a new shape. A hollow metal wolf the size of a pony landed in front of me, its skin an intricate metal lace held together by ancient spells. Like all of Roland's weapons, beautiful and deadly.

The wolf snapped its fangs, and its eyes ignited with a red glow. I dropped my bag and my cloak. The canteen on my belt was filled with vampire blood. Just enough for a single set of armor.

Making the armor would drain me. Once I put it on, it would protect me from heat until its magic was exhausted. My immunity to fire bought me some protection already, and I had to endure until the heat became too great. I had to save the armor until the end.

I grabbed a handful of arrows from my quiver and stabbed them into my thigh. The pain anchored me. The world turned crystal clear. My blood coated the arrowheads. I shoved them back into the quiver and turned to look at Derek one last time.

He looked demonic, all claws and fur, a monster corded with bulging muscle tearing into the wall of magic. Nothing human remained in him.

I put my hand against the ward. *Goodbye.*

Claws gouged the other side of the spell, leaving no tears. The ward held.

I spun around and jumped on the metal wolf's back. The magic would power it for twenty minutes. It would have to be enough.

The wolf charged in a dizzying sprint. Wind tore at my face. The cloud in front of me condensed and flashed with flames. The dense curtain of smoke churned faster. Dozens of red glowing fires ignited within the storm and streaked down. Fireballs rained on the plain, exploding left and right, shooting flames and dirt into the air.

The wolf zigzagged like a mad rabbit. *Come on, show yourselves.*

A fireball hit too close on my left. Heat bathed me. We tore through it, sprinting deeper, to the center of the storm.

I finally saw the pattern within the cloud, three churning maelstroms, three priests each generating smoke and fire in a dark spiral. An equilateral triangle, with a ma'avir in each corner. Individually they would be problematic; together, locked into a battle formation, they became unstoppable.

I guided the wolf into a turn and leaned back until my spine hit the metal. The left spiral spun directly above me. I nocked an arrow and fired. The arrow shrieked through the air and vanished into the cloud. A fireball answered. The wolf shied right, twisting like a cat in the air, and it took all of my skill to stay on its back.

Missed. Shit.

Fire pelted the ground around me, explosions so loud, I thought I would go deaf. I leaned forward, hugging the wolf's neck, and we streaked through, scorched by flames, showered with dirt, moving forward on instinct and hope.

Keep moving, keep moving. To stop was to die.

We dodged another fireball, and suddenly there was an opening to the left, all three spirals clearly visible on the side. I leaned to the right and fired, sending a burst of magic with it, the same way my ancestors had done thousands of years ago when horse archers of the Koorghans ruled the steppe.

The arrow screeched, its red arrowhead glowing, an ember against the black storm. It pierced the center of the whirlwind. A ghostly scream rang out. The spiral collapsed, revealing a ragged circle of clear sky and the ma'avir at its center, my arrow in his chest.

The priest arched his back. Fire spilled out of the wound. The arrow shaft ignited and burned to ash in an instant, but the arrowhead was still inside him, eating at his body, sapping his power.

Soot blinded me. I fired again on pure instinct. The second arrow bit into the ma'avir's side. I saw it strike home out of the corner of my eye, as the wolf and I raced out of the cloud of ash. Behind us fireballs drummed the ground, as if a giant was chasing me and pounding the ground with his feet.

The firestorm tore in half, the injured ma'avir convulsing.

A torrent of flames slashed into his side from the left. A second torrent hit him from the right. The other priests had anchored him.

The burning cloud melted away. The plain was ash around us. The three priests hung high above, connected by ropes of fire.

I fired an arrow at the priest on the left. It shrieked through the air and burned to nothing five feet from the ma'avir. Crap.

Moloch's priests twisted themselves in identical strange poses. Three pillars of fire burst from their feet, smashing into the ground with a deafening thud.

I steered the wolf into a wide circle and fired again, at the other priest. Once again the arrow melted into ash.

The pillars solidified into ornate metal columns, red and glowing with heat. Each column, about two and a half feet in diameter, towered forty feet high. Two priests in front, one behind, still arranged in a triangle.

And what the hell were they doing now?

The wolf angled around the pillars, keeping far enough back to tolerate the heat. The arrows weren't cutting it. I'd have to get close. Climbing up one of those pillars would be a bitch. Nothing I had could slice through them. Even blood weapons had their limits.

The priests clapped their hands. Fire shot out of them, colliding in the center of the triangle. A deafening thunderclap shook the plains, the sound of a colossal amount of magic released at once.

The fiery glow flashed with white and rained down, flowing into a bovine shape. A giant three-headed bull hit the ground. The steppe shuddered.

The beast raised his head. Twelve feet long, eight feet tall, and eight feet wide, with horns the size of sabers, it was flesh that emanated fire. Metal scales shielded its sides, chest, and back, and the heat surging from it warmed them to a dull red.

309

The Bull of Tophet. In Sienna's visions, she saw him rampage through Atlanta, setting the city ablaze.

Not today.

I emptied the canteen on myself and sliced across my thigh. My blood sparked with magic. The undead blood from the canteen reacted, shooting out in a multitude of streams and arching over my back, weaving itself over my body, forming a flexible cuirass over my chest, pauldrons and vambraces over my arms, cuisses and greaves over my legs, and a helmet over my head.

The bull dug a hoof the size of a turkey platter into the ground. Flames swirled along his hide. His six eyes sighted me. He blew fire out of his nostrils and charged.

I pushed the wolf into a gallop. It flew over the ground-raising clouds of ash with its paws. The drumbeat of the bull's hooves shook the steppe. Fighting him head-on would be suicide. I had to take out the priests. They were the ones feeding it power.

The arrows were out. Trying to climb the pillars would burn through the armor and my fingers. Throwing Dakkan was pointless. They were too high.

I glanced over my shoulder. The damn thing was gaining. How in the hell could something with that much mass run so fast?

That was a lot of mass moving at a great speed.

I twisted the wolf into a tight turn, leaning so far out of the saddle my body was parallel to the ground. It skidded, turned, and we sprinted back to the pillars.

The bull tore past us, unable to make the turn in time. A bellow of rage tore from the beast.

Chase me, you stupid cow.

The bull came around like a barge turning and zeroed in on me, picking up speed. *Faster. Put some of that bovine muscle into it.*

The bull bellowed again, coming fast. The wind fanned his

310

fire, and flames streamed from him like some hellish mane. He was gaining.

Seventy feet.

Fifty. The bull lowered his heads, six horns ready to gore me. I aimed straight for the pillars.

Thirty. Heat scorched my back through the armor.

The wolf shot between the right and rear pillar, its sides softening from the heat. The air in my lungs burned.

The bull plowed into the rear pillar. The metal column careened, tilting, the priest atop it scrambling to maintain his purchase.

I twisted the wolf into a turn.

Three of the bull's horns had pierced the pillar, biting deep into the red-hot metal. He lurched to the right, but the horns remained stuck, trapping two of his heads.

I dropped my bow and snapped Dakkan together.

Instead of backing up and pulling his horns loose, the beast pushed forward. The pillar held. He shook his left head back and forth, trying to rip the horns free through the metal. The pillar shuddered, swinging.

I darted in. Heat slammed into me like a suffocating wall. I plunged Dakkan into the bull's captive head, straight into his ear. He brayed in fury and pain. I stabbed it again and again, in the ear, in the eye, in the nose, over and over.

The bull roared, throwing all of his weight to the side, trying to get away from my spear. Something snapped. The horns ripped through the pillar's side. The metal column sagged, toppled, and plunged to the ground like a felled tree.

The priest atop it had no time to react. He flailed, his robes flaring out like wings, and fell. He hit the ground and found me there, above him. I plunged Dakkan into his skull.

The ma'avir convulsed, his robes flapping. I vaulted onto the wolf, and we broke into a gallop.

Go, go, go.

With a deep bellow, the bull gave chase. His hooves smashed into the jerking priest. The ma'avir exploded.

The blast wave slammed into us, the heat agonizing despite the fifty yards between us. The wolf stumbled, its melting legs too soft to hold our weight. I jumped and rolled through the ash. Pain stabbed through my left thigh.

A horrible scream deafened me, like a human howling in agony into a copper bell. I clamped my hands over my ears.

The scream rang out and died. The shaking ground announced the bull bearing down on me.

I jumped to my feet.

The beast tore toward me. Only two heads now, one of them with half a horn. Fifty feet, twenty...

Steady, steady...

Now.

I jumped aside. The bull's momentum carried it well past me, too fast to stab.

The wolf limped forward, its legs a soft mess of bending metal.

The bull slowed, turning. Stabbing those thick necks would be like trying to saw through a telephone pole with a pock-etknife. The legs were a better option. It couldn't run without its knees.

The world turned dark. Pain exploded in my head, chest, and stomach, as if my whole body was rebelling against me. The ground spun and fell on my head.

I clawed through the agony, desperate to hold onto consciousness.

Feedback from the broken blood ward. Someone had shattered my spell.

I floated through the sea of pain. Reverse the magic flow, pull it inward, exhale out, wrap it... Reality exploded around me in a cacophony of light and sound. Ten yards from me, the bull shook his head, trying to dislodge the metal wolf impaled on his horns and melting over his face. The construct had sacrificed itself for me.

Above me a nightmarish meld of wolf and human bounded onto a pillar, digging his claws into the metal, scrambling up.

Derek, you stupid idiot! It's too high, it's too hot...

He jumped onto the top of the pillar. The ma'avir vomited a torrent of fire. Derek dropped under it, planting one hand on the pillar. The fur on his arm burst into flame. He swung his legs, knocking the priest off, and leaped after him, ripping into the ma'avir as they fell. They crashed to the ground in a cloud of ash.

"Run!" I screamed. "Run!"

A lupine shape rushed out of the cloud: Derek, sprinting at full speed.

The priest detonated. The blast wave picked Derek up, every hair on his body igniting at the same time, and tossed him like a rag doll.

The metal scream erupted again. I clamped my hands over my ears. To the right, another head melted from the bull's shoulders. He was down to two horns now.

Derek staggered upright, swaying, stunned. Burns smoked all over his body. His skin crawled, sprouting fur, as Lyc-V tried to repair its host.

The bull sighted him.

"Hey! Here! Look at me!"

He didn't see me. I was off to the side and Derek was directly in his line of sight, still dazed.

No.

I sprinted to the bull, melting the armor over my thigh, pulling blood onto my hands in twin ribbons.

The bull spun toward me.

You can't have him.

The Bull of Tophet charged, but I was too close. He didn't have time to build up speed. I twisted to the side, rammed

Dakkan between the metal scales over its shoulder, and thrust my hands into bovine fireblood.

"Hesaad." Mine.

Magic tore out of me. The pain shook me to my core. It felt like my bones cracked open and the marrow was sucked out into the void. The threshold for taking the bull over was too high...

The bull brayed. On top of his pillar, the remaining ma'avir screeched in agony. Our magic collided, wrestling for control of the beast. Pressure clamped me, the power inside the bull a dense knot.

Derek would live. No matter what it cost me, he would walk away from this.

Blood drenched my lips. My eyes and nose bled, and I fed every drop of it into the creature. The Bull of Tophet had been crafted from Molokh's divine power. I was trying to rip a god's beast away from him.

"Amehe, amehe, amehe..." Obey, obey, obey.

My whole body went numb. Tears drenched my eyes, making it hard to see. I couldn't feel my hands. I was teetering on the edge of a chasm, about to plunge to my death.

"Amehe."

The cocoon of magic within the bull burst. My magic flooded through it. A malevolent primitive intelligence that was the creature's consciousness connected with mine, accepting the bridle of my will. I felt the overwhelming strength of the bull's body, its weight, its power. I jerked my hands out and shoved the bull's mind at the last ma'avir's pillar.

The creature charged and smashed into the metal column. The pillar quaked. The bull bounced back and struck again, like a battering ram. The priest above ripped his robes and fell to his knees, wrapped in flames.

The air shimmered and split, and through the gap a giant reached out with a perfect hand. He stood eighty feet tall, his face heartbreaking in its beauty. A mane of blond hair fell onto wide shoulders covered in ancient armor that glowed like a golden mirror. To look into his emerald eyes was to lose yourself. Moloch had come to see me.

He had to be burning through his magic at a crazy rate to manifest here and in the giant form. He couldn't possibly keep this up. I had to outlast him.

Moloch's fingers closed around the priest, lifting him in the air. He opened his perfect mouth. "YOU STILL RESIST."

I hurled the bull at him. It charged the avatar, thousands of pounds of fury and flame.

Moloch reached out with his other hand. The bull connected and melted into his palm. The loss of magic brought me to my knees.

"YOU BELONG TO ME. COME TO ME, PRINCESS OF SHINAR, AND KNOW PARADISE."

"Go fuck yourself." Moving my tongue was a colossal effort. I had lost so much magic...

"YOU CAN'T DEFY ME. MY WILL IS ABSOLUTE. YOUR MOTHER WILL DIE, YOUR GRANDMOTHER WILL BE MY SLAVE, AND YOU WILL SIT BESIDE ME."

"I'll kill you and obliterate your name. Nobody will remember you, and you will pass into nothingness."

He smiled, magic radiating from him, warm and brilliant. It pulled me like a magnet. It made me want to weep.

Moloch leaned forward, reaching for me.

I could do nothing. I was spent.

A silver werewolf thrust himself between us. Power boiled out of him, hungry and ancient, so potent it took my breath away.

Moloch stared at him. His eyes widened.

Derek raised his head and howled. It sounded like a vicious battle prayer.

The child-eating god took a step back. The rip in reality collapsed, the final echoes of his voice dancing on the wind.

"UNTIL WE MEET AGAIN."

I fell on my back, my arms wide, and stared at the blue sky. The air tasted so sweet. Everything hurt.

Derek howled again, singing a song of triumph and blood.

In the distance wolves howled, answering him.

18

The old ruin around me lay silent. I had no idea what it had been in its past life. A hotel, a concert hall, a school? Two stories tall, it was perfectly round, and rose fifty feet above us in a dome punctured by rectangular windows, their glass long gone. The center of it lay open. Dust stained the once polished marble floor. Along the walls, columns supported a narrow balcony. Somewhere within the ruin, there were probably stairs that led up there, but neither Derek nor I looked for them.

He lay next to me in the dirt. He hadn't bothered changing shapes to ease the strain on Lyc-V, and right now he was shockingly large, a true monster sheathed in silver fur.

The box sat between us on a dusty step. Moonlight shone through the windows above, and it set the enchanted bone aglow.

I stirred the coals in the metal pot in front of me with a long stick and tossed another handful of dried herbs into it.

I had fallen asleep on that battlefield, right in the ashes. Derek had moved me to the grass. When I woke up, hours later, he was the first thing I saw, still in his wolf form, sitting next to me, silhouetted against the setting sun. Soot and blood stained his silver fur. Bald patches marked his right arm, some still blistered and oozing fluid, where the heat had cooked him. I asked him if it hurt, like an idiot. Of course it hurt. He lied and said no.

The box waited next to him.

I had insisted on confirming that Saiman was still alive. Once I saw him with my own eyes, the lot of us walked out of the portal, and now we were here, in a ruin on the edge of Unicorn Lane, waiting to settle Derek's debt to a kind priest. The wolves had spread out and hid, forming a perimeter around the ruin. Derek told them to not interfere unless Unicorn Lane spat something particularly nasty in our direction.

I had been sitting here for hours, and we hadn't said a single word to each other.

He was leaving in three days. Two now. It was after midnight.

I didn't want him to go.

It was absurd, and stupid, and when I thought about him leaving, it hurt. He'd lived. It was enough. He had his life, I had mine, and after tonight we would go our separate ways. It was for the best.

There were so many things I wanted to ask. None of them mattered.

Derek sat up. His ears twitched.

A strange shape squeezed through one of the empty windows and perched on the balcony, staring down at us with disturbingly human eyes.

She was the size of a female lion and most of her was built like one, but instead of a sandy-colored pelt, her hide was covered with fine brown hair, like the flanks of an Arabian horse. Two massive wings thrust from her back, their feathers a matching tawny brown flecked with white and gold. Her feline legs didn't end in paws, but in monstrous hands with oversized cat-like fingers armed with sickle claws. Her thick neck supported a nightmarish head, her face a strange evolution of a lion muzzle with a flat feline nose, split upper lip, a large maw revealing fangs, and disturbingly human cheekbones and forehead. If lions had evolved the way humans had, they might have looked like her.

A golden circlet crowned her brow. Thick gold armbands studded with red stones clasped her wrists. The gold necklace around her neck was splattered with dried blood.

A female sphinx. My first time seeing one.

The sphinx stared at us with glowing turquoise eyes. Creepy.

She opened her mouth. "Do you burn the funeral herbs for yourself or for the wolf?"

Her whispery voice raised the hair on the back of my neck.

"I burn them for you," I told her. "I brought a coin with me so you may take it to the ferryman. I know the local Thanatos. He's a kind man. He will guide you well."

"How thoughtful of you, human." Her claws scraped the stone. "The wolf hasn't touched the treasure. He may go."

"You killed my friend," Derek said. "A holy man."

"He touched the treasure. He had to die."

"He helped many people," Derek said. "He healed the sick, he fed the hungry, and he shielded the weak. He didn't steal the box, yet you killed him."

Her eyes shone. "His heart tasted like any other."

"You knew he no longer had the box. He wasn't the one who stole it. You could have chosen to spare him," Derek said.

She seemed to think it over. "Yes."

"You could have given him a swift death."

She flexed her fingers, and her claws scraped the stone again. "I like prey that fights back. You have not touched the treasure. You are not my prey. Leave."

Slowly, deliberately, Derek put his clawed hand on the box. "How about now?"

The sphinx dove off the balcony. Derek leaped off the floor, meeting her in midair. The wolf and lion collided in a whirlwind of bodies and fur. They rolled around, snarling, growling, biting, and clawing.

I stirred my herbs. It was his fight. That's why he'd returned to the city. I had to let him have it.

The sphinx clawed Derek's side, ripping through skin and muscle. He gripped one of her wings and bit it where it joined her body. She screamed, and they rolled again, smashing against the columns. Dust rose in the air. I coughed.

Blood splashed the marble. Derek grasped the sphinx by her hind foot and swung her at the nearest column. Her back smashed into stone with a crunch.

Outside one of the wolves snarled. Hopefully, it was nothing. If they snarled again, I'd have to go and check it out.

The sphinx broke free and leapt at Derek, sinking her claws into Derek's shoulders and kicking, trying to disembowel him with her hind legs. He grasped her by her throat, tore her free of him like she was a feral cat, and bit her neck.

Blood washed over them, spurting out between his teeth. He chewed on her, carving through flesh with vicious focus. She raked him with her claws, but he kept biting.

The sphinx sagged. Her strikes lost their power. She went limp. The light in her eyes dimmed.

Derek let go. She fell to the floor in a crumpled heap. He drove his hand into her chest and ripped her heart out.

She shuddered one last time and went still.

Derek dropped the heart. He raised his bloody face to the moon and howled. It wasn't triumphant, it was mournful. It gripped your heart and squeezed it, telling you that life was not forever.

The last notes of the howl died, melting into the night.

Derek turned. His warrior form condensed in on itself, folding into a human shape. His eyes were full of golden light.

Uh oh.

He started toward me, naked, bloody, his eyes on fire.

I stood up.

He kept coming.

"Earth to werewolf, mission complete."

He lunged at me. I had no time to dodge. He pressed my back into a column. His face was inches from mine. An electric thrill dashed through me, fear and excitement rolled into one.

He was looking at my face, at my eyes, at my lips...

"I get that killing her was very exciting..."

He leaned close, resting his forehead on mine. No rational thought remained in his eyes. Only hunger and need. Mayday, mayday.

"Stop."

He took a deep breath, sampling my scent.

"Stop! Derek!"

Oh shit.

He leaned back an inch. A slow smile stretched his, lips but there was no humor in it. It looked harsh and bitter. "Well, look at that. The illustrious Julie Olsen remembered my name."

Cold drenched me. "You knew."

"Yes."

It had to have been the blood armor. "Since when?"

"Since the beginning. I saw you ride into the city."

"How? My face is different; my scent is different."

He leaned closer, his lips almost touching my ear. "I don't need to see your face or smell you. I could tell it was you by the way you rode your horse."

My brain screeched to a halt.

He straightened, giving me more room, and I saw his eyes. They brimmed with cold fire. He was pissed off beyond all reason.

Really? *He* was mad? He had some nerve.

"You knew and you didn't tell me. Was it fun?"

He pondered me. "Not sure. Let me think about it."

"I sense some hostility."

He pretended to ponder it. "Really? Now what could've caused that, I wonder?"

"Why don't you tell me? Just lay it all out."

He bared his teeth. His voice was a snarl. "You left. No good-bye. No explanation. You fucking left me behind like an old knife you didn't want."

"You could've found me any time you wanted. I called home. I told them exactly where I was. If you wanted to talk to me, all you had to do was pick up the phone."

"And said what? Please come back? You made your move, I made mine. I waited for you to come back. You didn't. You made it plain you didn't want anything to do with me. Was I supposed to wait for you here forever like a good boy?"

"Was I? I was in love with you for five years and you couldn't even be bothered to look me up."

"You were a little kid!"

"And if I hadn't left, I would've stayed a little kid in your head forever. I grew up. I thought that if I left, eventually you would track me down. Things would be different."

"Things were fine! We were a good team."

"I didn't want to be a team! I wanted to be a couple!"

He stared at me.

"My gods, how can you be so dense? If I stayed here, we would still be 'a good team.'"

"That was enough for me. I liked having you close. I liked knowing where you were and what you were doing."

"It's not always about you. If I hadn't left, we would still be right where we were before, with me hoping and hoping and you never making up your mind. Nothing would've changed."

"You didn't give me a chance," he snarled. "You left."

"I left because I had a gaping hole in my soul from the severed binding. I didn't ask you to come with me, because for

322

once in your life, I wanted you to show me that you loved me. I wanted you to fight for me. I wanted you to do the ridiculous werewolf mating thing, where you bring me food, and flirt with me, and growl at any other male who tries to hit on me. I had these ridiculous fantasies of you dramatically showing up out of nowhere. When you left Atlanta, I thought you were coming to find me. I waited by the fucking window like a moron every morning for three weeks."

"I left Atlanta because I had to figure out what I was. It had nothing to do with you."

"Nothing you do anymore has anything to do with me. I don't even know why we're having this conversation."

"We're having it because I want some fucking answers."

"I got tired of waiting for you, Derek. You have done quite well for yourself, Beta of Ice Fury. You became the man I always thought you would be if only you got out of your own way. That man didn't want Julie Olsen, but here we are, with you staring at me like you need me to keep breathing. What? Am I finally pretty enough for you?"

He stepped away from me. His gaze was impossible to hold. "Okay. I hear you. Be careful what you wish for, Princess."

He turned and walked to the sphinx.

"That's right," I called. "Keep walking."

He swiped her heart off the floor, turned to face me, and bit into it. Blood dripped down his chin. For a moment Derek froze, encased in moonlight, looking at something a million miles away with glowing eyes. A feral wolf smile bent his lips. He turned away and walked out.

I sagged against the column.

Too much. Too much magic, too much danger, too much Derek. Too much.

It didn't matter. He'd killed the creature he'd come here to kill. He would go back to Alaska now. It was over. I should be glad for him. I should be relieved for myself. I got things off my

323

chest. I cleared the air. I could finally let go of him forever and be free. Everything went according to plan.

So why the hell did it hurt so much?

I sat by Saiman's gravestone and watched the sky slowly lighten above Unicorn Lane. I was so beat up. My body, my mind, my heart, everything was bruised. I just felt hurt and hollow.

Sienna walked out of the shadows, her cloak swirling around her. She carried a plastic bottle filled with clear liquid. The liquid shone slightly, not exactly glowing, but filled with its own subtle light.

"Very mystical," I told her.

"I try."

She looked me over. Her eyes were distant. Magic shimmered along her skin. To my sensate vision, she glowed with an intense, brilliant blue, the tendrils of her magic stretching out in coils, as if stirred by a phantom wind. Her voice flowed, suffused with magic.

"You are so tired," the Witch Oracle said.

"I am. Did I do enough? Did I change the future?"

She shook her head. "No."

Fear drenched me like a bucket of icy water. I'd failed. I'd signed Kate's death warrant. I—

"But you've made it less certain."

The words took a moment to penetrate. "Damn it, Sienna."

"I want to show you something. I saw it for the first time just after midnight."

She crouched and poured the contents of her bottle on the ground. The liquid gathered in a depression of the pitted asphalt, and she touched it with one long, slender finger. Vapor streamed from the surface of the water, rising in a shimmering curtain. A dark-haired woman appeared within it, her features familiar, so much like my own. Kate. She smiled, picked up a small blond toddler, and set the child on her hip. The toddler looked at me through the curtain of time, her big brown eyes bright on her tiny face.

Goosebumps broke out on my skin.

"This is your sister," Sienna said softly. "This vision exists because yesterday you brought Moloch up short."

The vapor vanished, as the water dissipated into nothing.

"You bought them time," Sienna told me.

"How much?"

"Who can say?" Sienna gave me a one-shouldered shrug.

"Can I see them now?"

"No. You cannot see them, and you cannot leave." The Oracle looked at me with haunted eyes.

"What is it?" I asked.

"If one day I wrong you, Julie, will you forgive me?"

"Yes. We all come up short once in a while. You're my friend."

She smiled. She looked like she was about to cry.

"Is something wrong?"

She shook her head. "A promise is a promise. I hope you always feel that way."

Her magic spiraled around her and vanished, pulled in. An ordinary young woman stood in front of me. My friend was back.

"We should have tea and chocolate tomorrow," Sienna said. "I will take you to the new bakery on Smith Avenue. My treat."

"I'll take you up on that generous offer."

Sienna smiled.

EPILOGUE

The sun had risen, and the magic still held. Normally I would've waited till the beginning of a new wave, but this was too important.

I picked up the box, wrapped in purple velvet, with my left hand and a bag with my right, took a deep breath, and reached for the hidden connection, letting it carry me to a place at once near and impossibly far.

The scent of flowering trees washed over me. I stood on the balcony of a grand palace. Below me a breathtaking garden bloomed, trees and flowers flourishing among shallow ponds and gentle streams flowing through manmade beds. Delicate ornamental pavilions of pink and white stone dotted the greenery.

The Water Gardens. One of the wonders of the old kingdom.

"It's been a while," a familiar deep voice said behind me.

I turned. My grandfather strode onto the balcony, dressed in a white tunic and loose white pants. His feet were bare. His dark hair, strategically salted with grey, fell on his shoulders. He had the face of a sage, beautiful beyond human limits, yet wise and self-assured.

"I've been busy. But I come bearing gifts."

"Is that my wolf in your bag?"

"What's left of it." I let the bag fall to the floor. The fabric vanished, revealing melted remnants of the wolf. "I broke it. I'm sorry."

"You're standing in front of me, so it must have done its job. Did it serve you well?"

"It saved me. Can you fix it?"

"It is only a machine," Roland said. "Did you mourn it?"

"I did."

Grandfather smiled. "Be careful. I will rebuild it, but the more attached you become to it, the more agency it will obtain. Such is the nature of magical constructs. There may come a time when it will become an entity with an independent will."

"I'll keep that in mind."

I offered him the bundle of velvet.

"What is this?"

"An artifact Moloch desperately wanted. I think it might be one of yours."

Roland moved his hand. A table sprouted from the balcony's floor. The bundle landed on it, and the velvet fell away.

He laughed. Two bottles of Corona appeared on the table, ice forming on their sides. Two matching chairs materialized by the balcony rail.

Roland picked up a beer. "Tell me everything."

We had finished the beers by the time I was done.

"You've done well," he said.

"Thank you." Praise from Grandfather, both rare and precious.

"Would you like to know what this is?"

"Please."

"We will need the night sky for this."

Roland waved his hand. Sunset splashed across the sky and melted behind the horizon. Indigo flooded the sky, familiar constellations shining within its depths like diamonds. Inside of his prison, Grandfather was god.

Roland touched the box. The lid opened slowly. A gentle blue glow emanated from within and splayed out, forming glowing spiderwebs of constellations above and coastlines below. So beautiful.

"When I was fourteen years old, my tutor challenged me to make a moving map. It had to always know its user's location and adjust with the seasons and the tides. It had to be beautiful and effortless to use."

"You made an ancient version of GPS?"

Roland grinned. "Yes, but mine is so much more stylish. It sat forgotten among other trinkets I created, until years later, the merchants from the Middle Sea arrived. They brought delicate pottery, statues of marble, gold and copper, olive oil, perfume, and wine. We wanted to establish a persistent trade route, but they told us the sea was perilous and full of monsters. It was easy for the ships to be blown off course. So, I gifted them this map, and we traded for two centuries until no more ships came."

That was Roland. A discarded school project that guided fleets across the Mediterranean. Just an afterthought. The ancient Greeks or their ancestors must have treasured it beyond all measure, even binding a sphinx to protect it, and he treated it as a forgotten toy that had turned up in the attic.

"I'm going to leave it here with you," I told him.

"As you wish. I can probably make a better version of it. Yes, something smaller. More handheld." He waved his hand, and two new bottles appeared on the table. "Will you sit with me for a while?"

"Of course I will."

I took my shoes off and leaned back in my chair. The beer in my hand was crisp and cold, and the night sky above us was so vast.

"It will only get harder from here on out," Roland said. "I'm afraid you will suffer."

"Life is suffering. Why should it be different for me?"

"Because you're my granddaughter and very precious to me. I would spare you if I could."

"Aww. You say the sweetest things, Grandfather."

He laughed. We clinked our beers and watched the stars glow.

RYDER EXTRAS

The Letter

One month after the Battle of Atlanta

Order of Merciful Aid
The Citadel
Wolf Trap, VA 22182

14 Sep 2045

TRANSCRIPT FOR THE RECORD

FOR Grand Master, Angevin, Damian, 3rd Knight-Preceptor of
the Order of Merciful Aid

INDIVIDUALS PRESENT: Grand Master Damian Angevin,
Knight-Inquisitor Bruce Dolivo, Knight-Secretary Timothy
Hanson (recording)

Subject: Battle of Atlanta /Attempted Invasion by Roland aka Nimrod of Shinar

BD [Reading]: To understand the conflict that took place in Atlanta resulting in the Battle of Atlanta in August 2045, it is helpful to consider two theories.

First, the forces of magic and technology exist in a balance. Both must be present for life to survive. The complete absence of either results in a mass extinction event, as we saw during the Lighthouse Keeper incident in Palmetto GA. Using technology or magic through means of devices and spells increases its respective potency in the world at the cost of the opposite force. So, the more spells the population uses, the stronger is the magic and the weaker is the tech and vice versa. This continues until the imbalance becomes too great and the system autocorrects. This is known as the Balance Theory.

DA: I'm well aware of this. Last time I checked, I wasn't an idiot.

BD [Reading]: The Shift, the return of magic to our technological civilization is an example of such correction. The correction isn't instant but gradual, which is why we're now experiencing magic waves with periods of technology in between. That is also why magic destroys objects with a high technological concentration, such as tall buildings, aircraft, and computers.

DA: Bruce, my time is valuable. Get to the fucking monkey.

BD [Reading]: Second, the Shift isn't the first such correction our world has experienced. Evidence suggests that several advanced civilizations existed in pre-history, based on the practice of magic, and that they obtained a level of knowledge and innovation at least equal to or surpassing our own. They had experienced their own Shift, which brought waves of technology and ultimately resulted in their demise. This is known as the Second Shift Theory.

DA: *You're doing this on purpose.*

BD: *Yes, you asked me to do this, I dropped everything, and now you're going to sit and listen to my damn report.*

DA: *You always did love the sound of your own voice.*

BD: *And thirty years later you still can't pay attention to the lecture. I'm still doing your fucking homework for you, Damian.*

DA: *That is a lie, and you know it. I did my own damn homework. It's your job to investigate. It's my job to decide what to do about your findings.*

BD: *Oh no, I'm losing my train of thought due to the constant interruptions. I think I'm going to have to start from the beginning.*

DA: *I already know this. The kid knows this. Tim, is any of this news to you or were you awake during the classes at the Academy?*

TH: *No, Grand Master. Yes, Grand Master.*

DA: *Tim, tell me who Roland is.*

TH: *He's an exceptionally powerful wizard born in the prehistoric times when magic civilizations flourished. It's rumored that he is the basis for Biblical figure of Nimrod, the man who built the Tower of Babel. When the first Shift destroyed the magic civilization, Nimrod went into hibernation. The current Shift woke him up and he took the name Roland. He possesses god-like powers, he uses blood magic, and he may have created vampires. He seeks world dominion and is classified as extraordinarily hostile.*

BD: *How is it you have a kid who uses words like flourished? Give him to me, he's too smart for you.*

DA: *Get your own smart kid. This one is mine. Just give me the Cliff-Notes version, Bruce.*

BD: *Fine. Think of magic as water and technology as a dam holding it back. A little bit of water always flows through, but it's barely a trickle. Then we have the Industrial Revolution, a couple of World Wars, and the Space Race, and information technology. The more we progress, the greater is the pressure on the dam, until eventually the damn thing starts cracking. We think it really started sometime in the '70s, when all that psychic crap hit.*

So, the magic keeps leaking through the cracks, the cracks widen, and eventually Roland wakes up, probably sometime in the '90s. He crawls out of whatever cave he was sleeping in and starts running around waiting for the dam to break. Which we know it did, and we have our apocalypse.

Nobody exactly knows what happened to Roland in the past, but it was some heavy shit, because the man is unhinged. Mad genius, megalomaniac wizard, crazy cosmic powers, the whole enchilada. He's obsessed with rebuilding his ancient kingdom, the Shinar. He settles in Ohio, creates the People, and sets about building the foundation for his kingdom.

Shortly after the Shift, he meets a woman, Kalina, and falls in love with her. She becomes pregnant, and at first, he's happy, but then he decides to kill the child in the womb.

DA: *Why?*

BD: He's had children in the past, and it didn't go well. They were powerful and every one of them died or turned against him and then died. No one knows how many of his own kids he murdered.

DA: Clearly, father of the year material.

BD: Kalina had other ideas. She somehow seduced Roland's warlord and ran off with him. Magic may have been involved. Roland chased them. At some point she gave birth to a girl. Roland caught up with them, so she gave the baby to the warlord and confronted her husband to buy them time. She did a damn good job, by all accounts. Bought her daughter twenty-five years before Roland learned of her.

DA: What happened to Kalina?

BD: She stabbed Roland in the eye, and he killed her.

DA: This has turned into a lifetime movie.

BD: Do you even know where that saying comes from?

DA: Yes, do you?

BD: Timothy, bonus question. Where does the phrase lifetime movie come from?

TH: Lifetime was a basic cable channel that provided programing targeted toward women and featuring women in leading roles. Lifetime's original content included made for TV movies, which often portrayed women overcoming adversity resulting from men's actions.

BD: I'll trade you Lisa for him.

DA: Pass. What happened with the girl and the warlord?

BD: The warlord decided to make the girl into a killer, and he did. This woman can kill anything. There are reports of her fighting in the pits South of the Border when she was eight years old. Eventually, the warlord died, and from fifteen until eighteen she ended up in a guardianship under one of ours, Knight-Diviner Greg Feldman.

DA: We had her?

BD: Yep.

DA: Did Feldman know?

BD: Looks that way. He tried to enroll her into Academy twice and she bolted both times. You can check the enrollment logs yourself. She went by Kate Daniels.

DA: Well, fucking shit.

BD: Eventually she ended up in Atlanta and ran into Curran Lennart.

DA: The first Beastlord of the Pack?

BD: Yep. Apparently, there was some sort of instant attraction. It gets better. Ted Moynohan at this point is in charge of the Atlanta Chapter.

DA: That fuckwit again. The gift that keeps on giving. I still don't understand how he got to be the Knight-Protector. If that man was in charge of nothing except his own dick, sooner or later he'd suspect it of presenting a danger to humanity.

BD: He was one of the original 50 people Stone knighted. Stone liked him for dependability and promoted him to Knight-Sergeant, and after he died, Heath took over and Heath prized seniority over ability. We're taking about the same man who commissioned a life-size portrait of Stone and had it framed in gold...

DA: And if Stone was alive, he would've brained Heath with it.

BD: And I would've paid good money to see that. Greg Feldman, the Knight-Diviner who served as Kate's guardian, is murdered. Myonohan isn't investigating it.

DA: Why the hell not?

BD: Feldman had issues with him. Daniels shows up, and Moynohan hires Daniels as an agent of the Order to solve the murder.

DA: What the actual fuck?

BD: Your guess is as good as mine. This thing is actually a lot more complicated, but you asked for highlights. She works for us for a bit. Meanwhile, her daddy wakes up his sister. Her name is Erra and she is the human equivalent of a nuke. In ancient times, she was his warlord. She's got a list of titles a mile long, things like Plaguebringer and City Eater, and she is even less sane than her brother. For some reason, Roland sends her to Atlanta, and she runs into her niece. Shit hits the fan. A plague almost wipes out the city, crazy crap happens, but eventually Daniels kills her. In the process, it becomes clear that she and Lennart are an item and Moynohan thinks shapeshifters aren't people and should be put down. So our girl quits and goes off to be the Beastlady.

DA: ...

BD: You okay?

DA: *Just think about it. If only we'd managed to reel her in. We could've had our own nuke.*

BD [sigh]: *Yep. This is what happens when you promote people beyond their intelligence. Anyhow, some years pass and Roland and Daniels keep coming into conflict with each other remotely. Meanwhile, Heath is leading us into a political nightmare ass first. The Order's reputation plummets. Moynohan, who is gone full lunatic by now, becomes convinced that the only way the Order can survive is to have a holy war against an evil enemy.*

DA: *And we know this how?*

BD: *He wrote a memo to Heath about it.*

DA: *... Continue.*

BD: *Moynohan looks around for some enemy to fight and settles on Roland. Roland decides it's time to meet his daughter in person, so he sends his warlord to get her.*

DA: *Hugh d'Ambray, another massive pain in the ass.*

BD: *He was a pain until Roland threw him away.*

DA: *That man is a butcher. Right now, he sits safely in Kentucky playing house with his new wife, and the moment he steps foot outside of that state, I'll be on him like white on rice.*

BD: *Okay. Moving on. Moynohan makes sure that d'Ambray slaughters the entire Atlanta Chapter and burns a deep-cover agent embedded with d'Ambray. That agent is...*

DA: *Are you going to tell us?*

BD: It's a dramatic pause, Damian. That agent is Knight-Crusader Nikolas Feldman, Greg Feldman's son. Didn't see that coming, did you?

DA: How does this woman keep doing this? How is it every time her trajectory intersects with the Order, we have a major disaster on our hands and she sees us in the worst possible light?

BD: Luck? Coincidence? Fate? Anyway, Heath refuses to go to war with Roland and for some reason decides to promote Feldman to Knight-Protector and set him up in charge of the Atlanta Chapter. Mariana de Leon calls for Heath to step down and your name is brought up as the possible replacement. You know what happened next. While we were busy sorting all that out and fighting our civil war, Roland and Daniels come into open conflict. This family has an inborn ability to claim land.

DA: Define claim.

BD: They become bound to the land and all living creatures within it. If a significant magic power enters their domain, they know and can track it. It's something that had been deliberately bred into them to make them better rulers. Apparently, there is a big price tag attached to all this, but we won't go into that. Short version: Roland tries to claim Atlanta and Daniels blocks him and claims it instead. They make a deal. Lennart gives up the Pack, and Daddy dearest will mind his manners for the next hundred years. Basically, Lennart and Daniels bought some time.

DA: Didn't last.

BD: No. He keeps poking her with a stick. She and Lennart get married and she gives birth to a baby boy, and that just makes her father's meddling worse. While he's harassing her, an ancient dragon

341

decides it would be a great idea to invade the world. He opens a secret dimension where he's been hiding with his slave army and starts capturing people and boiling them alive. The entire city comes together to fight him and somehow Daniels convinces Roland to help her. They kill the dragon, and the moment he croaks, Roland turns on his daughter. When the dust settles, Roland is gone, jettisoned out of our world.

DA: Where?

BD: Nobody knows. Feldman has written a report in which he claims that Roland is imprisoned in the realm outside of our existence and can never escape. I pressed him for an explanation, but he hasn't given one yet. He doesn't have the highest opinion of us. Like Moynohan, he's been writing memos for years explaining that Roland is going to invade and Daniels is a danger to democracy.

DA: I've read them. His points were valid, but we had more urgent things on our plate. What happened to Daniels?

BD: She unclaimed the land and went back to living in the suburbs with her ex-Beastlord husband.

DA: Just like that?

BD: Just like that. Here's the kicker. You remember the aunt she killed? Erra, the Plaguebringer? The one with all the titles?

DA: Yes.

BD: She got resurrected on the battlefield.

DA: Bruce, death is forever. In all the decades since the Shift nobody has ever come back to life.

BD: Well, she did. Rumors said she wasn't fully dead, and she and Daniels have some sort of arrangement. Shortly after the dust settles, she leaves. And here is another tidbit for you. Years ago, Daniels rescued a street kid, a little girl named Julia Olsen. Lennart and Daniels formally adopted her. Julia, they call her Julie, was a sensate and had some weird powers. Word is, she and Erra left together. Their whereabouts are officially unknown.

DA: So, we have an ancient warlord princess running around the country, possibly starting plagues and, good news, she found an apprentice with weird powers. Fantastic. How sure we are that Roland is no longer a threat?

BD: One hundred percent sure. Daniels is unconcerned, and she would be his primary target. As to Erra, we will find her.

DA: What makes you so sure?

BD: Because she looks like this. [passes photograph]

DA: ... How tall is she?

BD: Six two.

DA: When you said she was thousands of years old, I didn't expect... that.

BD: No. I know this look.

DA: What look?

BD: Damian.

DA: Yes? Is there something you want to tell me off the record?

BD: *No, I want it on the record. It's Timothy's job to record every word that passes here, and I want to be damn sure that he puts this in writing. Do you understand, Knight-Secretary Hanson?*

TH: *Yes, Knight-Inquisitor.*

BD: *This woman is a weapon of mass destruction. She can do things we can't even imagine. She can make indestructible weapons and armor out of her own blood. She has centuries of education and experience. The Shift happened less than fifty years ago. Our most advanced mages are babies compared to her. Leave it alone.*

DA: *Mhm.*

BD: *I'm dead serious, Damian. This woman is trouble. Don't get involved. I mean it.*

DA: *I heard you. Thank you for the report, Knight-Inquisitor. The Order appreciates your efforts.*

BD: *I warned you. Besides, it's Julia Olsen we need to focus on. Roland had taken an interest in her. She was seen at his Swan palace and his subordinates referred to her as* talmir, *that means disciple. Daniels taught her to use bladed weapons, Roland taught her magic, and now, Erra took her with and God alone knows what she's teaching her. Three individuals from that family have chosen to pour their knowledge into this child. Why? On top of that, this girl had a front row seat to the mess that is Atlanta's politics for years. She has close ties to the Pack and the Witch Covens. Also, she's welcome at Hugh d'Ambray's Kentucky castle. She worries me.*

DA: *She's what, eighteen?*

BD: *Just about. We don't have an exact birth date.*

DA: *Young. Impressionable. And probably has a shit load of power. Find her for me, Bruce. We can't get Erra, and we lost Daniels, d'Ambray was never an option, but we can still get Julie Olsen. We can't afford to pass on this one. The ruling family of Shinar isn't the only one waking up. We need the knowledge in her head, or we're going to get outclassed fast.*

BD: *I'll find her. The question is, how are you going to convince her to join us?*

DA: *She is an impressionable eighteen-year-old kid. Between the knights and the support staff, we have eighty thousand people who chose our side. Just get me to her, and I'll take it from there. Make this a priority, Bruce.*

BD: *Understood, Grand Master.*

Knight-Inquisitor Dolivo left the room.

DA *[holding photograph of Erra]: What do you think about woman, Tim?*

TH: *She's very dangerous, Grand Master.*

DA: *I'm sure she is. What was it Bruce said? Trouble.*

TH: *Yes, Grand Master.*

DA: *When you get to my age, Tim, you realize that playing it safe isn't always the best strategy. After all, what's life without a little trouble? Don't write that down. We wouldn't want Knight-Inquisitor Dolivo to lose his beauty sleep.*

The King of Fire

Four years after the battle of Atlanta

"Why do you do this to yourself?" Grandfather sighed.

I sat on the floor of the library, basking in a pool of gentle light slipping through the narrow, arched window behind me. Blood and dirt smeared my jeans and my T-shirt. Everything hurt, and sorting through the maze of pain and aches was exhausting. My body was pretty much a single bruise. The right side hurt the most, sending a sharp spike of agony through my insides every time I inhaled. The seventh rib was broken. Probably when the bigger one kicked me. I was covering my head at the time, and the broken rib was the lesser of two evils. I was working on it, but I had to conserve magic. They would be coming for me soon.

"I have my reasons," I told him.

"Are they good reasons?"

"The best."

Grandfather sighed again. His handsome face, edged with a neat silvery beard, wore a long-suffering expression.

My brother stalked over from the spot by the wall. He moved on all fours, silent like a ghost on padded paws. When I materialized in Grandfather's palace, he'd taken one look at the blood on my face and changed shape in a burst of flesh. In his human version, he was three feet eight inches tall, a perfectly reasonable height for a five-year-old. I knew this because we measured his height every six months. The current freaked-out iteration was about my height, armed with powerful muscle, leonine jaws with four-inch fangs, and claws that could gut a human like a fish. His fur was so dark, it was nearly black, and against that darkness, his gold eyes glowed, two blood moons hypercharged with shapeshifter hormones.

"It's not that bad." It was worse.

My brother pawed at the thick chain stretching from the shackles on my leg into empty air.

"Please leave it," I told him.

He caught it with his right hand and pulled, testing the strength.

"Stop." If he yanked it out of the wall, my whole plan would collapse.

He whirled around. The massive jaws gaped and snapped shut, fangs sliding against each other like teeth of a steel bear trap.

"That's not nice."

He snarled.

Grandfather stepped forward and rested his hand on my brother's shoulder. "You are late for dinner."

The kid let out a soft half-growl, half-sigh that turned into a whine.

"I know. Your sister never does anything without a plan. Off you go."

"Do I get a hug?" I held out my arms.

He grumbled, but padded over, and nudged himself into my arms. I hugged him, petting the soft fur. "Don't worry. I've got this."

He sighed and then I was holding empty air.

"He missed my fingers by less than an inch."

"Your brother is upset." Grandfather snapped a huge old book closed. "Can you blame him? I am upset. Your mother, if she knew, would be upset."

If my mother knew, she would drop everything and ride out to save me. I had to keep that from happening at all costs.

"Your grandmother will be livid."

My grandmother was the one who sent me into this hell in the first place. She wanted to come herself, but she was too much. Too tall, too strong, too beautiful, and too full of magic.

She would draw attention and be treated with fear and caution her power deserved, while I had learned to hide my power. I was unknown and easily overlooked as a threat.

"Why Moloch?" Grandfather asked. "Why now?"

"There are children in the hell fortress. He has over five hundred people building his citadel. You should see some of them. They're walking skeletons. You look into their eyes and there is nothing there."

The stench of it, sweat, urine, blood, feces, rot of infected flesh permeating the narrow tunnels filled with cells, barely lit with oppressive watery fey lanterns. The voices. The newer captives cried, the ones who had been there for a little while moaned wordlessly, like animals, and those who have lasted the longest just stared, wordlessly, glassy-eyed. The air saturated to the brink with a miasma of pain and misery. I'd cried when they dragged me to the cell from the sheer impact of so much human suffering. I had to get out. It was that or I would break and do something rash. That's why I came here. I had to anchor myself to something light.

"This is what Moloch does," Grandfather said. "He views his people as fuel to be consumed in order to achieve his means. He feels no remorse. He believes it is as it should be. This is the danger of proclaiming yourself to be a god-king. You start believing your own press."

"He isn't a god."

"No. He is a man, but he is at least as old as me with all of the education and magic his ancient line bestows and that makes him infinitely dangerous. I know you are aware of this fact, so I will ask again. Why are you there? You can answer me, or...'

"Or?"

"Or I will tell Kate. Your choice."

I was out of options. I would need his help anyway, eventually. "The seer of the Witch Oracle called me."

Grandfather's eyebrows rose. "I didn't know you kept in touch."

"We're friends. She is only two years older than me. We used to have girl days and shop for makeup together. I call her once in a while."

Grandfather frowned, obviously struggling with this information. I gave him a moment.

"Is there a prophecy?"

"There is." And she'd called me frantic in the middle of the night to deliver it.

"Let's hear it."

"When magic crests at its peak, the King of Fire will leave his citadel of misery in the Western Desert to travel east to devour the queen who doesn't rule and sever bloodline reborn. Only the one who shares his power may oppose him."

As soon as I heard it, I told my grandmother and we were on the leyline to Arizona before the sun came up.

I met Grandfather's gaze. "He's going to kill Kate."

Nobody would ever harm Kate. Not as long as I was breathing.

He pondered my words. His eyes grew distant and for a moment a different man emerged from his wise and kind facade, younger, harder, vicious and sharp, like a shark coming to a surface from the depths of the ocean. The immortal wizard-king who nearly killed everyone he loved to rule the world. Ah, Grandpa. I missed you.

"You cannot kill Moloch."

"I'm going to give it a very good try." I had planned a lot of fun surprises.

"No, child. When I said you cannot kill him, I meant he regenerates. Our family bred for power over the lands we claim. His line bred for the ability to restore themselves.

"I'll chop his head off. I'd like to see him regenerate that."

"He will," Grandfather said. "I haven't seen it, but my father has."

He was serious. My careful plan collapsed on itself like a house of cards. "How is that possible?"

Grandfather shrugged. "Magic of a bygone age. The best you can do is destroy enough of him to buy you time to get out. The magic of this moment in history isn't strong enough for rapid reconstruction and the periods of tech will slow him down even more. Inflict enough damage to assure a temporary death and he won't be a problem for at least a few months. Dismemberment is your friend."

I gave him my sweet smile. "Thank you."

"You didn't ask the most important question."

He paused. This was a test. If I asked the correct question, I would be rewarded. If I failed, he would be disappointed. I needed his help desperately.

I ran through it in my head. Magic at its peak, the King of Fire, citadel, Western Desert, the queen who doesn't rule, the one who shares his power...

Here goes nothing. "How do I share in Moloch's power?"

Roland smiled, his magic shining from within. The sun had risen, the clouds parted, the flowers bloomed, and the world smiled with him.

"The eyes, Julia. Moloch's power is in his eyes."

The library vanished. I was back on the piss-soaked straw in a dank cell, chained to the wall. The gaunt woman across gave me a blank stare. She probably didn't even notice I was gone.

The heavy footsteps echoed through the hallway. A metal bar clanged open. Men filed into the room. Hands grabbed me and hauled me up, as someone unlocked my shackles. I hung limp. It was time.

I climbed to the apex of the hill, scrambling up the rocky slope. A strong hand caught my wrist and hauled me up like I weighed nothing. My grandmother grabbed me and squeezed me in a crushing hug. All my wounds cried out with a trickle of blood.

"How did it go?" she asked.

I glanced over my shoulder at the citadel burning behind me. The flames roared, turning the fortress into one massive bonfire staining the night with orange.

"He took my eye," I told her.

Erra sucked in a sharp breath.

"That's okay," I said and opened my eyes wide, one brown and the other a brilliant glowing green. "I took one of his."

ACKNOWLEDGMENTS

This book was started during the first wave of COVID pandemic, when pictures of bodies loaded into refrigerated trucks were coming out of New York. It came about because an ICU nurse emailed us and asked us to post something, anything, because reading our work on her short break between grueling shifts kept her sane. We don't have permission to share her name, but she has our deepest gratitude for everything she and other medical professionals, first responders, and essential workers have done for us.

We'd like to thank out agent Nancy Yost, and the awesome crew at NYLA: Sarah Younger, Natanya Wheeler, and Cheryl Pientka, for their support, friendship, and very hard work.

We are grateful to Rebecca Brewer, Stephanie Stogiera, Stefanie Chin, and Katherine Heasley for their editorial services and shaping the manuscript into a book and to Jill Smith and Jessica Haluska, who have read it on short notice and offered feedback.

A lot of people generously helped us make the book better. We'd like to acknowledge Rev. Dr Victoria Hart Gaskell for help with Christian research, Lail Edelsztein and Shani Hochberg for the assistance with Hebrew language and coming up with the name for Moloch's priests, Pamela Freeman for helping us with Marten's nickname, and Jesse Wendel, Camilla Cracchiolo, and Karen L Beasley, MD for their knowledge of injuries and medical expertise. We apologize if we have forgotten someone. All errors of fact are our own.

Finally, we'd like to thank our fans. You wanted this book and here it is. We hope it will be fun to read.

ALSO BY ILONA ANDREWS

Kate Daniels World

BLOOD HEIR

Kate Daniels Series

MAGIC BITES

MAGIC BLEEDS

MAGIC BURNS

MAGIC STRIKES

MAGIC MOURNS

MAGIC BLEEDS

MAGIC DREAMS

MAGIC SLAYS

GUNMETAL MAGIC

MAGIC GIFTS

MAGIC RISES

MAGIC BREAKS

MAGIC STEALS

MAGIC SHIFTS

MAGIC STARS

MAGIC BINDS

MAGIC TRIUMPHS

The Iron Covenant

IRON AND MAGIC

UNTITLED IRON AND MAGIC #2

ABOUT THE AUTHOR

Ilona Andrews is the pseudonym for a husband-and-wife writing team. Ilona is a native-born Russian, and Gordon is a former communications sergeant in the U.S. Army. Contrary to popular belief, Gordon was never an intelligence officer with a license to kill, and Ilona was never the mysterious Russian spy who seduced him. They met in college, in English Composition 101, where Ilona got a better grade. (Gordon is still sore about that.)

Together, Gordon and Ilona are the coauthors of the *New York Times* bestselling Kate Daniels urban fantasy series and the romantic urban fantasy novels of the Edge. They currently reside in Austin, Texas, with their two children and numerous pets. For sample chapters, news, and more, visit www.ilona-andrews.com.

CPSIA information can be obtained
at www.ICGtesting.com
Printed in the USA
LVHW051537240121
677358LV00010B/1160